THE WORLD SO WIDE

Advance Praise for THE WORLD SO WIDE

"Historical fiction packs the same punch as a five-act opera in Zilla Jones' much-anticipated *The World So Wide*. With a heart as complex as Grenada's turbulent past, heroine Felicity Alexander witnesses her homeland brace against waves of political change. Standing ovation and flowers thrown at Jones' feet for this brilliant first novel."
— Catherine Hernandez, author and screenwriter of *Scarborough*, the book and film, also a Canada Reads finalist

"I adore Felicity Alexander, the woman at the heart of this novel. She is complex, delightfully melodramatic, and passionate about sex, opera and politics. Hers is a voice, oh so full, that refuses to be neither circumscribed nor colonized. Read this novel and fall in love."
— David Bergen, author of *The Time in Between*, winner of the Giller Prize

"[*The*] *World So Wide* immerses us in the complex inner life of opera prodigy Felicity; a defiant, tumultuous spirit with an insatiable heart. Propelled by loss and family history, Felicity's ambitions and desires collide against the reverberations of Grenada's colonial history. Jones addresses the complexities of diasporic identity with candor and sensitivity in this affective story about a woman and a nation constrained by the horrors of the past. Jones explores the transcendent connections forged through art and love, and the ways in which political acts of bravery are driven by a profound yearning for acceptance, community, and a sense of belonging. From the grey streets of London, to the verdant landscapes of Grenada, to the stage ... Felicity emerges as a beacon of light. This work is a captivating, exquisite, and unforgettable journey."
— Denise Da Costa, author of the Toronto Book Award–longlisted *And the Walls Came Down*

"Zilla Jones' lavish saga spanning four countries and fifteen years, is a coming-of-age account of its star diva, Felicity, and indeed the island of Grenada itself. Jones makes the glorious and tragic island story one about people, both the architects of ideological hope, and the victims of their own hubris, miscalculation and disappointment. Their passions, political, cultural and romantic, unfold to create layers of tension and misunderstanding, unity and division in their personal lives as surely as their bold dreams create hope and pride and then disaster on the international stage. Felicity, who straddles two worlds, black and white, finds her voice through music, which becomes her life's calling. In this telling, she bucks suffocating strictures of family, religion and the various mores of society. Jones' distance from formal facts of history frees the reader from nit-picking the details, but it also widens our perspective to human and therefore universal truths — and to the effects of the colonial experience and the agonizingly personal toll it takes in the drive to free ourselves from the toxic yoke of colonialism."
— Rachel Manley, author of *The Fellowship*, *The Black Peacock*, and the Governor General's Literary Award–winning *Drumblair: Memories of a Jamaican Childhood*

"*The World So Wide* is a nimble, clear-seeing portrait of a generation's complex inheritances preceding and extending from the Grenada Revolution. As sharp and clear as a stream in sunlight, *The World So Wide* is Jones' beautiful, musical, astute, and richly earned entrance into the tome of vital Caribbean diasporic literature."
— Canisia Lubrin, author of *Code Noir*, finalist for the Governor General's Literary Award and the Atwood Gibson Writers' Trust Fiction Prize

THE WORLD SO WIDE

ZILLA JONES

CORMORANT BOOKS

The lines quoted on pages 55 and 367 "The time has grown so short, the world so wide" are taken from the opera *The Tender Land*, libretto by Horace Everett and music by Aaron Copland. First performed April 1, 1954, a production of the New York City Opera.

We acknowledge financial support for our publishing activities: the Government of Canada, through the Canada Book Fund and The Canada Council for the Arts; the Government of Ontario, through the Ontario Arts Council, Ontario Creates, and the Ontario Book Publishing Tax Credit.

LIBRARY AND ARCHIVES CANADA CATALOGUING IN PUBLICATION

Title: The world so wide / Zilla Jones.
Names: Jones, Zilla, author.
Identifiers: Canadiana (print) 20240460383 | Canadiana (ebook) 20240460421 | ISBN 9781770867758 (softcover) | ISBN 9781770867765 (EPUB)
Subjects: LCGFT: Novels.
Classification: LCC PS8619.O543 W67 2025 | DDC C813/.6—dc23

United States Library of Congress Control Number: 2024944651

Cover and interior design: Marijke Friesen
Manufactured by Friesens in Altona, Manitoba in March 2025.

MIX
Paper | Supporting responsible forestry
FSC® C016245

Printed using paper from a responsible and sustainable resource, including a mix of virgin fibres and recycled materials.

Printed and bound in Canada.

EU RP eucomply OÜ
Pärnu mnt 139b-14, 11317 Tallinn, Estonia
hello@eucompliancepartner.com, +33757690241

CORMORANT BOOKS INC.
260 ISHPADINAA (SPADINA) AVENUE, SUITE 502,
TKARONTO (TORONTO), ON M5T 2E4

SUITE 110, 7068 PORTAL WAY, FERNDALE, WA 98248, USA
info@cormorantbooks.com / www.cormorantbooks.com

Grenada is a green book
Spread out
On the blue table of the Caribbean sea
Its pages written in blood and struggle
Our history

— Taken from "From Camerhogne They Came," a history of Grenada produced and performed during the Revolution, as quoted in *The Grenada Revolution in the Caribbean Present: Operation Urgent Memory* by Shalini Puri

LIVICATION

I livicate this book to the people of the Caribbean and especially to those of Grenada, in the Diaspora and at home, for telling our stories and keeping the resistance alive, in the certainty that someday we shall overcome.
To the Revo!

And in memory of Gerry Atwell, for believing in the power of my voice. Soon come in Zion.

PROGRAM NOTES

This book is a work of historical fiction, written to place a spotlight on events that are not discussed sufficiently today. In service of the story, I have taken liberties with some of the historical facts. The historical sources that I consulted are listed in the Acknowledgements at the back of the book.

The characters in the book are creations of my own imagination. Any resemblance to actual persons, living or dead, is coincidental.

CONTENT WARNING

Since 1492, the land and people of the Caribbean have been colonized, and they bear many scars. The people of the Caribbean Diaspora have been subject to decades of systemic discrimination and exclusion. Arising from these histories, this story is a journey through collective and individual trauma. There are incidents of sexual violence and attempted sexual violence, physical violence against women, gun violence and armed conflict, racist language, infidelity, and infertility. But there are also depictions of the care and comfort of community, of non-violent protest, of the joy of friendship, of the beauty of music, and of self-love, self-discovery, and liberation.

Crick, crack
Break my back

OVERTURE
CHAPTER 1.

St George's, Grenada, October 9, 1983

A SOLDIER WITH a gun and a conductor with a baton: both men who derived power from pointing sticks at women. Felicity Alexander had seen many sticks in her time, and she knew the best way to respond was to ignore the men who wielded them. Continue to sing her tempo, or keep digging this hole under the fence with her bare hands.

"I askin' you, what you doin'?" The gun shook. The holder had a smooth face, with gangly limbs protruding through the sleeves and cuffs of his uniform; he was a boy, not yet a man.

"I'm trying to get out of here." Fireflies lit the night with circling brightness, tiny moving stars. The heat draped over Felicity's shoulders was a wet towel, laced with the scent of the ocean that glinted in the distance. She had chosen a spot shielded from the rest of the yard by a cluster of banana trees, but somehow this kid had found her.

"You know everyone in the house does have to stay in." He jabbed the gun in her direction. Its mouth wavered and dipped to the ground.

"Everyone in the house who's a member of the government of Grenada."

"And you. You from the enemy, from USA."

Felicity regretted that lie. It had been told on impulse, when the army first arrived.

"Why on earth do you want to waste your time performing in a showcase for the People's Revolutionary Government of Grenada?" her agent had asked her, when she was still safe in Winnipeg. "Besides the political implications, the arrangements seem rather lacking. Quite amateur."

Felicity had lied then too. "It has to do with my ancestry. Finding myself."

"Yes," her agent said. "You knew Neville Carpenter as a student, didn't you? The thing is, Felicity, Neville Carpenter is a controversial figure. He's a media darling, he's sexy, he's an international womanizer, but then there are lots of people who think he's a bloodthirsty Communist. A roll in the hay for old times sake isn't worth the potential blow to your career."

"I could just fire you and go anyway."

Her agent swallowed so hard Felicity heard it on the other end of the line. "Well, all right, go, but for God's sake, keep it low profile. Get in and get out quickly."

When the soldiers asked Felicity to identify herself, she remembered her agent's words, and she gave them the name she had used at the clinic in Sauteurs twelve years before. Lydia Felix: her middle name, and her former husband's last name. Lydia Felix, an American, a friend of Prime Minister Neville Carpenter. Not Felicity Alexander, Canadian opera singer, still in love with Neville's deputy, Claude Buckingham, eighteen years after they had met.

"You're a dirty American," said the boy with the gun. "All you have a real ass of a president."

"Black Americans don't like him either," said Felicity. "America won't lift a finger to help a Black woman."

"Who is Black? You?"

Felicity remembered that her racial identity was not in question in Canada, or England, or the United States, but here in Grenada, her lighter shade of brown and her thick curly hair came with distinctions, and with privileges.

"You has to go inside," the boy soldier said. He grew brave and jabbed Felicity in her side with the butt of the gun. "All of you is under heavy manners."

"You're holding it wrong," Felicity said. "Your hands go here. Look." She stood next to him and allowed her body to brush against his. She wore only Neville's Malcolm X T-shirt and a pair of his boxer shorts with the waist rolled over to hold them up.The young soldier shuddered as she peeled his fingers from around the weapon and placed one hand near the scope, one near the trigger, as Hans had shown her at the shooting range in Vienna. "What's your name?" she asked.

"Elrick," he said. His teeth chattered in the warm breeze that stirred the broad leaves of the banana trees.

"How old are you, Elrick?"

"Sixteen."

"You should be in school." Felicity raged at Neville's intransigence and stupidity that had led to boys like this taking up guns instead of books.

"Who can afford school?" asked Elrick, and Felicity was reminded of her cousin Arnold so many years ago. *School is for you people from foreign,* he had told her.

"I thought Neville made schools free."

"Free? It ain't free if you have to eat." Elrick spat on the ground. "Brother Carp ain't done nothing to feed we families. That's why we had to remove him from power." He brandished the rifle at Felicity again. "And all you who support him have to stay inside."

"Okay," Felicity said. "Okay." She held out her hands, palms up. "I'll go." She knew he wouldn't intentionally shoot her, but she didn't trust him not to discharge the gun by accident. She turned towards the white walls of Government House that gleamed through the shadows. Mosquitos had settled on her arms and legs, but she dared not slap at them, lest the motion or sound alarm

Elrick. She started to walk, and the gravel, also painted white, crunched under her bare feet. After a few steps, she turned back to see Elrick still watching her. "Elrick," she said. "How does this all end?"

She couldn't read his face in the dark as his voice rolled towards her. "It ends," he said, "when Brother Carp accepts the transfer of power, Brother Henry is we new leader, and we all has worker solidarity and no more bourgeoisie."

Felicity doubted he knew what those words meant. To be honest, neither did she.

THE KITCHEN DOOR was still unlocked, and Felicity slid quietly through. As she pushed the bolt shut, a hand grabbed her arm. She screamed.

"Shh." The hand came over her mouth, and now she relaxed because it was Claude. At last, she was alone with Claude. She had the prize that she had come to Grenada to reclaim. But the lights flashed on, and there was Neville too, blinking in the sudden brightness.

"Felicity, what the ass are you doing?" asked Neville. Claude took his hand from her mouth and let her go.

"Nothing." She shook her thicket of hair back from her face where it clung to her sweaty temples, noticing as she did so that the hairs on her arm had stood up in response to Claude's touch.

"You were outside. We're confined to house arrest. That's not nothing."

"I was looking for a way out of here." She wondered what would happen if she cried. But she couldn't manage to raise tears in the moment, not with the heat of her rage still blazing.

"Are you crazy?" Now it was Neville who raised his voice and Claude who placed a hand on his arm to shush him.

"House arrest is house arrest," said Neville. "We're surrounded by armed men. In case you hadn't noticed."

"Oh, I noticed," Felicity said. "I had a nice chat with one of them. He's sixteen years old. Neville, what the hell have you been doing? How did you piss these people off?"

Claude's eyes signalled a warning, but Felicity no longer cared. Her days of pandering to Neville were over.

"You met up with one of Mark Henry's people, and he didn't shoot you?" Neville's voice took on an admiring tone.

"He's scared to use the gun. I had to show him how to hold it."

Neville grinned. "Fucking your way out of here. I have to admit, if there were any women out there, I might try it too. Brilliant, Felicity."

"I think you've done enough fucking around, Neville." Felicity ran her hand through the tangles in her hair. "I hope you have a pick and an afro spray," she said. "This is a mess."

"You can't go wandering around out there at night, do you understand?" Claude's jaw was set, the way it always was when he was annoyed. "It's dangerous. We don't need an international incident with some foreigner who got in the way."

Felicity's body sagged under the weight of his disdain, and two sleepless nights on Neville's couch. She was too tired to maintain the flirtatious facade that had been her armour until now.

"I was trying not to be in the way." Tears poked at the edges of her eyes.

"You should never have come," Claude said.

The tears began sliding down her face; she had come here to be with Claude. She pressed her forearm into her leaking eyes. "Neville said it could help. That I was collateral."

"You did," Claude said to Neville.

"Shit." Neville bounded across the kitchen. "Felicity, I'm sorry. You were in the wrong place at the wrong time. I should have just told them to let you go."

No, she had been in the right place, exactly where she wanted to be. Neville pulled her to his chest, and she jerked away. It was always Claude who had comforted her, Claude who had been there after each failed audition, Claude who had recognized her longing for her absent father, even if he didn't understand it. "It's okay," Neville said in her ear, and his closeness overrode her power to resist. She allowed herself to go limp in his arms, and Neville patted her back with practiced expertise. "Don't try that again," he said. "Let me figure out what we should do. I'll decide if we're going to escape."

Felicity raised her head. "Why don't you just surrender? Let Mark Henry be the prime minister if he wants it so bad? Let him find out it's not as easy as he thinks." She sniffled and wiped her palms across her face.

Claude said, "Or agree to share power. Like you said you would."

Watching Claude challenge Neville was as if the sun had suddenly shattered the night, or snowflakes had started to spin through the tropical air. Felicity's tears stopped. Neville's arms stiffened around her. "You too, brother? You're against me now?"

"Of course not," Claude said. "It's just that there is the safety of other people in this house to consider." Felicity knew he was thinking not so much of her but of Pat, sleeping upstairs, with Claude's baby curled inside her.

Footsteps sounded on the stairs, and Neville smoothly pushed Felicity away from him and went to the fridge. By the time Alison entered the kitchen, Neville was pouring water into a glass from a jug and Felicity was leaning against the wall. "What's going on?" Alison asked. Her eyes narrowed and Felicity saw the scene from her perspective — wet patches across the front of Neville's light grey T-shirt, Felicity with red eyes and hair even more dishevelled than it had been at bedtime, tangible tension in the air.

"Nothing," said Neville. "Felicity isn't feeling well, so I'm just getting her a drink of water. Claude and I were chatting. I'm coming to bed in a minute."

"You said that an hour ago." Alison would never stop trying to claim Neville, attempting to cajole, trap, or guilt him into a relationship, a marriage, everyone could see he didn't want. Felicity wouldn't stoop to that with Claude. She wanted Claude to choose her, to forsake Pat and throw himself at her feet, as so many other men had done. She took a sip from the glass Neville shoved at her, unable to meet his eyes.

"I think I'll be okay," she said. "I was just feeling a little anxious, but I'm better now. Thanks, Neville. Don't forget, I need that pick and hairspray." Alison moved closer to Neville and rested her head on the shoulder where Felicity had just cried. Claude loped up the stairs to Pat, leaving Felicity alone again.

FELICITY LAY ON the living room couch looking up at the ceiling fan that spun lazily, barely stirring the thick, hot air. The faint scent of cigarette smoke seeping under her door and the creak of the floorboards in the hallway told her Neville had not returned to bed with Alison but was in the hall, pacing.

She wondered who the Metropolitan Opera had found to replace her in what should have been her first *Traviata*, whether they had trusted the understudy with the role or brought in a more experienced Violetta. The music she had studied so intently over the past few months ran through her brain. She lingered on the opening scene, an elaborate party in an opulent room. She wondered what kind of gown the wardrobe department would have constructed for her. All eyes would be on Felicity, draped with jewellery designed for maximum sparkle under the lights as she glided onstage. She would take a deep breath that lifted her diaphragm and expanded her ribs, and she would sing "Al piacere m'affido, ed io soglio, con tal farmaco i mali sopir." *To pleasure I give myself and in pleasure I trust, because its medicine banishes my troubles.*

Hans was to be the conductor. The man who had taught her how to shoot a gun, and who had directed her in her first leading role on the European continent. *L'elisir d'amore,* more than twelve years ago, when Felicity was a child of twenty-three. Her daughter

Mara was two, and Adele was not yet born. Felicity was still married to Anthony, though that was but a minor inconvenience.

"Your job is to bend to my will," Hans told her. "I don't want you to pause so long on that phrase. It's schmaltzy." He bit her ear. "You understand?"

"I understand, Maestro." But on opening night, Hans's baton was a thin white blur, no more than a pencil. Insignificant. Felicity could feel the curiosity of the audience as she entered the stage. A Black singer in a white space. An interloper from the New World to the Old. They were here to see what she could do, and no matter how hard Hans waved his stick, she took her pauses, feeling the audience hold its breath with her and then, at the end of the aria, the crash of their applause, like waves of the sea. The next day, the reviews praised Hans for his impeccable sense of style and flawless direction. *White people,* she remembered Claude saying. *They take everything from us, take credit for everything we do.*

Felicity shifted position on the hard couch. She imagined she could feel Claude's breaths through the ceiling, and yet he was no closer to her than when she had lived an ocean away and spent her nights with the likes of Hans, giving herself to pleasure. The soldiers outside the window shouted commands to each other and the flames from their bonfire cast flickering shadows into the room, reminding Felicity of the time when the cocoa estates had burned and the skies above them had glowed red.

The crackling crescendo of the flames collided with the music playing in Felicity's head. She rolled onto her other side. She could not escape and had only herself to blame, because she had opened the letter.

ACT I
CHAPTER 2.

Winnipeg, Manitoba, September 8, 1983

IMPORTANT NEWS NEVER came by mail. Felicity's agent and publicist took care of her professional communications. If they had anything important to tell her, they would call. Her lovers were not the letter-writing kind, and there was only one missive she wanted to read. The mail was for bills, junk, and desperate appeals for attention from people grasping at straws, seeking access to her without understanding that they were supposed to go through her agent. Her mother had left a pile of envelopes on the hallway table that Felicity was only now tackling, three days after her return from singing *Magic Flute* in Tokyo. She was still waking at three in the afternoon, her brain jumbled after flying through half the world's time zones, and she sat at the kitchen table in her robe waiting for the coffee as she flicked through the envelopes.

The crest on the corner attracted her attention. Red, yellow and green; they were the colours of the Grenadian flag, currently flown by the Revolutionary Government of the People of Grenada, and its name was stamped underneath the image. This was the letter she had longed for over the past twelve years. Alone in countless hotel suites and dressing rooms, she had closed her eyes and manifested it sliding from the mail carrier's hand into her black metal mailbox, the way she had been able to visualize so many of her professional successes before they happened. To Felicity, a dream was an item on a to-do list that would eventually be checked off — it was just a matter of when.

Her lungs gathered breath as if she were about to walk onstage, as if the introduction to her opening aria was already playing. She ripped the envelope open, pulled out a sheet of paper with the same crest at the top of it, and read:

Dear Miss Alexander:

Greetings, in solidarity with the workers on the land, from the Black Pearls of Freedom, the Revolutionary Government of the People of Grenada, led by the Honourable Neville Carpenter, Prime Minister.

You are receiving this letter because you are a performing artist of high standing with a known connection to the island of Grenada, and it is believed that you may be a friend of the Revolutionary government of our independent nation. The government wishes to increase its profile and standing abroad, and to that end, we are planning a showcase of music and arts for October 7, 1983, in St. George's, Grenada, to which we will be inviting leaders from neighbouring countries and other sympathetic governments. We are hoping that you will participate by performing a few musical selections. If at all possible, your presentation should be on the themes of Black liberation, economic cooperation, socialism, land reform, or worker solidarity.

If you are willing to be part of this event, please contact the Minister of Leisure and Culture, the Honourable Melvin Cleveland, and we will add you to the program. Travel to Grenada will be at your own expense, but if the showcase is profitable, we will offer reimbursement.

Power to the people,

The Honourable Assistant to Melvin Cleveland

Frank Potts

So much of the letter was clueless. It was inappropriate to send a performance request directly to an artist at Felicity's level — she was not a high school kid providing entertainment for a Mother's

Union tea. Her schedule was full for years, and it was only by coincidence that this showcase coincided with the break that she had engineered to do some coaching before singing her first *Traviata* at the Metropolitan Opera. And imagine asking a world-class artist to cover her own travel. It was laughable. Yet none of that mattered, because the letter signified only one thing — Claude's government, the one in which he was deputy prime minister, wanted her to come to Grenada. Claude wanted to see her. He had finally responded to the letters she had sent him, belatedly accepting the offer he made to her at the sugar plantation in Vincennes. Claude's absence was the one hole left in her life, and, like all the others before it, she had filled it. She had manifested the reality she desired.

The boys had made it, and this letter was proof of their success. Claude and Neville were heads of government on their beloved island, and Felicity, too, had reached the heights of her profession. Now they all performed on the world's great stages; for her, the Met and La Scala, and for the boys, the United Nations.

FELICITY'S MOTHER STOPPED by with Aunt Rose, after work, before the girls came home from school. Felicity still sat at the kitchen table with another cup of coffee and her score of *Linda di Chamounix*; not the one that she had used for her Met debut six years ago, in which she had overzealously noted the stage directions above every measure, but the older copy from which she had sung her first student show in London. She had decided to perform its most glorious aria, "O luce di quest'anima," at the showcase in Grenada.

Mom opened the door with her key and walked in as if this were her house. She didn't bother with greetings or pleasantries. "Felicity!" she said. "You're still in your pyjamas? And you haven't combed your hair?"

"I just flew in from Tokyo," Felicity said.

"Three days ago." Mom looked around the kitchen and Felicity saw her assessing the dirty dishes in the sink, the takeout containers on the counter, the wilting plants she had never wanted in the first place.

"I'm still jet-lagged. I was working my ass off. Rehearsals every day for two weeks."

"Language, Felicity," said Mom.

"Flower!" said Aunt Rose from the hallway. "It's so good to see you. Welcome home." She opened her arms, and Felicity rested her head on her warm, solid chest and breathed in the fruity scent of her hair oil, the sweetness of the baby powder she sprinkled on her damp skin after a bath, and the faint aroma of onions.

"Josiah will be happy to see you too," Aunt Rose said. "He's getting out on Monday."

"How long has it been again?" Felicity asked.

"Almost a year," said Aunt Rose. Almost a year since Felicity had spent the last hours of Thanksgiving with Josiah at Jack's place. A flush spread through her body. She squirmed in her seat and stared down at the letter from Grenada. She tried to remember what else she had been doing a year ago. Pining for Claude and preparing to sing *Candide* in Sydney. After that, flying to Amsterdam for a recital, and pining for Claude. Working on a plan to fly to Chicago to record a blues album and make private music with Russell Pinto. Aunt Rose would have spent the past year praying for her son, having not yet realized the ineffectuality of her actions, and playing her blues records, which she called her "crying music."

Felicity lifted her head from Aunt Rose's embrace and picked up the letter from Grenada. "I'm glad you came by, Mom," she said, "because I was about to call you. I got this invitation to sing in Grenada. I thought it might be nice if you and the girls came."

"Grenada?" Mom sounded as if Felicity had asked her to go to Iran, and not the country of Mom's birth. "Why on earth would you sing in Grenada?"

"The government is having an international showcase of Grenadian talent from home and abroad."

"This invitation is from the government? You mean Neville Carpenter and his gang?"

Felicity slammed the letter onto the table. "They're not a gang, Mom! They've increased employment and literacy rates. They're using more land for agriculture — they're doing really good things." She regurgitated everything she had devoured from the newspapers, all the information she had gleaned listening to radio talk shows as she sat in the back seat of one cab after another.

"And rounding people up and throwing them in jail," said Mom.

"That's not true. That's just their enemies trying to make them look bad. Anyway, they're better than Percy Tibbs was."

"I don't know about that," Mom said. "You know there's a song, 'Lord have mercy, bring back Uncle Percy.'"

"The Black Pearls of Freedom have massive popular support. And they took power from Tibbs in a completely bloodless coup. Tibbs was killing people." Felicity shuddered as she recalled the soulless eyes of a man who cared for nothing but holding power for its own sake.

"Never mind all that," Aunt Rose said. "You're in Canada now. We live in the best country in the world. We have freedom here." Felicity was infuriated by her aunt's ability to speak such a blatant lie, when just two years ago, Aunt Rose's own son had been beaten so badly by Winnipeg police that he almost died.

"What do the Black Pearls want with you?" Mom said to Felicity. "I wouldn't trust those people. Why are you even considering helping them?"

"I knew Neville Carpenter in university, remember I told you? And some of the others in his government." Felicity looked at her discarded score, longing to pick it up and fill her head with the beauty of "O luce" instead of this bothersome conversation.

"I don't know why you were wasting time with that when you had your studies to attend to. Perhaps if you had done better in your classes, you could be teaching today instead of having to travel all over to sing, no steady job."

"Oh, no, Dolores," said Aunt Rose. "Felicity is doing so well, and we are all so proud of her. You're a wonderful teacher, but Felicity is using her gifts, just like Corinthians tells us to do. She's a credit to our race."

"That's exactly it," Felicity said. "The Grenadian government recognizes me as a musician of Grenadian heritage and they want me to perform, and I want to do it. It would be nice for Mara and Adele to come with me. They've never seen Grenada. I'll be busy with rehearsals so I thought if you came you could show them around." She ran her fingers along the fold of the letter, trying to hide her discomfort at the thought of being alone with her daughters.

"I don't want anything to do with Neville Carpenter's government," Mom said. "I don't support Communists."

Mom had staked her position, and she would not retreat. With her or without her, Felicity would go to Grenada, and she would bring her girls. It was time she told them the truth about their origins.

AFTER MOM LEFT, Felicity pushed aside the cold cup of coffee. She stood up and paced the room. She was desperate to see Claude, but she feared seeing him. Her skin had retained the memory of his, but her heart had grown knotty with scars. Twelve years since she had last seen him in Grenada. Eighteen years since they had met in London, when she was eighteen and he was twenty-one.

Felicity should have known that it was useless trying to talk to her mother, but there was one person who had never failed her. She called Jack before she went to see him. Abby had begun insisting upon it when she ended the separation, instead of merely complaining about Felicity's visits. "But Abby, we don't do that," Felicity had said, relying on their old bonds of culture and community, since that was all she and Abby had now.

Abby's face tightened, and the shadows settled under her eyes. "We?" said Abby. "You are the one coming to my house to talk to my husband. I'm not coming to your house."

"You could if you want," said Felicity. When they were children, Abby had spent almost every weekend with Mom, Felicity, Aunt Rose, and Josiah in the little bungalow they had shared. Abby's house was even smaller and held the whining mouths of her many siblings and the clothes iron that in her mother's hand sent bruises marching across Abby's back. Felicity's home was a respite for Abby, and Felicity, with no friends at school besides Josiah, had relished the time with her church companion. "We were like sisters, Ab," Felicity had said. "You met Jack through me. You knew he was my friend."

"Friends," Abby had said. "I don't know what you are now, but it isn't friends. You call before you come."

So Felicity called. "Sure, Fizzy," said Jack. "Come on over. We've finished supper."

Jack was unshaven and his hair straggled loose from his ponytail. Felicity's eyes swept across the guitar occupying a seat at the kitchen table and the plate before Jack, scraped clean. She smelled tomato sauce. Homemade; Abby never bought the jarred version. "Pasta?" she guessed. She hadn't made anything for supper. The girls would get home to find her gone, as was her normal state, and they would fend for themselves.

"Lasagna." Jack got up and retrieved another plate from the cupboard. "Your favourite. Kept some for you."

"Abby must be pissed she made it, now I'm here to eat it."

"Come on, Fizzy." Jack passed a trembling hand across his eyes.

"Where is she?"

"Lying down," Jack said. "It's her ... you know." Felicity swallowed the rush of envy, the fear that Jack and Abby would get what they most desired, the relief that it wasn't going to happen for at least another month.

"Sorry," she said. "Do you want me to go? Do you need to be with her?" *Please say no, please say no,* she chanted to herself.

"It's okay, Fizzy. I think she just needs some time alone." Jack spooned a slice of lasagna onto Felicity's plate.

"Well, she can fucking cook, anyway," Felicity said. Then, chastened by the real sorrow in Jack's eyes, "You guys could adopt." She knew Abby wouldn't. *I'm not a child thief,* Abby had said when Felicity made the same suggestion to her. Felicity wanted to shout that having children wasn't all it was cracked up to be, that Abby was lucky to be freed from domestic slavery, that she could have her life to herself. Jack could too, and instead he was wasting time moping about not having something that was not worth having.

Jack said, "I worry that if Abby and I —"

"If you have a kid, they'll be like me," Felicity said. She told herself not to be bitter even as she said, "An outcast." Half Black and half white. In Canada, indistinguishable from the other Blacks — called the same names, sniffed at by the other parents in the same way. In Grenada, pointed at for being "red-skinned," for "acting sociable," for thinking she was better than everyone else. In London with Claude, suspected of being a trophy, or evidence of his hypocrisy, always feeling that she had to work harder to make people realize that she had only ever been Black. That the Ukrainian man who sired her, of whom her mother had spoken only once to tell her that he was dead, had no impact upon her allegiances. But Jack would not be like Felicity's absent father. He would be at the centre of his child's life; a child who would carry not just Jack's blood into the world, but also his wisdom. In a haze of anger and grief, Felicity had renounced white men a year ago, but she could not give Jack up.

Felicity felt a welling in her throat and lowered her head. Jack had seen her tears countless times, but these ones were just for her. She picked at the label on her beer bottle, noticing that it was time for a manicure.

"You're not an outcast, Fizzy," Jack said. From under her eyelids, she saw his Adam's apple jump, and he smoothed fine, stray strands of hair from his face. "But never mind me. What's going on with you?" He got up again and returned with another beer for each of them.

She had allowed herself to get sucked into Jack's problems and had forgotten why she came over in the first place. "I got this letter, Jack. From Claude." She passed it across the table.

Jack's head bent over the page. "This isn't from Claude. It's from Frank Potts. He works for Claude. Claude's the deputy prime minister."

"You know what I mean." Felicity stifled the urge to kick him.

"Hmmm." Jack shed the role of frustrated husband and transformed into pastor and counsellor. "What does this letter really mean to you?"

"It just seems like it's meant to be," she said. "I'm always booked up, but then this fall, I'm set to debut *Traviata* and I book off time to go to New York and coach it and, boom, an invitation from Grenada."

"You should go, if you really want to." He reached for his guitar. "It's just that I saw on the news that there's talk of an invasion. The Americans are getting fed up with your friend Mr. Carpenter. They say he's building a runway to land Russian warplanes. You'd better come back in one piece, or" — he grimaced, cast his gaze upwards towards the bedroom — "I don't know what I'll do."

AFTER RETURNING FROM Jack's place, Felicity raised the letter from the Revolutionary Government of Grenada to her face. Brushing the paper across her cheek, she wondered if Claude had touched it before it was placed in its envelope. If his fingers had lingered where hers now rested. She imagined those fingers running along her arm, the scent of him filling her nostrils. But the letter held no further clues.

She ordered pizza for dinner. When Mara and Adele came down to eat, she told them about the invitation. "What do you think? Do you girls want to go to Grenada?"

"Can I meet my dad's family?" Adele asked. "And see his grave?"

Felicity had denied Adele her history long enough. "Yes," she said. "You can meet your father's family." It had to happen sometime, she told herself.

"Well, good for you," said Mara. She kicked at the table leg.

"You don't want to come, Mara?"

"What does Grenada have to do with me? My dad lives in Alberta, but I never get to see him."

Felicity gulped back her nausea. There was no room for Brian in her head just now. "You will," she said. "After." That also had to happen sometime.

"I don't want to go to Grenada," said Mara. "I don't even fit in with the Grenadian League."

"What do you mean, you don't fit in?" asked Felicity. Years ago, her mother had enrolled both girls in the Grenadian League dance group, which performed traditional Grenadian maypole and harvest dances for cultural celebrations.

"I don't look like the other girls," said Mara. "She does." She pointed at Adele.

Felicity understood Mara. At fourteen, her eyes had been opened to the difference in skin tone between herself and her eleven-year-old half-sister.

"Can I stay here with Grandma?" Mara asked. But Felicity needed her mother to come to Grenada. She didn't want Adele tagging along to rehearsals and the meeting she hoped to engineer with Claude. Adele was too young to leave alone with family members who were strangers, separated not only by distance and time but by another ocean of resentment and bitterness.

"I'm going to call Grandma and talk to her again," said Felicity.

The calypso music was so loud that Mom couldn't hear Felicity at first. When she realized who it was, she called, "Just a minute, Rose." Back with Felicity, she said, "I have company, Felicity."

"I hear that." Felicity twisted the phone cord around her fingers. "How come?"

"I meant to tell you when I was there," Mom said. "The school's making me a principal. First Black principal in a school in Manitoba. I thought you and I could have a nice dinner to celebrate with Rose and the girls, but then I invited some of the ladies from church to my place instead."

Cackling laughter spun down the phone wires. Felicity had been excluded from her mother's moment of triumph. Her mother had found better company. "Congratulations, Mom." The words sounded dull, even to her ears, although she meant them. She could see now how hard her mother's struggle had been, raising Felicity by herself, insisting on their dignity, clawing her way to an education in a world that barely acknowledged her humanity. A thought formed, and Felicity said, "Wouldn't it be nice to go back to Grenada and tell them about it?"

"They told us never to come back," Mom said. "Don't you remember? After my mother died."

They had not discussed that day. Felicity was ten. Her mother had taken her back to Grenada because her grandmother was dying, and Mom's sisters were angry because Grandma had died when they had all gone to a workers' strike meeting, leaving Felicity and Mom alone in the house with her. Their fury was compounded by Mom's failure to call a priest for the last rites, which they blamed on the fact that Mom had left the Catholic faith to become a Baptist. "I doubt they remember that," Felicity said. "I don't think they meant it." She cast another glance at the letter. "Anyway, that was over twenty-five years ago. You're a principal now," she said. "You're president of the Grenadian League. Shouldn't you sometimes see the country you're always talking about?"

"I suppose," her mother said.

Felicity's mother had lived in Canada for almost forty years, and she still called Grenada home. Mom was born there, but Felicity had entered the world in Winnipeg. She had never felt that she belonged in this flat, cold prairie town, and yet she had not left it; her house and her family were here. Her own life was lived between hotel rooms, getting in and out of planes and cars that flashed from stage door to stage door. Even though she had only been to Grenada twice, Felicity imagined that scrap of green floating on the blue skirts of the ocean as her home too.

CHAPTER 3.

St. George's, Grenada, October 10, 1983

UP IN THE hills, Grenadian mornings began with the cries of roosters piercing the darkness along with the first pale yellow streaks of light. But at Government House, the day started when tanks rattled into the courtyard to relieve the soldiers of the night shift. Their arrival was Felicity's cue to give up on sleep. She sat on the lumpy couch and rolled her shoulders, cracking away the stiffness. There were so many things she longed for. A cup of hot coffee, ground from dark roasted beans, or a frothy cappuccino at a café in Rome and a plate of lightly oiled linguini, sprinkled with fresh parsley. A piano, and a pile of scores. The freedom to sing. And Jack. How she wished she could talk to Jack. But he was lost to Felicity now, cut off from the rest of the world. She wondered what news had filtered out to him.

Felicity initially expected to see Claude at the dress rehearsal, three days after she arrived on the island. But when the roosters woke her on her first morning in Grenada, she knew she couldn't wait. She told her family she was going to find somewhere to practice, but as soon as she got to St. George's, she called Claude's former law office. She wasn't sure if he was still connected to it, but it was a starting point. She was surprised when a young male voice answered, "Black Pearls of Freedom headquarters."

Felicity pulled her courage to her like a shawl, and said, "I'm looking for Claude Buckingham."

"And who might you be?"

"One of the performers for the showcase."

"Oh, are you wanting to see where the showcase is going to be? I think Brother Buck is over there now. It's at St. Thomas's church hall. You know where that is?"

She did. When she got there, she stood outside, adjusting her clothing. Her underwear was damp from the anticipation of seeing Claude and her bra was saturated with sweat. Her curls were on full display, the way Claude liked them. She tugged at the skirt of her blue flowery sundress. She was thirty-six now — Claude had last seen her when she was twenty-four, if she didn't count those few seconds in London. She wondered what changes time had wrought upon him. Upon them both. Calypso music boomed from the hall as she shouldered the door open.

The first person she saw was Alison, much bigger than she had been in London and now wearing glasses, conferring intensely with a heavily pregnant woman. She noticed several other people putting up decorations, or milling around, before her gaze fell on Claude. He was the tallest person in the room. He was directing the placement of large banners on the wall. "FORWARD TOGETHER," "BLACK POWER," and "BLACK PEARLS ARE THE MOST PRECIOUS."

"Neville, what do you think?" he bellowed over the music as he turned around. Then his gaze rested on Felicity, standing in the doorway. He paused for a moment too long. There was no smile, nothing but a cold recognition. He walked towards her and when he reached her, he said, "What are you doing here, Felicity?"

The drums began pounding in Felicity's chest. She reminded herself, *I am Felicity Alexander. I am a bona fide star. I am a regular at the Metropolitan Opera, La Scala, and Covent Garden. Audiences go wild for me. I have been on the cover of* Opera News *thirteen times. I have nothing to be ashamed of. I am every bit as much a success as he is, maybe even more. There is no one else as good as me in this showcase. He needs me more than I need him.* She looked directly at Claude as she said, "I'm here to see the performance space."

"Oh," Claude said, "that's right, you're in the showcase." His tone implied that this was a decision that had nothing to do with him, maybe even one with which he did not agree.

Felicity was in full diva mode, the one that had earned her the nickname "Alexander the Great" at the Met for using lines such as the one with which she had skewered a hapless tenor who dared to try to steal the spotlight from her in rehearsal: *With a face like yours, you really need to sing and fuck much better than you do.* The Met sold "Alexander the Great" T-shirts in its gift shop, decorated with a caricature drawing of her face, ringed by chaotic springs of hair.

"I was planning to do the showcase, but I expected a more professional venue."

Claude responded, "We're just getting ready. We're not finished. We're getting a nice piano brought in from one of the hotels." His gaze floated past Felicity. "You should talk to Neville if you have questions. This is all his idea." He gestured across the room, and Neville loped over, a slow smile simmering.

"Felicity!" he said, holding out his hand. Before she could take it, he withdrew it and enveloped her in a hug. "You look fantastic, as always. It's been years!"

"Prime Minister Carpenter." Neville's smile grew broader.

"I told you it was going to happen!" he said. "Didn't I tell you?"

"You did," Felicity said, transported back to London.

"You've reached the top, too," said Neville. "Everyone we called for the showcase, all the music students" — Felicity felt a stab of dismay that she was to perform with students — "they all couldn't believe you were part of this. They say you're big time. Really big time."

Felicity nodded as her smile curved into a death mask. Claude had eased away from them. He was standing very close to the pregnant woman, his hand resting lightly on her lower back as he looked down at her and she leaned her head on his chest. Something about her seemed familiar. Felicity didn't have to hear their conversation to know that she was complaining about her aches and pains and the heat, and he was giving comfort to her, the way he used to give Felicity comfort. The way no one gave her comfort now. She was too late. Claude had ended things with Marlene after all, but not for her.

She should leave now. But then it would be obvious she was a scorned lover slinking away. And, whatever was going on with Claude, Felicity believed in the Revo. Grenada was a tent with its pegs planted in her heart. She lay in hotel beds in one foreign city after another and remembered the true blackness of the nights, the sandpaper scratch of the cicadas, and the glowing red skies.

As she stood in the doorway, reviewing the frame of her leaving and the one of her staying, a convoy of Jeeps rattled into view. Neville grew rigid, staring past Felicity as the Jeeps stopped on the road opposite the church. Men in camouflage outfits, guns with metal teeth slung across their bodies, ran towards them. "Aw, shrimps," said Neville. The camera in Felicity's mind slowed down as the men surrounded the building. Two of them marched up to Neville, holding a piece of paper.

"Neville Carpenter, you are being placed under arrest. Norman Porter has seized control of Grenada and is now the leader of the Black Pearls of Freedom and prime minister of Grenada. All the rest of you" — he made a sweeping motion with his arm that included Felicity — "are under arrest too." The paper trembled in his hand.

"You're doing good, brother. Let me see that," said Neville, plucking the sheet of paper from the soldier's hand. He scanned it and said, "Come on, man." Ripping it in half, he let it drop to the ground. The pieces fluttered forlornly, dying butterflies returning to the dust. "You can't be serious. What does Norman think he's playing at? The people will never accept him over me."

The soldier stood his ground, though his voice now shook more than the paper. "You are under arrest. All current ministers not loyal to Brother Porter are under arrest. I — the paper say what go happen. We are to march you to your house and keep you there so you cannot interfere with Brother Porter."

"Claude!" Neville shouted, still not sounding worried. Claude looked up. He had settled the pregnant woman in a chair and was now kneeling on the ground, rubbing her feet. He patted her reassuringly on one knee and came over, never even once looking at Felicity.

"Claude Buckingham," the soldier said, his forehead now jewelled with beads of sweat, "I am placing you under arrest on behalf of Prime Minister Norman Porter —"

Claude shot Neville a look of exasperation. "Fucking Norman!" he said. "I told you to deal with him at the last Party meeting. We should have put him under heavy manners." A whole story was exchanged between Neville and Claude in seconds.

Neville looked sheepish. "Maybe we can talk to him now." The soldier and his companion, however, had decided that the time for talking was past, and raised their guns to their shoulders. Felicity had heard enough. She did not want to be caught in the middle of a Third World coup. She turned to slip away, but one of the soldiers on the outside of the perimeter spotted her, and stepped forward to meet her, pointing his gun.

"Stay where you are!" he yelled. He cradled the long metal tube as if he were curious to know what would happen if he used it.

"Let her go," Neville said. "She's just —" He paused, in response to a jab in the ribs from Claude.

With everyone watching, Felicity realized that all she had to do was identify herself as a Canadian citizen, and she could be on her way. Whatever quarrel these men had had nothing to do with her. She opened her mouth, but then she looked back at Claude. Their shared past hung between them and the limitless future she had once hoped for with him still stood in his eyes, along with something else. A warning? His body that had so often lain so close to hers, that she could still read, crackled with a message to keep silent. If she used her status now, there would be no more chances with Claude. Another more pragmatic thought nudged out the ones about Claude — her agent would not be happy for it to be reported that she was mixed up in this amateur coup attempt. She shrugged her shoulders and eased back towards the church. The soldier lowered his gun.

"Carp, your woman can stay right there," said one of the soldiers, and Felicity realized they had taken her for Neville's girlfriend. "Carp, Buck, you stand here. Everybody out! Let's see who we have in here!" he yelled into the church hall, where the occupants crowded silently around the windows. They shuffled out at gunpoint, as their captor called their names.

"Melvin Cleveland," he said. "Frank Potts." That was the minister who had written to Felicity, and his assistant. "Lee McPhail. Lawrence Francis. Kingdon Miller. Alison Greaves. Patricia Jack." Patricia was the pregnant woman, who was leaning on Alison as she shuffled through the door. And Felicity recognized that name. Patricia Jack was Miss World, the one she had seen coming out of the Albert Hall the night she and Claude had confronted Percy Tibbs in London. Her face had matured, the sleek hair was replaced with a large afro, her formerly slim legs now ended in swollen ankles, but she had the same fine features. The same mix of haughtiness and shyness that had stamped itself on Felicity's memory.

"You don't need the women, do you?" Claude asked.

"Are you loyal to Neville Carpenter?" the soldier demanded of Alison.

"Yes," Alison said without hesitation, her voice carrying over the uneasy tableau. "Yes, I am."

"Over there." The soldier pointed to the line of ministers. "And you?" he asked Patricia.

There was a long silence before she said, "Yes."

"Then, go." He pointed to the group of Neville's people and she trudged over, one hand still on her aching back.

"What's your name?" the soldier asked Felicity.

The name, used only with Claude at the clinic, presented itself without thought. "Lydia Felix."

"We will be marching to Neville Carpenter's house where you will be confined," announced the lead soldier, his confidence growing by the second.

"Can't you drive Pat there in the Jeep?" Claude asked.

"It isn't far," the man said. They began walking. Felicity was aware of the sound of her high-heeled sandals clacking on the cobblestones, drawing attention. Alison and Patricia wore flat, serviceable shoes and she imagined them smirking at her. Even now, she could still say, "Actually, there's been a mistake. I'm from Canada, and I need to get back." But she walked on, a gun at her back. She didn't know where she was going, but Claude would be there, and where he was, she was going too. She left Jack, and her mother, and her children, to go with Claude. This time, she would not leave Claude, and she would not leave Grenada.

CHAPTER 4.

Vincennes, Grenada, July 5, 1958

AFTER THREE MONTHS visiting Grenada with her mother, Felicity was becoming used to the heat and the way it coated her body with its steamy weight. She could tell how far away the rain was from the speed at which the clouds moved in from over the sea. She had adapted to her new routine in the crowded wooden house without electricity or running water, where she and Mom slept in a room with a leaky roof and a net tied around their bed to keep out the mosquitos. She walked three miles with her cousins through the hills every morning to school, and then came home and listened to Mom arguing with their relatives about religion and the right kind of church.

When Felicity lay in bed, she could hear music rolling through the floor from the radio downstairs, and she sang along to Elvis Presley and Chuck Berry until her eyes closed. Someone snapped the radio on again in the morning, sometimes before the roosters had started to crow. Mornings in Grenada were brighter than in Canada, and the nights were blacker, without a single streetlight or headlight.

Aunt Beulah was the one who argued the most; but, today, she was smiling as she announced that Ina Smith from up the road was getting married.

"Everyone going. All of we invited." She looked sideways at Mom. "But what about Ma? We can't leave she."

Felicity's grandmother was sick; that was why they had come.

Mom said, "I'll stay."

"Can Felicity go with us?" asked Aunt Rachel.

"Yes!" said Aunt Ida. "We could press her hair. It go look so nice-nice."

Felicity longed to have her hair pressed straight. "Can I, Mom?"

"I want Felicity to stay with me."

"That's not fair!" Felicity's chest began to swell and so did her eyes.

"What if I need help?"

"Oh, shrimps, man! Ma been all right lately," Aunt Beulah said.

Mom raised a hand, then dropped it. "I don't know —"

"Oh, never mind!" Aunt Beulah said. "Keep her here, then. Our weddings not good enough for you anyway."

When her aunts left the house on the day of the wedding, in their best hats and dresses, their stiff-straight hair insured against the humidity with layers of Vaseline, Felicity stormed up the ladder to the bedroom. But she was forced to come back down an hour later by a need to use the bathroom. When she pulled down her panties, she knew that something was wrong. She screamed, "Mom! Mooooom!"

"Felicity Lydia Alexander!" Mom shouted back. "I don't want to hear another word."

"I'm bleeding," Felicity wailed.

Mom ran into the bathroom. "Are you sure?" she asked. Her voice sounded funny.

Felicity held up the stained panties.

"This is normal. It happens to every woman once a month."

"But I'm not a woman. I'm ten years old!"

"You're turning into one. And you're almost eleven."

"I don't want to turn into a woman!" Felicity said. Not if being a woman meant that blood came out of you every single month. Not if it made you frown and bite your lip, like Mom was doing now.

"You don't have a choice, Felicity. This means you can carry a baby now, and so you have to keep away from boys. Don't let them touch you, don't let them see you without your clothes on, don't believe them if they try to sweet-talk you. If you have a baby, your life is ruined."

Felicity didn't want to have a baby. There were lots of babies at Salvation Baptist. Everyone said how cute they were, but their crying made Felicity's head hurt. The stink from their diapers hung in the air in the washroom, causing her to gag. And sometimes she stumbled upon a mother nursing in one of the back rooms. The thought of a tiny mouth on her chest, sucking and pulling, made her feel sicker.

"Did I ruin your life?" Felicity asked. She already knew she had. She had heard Mom tell Aunt Rose many times how hard it was to go back to school and still make ends meet while having another mouth to feed.

"No, of course not, but I had you when I was old enough. I mean it, Felicity Alexander. You listen to me. No boys."

"What about Josiah?" The things Felicity missed most from Canada were arm-wrestling Josiah in the living room after school, throwing a football around his grandparents' backyard while his grandma made Sunday lunch after the service at Salvation Baptist, lying on his bed with their heads touching, reading Josiah's Dennis the Menace comics, Felicity waiting at every page for Josiah to catch up. Aunt Rose and Josiah lived with Mom and Felicity, so Josiah was like her brother even though they weren't actually related by blood. "Can I tell Josiah that I'm a woman now, and I can make a baby?"

"No!" Mom snapped.

"Well, Arnold, then." Josiah had been temporarily replaced by Felicity's cousin, who walked her to school and defended her to the kids who made fun of her accent or her light brown skin or the white father they said she had.

"You don't talk about this time with men, ever," said Mom.

Felicity's back twinged with a sudden awakening of pain. She winced and pressed her fist against the ache. Mom looked at her but said nothing.

"My back hurts, Mom," Felicity whined. She knew she was acting like a brat, but she would rather be a brat than turn into a woman.

"That happens sometimes," said Mom. Felicity waited to see if Mom would hug her. But she didn't.

FELICITY SPENT THE rest of the morning wondering how exactly babies were made. She didn't know much about it, but she was pretty sure you needed a woman and a man.

"Mom," she asked at lunchtime. "Who's my dad?"

Mom's arm jerked and rice spilled across the table. "You don't have a father, Felicity. I've told you before."

"But don't you need a father to make a baby?"

Mom rubbed the sweat from her forehead with her arm. "Your father is dead, Felicity."

Mom had said this before, but Felicity had secretly hoped that Mom was wrong. That her father had been separated from her and Mom against his will, but he was still searching for them and one day would find them again. Thinking of the taunts of the Grenadian kids, she asked, "Was he white?"

Mom shuddered. "Yes, he was." After a minute, she said, "He was Ukrainian."

"Did he love me?" Felicity asked.

Mom's pupils dwindled to tiny black specks and she spoke through a tiny space in her lips. "What a stupid question to ask! Felicity Lydia Alexander, you are a foolish girl."

For the second time that day, Felicity rushed up the ladder and threw herself across her cot. Her body felt achy and funny. She listened to the rain striking the roof.

GRANDMA DIED THE next day, early in the morning, when Mom was alone with her because the aunts were at a workers' meeting. When they got home, they were furious that Mom had not called for the priest. The argument that followed was long and loud and, from what Felicity could tell as she listened from the top of the ladder, it ended with the rest of the family demanding, and Mom agreeing, that Mom and Felicity would go back to Canada as soon as Grandma was laid to rest, which would take place the next day.

It rained that morning, and the adults stayed inside, trying to preserve the smoothness of their pressed funeral hair. When it subsided, Felicity and her cousin Arnold squatted in the mud behind the house to play marbles. Arnold drew a wobbly circle in the dirt and lined up the marbles. "You can go first," he said, clearly of the belief that his skills were superior to hers. *Like all boys*, thought Felicity. She placed the marble he gave her at the edge of the circle. There was a swirl of green and blue at its centre. Arnold's marble, in the middle of the circle, contained a smear of orange, like marmalade. She peered down the length of her arm and flicked the marble with her thumb. Arnold's marble exploded in a spray of glass.

"Oh shrimps! Oh gosh!" he shouted. Felicity expected him to be mad, but he looked at her with growing respect. "How you do that? When you got here, you couldn't play at all."

"I practiced," said Felicity. When the Grenadian kids ignored her, she had drawn her own circle in the dust in the schoolyard, lined up stones, and sent them colliding into each other, over and over.

"You could play with us, you know," he said. Now she was a good player, they would tolerate her.

"I can't," Felicity said. "I'm going home." She wondered if *home* was the right word. When her mother spoke of home before, she had always meant Grenada. But in Grenada, home meant Canada. To Felicity, home was a place where you were not, a place where you didn't quite fit in.

"You going on the big boat?"

"Yes." Felicity dreaded the trip; the nausea and dizziness at the beginning, and once she recovered, the hours of boredom standing on deck staring at the grey sea.

Horns and whistles sounded from the street and the loud bang of a drum grew closer.

"What's happening?" Felicity asked Arnold.

"Is the strike, must be the strike."

The strike was the reason that none of Felicity's aunts had been going to work on the cocoa estates. "Why we should go?" Aunt Beulah had demanded the week before, when Aunt Mary's resolve had wavered. "We already starving on what they pay we. And now they saying cocoa prices crash so they cutting we wages. How we supposed to live? And they want we bow we head and put we hands behind we back when we talking to the estate manager? Why, because they white and we Black?"

Aunt Ida added, "Uncle Percy say we must stand tall to stand for all."

Uncle Percy was the leader of the estate workers. In Aunt Beulah's house, he had taken on higher standing than Jesus, and his picture was higher on the wall than the one of Christ on the cross. Felicity yearned to see Uncle Percy up close, this man who had dark skin, far darker than hers, who drew people from across the island to see him. They walked miles, packed minibuses or crammed donkey carts to go wherever he was giving a speech. Felicity, too, wanted to be someone crowds would come to see, someone they would cheer for.

Felicity ran behind Arnold to the bottom of the road. He stopped at the rum shop, where he swept her back with his arm just as an endless curling tail of strikers surged past. They waved hoes, pitchforks, and shovels. and shouted, "Fight, fight, fight!' as they marched in the direction of the capital city of St. George's. They wore the coveralls and aprons of the estate workers. Their bare feet and ankles were pale with dust.

Arnold lifted his arm and held it up, repeating the chant, "Fight, fight, fight!" The workers grinned and shook their tools in the children's direction. People kept coming down the hill, merging with groups of more workers arriving from either side.

"Bangarang!" shouted Arnold. "Whe look at dat!" Felicity had not seen him smile so brightly. "I want to march with them," he said.

"But you're not an estate worker," said Felicity.

"I will be."

"How do you know that? Maybe you'll be —"

"What, Felicity?" Arnold's voice turned rough and got louder, not the happy celebrating loud of before, but a raw, dangerous loud. "I can be doctor? Lawyer? That is for you people in foreign. My father worked on the estate, his father worked on the estate, and I go work on the estate too."

"But you're good at arithmetic," Felicity said. Arnold helped her with her own work when the numbers confounded her.

"So? What that got to do with anything?" he shouted. "Shrimps, Felicity, my ma can't afford secondary school. How I can go?"

A truck rumbled by, and Arnold grabbed Felicity's arm and pulled her off the road. It was full of white people, in soldiers' uniforms, wearing helmets, their shields and rifles poking through the window as it followed the crowds into town.

"Oh, shrimps," said Arnold, just as one of the marchers ahead of them bent to pick up a rock and threw it at the van. Other rocks followed. The first shot made a boom that could be heard above the screaming and the chanting. "Run!" said Arnold, and Felicity ran. Even as she was terrified, she registered a feeling of happiness. She was connected to something, to people standing tall, to people fighting, refusing to accept less. Arnold thought that because she lived in Canada, everything was easy for her. But Felicity remembered how many times she and Mom went into a store and left empty handed because the clerks wouldn't serve them. How no one sat near them on the bus. "That's all right," Mom always said. "More room to put our things." But Felicity knew it was just one more way they didn't belong.

ONE OF FELICITY'S cousins was dispatched to the rectory to find out if the funeral would be postponed due to the unrest sweeping the island. He returned to announce that Father said it was going ahead. The pallbearers came to their duties fresh from the march, and the proceedings were interrupted by the shouts of workers coming and going from town.

There was a funeral mass in a Catholic church. Felicity couldn't understand any of it because it was all in Latin, read by a priest wearing a long robe with wide sleeves. When he turned his back to them and lifted first a big white circle, then an ornate silver cup, Mom whispered to Felicity to look away, and said, "Remember, salvation is by grace alone." After the mass, the men of the family dug the grave by the side of the road. As the coffin was lowered into its earthy pit, the mourners sat in a circle around it, singing hymns to the rhythm of spoons clinking against the glass bottles of the kerosene-filled *masantos* as flames shivered within. People in Grenada normally feared the night, and as soon as the rim of the sun turned pink and dipped lower in the sky, they rushed home lest they be accosted by a *ligaroo* — a blood-sucking werewolf-like creature — or a *bageede*, a ghost. In the darkness, their reedy singing sounded like the voices of the undead creatures.

Later that night, lying under the mosquito net, Felicity watched a paper coil burning beside her bed as further defence against insects. She swung between a longing to return to Canada and a mourning for Grenada. "Felicity?" whispered Arnold from the doorway. "You sleeping?"

"No," she whispered back. The place between her legs throbbed where she was still bleeding, and her chest ached.

"You want to go see what's happening?"

Of course she did. She rolled away from Mom's sleeping form and followed her cousin downstairs. Arnold waited while Felicity put on her shoes. Like the rest of her family, Arnold didn't own a pair. Felicity felt hot and squirmy about wearing hers, but Mom insisted. "They have feet like leather from walking in these hills all their lives," Mom said. "You don't."

The moon was a tiny sliver of light, and the only other things to pierce the dark were the pinpricks of the fireflies and the stars. There were no *masantos* to light the way; sound was the only guide. The blackness was alive with the scratching cries of the crickets. They followed the distant trail of song laid down by the strikers.

As they grew closer, the sound rearranged itself into words.

We stand tall
We stand for all
We love we leader
Best of all.

Felicity knew the song was about Uncle Percy. A flash pushed the darkness aside; a searing yellow ball that expanded in ripples, growing orange, rimmed with grey smoke. Its hungry crackle silenced the singing. The scent of hot chocolate rose into the air.

"Dey burning down the crops!" Arnold said. "All the cocoa trees." He grabbed Felicity's hand, and they stood by the road, watching as the sky grew red, reflecting the flames below. It was as bright as if the sun had risen early and was beaming its light upon the island. Felicity's eyes grew wet, and she didn't know whether her tears came from the smoke or from the sudden flame of pride that swept through her with the speed of the fire leaping from estate to estate.

"I'm going to fight too," Arnold said to Felicity. "I want Grenada to be free. I want to stand tall."

IN THE MORNING, the donkey cart rattled past blackened trees. Shrivelled leaves clung to branches. Smoke rose into the sunshine. "It's criminal," Mom whispered. "A waste of good food." Mom was also mad about what they had heard on the morning news: a British soldier and several estate workers had been killed in the clashes that had happened before the fire. But the strikers were not giving up. According to the cart driver, the governor was meeting with Uncle Percy later in the day to discuss fair compensation for the workers. Felicity boarded the ship feeling so full of air she might float upward at any moment.

Mom and Felicity stood on deck as the crew hauled the anchor up and the great ship began to move. Felicity felt an urge to sing. Singing was the only place she had to put everything that she was feeling: the loss of Arnold, the gain of Josiah. The strikers and the red skies. She sang, "We stand tall, we stand for all," but the notes were lost in the gusts of wind, the relentless slap of the waves, and the cries of the sea birds. The people standing on the wharf called their last goodbyes to passengers on the deck who shouted back at them, waving and sobbing.

"No one came to see us off," Felicity said. She turned her head so Mom wouldn't see her tears. Mom told her she cried too much, but she couldn't help it.

"No, they didn't, but there will be people to meet us when we get home."

"Aunt Rose," said Felicity, "and Josiah." She gripped the rail of the deck. Seagulls swooped close. The green hills of the tiny island faded into the grey haze of sea spray and the never-ending expanse of ocean.

CHAPTER 5.

St. George's, Grenada, October 11, 1983

FELICITY LAY ON the couch as the ceiling fan stuttered above her. It whirled for a few seconds, came to a halt, and then started up slowly. It was doing nothing to push away the hot air. Her T-shirt had become part of her skin, glued down with a layer of sweat. Outside the window, the soldiers barked commands and marched pointlessly from one end of the yard to the other. A wall of protestors stood outside the gate chanting and waving signs, heaping insults upon the soldiers. Inside the house, the clang of pots and the jangle of cutlery echoed in the kitchen where Alison puttered. A loud conversation was taking place in the dining room. In a house full of people, Felicity was as lonely as she had ever been in a foreign hotel room.

A beetle, its wings an iridescent green, had crawled halfway up the wall and stopped. Felicity watched as it resumed its ascent. Its legs, like tiny pieces of thread, pushed forward into unknown territory. Felicity marvelled at its courage. It passed a brown water spot and stopped.

Neville, Claude, Frank, Lee, and Pat entered, in the throes of their argument. None of them knocked, although the room had been officially assigned to Felicity as her bedroom by Alison. Felicity wished they had found her naked. Frank Potts went to the television and turned it on to nothing but a grey buzzing. "They're blocking the signals," Claude said. "Try the radio." Static cleared into a voice repeating that there had been a coup and Mark Henry was now prime minister. It rattled on, delivering the same announcement it had for days. The voice spoke each word with a pompous over-enunciation as if the speaker knew that this was the most important task he would ever perform.

"It's the Americans," said Neville.

"We should have asked the Russians for some jammers." Lee twirled the radio dial. "We could probably reach Florida with them."

"You know the Russians won't give us anything," Claude said. "Cuba might, but I've told you, they give with strings attached."

The beetle was hurrying now, desperate to reach the ceiling, its wings flashing in the sunlight. The noise from the courtyard grew louder. Felicity felt irritation creeping over her like a rash. Nothing had changed since their university days, she thought. Here were Neville, Claude, and some new players sitting around talking politics like kids, and Alison still running behind, cooking for them. All of them were still more idealistic than practical. She made a sound of disgust without realizing it was audible. The room fell silent. "You have something to say, Felicity?" asked Neville. All eyes swung to her.

She was Alexander the Great. She had sat in the corner long enough. "Yes, I do," she said. "You're all sitting here talking about Russia and America like you're any more than a pawn to them, and you're completely forgetting that this is a human problem."

"How so?" asked Claude.

Felicity said, "Back in London, Claude, you told me that Mark Henry was a good friend of Neville's." She saw Pat lift her head and stare at Claude.

Neville cleared his throat. "Mark and I were best friends in school."

"And Claude came into the picture later, didn't he?"

"I knew who he was," Neville said.

"But you were Mark's friend first," Felicity persisted.

"Well, yes," Neville said, "but Felicity, this is geopolitics. This isn't one of your soap operas."

Felicity used her most commanding voice. "Mark Henry is pissed that you chose Claude over him. What's Mark's position?"

"Minister of defence," said Neville. "It's a very important —"

Felicity cut him off. "You're telling me you took the guy who's jealous you passed him over for someone else and put him in charge of the fucking army? The guys who have us trapped in here?"

"No one asked you to come," said Lee. "We don't know who you are. For all we know, you're an American spy."

"Nah," Neville said. "Easy. Felicity's an old university friend."

Pat swung her legs out of Claude's lap and sat up. "That's what you said, isn't it, Claude? Neville should split the deputy PM position between you and Mark, and Mark shouldn't be so close to the generals."

Claude laid a hand on her arm, and Pat mumbled, "Maybe I misunderstood."

"It's complicated," said Claude "Mark is a hardline Marxist. He thinks we're not socialist enough. We're Black Power socialist revolutionaries. We connect with oppressed people everywhere. Mark wants to reach out only to Russia and Cuba. He's upset that Neville and I went on a government visit to the States. But Black Americans have more in common with us than white Russians. And their president is our biggest threat. His administration is trying to destabilize us. We're trying to build a new runway to land jumbo jets so that tourists can get here more easily, and the president's saying we want it for warplanes, to attack America. We went to America to get support from Black Americans and from white Democrats too. Mark is angry about that."

Alison entered the room and passed around bowls of rice and peas.

"Did you cook this yourself?" Neville asked, sniffing his bowl. "You never took your eyes off it?"

"I watched the pot the entire time," Alison assured him, but Neville didn't touch his food. Claude got pillows for Pat to put behind her back and fetched her a glass of water. Felicity looked up at the beetle. It had reached the ceiling and was now crawling across the maze of cracks in the plaster. Felicity wondered if it, too, was wondering how it got there and was searching for a way out.

"I think going to America was a waste of time," Lee said. "Getting pussy isn't worth where you have to put your dick."

Alison slammed her bowl down and glowered at him.

"Why are you so interested where I put my dick, Lee?" asked Neville.

"The whole world knows about Neville's dick," Felicity put in. She wanted Alison to suffer, to feel the same sick, sad, unwanted, unloved feelings as Felicity.

"Those in western countries should shut up and think about their own racism," said Lee. "How old were you, Felicity, the first time someone called you a *nigger*?" He looked up at the beetle, which had stopped moving near the light fixture, and pulled off his shoe. His arm scythed through the air and the shoe hit the beetle with a thud. The shoe and the dead insect fell to the floor.

CHAPTER 6.

Winnipeg, Manitoba, September 6, 1958

FELICITY AND JOSIAH were surrounded. There was no way to get around this many attackers. They would have to wait for the enemy to give up and go away or fight their way past them.

"Monkeys! Monkeys!" shouted Robert. He danced around, scratching his armpits and screeching.

"Go back to Africa!" added John. "You don't belong here."

"I am not from Africa," Felicity said. "I am from Grenada." The name made her smile as she remembered the sky flaring red.

"Grenada? Who even heard of such a stupid place?" said Robert.

Josiah's hands curled into fists. Then he put his head down and tried to charge through the crowd. Felicity did the same, but Robert grabbed her. "Let's see what a black butt looks like!" he said. "Does she have a tail?" He pulled up the skirt of the new dress Felicity's mother had made her for the first day of school.

"Don't touch me," Felicity said. Her voice shook. Her mother had taken her shopping to pick out the pattern and the fabric and had pinned the cloth around her to make sure the dress fit perfectly. Robert had no right to put his hands on it.

"I'll touch you if I want to, monkey," said Robert. John and Greg laughed, droplets of their spit landing on Felicity's face.

"Josiah!" she cried.

Josiah turned towards the boys, his lips curved into a snarl.

"Leave her alone," he said, as Robert's hand went up under Felicity's skirt.

Robert responded with more monkey noises.

"She's ugly anyway," said Sheila, sounding almost bored. "Ugly nigger hair, and they're all sluts."

Slut. There was that word again, the one Grandma had called Mom, before she died. It must be a really bad word. And *nigger* sounded just as terrible. "I'm not a slut," Felicity said.

"You are," said John. "You're a whore." Felicity didn't know what a *whore* was either.

"You take that back!" Josiah swung his fist back and there was a pop as it hit John's nose.

"You stupid nigger!" Robert swung a punch back at Josiah. Sheila and Diane grabbed Felicity, each holding one of her arms. "You're a slut, your mother's a slut," sang Sheila. Felicity reared up, wrenching one arm free, and grabbed a handful of Sheila's hair. Sheila had golden-blond hair, down to her waist, which she brushed until it shone. All the girls loved Sheila's hair, and every day, Sheila chose the lucky girl who got to sit with her at lunch and braid it, and then play with her Revlon doll or her Lassie board game.

When Sheila sat in front of Felicity, Felicity ached to reach out and stroke the shimmering strands. Felicity's own hair was frizzy and refused to lie flat. Sheila was right — it was ugly. Felicity was ugly. But that still didn't give Sheila the right to stand in Felicity's way when she was trying to walk home. Felicity yanked as hard as she could on Sheila's hair and Sheila screamed. Felicity came away with a wispy blond handful that she examined with curiosity. Sheila's hairs were so much less substantial than her own, so light they were almost invisible in the sunlight, and could blow away like nothing.

"My hair!" Sheila sobbed, putting a hand to her scalp. "You dirty, rotten nigger!"

Frank seized Felicity's waist. "An eye for an eye," he said. "Hair for hair." But Felicity's mother had, as usual, parted her curls with a perfect straight line and secured them in two thick braids tied with ribbons. Frank would have to undo the braids if he wanted to pull out her hair. He struggled with the knots on her ribbons, loosening the bows but unable to get further. Josiah darted around and aimed his knee at Frank's crotch. Frank grunted and let Felicity go. As she stumbled to the ground, she felt her skirt tear. Her knee scraped across the sidewalk.

A blue car with giant tailfins and a gleaming chrome front honked its horn. It pulled over beside the group and a woman leaned across the leather passenger seat and rolled down the window. An enormous string of pearls stretched across her throat. "What are you kids doing?" she demanded. "Are you playing rough? Sheila McLean, I'm surprised at you, horsing around with the boys like this. Do I have to speak to your mother?"

The group scattered, leaving Felicity and Josiah standing alone. Felicity's nose and eyes were running. "I should have known," the woman said. "You people come to this country just to make trouble. I'm surprised they even let you in." She drove off.

"Josiah," Felicity wailed.

"It's okay, Felicity," Josiah said. "They're gone." He was breathing hard. His shirt was torn, and three buttons were missing.

Felicity looked down at herself. Her skirt was ripped from the hem to her waist. Her sash was dangling, one half of it separated from its loop of string. Her hair ribbons flapped in the breeze. Her knee was bleeding into her sock. "Mom's going to be so mad," she said. A clump of Sheila's hair blew in a ball down the sidewalk.

MOM WASN'T JUST mad. She was furious. And, if it was possible, she became even more incensed when Felicity said, "They told me I had ugly nigger hair, and I'm a slut. And they said we don't belong here. They told us to go back to Africa."

Mom's eyes widened, looking like they were bursting from her skull. "And you believe any nonsense someone tells you? We have every right to be in this country. And now that Mr. Diefenbaker is prime minister, he's promised that discrimination on the basis of colour will be outlawed. You just wait, people like them will be sorry soon."

Felicity didn't see how the prime minister could tell a bunch of kids what to do. "The lady said she was surprised they let us in."

Mom gave a laugh that wasn't really a laugh. "I came here as a British citizen," she said. "I worked in a munitions factory in London during the war, and then I heard that Canada was looking for people. They thought I was a white English lady. Imagine their surprise when they saw my Black face, and it was too late to do anything about it. And Rose is American. She fooled them too."

As interested as Felicity was, there were more things she wanted to know. "What's a slut?"

"Don't you worry about that. Worry about your own behaviour. Fighting in the streets like common hooligans! Stooping to their level!" Mom gripped one hand with the other, the bones protruding, as if they were about to pop out of her skin.

"I want to be on their level. I wish I was like everyone else," Felicity said.

Mom took a deep breath. "You are just as good as them," she said. "Psalm 139. You are fearfully and wonderfully made."

Fearfully? Felicity thought. *Why should I be fearful? I thought God loved me, so why should I fear Him?* But Mom was right. She was as good as those kids. She remembered the estate workers chanting *Fight! Fight! Fight!* She and Josiah had fought. Then more doubts slid in alongside that memory.

Felicity said, "I'm not as good though, Mom. Sheila McLean's so pretty, she has long blond hair, and she plays the piano, and —"

"Piano?" said Mom. "If you want to play the piano, you can play the piano."

Every time they had music class and Sheila volunteered to perform, Felicity closed her eyes as the music rippled around her. Even when Sheila made a mistake, Felicity could hear how the piece was supposed to be played; a curving arc of notes flowing together, beads on a string. "But we can't afford lessons," Felicity said. "You're still going to college, and you said we can't have extras until you get a job as a teacher."

"If you want lessons, Felicity, I will find a way for you to have lessons. Jean at work has a son who plays the piano. I'll ask for his teacher's name."

"You will?" Hope blossomed in Felicity. Maybe her mother loved her after all.

MRS. HAMMOND LIVED in a large, stately home on a street lined with elm trees. She came to the door dressed in a smart-looking green and navy plaid wool skirt, pale blue blouse, and pearl necklace and earrings, her grey hair carefully waved. "You must be Felicity," she said. Mom nudged Felicity.

"Yes, ma'am."

"And you are Dolores?" Mrs. Hammond said to Mom. She pronounced it Do-LOAR-es.

"It's DOLLAR-eze."

"Oh, that's right," said Mrs. Hammond. "You did tell me that. Such an unusual way to pronounce it."

"It's the way we say it in Grenada," said Mom. Felicity cringed at this exchange. It happened every time someone new saw Mom's name. Why couldn't she just say Do-LOAR-es, Felicity begged silently.

"Grenada?" Mrs. Hammond wrinkled her nose. "Where is that?"

"The British West Indies," said Mom.

"Oh," Mrs. Hammond nodded. "That's why your English is so good." People said that to Mom a lot. Mom smiled and thanked Mrs. Hammond as if she had never been told that before.

"Come in," said Mrs. Hammond. "Let's sit at the piano and see what you can do."

"She's never taken lessons," Mom said.

"I know that. I am looking to test her musicality. How old are you again, dear?"

"Eleven, ma'am," Felicity said, following another nudge from Mom.

Mrs. Hammond showed Felicity how to sit and how to hold her hands. She tapped a rhythm, and had Felicity play it while she provided the melody.

"That was very nicely done," Mrs. Hammond said. "But you people do naturally have a good sense of rhythm. Let's see what you can do with melody." They switched places. "I will play a triad now," said Mrs. Hammond, "and then I'll play a melody two or three times, and you see if you can sing it." She played. Felicity didn't need to hear the melody more than once. It was already in her head, so she sang. Mrs. Hammond's hands stilled on the keyboard. "Sing that again, dear," she said. Felicity sang. "Can you sing it higher? Start on this note, but sing the same tune?" Felicity sang.

Mrs. Hammond looked over Felicity's head to Mom. "Your daughter has the gift of song, like many of your people do. You should consider having her take singing lessons as well as getting a foundation in piano."

"You need lessons to learn how to sing?" Mom asked.

Desire rushed into Felicity. More than she wanted piano lessons, she wanted — she needed — singing lessons.

"It is hard to tell with a girl so young," Mrs. Hammond said, "but she has an unusually bright and pure voice, and it could be that this will be a voice of importance in twenty years. The only way to find out is to train it — gently, working on her ear, and her sense of line and phrasing, and how to breathe." Felicity already knew how to breathe, didn't she? Didn't everyone?

"How much are lessons for both?" Mom asked, and Felicity felt herself slump on the piano bench. She had forgotten about money.

"Normally, I would recommend two half-hour lessons a week. But what I can do, because your daughter has such potential, is offer you the rate for one half-hour a week but give you forty-five minutes. Twenty-five for piano, and twenty for singing."

"Thank you, that's very kind."

"Good," Mrs. Hammond said. "That's settled. Now, Felicity, dear, let me show you how to play a major scale, and then we'll sing one together." She placed her hand on the piano next to Felicity's.

CHAPTER 7.

St. George's, Grenada, October 12, 1983

AFTER SPENDING MUCH of the night awake, Felicity napped for most of the day. She had just settled in for one when the living room door banged open.

"Sorry, Felicity," said Neville, not sounding sorry at all. "We need the radio. There's someone broadcasting news offshore." He bounded over to the cabinet and turned the dial.

"How do you know that?" Felicity asked. Her throat was dry, and her head felt fuzzy, thanks to her consumption of a large portion of several bottles of sherry from the government reserves, consumed over last night's dinner.

"Them." With his thumb, Neville indicated the protestors outside the gates. "One of them managed to get a note under the door." The unremitting static broke for a second and admitted a fraction of a word. "There it is." Neville turned slowly, and the voice came into focus. Neville, Claude, Lee, and Melvin cheered.

"... to evacuate American students," said the announcer.

"Americans? Are they coming here to —" said Lee. Everyone shushed him.

"... six hundred and fifty, at St. George's University —" the announcer continued.

"Most of it isn't even in St. George's," Lee said.

"Sssh!"

"... but so far, this is only a rumour. What we do believe to be true is that the American president has asked the Mark Henry government to guarantee their safety —"

Now the room exploded into commentary. "The Mark Henry government!"

"Look at Mark, so bold-bold."

"Their safety! What about ours?"

"Who is we? Who is that on the radio?"

Felicity sat up and hugged her knees. She vacillated between not wanting to show her ignorance and needing information. She chose. "Someone want to tell me what's going on?"

Neville said, "There's a medical school here, for Americans. Ones whose scores are just a bit too low for US med programs, so they come here, and we educate them and they go back."

"I said we should shut it down," said Lee. "Now look, it's bringing us nothing but trouble."

"You wanted to shut down everything, Lee," said Claude. "We needed the money. Six hundred and fifty Americans with rich parents, who could turn that down? They don't bother us, and we don't bother them."

"Well, now they are," said Lee.

"No, they're not," said Neville. "It's just that evil president they have. The donkey's arse doesn't know anything. Like how he's convinced that our runway is for Russian warplanes."

"It won't be good for anything," Claude said. "If they don't stop interfering with our tourism." He turned to look at Felicity. The ferocity of his gaze made her throat constrict. "They're telling lies in America and Europe, saying our beaches are full of barbed wire, that it's not safe here."

The door opened. Pat entered. She walked straight to Claude, and he put his arm around her. "What are you doing?" she asked. Her gaze swung to Felicity, a laser beam of suspicion.

"We found a radio station," Claude began to explain to her, their bodies angled away from Felicity on the couch. Felicity closed her eyes and concentrated on trying to hear more of the broadcast over the babble in the room.

"The curfew remains," said the voice. "Anyone found violating it will be shot on sight. Take it very seriously."

The word *shot* arrested Felicity's heartbeat, holding it hostage within the cavern of her chest. A bullet would stop it forever. She tried to calm herself the way she did before a performance — breathing deeply, in and out, focusing on the task before her and nothing more.

CHAPTER 8.

Winnipeg, Manitoba, March 18, 1965

FELICITY WALKED OUT from the wings, across the gleaming wood of the stage. She stopped where she had been directed to stand, in the crook of the shiny black grand piano. She bowed her head and waited for the room to settle. The Salvation Baptist women had been moved to the sides of the auditorium where their immense hats would not block the vision of those behind them. The piano introduction dropped into the silence, stars appearing in the night sky. She took a breath, harnessing all her energy and power to become the character of Laurie, a small-town girl who, like Felicity, was soon to turn eighteen and embark upon her adult life.

Felicity had been invited to give a recital by the Winnipeg Ladies' Musical Circle. "The youngest singer to ever be given that honour," said her teacher, Miss Fisher. When Felicity shared her triumph with her mother, she had not been as enthused. "I told you, I don't know about this business of singing for a career," said Mom. "It's most ungodly, the lifestyles those women live, going from city to city, hopping from bed to bed. Music should be for the church, for the glory of God. You can teach kindergarten, do singing with the little ones, or teach lessons and bring in a little more to help with what your husband's earning." The thought of such a small life made Felicity want to howl. Mom was even less excited when Miss Fisher insisted on taking Felicity to Vancouver on the train to audition for the Guildhall School in London.

But none of that mattered now, because Felicity had had a letter from the Guildhall that she had shoved in her purse unopened, sure it was a rejection, and Miss Fisher was mad at her. Miss Fisher wanted Felicity to start her recital with Handel or Purcell, and Felicity had insisted on "Laurie's Song," from the opera *The Tender Land* by Aaron Copland. She had discovered it the previous summer when Salvation Baptist Church took up a collection to send her to a music camp in Minneapolis. "This is a new opera," the music director told Felicity. "Opera doesn't have to be kings and queens and fat ladies squawking. It can be about your life, and mine." Felicity wanted the audience to see that, too.

"Well, if that's your decision, I wash my hands of it," Miss Fisher had proclaimed, smacking her palms against each other to make the point. Felicity had moved on to Miss Fisher when Mrs. Hammond said she had nothing more to teach her, but Miss Fisher was not in awe of Felicity's talent. Miss Fisher had sung at the Metropolitan Opera in New York, and she said Felicity had a lot of work to do if she wanted to do the same. Now, Felicity sang the opening verse of her chosen aria that described a little girl, shorter than the fence in her backyard, feeling time creep until it started to run.

Felicity remembered playing with Josiah in a time before she thought about men or sex or dead fathers or the colour of her skin. Those days were gone now, never to return. She and Mom had moved away from Aunt Rose and Josiah into their own house when Mom got a job as a teacher, and Felicity had fallen in love with Brian Campbell.

She fought the urge to choke up and forced herself to focus on the words. There was a new hardness at her core. She had been frantic to have sex for the first time before the recital. Laurie's character was innocent, and the moment captured by "Laurie's Song" underlined the moment that she would start walking towards knowledge. Felicity wanted to cross that line herself so she would know how it felt to be on either side of it.

She had been dating Brian since Christmas. It had been too good an opportunity to pass up — the quarterback of her high school football team, who had big eyes, blue as the summer sky, and soft, golden hair, asking her if she wanted to go steady. They had necked a few times but hadn't gone all the way, and so she had hinted and suggested until she learned that the night before her recital, his parents were going out for dinner, leaving the house empty.

Brian's house was immense, with a long, curving driveway and marble pillars flanking the front door. When they reached his bedroom, Felicity pushed him inside and onto the bed. She looked around for a few seconds, noting the posters of the Beatles, the Rolling Stones, and of Mickey Mantle. Then she threw herself on top of Brian and began to kiss him all over his face. When he came up for air, he asked, "What are you doing, Felicity?"

"I need you now, Brian. I've waited so long."

"But, Felicity, what if —"

"If I get pregnant? It's okay, Brian. I counted the days since I last had my period and I'm about to get it again, so that means it's too late to fertilize my egg." That much she had learned in biology.

Brian turned red and fixed his eyes at a point past Felicity's head. "But your mom —"

"Who cares about her? I want you," Felicity whispered, and she reached down and cupped a hand over Brian's crotch. The hardness she felt there thrilled her. She began undoing his belt. Brian offered no resistance.

She pulled Brian down onto the bed and pulled off her own sweater and bra. Brian's eyes bulged when he saw her soft brown breasts spill across her chest. He reached out with his forefinger and touched one of them. Felicity took his hand in hers and traced the outline of her nipple.

Brian gulped. "I've never gone all the way before," he said.

"Neither have I," Felicity said. "That's why it's special." She shivered as she reached out. She peeled off her girdle and threw it to the floor to join the rest of her clothing. Then she wriggled until she had positioned her pelvis under him, both of them squeezed onto the single bed. Brian's mouth twitched as he slid down over Felicity and began fumbling.

"Where does it go?"

Felicity directed him to the place where she was warm and slippery. With panting and fidgeting, he slid inside. Felicity closed her eyes and breathed in the feeling. Despite the spears of pain, she thought she felt a warm ripple of contentment. Brian flopped sweaty onto the pillow beside Felicity. She turned to look at him, and his face gleamed silver in the moonlight streaming through the window. There was a rawness between her thighs and her body felt hot, but she couldn't figure out if her mind was any different.

Brian sat up. "You should get dressed," he said. "My parents will be home soon." He was already stepping into his briefs.

Felicity scanned the audience as she sang. Brian had promised to come to her recital, and he wasn't here. She had given herself to him. Was this how he repaid her love? She wondered what the audience saw — a young innocent girl in a black dress, poised on the stage, or someone who had foolishly given herself away to a boy she could never have, now pouring her all into a recital because it was all she had left.

Felicity reached the end of the aria and sang:

The time has grown so short, the world so wide.

She sent the last high G arcing to the back of the hall and kept the tone spinning and pure for as long as she could. When finally all sound had dissipated, she still stood, fixing her gaze on an imaginary horizon that at that moment seemed more real to her than the stage beneath her feet. The audience was silent until she allowed her gaze to drop. Then the applause began. Slowly, uncertainly at first, like the tires of a lone car turning onto a quiet street, but then the great rush and roar of a mass of traffic with honking horns and sirens; all that sound and energy just for her. She was a goddess, and this stage was her altar.

AUNT ROSE HAD come over that afternoon to press Felicity's hair, flattening into submission the clouds of reddish-brown curls that spiralled off her forehead. Then she helped Felicity into her sleek black gown and did up the zipper. Felicity put on her black gloves and looked down at herself, bothered, as always, by the square, solid body she must have inherited from her father rather than her mother's willowy frame. Her unknown father was in her face, from its round shape to the prominent nose. He had also diluted her mother's skin to create Felicity's warm, light brown colour. Her eyes, big and wide set, could not be said to have any particular colour. All her life, people had commented how they shone green, brown, silver, or gold, different every time they caught the light. Brian called them her "rainbow eyes."

"You're beautiful, flower," said Aunt Rose. Felicity didn't feel beautiful. She was still dissatisfied after the recital when she went out to greet the audience. Someone said her name, and she turned to see Jack Mueller from school, lolling in his seat. "You look fantastic," he said. Before she could respond, he indicated the stout woman beside him, her blond hair twisted around her head in two braids. "Felicity, this is my mother. Muti, this is my friend Felicity."

The woman smiled and reached over Jack to clasp both Felicity's hands between hers. "Felicity, I've heard so much about you," she said. "In Germany, I sang in a radio choir. I really love music." She pronounced her RS with a scrape at the back of her throat and her vowels were flatter, more squeezed, than in English. "But you didn't sing anything in German."

"I have trouble with German," Felicity said. She didn't add that she found the language spiky and unmelodious.

"Come and see me. I will fix that."

Felicity looked up and saw Brian with five other people. Sheila McLean, and what looked like both Sheila's and Brian's parents. Brian's eyes widened when he saw Felicity, then fluttered worriedly to the rest of the group. He said, "Hello, Felicity. You look nice." It was as if last night had never happened.

"Mom, Dad, this is Felicity from school," he said.

As Felicity looked at Brian, so handsome in his blue shirt, that matched the colour of his eyes, she could feel her heart turn to water with longing for him. But he wasn't looking at her.

"Oh, you must know Sheila, Felicity," said Brian's mother to Felicity. "She sings too. Her teacher is Mrs. Hammond, one of the best, you know."

"I used to study with Mrs. Hammond," said Felicity. "She said I needed someone more advanced, so she passed me on to Miss Fisher."

"Not Gloria Fisher!" said Brian's mother. "But she's —" She stopped and squinted at Felicity. "Tell me, how is a girl still in high school singing this music? Isn't that rather ambitious of you? I mean, opera isn't even your people's music."

"Felicity is exceptional," said Jack from behind Felicity. Her bones bent with relief. "She isn't a high school singer. She has a gift." He put an arm around Felicity's shoulder, and Felicity leaned against him, watching Brian's face grow white and pinched.

"It's Jack Mueller, isn't it?" said his mother. "The German boy?"

"Canadian," said Jack.

"Your mother allows you to wear your hair like that?" Brian's mother pointed to Jack's long, wavy ponytail. "Like one of those good-for-nothing beatniks?"

"My mother doesn't treat me like a baby." Jack pulled Felicity a few feet away. "Want to get out of here?"

Felicity was overjoyed at the idea of not going home alone. "What about your mom?"

"My dad will pick her up."

"Are you sure?"

"Of course I'm sure. This is your big night. Someone's gotta make it a celebration."

Felicity's mother was talking with her church friends. When Felicity asked if she could go out with friends, Mom said, "Curfew is midnight."

"It's already almost ten," Felicity protested.

"Then one o'clock. No later. There's church tomorrow morning."

AFTER A FEW minutes of driving in silence, Felicity asked, "Why was Brian —"

"Ssh," Jack said, "don't make me mad when I'm driving."

"You're mad at him?"

"I'm fucking furious at him. I want to bash his fucking face in," said Jack. No boy had ever said that word, *fuck*, in front of Felicity. She rolled it in her mouth, liking its sharp, succinct feel.

Felicity nestled closer to Jack. She was Brian's girlfriend, but Brian had just rejected her. Jack wanted to spend time with her. He put his hand on her knee. "I've known Brian since elementary school," he said. "He was always a shit. I went to his birthday party, and his mom wouldn't let up about me being German. She kept asking if my dad fought in the war — he did, but only because he was forced — and bragging that Brian's dad got a medal for his service. Brian never said a word, even though he was always calling me his best friend. Some friend."

They entered Jack's house through a side entrance, and Jack directed Felicity down a flight of stairs into a slightly chilly, wood-panelled room. "Welcome to my lair."He sat down on the sagging green couch and patted the spot next to him. "Want a beer?"

Felicity had never had one, but she said "Sure," and Jack pressed a bottle into her hand, clinking it against his. It was bitter, but she continued to sip. Her insides felt warm. Her head spun a little. Jack said, "I need a smoke." But instead of lighting a cigarette, he went to a drawer, pulled out a bag of what looked like dried oregano, and began rolling a pinch of it in a small square of white paper.

"What are you doing?"

"Having some weed. You want to try?" He licked a finger to stick the ends of the paper together.

"Uh, sure."

"You don't have to."

"I want to."

Her first drag led to a coughing fit, but she persisted, eventually getting a taste of the smooth, spicy smoke.

"Like it?"

"Mmm, yeah." Her mind was beautifully fogged. She turned to Jack, pressed her lips to his, and began kissing him. She pressed her body against his. He responded hungrily and they fell onto the carpet. Felicity reached for his crotch.

Jack put his hand over hers. "Are you sure?"

"I've never been so sure," she said, unzipping his fly. Jack peeled off her dress, unhooked her bra, and sat back to behold her. "What a body," he said.

Felicity pulled him to her. She caressed his hardness. "You've done this before?" Jack asked, and she nodded. He made a face of surprise. "Brian?" he said. "Didn't think he had it in him." He paused. "What about birth control?"

"I'm getting my period, so it's fine." Seemingly satisfied, Jack began kissing her all over her naked body and she shivered, overwhelmed by the sensations. When he entered her, her world erupted. She screamed and writhed on the carpet. Sex hadn't felt anything like this with Brian.

"Felicity, you are something else," Jack said when it was over. "I need another joint." Naked, they passed it back and forth.

"I feel fizzy," she said.

"Fizzy," said Jack. "That's a good nickname for you." He picked up his guitar and strummed. Felicity recognized "A Hard Day's Night" and "Please Please Me." *The Beatles*, she thought, and thinking of the Beatles made her think of England, and the envelope in her purse.

"Jack, I got a letter from the Guildhall!" she said. "You know, the music school I auditioned for in London."

"What did it say?"

"I don't know. I didn't open it."

"Well, let's see." He put the guitar down.

Balanced between hope and fear, she handed the envelope to him. "Can you, Jack?"

He used his thumbnail to slit the top of the envelope. Felicity struggled to breathe. Jack put an arm around her as he continued to pull out the letter. He scanned it and said, "Well, Felicity, the answer is —" Her chest began to seize. She fisted her hands against it. "Hell, I don't want you to die on me. You got in, you idiot. Full scholarship."

Felicity screeched and threw her arms around Jack so hard he fell backward. "I'm so grateful. I would thank God, but I don't think I believe in him, or it, or whatever God is."

"You go to church?" asked Jack.

"Only because my mother makes me."

"She's pretty strict?"

"The main thing for her is that I must not have sex. I cannot get pregnant. That would be displeasing to God and embarrassing to her. And she's scared that if I go to London, I'll be out of her sight and I'll live a life of immorality with the theatre people."

Jack laughed. "You've already started on that."

"That's why I need to get away," Felicity said. "I can't hide what I'm doing from her forever. I can't stand listening to her talk about the Bible anymore. I'm interested in people, not God. I think about love, and pain, and so many things, Jack. But not God."

"I think about God. A lot," Jack said. He picked his guitar up again and struck a chord. The Beach Boys this time. "I Get Around." Jack bent his head over the instrument. "My parents don't go to church. We're Lutherans, but they lost their faith because of the war. It killed them inside, man."

Felicity lay on the couch listening to the chords he strummed. The sex and the beer and the marijuana collided pleasantly in her brain and traced a path down her spine.

CHAPTER 9.

Winnipeg, Manitoba, June 23, 1965

TWO DAYS AFTER Felicity's graduation, it was Josiah's turn. Josiah's father, Zeke, came to Winnipeg from Nova Scotia for the occasion, at the expense of Josiah's grandfather, Pastor Jefferson. It was the first time Josiah had seen his father. Aunt Rose and Zeke came with Josiah to pick Felicity up for the graduation dinner. Despite Brian's objections, she was Josiah's date. "He's like my brother, Brian," she assured him. "Our mothers are best friends, and we grew up together. I'm just going with him to say goodbye, before I leave." In actuality, she was punishing Brian for snubbing her at her recital. His flowers and his apologies had not put a dent in the crater that had opened in her soul with his public indifference.

Aunt Rose made a dress for Felicity to wear on the big day. It was not to Felicity's liking; it was a soft peach with fussy ruffles, far too girlish and cute, but when she came down the stairs wearing it, Josiah's eyes opened wide, and he said it was a dress for a fairy princess.

Zeke kept everyone at the table laughing. Felicity sipped a glass of wine, which Aunt Rose chose to ignore, and felt comfortably warm, in contrast with her own graduation dinner, where she, her mother, Brian, and the Campbells had sat stiffly across from each other making inane comments about how nice the ceremony was. After dessert, as music started playing, Aunt Rose turned to Zeke and said, "Well Zeke, we should let the young people enjoy their night, shouldn't we?"

"Dance with me first?" said Zeke.

"And then maybe we can —" Felicity recognized the look of longing that Aunt Rose cast up at him. Now that she had had sex, she understood desires of others as well as her own. She saw from Josiah's rigid posture that he understood them too.

Zeke laughed and drew Aunt Rose onto the dance floor. Josiah followed behind, guiding Felicity. The speakers blared "My Girl," the current big hit by the Temptations. Josiah had dressed the way they did in the picture he had tacked to the mirror in his bedroom. His suit had the same white-trimmed lapels, and he also wore a ruffled shirt and white socks. Felicity and Josiah danced together, not too close, Felicity's dress swinging against her ankles as she swayed her hips. Josiah snapped his fingers and swung from foot to foot as his classmates gathered to watch them. None of them could move with the fluidity Josiah had.

As Felicity danced, a hand grabbed one of her buttocks and squeezed through her dress. She whirled around, expecting to see one of Josiah's classmates, but Zeke stood there, winking at her. Nausea rose in her throat. She looked up at Josiah, but he was still jiving, oblivious. Aunt Rose continued to press her hips against Zeke's thighs. "Josiah, I need a drink," Felicity said.

Josiah turned to his parents. "We're going to the bar," he said.

Aunt Rose replied, "I think it's time for us to go anyway, isn't it, Zeke?" She nestled close to him. Zeke glanced at Felicity, and she looked away.

"You two have a nice evening," Felicity said.

Felicity, sweaty from dancing, fanned herself, and tried to forget the feeling of her flesh grabbed by Josiah's father's fingers. Josiah ordered a beer. "You want a soft drink, Felicity?"

"No. I'll have a beer, too." She saw the surprise flash in his eyes, but he ordered it. They carried their drinks through the back door and sat on the concrete stoop.

"In a couple of months, you'll be gone, Felicity," Josiah said, his voice mournful, or maybe it was wistful.

"You could leave too, Jo."

"My mom wanted to send me back to the States for school. But I dunno, this is my place now."

"And you got that football scholarship," Felicity said. "You'll be playing with Brian."

"That asshole."

"Why do you say that?" Felicity had tired of Brian, and she could complain about him if she chose, but she didn't like Josiah criticizing him.

"I don't like how you are since you met him. Always sad, always worried. Trying to measure up, but you don't have to ..." Josiah shrugged and lowered his head.

Felicity felt bile in her throat. "I'm leaving soon, Josiah. He'll be ancient history. And I'm glad I'm leaving. My mom doesn't want me. She never did."

"What makes you say that?"

"Well, she had me when she wasn't married, didn't she, and now she goes preaching about morality and such."

Josiah put his hand on her knee and his face close to hers. "Felicity, you can't hold that against her," he said. "When a woman is forced, it's not her fault."

Felicity jerked away, kicking her beer bottle. It crashed onto the ground. A foamy puddle formed on the step. "Forced? My mother was forced? You mean ..." The word stuck in her throat. "Raped?"

"Oh, shit. You didn't know?"

"How do you?"

"I found a letter," Josiah said. "My mom must have written it to your mom, when she was sent away." Aunt Rose, Felicity knew, had had Josiah in a home for unmarried girls, but she had refused to give him up for adoption, and Pastor Jefferson eventually relented and let her bring him home. "I don't know why she never mailed it," Josiah went on. "But it talked about what happened to your mom."

"Where is it?" Felicity demanded. "I want to see it."

Josiah patted his jacket pocket. "I was going to confront my dad with it, that bastard, but it seems my mom has other ideas." His eyes sharpened like knife points. Felicity lunged at him, but Josiah had already placed the paper in her hands.

Dear Dolores, Felicity read. *It's so dreary in this place. I hear the other girls crying all the time, but I'm not sad. You would think I would be, away from my home, and the people I love, including you, sweet friend, but who can be sad when life is blossoming inside them?*

Felicity skimmed down the page, uninterested in Aunt Rose's pregnancy.

Daddy is so furious at Zeke for having his way with me before we were married. But he'll never understand that Zeke didn't take advantage of me. You remember, I told you, I wanted to do it, and it was wonderful and I'm not sorry. Even though as you know, Zeke broke my heart and went off with Martha. Fancy me thinking her a friend. But the betrayal by Zeke was way worse than anything she could do. He still won't answer my letters.

She skipped ahead.

I want to encourage you now. You are going through your pregnancy on your own, which I know is hard, but you work for your own money, you make your own decisions. And no one thinks any the worse of you, because everyone knows that what happened between you and that horrible Ukrainian man, that so-called landlord of yours, could not have been your choice. I remember when you called my father to come and get you from the New Imperial Hotel, how your clothes were torn, and your cheek was bruised, and it was so obvious what that man did to you. But, my dear, you too got a wonderful ending after all that pain.

"Oh my God." Felicity put her head in her hands.

"Felicity." Josiah's voice seemed to be coming at her from

down a tunnel. "Let's get out of here, okay?" She tried to move, but she couldn't. She was vaguely aware of Josiah helping her up. She began shivering, great shudders that rocked her from head to foot. Josiah took off his tuxedo jacket and placed it around her shoulders as he guided her to his car. He settled her in the passenger seat. She hunched over, clutching her knees.

When Josiah stopped the car, she realized that he had brought her to their elementary school playground. He led her through a gap in the fence, placed her on a swing, and took the one next to hers. They had swung together every day, excluded by the rest of the kids. Felicity was bereft when their paths diverged in junior high, when her mother sent her across town to a school with a stronger academic program and Josiah stayed in the old neighbourhood school.

Josiah said, "When the kids at this school were mean to us, remember what my mom would say?"

"You were made in God's image."

"That's right. And it's true," Josiah said.

Thoughts spun in Felicity's mind. She was a child of rape. Her mother had felt shame, despair, pain. Bearing her must have been the worst thing in her mother's life. Felicity was never wanted. This was why her mother didn't love her; she couldn't. Whatever Felicity was, she certainly was not made in God's image, if there was a God. If there was, it was hard to imagine why he allowed the things he did.

Josiah muttered to himself, "Sure could use some weed right now. Shouldn't have left it at home."

Felicity's head snapped up. "I know where we can get some."

She directed Josiah past the park with the merry-go-round listing to one side, the see-saw pointing skyward, onward to Jack's cul-de-sac. The long driveways were lined with bushes beaded with flowers. Josiah whistled and said "Fancy."

She led Josiah through the white wooden fence across the lawn to tap on the basement window. A moment later, Jack poked his head out. "Hey, Fizzy," he said. "Hey, Josiah," he added, as if Josiah were an old friend. "Welcome to my lair. I'll come up and let you in." Felicity's footsteps felt heavy on the stairs to the basement, the green shag carpet sucking them down.

When they were seated on the couch, Jack asked, "What happened?" Josiah whispered to Jack. Then Jack leaned over and placed a pillow in her lap. "Hit it," he said.

"What?" Felicity looked up at him, her brain sluggish.

"Hit it, Fizzy. It's your fucking dad, that bastard."

"Shut up!" Felicity screamed. "Shut up! I hate fucking men, I hate them!" It was the first time she had said *fuck*, and she liked the metallic feel of it, the way it could carry her anger out into the world. She rammed her fist into the pillow, then the other fist. "Fucking asshole! I hate men!" Her throat felt raw. She fell forward, sobbing. She heard whispering between Jack and Josiah, and then Josiah sat next to her, holding the pillow as she punched it and screamed and cried. At last, her arms were spent, and she flopped against Josiah's shoulder, still crying hard.

"Felicity," he whispered. "Felicity, I'm here." Felicity clung to him, shuddering. Gradually her sobs tapered off.

"Feel better?" asked Jack. Felicity nodded, lolling against Josiah. "You just needed a good cry," Jack said.

"You know that about her," Josiah said. Jack didn't respond.

Through her burning throat, Felicity whispered, "Jack, do you have weed?"

"As the doctor ordered. Josiah, you joining us?"

"Yeah, man," Josiah said. Jack prepared three joints, and then sat on the other side of Felicity. Under the blanket, the smoke pouring into her lungs, Felicity felt the world begin to settle around her.

"How is it you know Felicity so well and I've never heard of you?" Josiah asked.

"Jack's my friend," Felicity said.

"Yeah," Josiah said. He addressed Jack, "Yeah, and you got her drinking beer and smoking weed, I see."

Jack shrugged. "Guilty."

"I don't really hate men," Felicity said. No one answered.

After a moment, Jack stood up. "Gotta take a leak," he said.

Josiah turned his body to face Felicity. "Are you really okay?"

She nodded. His eyes were brown pools, like melted chocolate, reminding her of the father she should have had.

Under his breath, Josiah sang the song they had danced to a few hours ago in a different universe. *My Girl.*

Before she knew it, Felicity had pressed her lips to his and their bodies melded, their hands hungrily groping each other. She wanted, needed someone to take away the horrible feeling of worthlessness that had come over her once she knew her origins.

"You look gorgeous tonight," Josiah said when they came up for air, and then resumed kissing her.

Felicity heard a muffled sound and saw Jack discreetly easing back out of the room. She pulled away from Josiah, registering his confused expression.

Jack said, "Don't mind me. I can go upstairs for a bit."

"No, Jack, stay," Felicity said. She couldn't make Josiah part of her scheme to restore her to herself and seek revenge on her unnamed father. It was not Josiah's fault she was unlovable.

CHAPTER 10.

St. George's, Grenada, October 13, 1983

ALISON MADE OIL down for dinner, the national dish of Grenada. She used breadfruit and coconuts grown on trees in the yard of Government House and dasheen and herbs picked from the garden. The soldiers brought the salt fish and ham to the back door and stood, pressed to the windows, as the scent from the simmering pot seeped out.

Felicity had always scorned domestic tasks. As a teenager, she had rejected her mother's tentative offer to teach her to cook oil down. "Why would I want to do that?" she asked. "Oil down is a disgusting dish." The breadfruit, absorbing the taste of the mishmash of ingredients surrounding it, the greasy liquid bubbling like a swamp, the thick, dark layer of burnt-off oil settling to the bottom of the pot; it all made Felicity feel nauseous. She almost missed the sadness that flashed across her mother's face; but, even when she saw it, she didn't change her mind. Felicity was not going to be a woman who wasted her time on useless things like cooking.

She revised her opinions when the fragrance from the kitchen washed into her nostrils. She had overlooked the power that a cook held over the hungry. How one truly talented in the culinary arts could produce a reaction almost like sexual desire. Alison was a witch preparing a love potion.

Felicity had been looking for an ally, without considering Alison. It seemed obvious now. Alison was lovesick, like Felicity. She was an artist, like Felicity. Felicity got off the couch and went into the kitchen.

"Need any help?" she asked from the doorway.

Alison swung around from salting the pot. "From you?" She laughed, without warmth or joy.

Felicity knew this wouldn't be easy. "I thought we women might have some common ground," she said.

"You're a foreigner. You're not one of us. You haven't been through the Revo with us." Alison laid down the wooden spoon she had been brandishing.

"I know," Felicity said. She would not argue the point, though she had in fact lived the Revo night after night with Claude as he worked himself into ideological zeal. "You're the one who has access to Neville. He listens to you," Felicity said. The words had the desired effect. Alison's face began to lift into a smile. "We need this house arrest to end, to get back to our lives. There's got to be a way."

"There is," Alison said. She passed a knife to Felicity. "You can cut those onions."

Felicity tried not to show her dismay. She was very sensitive to onion gasses. But she took her place next to Alison at the counter.

"Mark Henry wants to send someone to negotiate with Neville, to figure out the terms of release," said Alison.

"And Neville won't?" Felicity imagined the knife sinking into the flesh of the onion being drawn through Neville's neck. He was risking everyone's well-being for his own selfish pride.

"The Cubans don't want him to. Their leader loves Neville, thinks he's the only one who can truly advance workers' rights in Grenada."

"The Cubans don't have to live here," said Felicity. She turned her head to the side as a gust of tears slashed down her nose.

"Try this," said Alison, "it helps." She splashed water over the onion.

"What does Claude think?" Felicity tried to speak his name neutrally, so that it didn't sing in her voice, didn't waken every dying cell in her body.

"Oh," said Alison. "You know Claude." Felicity loved her for the way she said that, as if Felicity had a claim to Claude still. "He probably has the entire terms of surrender written already, but he'll wait until Neville is ready, and then he'll hand them over as if it was Neville's idea."

Felicity was appalled that this was still the pattern between the two men. "Why does Claude put up with that?"

"You should know," Alison said. "He just cares about the result. He doesn't think he has the personality to carry the Revo to the people, but Neville does."

"Claude wants to die for the Revo," remembered Felicity. She blinked back more burning liquid. Wetting the onion had not really done anything to mitigate the effects.

"Well, exactly," said Alison. "And if that's what he wants, then he's not going to fight that hard to save himself, is he?" She took the pieces of onion Felicity had chopped, threw them in the pot and gave the soup a fierce stir. "I will die for it too, if that's what I have to do to be with Neville. But that's not what you want, is it, Felicity? And if it isn't, what are you doing here?"

Felicity wasn't so sure she didn't want that. Death had never scared her. She didn't believe in her mother's heaven; it would be terrifying to live forever, to have to be with the people you thought you'd left behind. She thought of death as a cool, dark, quiet room, where you no longer had to strive or impress.

Alison went to the cupboard. "We can eat out of these bowls," she said, "and I'll give them" — she indicated the soldiers in the yard — "the pot to eat out of."

"Why give them anything?" Felicity asked.

"A hungry man is an angry man," Alison said. "We don't want them hungry."

Felicity remembered Anthony coming home from work at seven in the morning, two days after their wedding. She heard the front door open and then he slouched through the bedroom door, his eyes drooping with fatigue. She woke up and rolled over in bed, ready to give him a back rub, but he said, "Where's my breakfast, woman?"

"Breakfast?" It hadn't even occurred to Felicity to prepare food at this early hour. She had been hoping Anthony would give Mara her morning bottle and that they would both get some sleep. Then they would scrounge the leftovers from the wedding meal her mother had cooked and Felicity had crammed into the fridge. Felicity would feed her new husband food prepared by other hands and offer him her body; her language was touch.

"That's what a wife makes her husband in the morning," Anthony said.

"Oh," Felicity said. No one had told her this was expected. "I didn't think of that."

"You didn't think." Anthony's lip trembled. "You didn't think!" He slammed his fist into the door, so hard that it popped off its hinges and smacked into the wall. He turned and ran down the stairs as Mara began to wail.

A few days later when Jack came by, he returned from using the bathroom and asked, "How'd you get that hole in the wall upstairs?"

"We were moving furniture and we banged into it with a dresser," Felicity lied.

IF A HUNGRY man was an angry man, Neville must have been furious, because he again refused the meal. "What's it made of?" he asked.

"Mostly things from the garden," Alison said.

"But did Henry's men bring anything?"

"Just a little meat. It's fine, Neville."

"I can't eat anything they touched."

"Want me to pick you a mango from outside?" Alison's eyes bore a panicked sheen.

"They could have sprayed it."

Felicity decided to ask the question that had been circling her brain since her first evening of detention. "Why aren't all of you smoking?" A joint would relax Neville.

"Smoking?" said Pat. Neville and Claude narrowed their eyes at Felicity, and she sensed them warning her off. "You mean cigarettes?" Pat went on. "Neville smokes those all the time."

"Yeah," Felicity said, too quickly.

"No, that isn't what you're asking about," Lee said. "Neville doesn't smoke marijuana anymore," he proclaimed in an overly formal voice. "Because we've detained the Rastas for doing it."

"Detained?" Felicity asked.

"They were counter-revolutionaries," Alison said. "They had to be put under manners."

"Jesus, Neville!" Felicity said. Claude met her eye and shook his head. She dipped her head over her bowl of oil down and said no more, but she was troubled. Neville had betrayed his people, just like Percy Tibbs before him. The oppressed had learned from the oppressor.

Felicity and Alison cleared and washed the dishes. The look of surprise on Claude's face when she got up to help almost made it worth it. When they were finished, Felicity came across Pat and Claude in the hallway. Pat was crying, her face pressed into Claude's shoulder, her middle bulging between them. "I told you, I'm scared, Claude," she sobbed. "I don't want to have our baby here in this house."

"We still have time," Claude said. "This will be over by then. Our baby will be born under a Black Pearls of Freedom government, don't you worry, sweetheart."

I'm his sweetheart, Felicity thought as she slipped away. She knelt on the couch and pulled at the window above it. The frame swung open a few inches to reveal the mosquito netting. She filled her lungs with the evening air, the sea salt and the scent of nutmeg from the trees that lined the driveway; the only drug left to her to inhale. She watched the soldiers scurry back and forth, and scanned their faces until she saw the one she sought.

"Elrick," she said as he passed.

The young soldier looked up. "Lydia?" He lifted a bottle of rum to his lips.

Felicity longed for the amber liquid. "Can I have some?"

He passed the bottle through the window. Felicity swigged and passed it back to him. The other soldiers had made a small fire in the courtyard and a steaming pan of tea hung over it.

"How are things?" asked Felicity.

"They good," said Elrick, but his face was despondent. Felicity held his gaze until he said, "I hate guarding the Carpenter and Brother Buck. They bring us the Revo. This is wrong."

"So why are you doing it, then?" Felicity asked. She reached for the bottle of rum again.

"I'm in the army." His eyes darted back and forth. "We all loyal to Mark Henry."

"Or what?" Felicity asked.

"We get put under manners."

"They keep saying that," Felicity said. "What does it mean?"

"Put under manners? It mean kept in line. Taught a lesson."

"Why did you join the army in the first place?" Felicity asked him.

"I'm from Vincennes," he said. "Is poor up there."

Felicity was about to tell him that she knew, when she remembered that she was Lydia Felix, American citizen. "So the army was your only option?" she asked.

"Not the only one, but probably the best one," he said. "Farming, fishing, that's hard. The army don't pay much, but is a place to sleep, and you get food." He looked at her wistfully. "I wish I could go to America, go to school."

"Isn't America the enemy to you guys?" Felicity asked.

"Well, yes, but is different for people like me," Elrick explained.

"See this big house the Carpenter lives in? My house in Vincennes not like this. I could never have this here. The Carpenter only having this because he went to England and came back."

"So what's going on out there?" Felicity asked, indicating the world outside the fence.

"Is protests all over the island," Elrick said. "Brother Henry can't keep them down. And all work is at a standstill. Everyone on strike. People shouting 'No Carpenter, no Revo' all over town. Shrimps, man, this one big commess." He lowered his voice further. "Brother Carp should take the proposal. Brother Henry and Brother Carp as joint prime ministers, Brother Buck as the deputy."

"What's the plan if he doesn't?"

Elrick puffed out his chest. "We fight for the Popular Front, and we take control of the country, and we bring true socialism."

"But you told me you like Neville Carpenter."

"I love the Carpenter, but is a matter of national security."

"Is Mark Henry forcing you to be here?" Felicity asked.

"Not forced, ma'am. But he says after we take the fort —" He clapped a hand to his mouth. "I didn't tell you that."

Felicity sensed movement at the door. She turned to see Neville and Claude entering the room. Still together, she thought with a sense of hopelessness. Elrick slid away. Felicity hid the bottle of rum behind a cushion.

"That's enough," Neville said. "I told you not to talk to them, Felicity."

"I can talk to whoever I want," Felicity said. "You two aren't telling me what's going on, so I'm finding out elsewhere."

"What the hell makes you think Henry's troops will tell you anything?" Claude asked. The veins on his forehead bulged. Felicity longed to run her hand over them, smooth away his tension. Soothe him.

"He was telling me the plan, until you two showed up."

"Oh?" said Neville. "And what was it?"

"They're planning to take the fort."

"That's what I thought, Neville," said Claude. "They're going to Fort Albert. We have to get there before they do."

Felicity asked, "What's Fort Albert?"

"It's our military command complex," Neville said. "Used to be called Fort Nelson, but after Claude's dad died, we named it after him."

Felicity recounted Elrick's description of the protests. Neville beamed. "'No Carpenter, no Revo'," he said. "You hear that? We have all the ministers here. Henry doesn't have people who can do what we do."

"What is Pat minister of?" Felicity asked.

"Women's Affairs."

Felicity laughed. "Women's affairs? She's definitely mastered those."

"She was a teacher before she was in the government," Claude said. "Head of the Classics department at St. Anne's, the top girls' school in Grenada." He folded his arms. "Stop talking to the enemy."

After they left, Felicity lay on the couch, humming "Addio, del passato" from *Traviata*; the scene where Violetta, on her deathbed, recounts the sacrifices she has made. Felicity would miss that engagement, but she needed to keep her voice in shape. A hand tapped on the window. She looked up and saw Elrick, miming drinking from a bottle. She pulled it from its hiding place and handed it to him.

"So Brother Carp don't want me talking to you?"

"I don't care what he wants. I do what I like." Felicity tossed her hair, imagining she was standing in the spotlight, centre stage at the Met.

"He's your man, then?"

"No," Felicity said. She had to share a little of her bursting heart with someone. Who could this child tell? "I'm more friends with Brother Buck." She looked at the moon, hovering above the nutmeg trees. Her ears gave themselves over to the melody of "Casta Diva" and the flute's introduction of the chaste silver goddess. It was the sound of betrayal. "I met him a long time ago. And I still want to be more than his friend."

"How long you know him?" asked Elrick.

"Eighteen years," said Felicity. Two years longer than Elrick had been alive. In eighteen years, an international singing career could be built from nothing, conquering one opera house at a time. A life could open and close to include one marriage, two children, lovers. A body could go from unmarred to spent, unseen to adored. And love could sprout, flourish, and dwindle, expand and contract the heart.

CHAPTER 11.

London, England, September 3, 1965

IT WAS GREY again. Always grey. Grey pigeons, grey skies, grey-suited men hurrying into the Underground alongside Felicity. Black umbrellas, carried by the self-contained Londoners, were their only defence against the grey drizzle and the only thing that broke up the grey all around her.

Felicity sat on the train for the short ride from her hostel to college. A faint ache between her legs made her wish that she could feel a man there, any man. But today was not a day to think about sex or men. Today, she had work to do to prepare for the opera auditions at the Guildhall.

As Felicity walked down the hallway, voices emerged at all angles from the practice rooms. The pure, piercing notes of another soprano made her question her talent and ability to compete. She stopped at the bulletin board to check for the daily announcements, buried in a tangle of posters. One piece of paper amongst the clutter caught her eye with the words: *West Indian Students Association General Meeting for all students in London of West Indian origin.* The meeting was set for that evening, at Nelson's Column in Trafalgar Square.

Felicity wondered who could have put that poster there. She had not met another Black student at the Guildhall, despite the fact that there were many in London, far more than she had seen at home in Winnipeg. As they moved through this grey world, some of them carried themselves with purpose, carving out space with their elbows up to meet the unforgiving world. Others scurried, afraid, trying to shrink themselves, hiding in the crowds. All of them smiled when they saw Felicity — a moment of community that she held onto for the rest of the day.

A WEAK SUN had replaced the rain by the time Felicity got to Trafalgar Square. Red double-decker buses continually disgorged passengers speaking a cacophony of languages. Children splashed in the basins of the fountains, slapping the frothy water towards the pigeons, the birds ever on the lookout for the crusts tourists tossed them. Teenagers strolled by, snatches of Simon and Garfunkel, the Righteous Brothers, and the Beatles rolling from the transistor radios on their shoulders. Felicity assumed that Nelson's Column must be the great stone plinth with a tall concrete cylinder, topped by a statue wearing a triangular hat. Pigeons settled on its head and pecked around its base, where a number of Black people were gathered.

Felicity's heart stuttered. She could hear their laughter from across the square. The distance of a few feet felt interminable. She wondered what she would do if no one spoke to her. But she had come this far, so she forced herself to move her feet across the paving stones. When she reached the group, no one appeared to notice. She tipped her head back, squinting up at Nelson at the top of his column, where he seemed to rule over all London. Felicity remembered learning something about him in school. He had fought in some war, but she couldn't remember the details.

She wondered if this had all been a mistake and she should just get back on the Tube when a young man with a moustache appeared beside her. "Hello," he said. "I'm Gerald Mason. From Barbados. And you?"

"Felicity Alexander. From Canada."

"This is the West Indian Students Association, miss. Are you looking for Canada House? It's over there."

"No," Felicity said. "I'm — my mother is from Grenada."

"Grenada! You'll want to meet Buck and Carp, then." He peered at her more closely. "Your father is white?"

"Yes, and dead." The thought of her father caused pain to trickle through her stomach. She imagined a desert too vast to cross.

"Come with me," said Gerald. He led her a few steps away to where several young men clutched handfuls of hand-lettered signs stapled around sticks. "Hello!" Gerald shouted, "I found another Grenadian!" They all looked up. Felicity's heart swayed as she met the brown eyes of a tall man with spongy black hair cropped close to his head. His skin was a warm brown, like polished wood, and his eyes were limitless — in them, Felicity read her future. Beside him was a shorter, darker man.

"I'm Neville Carpenter," said the shorter man.

"I'm Claude Buckingham," said the taller one. *Claude Buckingham*. Felicity rolled the name around silently in her mouth, then realized she hadn't said her own.

"Felicity Alexander."

"From Grenada, you say?" asked Neville.

"My mother is from Grenada."

"But you sound American."

"I was born in Canada."

"Alexander," said Neville. "That's a good Grenadian name. Where is your family from?"

"Vincennes."

"Oh, in St. David!" Neville said. "Did you come here to march?"

"Um, yeah," Felicity lied. She didn't know what he meant by *march*. She wished Claude would say something. Sunlight curved through the spurting fountains. A cloud of pigeons took flight as a child ran through them.

"You're marching in those?" Claude pointed at the high-heeled shoes Felicity had worn to her vocal coaching appointment. "Are you actually a student?"

"I'm in my first year at the Guildhall," Felicity said. She was accustomed to the name of her college drawing impressed whistles or the raising of eyebrows, but Neville and Claude exchanged quizzical glances. "It's a music school," she said. "I'm studying opera."

"Opera?" Neville opened his mouth and pretended to stick two fingers down his throat. "Like those fat white women in horns?"

Felicity knew she should be insulted, but she could only laugh. "It's not really like that," she said. "I'm eighteen. I'm learning the fundamentals of singing."

"How does that help our people?" Neville demanded. "We need nurses, doctors, teachers, engineers. People who can bring progress to the next generation."

He sounded like her mother. But music pulsed under Felicity's skin, sang in her veins, and it would not be silent. Six weeks earlier, she had locked herself in her bedroom in Winnipeg and refused to eat or drink until her mother relented and permitted her to come to London on full scholarship.

"The world needs music," Felicity said. Neville snickered and nudged Claude, but Claude looked at Felicity with solemn eyes. Gerald Mason, too, seemed to be contemplating her with interest. "What do you do?" Felicity asked.

"Claude and I are in law school. I'm going to be prime minister of Grenada one day," said Neville.

Words scrambled in Felicity's head as she contemplated Claude's jutting cheekbones and full lips. She managed to say, "And where do you fit into that plan, Mr. Buckingham?"

Claude smiled. "I will make my mark, too. You'll see." A cloud scudded across the sun, turning the square temporarily dark. "Are you here to march against apartheid?"

"Apartheid. Yeah." A gust of wind disturbed Felicity's hair, and she grabbed a handful of it and held it back from her forehead.

"You don't know what apartheid is, do you?" asked Neville. Before Felicity could respond, he said, "Europeans. Scourge of the earth. They went into South Africa, displaced the native Black population, and brought in a system of laws that keeps whites in government, in control of all the land and the wealth. Africans have their movement restricted; they can't vote, they can't protest. And they're jailing all their leaders. Black people all around the world are supporting them. Have you heard of Nelson Mandela?" Felicity shook her head. "He's the head of the African National Congress, the resistance. Two years ago, the fuzz raided a farm in South Africa and captured fourteen people, and they charged Mandela too, even though he was already in jail. They called it the Rivonia Trial. Everyone was convicted and sentenced to death. Last year, we stayed out here for days, slept right by those gates, and people all over the globe demonstrated with us until they changed their sentences to life imprisonment."

"Bon jay, that was something," said Gerald.

Claude pointed up at Nelson's Column. "They put up statues to men like that, who raped and plundered our lands, and he sits in the sky while the real heroes are here on the ground fighting for our people's freedoms."

"Wait, brother, wait." Neville pulled a notebook from his pocket. "Let me get that down, for my speech."

Gerald said, "Miss Alexander, are you sure you can march, dressed like that? Your feet are going to hurt."

"She'll be all right." Neville stopped writing to sling an arm over Felicity's shoulders. "This is Grenada's corner. You go back and organize Barbados."

"Neville! We've been looking for you everywhere!" A figure came rushing around the corner, arms outstretched towards Neville, then stopped short.

"Alison." Neville lifted one arm and let it drop to his side. A second woman came puffing up beside her. The heaviness of their glares made Felicity's insides wither.

"Is this your girlfriend, Mr. Carpenter?" Felicity asked. If she was, then the other must be Claude's.

The woman turned her stare to Neville. He grinned, shrugged his shoulders, and said, "Just a friend." Claude said nothing. Neville said, "Alison Greaves, Marlene Francis, Felicity Alexander," as if at a tea party. "Felicity is going to march with us." He handed her a sign that read "FREEDOM AND JUSTICE FOR ALL."

"You're marching like that?" Alison pointed down at Felicity's slim-fitting wool skirt, her stockings and heels. Alison and Marlene both wore pants and practical brogues with laces.

"She's an opera singer," Neville said. The two women broke into laughter.

Felicity swallowed hard. She was not going to cry. "I've marched before," she said, her throat softening with longing. "When Malcolm X got shot." It was Josiah who had introduced her to the teachings of Malcolm X. Malcolm X represented everything that stood in opposition to the church; his Blackness was unapologetic, unfiltered, and not dependent on eventual liberation by Jesus. His death had felt like the death of courage, and though it had nothing to do with any government she lived under, it had felt right to go to the rally at the Manitoba Legislative Building and shout her grief to the sky.

"You care about Malcolm X?" Marlene sniffed and made a spitting sound. "Brother Malcolm ain't for the likes of you. You're part of the problem, prancing around with your light skin, like you better than us."

Felicity reared backward. Marlene might as well have struck her. Her heel caught in a crack in the stone. She stumbled. Her face felt hot. Her eyes stung. Claude took her elbow and steadied her. His gaze held hers and she read concern there. She made her body limp. Claude put both arms around her to hold her up. He took the sign from her.

"Marlene," Claude said, "I have told you before. In this country, they do not see the distinctions of colour we do at home. Miss Alexander — Felicity — is Black like us, here. We need unity, not squabbling. That is what apartheid does — it seeks to divide and conquer us, and we must stand against that."

Felicity could feel his heartbeat against hers, his body warm.

"Oh, that's good, Claude. Let me add that to the speech too." Neville pulled his notebook out again.

"Make sure you tie Grenada into the speech," Claude said, still holding Felicity close. "Lots of people from home are here today, and we must not let them forget that we have our own struggle." He spoke more quietly, so that only Felicity could hear. "Do you know about Percy Tibbs?" he asked.

"Uncle Percy."

"Shrimps, man," Claude said in her ear. "He's no one's uncle. Out for himself now, and he doesn't do anything for the people. Neville is going to take over from him and bring real improvements to Grenada."

Felicity struggled to comprehend the words. "Uncle Percy is bad?"

"Terrible," Claude said. "Just one more person raping Grenada. Only he's worse, because he's one of us."

"Hello, hello!" Neville shouted. "We've got a march to do here."

"Right," Claude responded. He released Felicity and handed her back her sign. "Sorry!" he called to Neville. Neville met his eye and winked exaggeratedly. Felicity had to crane her neck to see Claude's reaction — a smile. Alison and Marlene muttered to each other as Felicity took her sign in one hand and Claude's hand in the other.

"Let's march, then," she said.

Neville bellowed into his megaphone, "We shall not, we shall not be moved," and a braying chorus joined him in about five different keys.

Felicity lifted her voice above theirs. "We shall not, we shall not be moved," she sang. "Just like a tree that's planted by the water, we shall not be moved." It was what they had sung when they protested Malcolm X's death.

"Hold on, hold on," said Claude. "Neville, give me the megaphone." He handed it to Felicity. "Take this," he said. "Keep singing."

Felicity held the megaphone with the hand that had clutched Claude's. "We shall not, we shall not be moved," she continued. The wavering lines of sound behind her began to coalesce into a coherent melody as the marchers moved forward.

"Music isn't so useless after all is it, Neville?" said Claude, as Felicity's voice rose like a sigh, and the crowd followed her.

CHAPTER 12.

London, England, September 5, 1965

FELICITY REMEMBERED WHAT her mother had told her about renting a room. "Look respectable," she had said. "Landlords want decent young ladies who won't bring men around or make a scene." Once she had accepted that Felicity was going abroad to study singing, Mom had dispensed quite a lot of helpful advice, as well as some that was unhelpful. Felicity had let "Find a Baptist church, and read the Bible every day," rise into the air like smoke. Freedom from Sunday servitude was one of the things she liked best about her new life. And as to not bringing men to her room, Felicity could tolerate that edict since she was living in a big city where there were plenty of other places to meet with the opposite sex.

She made sure her hair was sleek and smooth. When Felicity and Josiah had listened to Malcolm X on the radio talking about how it was more important to use the brains under your hair than waste time trying to make it look like European hair, she had run to the bathroom and washed out her press. She had enjoyed the shocked looks of her mother, Aunt Rose, Brian, and the kids at school when she showed up at the dinner table, at church, or in homeroom, with a full, fluffy mane. But her enthusiasm for her new look waned when she found it impossible to comb and style, and she reverted to wearing it straight.

Aunt Rose explained that it was a lot easier to wear natural hair when you lived in a city that had enough Black people to also have Black salons selling hair products that moisturized, detangled, and shaped curls and kinks. She promised to bring Felicity some the next time she visited her family in Minneapolis, but before then, Felicity had come to London, and she was now able to buy her own products. She would find a Black salon once she had rented a room.

Felicity had cross-referenced her map of London with advertisements for available lodgings in the *Times* to find ones within walking distance of the Guildhall. She walked up to the first one, a small terraced house at the end of a row that seemed to lean slightly to one side. There was a brass door knocker, which she used. No one answered, although the ad had said someone would be home at that time, and a FOR RENT sign was tacked up in the window. She knocked again. Hearing no answer, she turned to go to the next place when the door creaked open.

"What is it, girl?" A woman blinked in the light, her eyes filmy with cataracts. She held a burning cigarette in one hand and clenched a silver-tipped cane with the other.

"Good afternoon." Felicity put on her most polite smile. "I'm here about the room you're renting."

"The room I'm renting," the woman repeated, as if this was a new concept to her. "Are you an American?" she asked.

Felicity had faced that inquiry many times since arriving in London a week ago. "No, I'm Canadian," she said. She wasn't sure exactly why, but she knew that it was imperative that this distinction be drawn.

The woman's mouth turned downward and her whole face drooped. "The room isn't available anymore," she said.

Felicity looked at the sign in the window.

"It was rented ten minutes ago. Just before you came," the woman said. "Forgot to take it down. Sorry."

Bad timing, Felicity thought. She moved to the next place on her list. Another woman answered the door, this one with grey hair covered by a hairnet. In the hallway behind her, the smell of stale cooking oil hung in the air.

"Good afternoon. I'm interested in your room —"

"Are you West Indian?"

"What? I mean, excuse me." Felicity held up the newspaper. "I'm asking about the room." She wondered if the woman had heard her.

"Are you West Indian?" The door had already begun to close.

"My mother is," said Felicity.

"Well, the room is already rented. Goodbye." The woman slammed the door.

Felicity's scalp prickled. A sharpness formed in her chest. She foresaw that she could knock on ten more doors, and the answers would be the same. And yet, she made the ten attempts, just in case. One landlady got as far as asking what she was studying, and when she heard it was opera, said, "Oh, I don't know dear, won't it be awfully loud?"

"I won't practice here," Felicity said, allowing herself to hope. "I can do that at my college."

"Well, I don't know." The woman twisted her hands together. Her blue veins bulged. "My husband wouldn't like it. I'm sorry, dear."

Though most of the time Felicity encountered women, at one address, a landlord answered. "Looking for a room, are you?" he said. "Well, come in and look at it, then. And I'll have a look at you."

The way he grinned at her with his silver-capped teeth was unsettling, and Felicity said, "No, thank you." She stepped away from him.

"Someone like you, you're not going to find many other people willing to rent to you," the man said. As if Felicity wasn't aware of that.

"I'd rather sleep on the street than with you," Felicity told him, and she ran. It was not a respectable thing to say, but it temporarily restored her dignity after an afternoon of being treated like vermin, something to be chased away. She took the Tube back to her hostel, tears already flowing by the time she took her seat on the train.

"Here you are, darling." The man opposite passed her a handkerchief pulled from his suit pocket, and then sat watching her expectantly as she sniffled into it. "He isn't worth crying over, love," the man said. "Chin up, there are plenty more fish in the sea."

Felicity looked away, not wanting to encourage him. She recalled how her mother often complained, "You cry too much. I've never known any child to cry as much as you."

If Aunt Rose was around, she would kiss Felicity and say, "Everyone feels blue sometimes." As a child, Felicity had never known why "feeling blue" meant being sad, and she still didn't really understand the expression. Blue skies were much preferable to grey ones. Grey was a far more despairing colour than blue.

CHAPTER 13.

London, England, September 8, 1965

FELICITY CLOSED THE door of her practice room. The usual gauntlet of competing voices seeped under it. There were shadows on the oak-panelled walls and on the floor, tiled in black and white hexagons. From the outside, the Guildhall School was nothing special; a nondescript brick building, tucked behind another building. But in this hallway, the air buzzed with dozens of youthful dreams, and the walls echoed with past glories.

Felicity warmed up, sending her own voice out into the hallway to battle with the others, and then she tottered out on her new high heels to sing for a stone-faced panel who cut her off halfway into each aria and dismissed her.

Her first audition was a failure. She was a failure. She should go back to Canada and take her mother's advice. Get a teaching certificate, marry a nice boy from Salvation Baptist. She would go to the Tube station to take a train back to the hostel, cover her head with a pillow, and cry. She noticed a side exit she had not seen before and wrenched the door handle open onto a small courtyard. A young man was sitting on a bench. He had a pale, narrow face and wore an equally narrow tie.

"Well, hello," he said. "Fancy seeing you here today." His voice was British, like many of the voices here, but it lilted upwards in a way that was different, that reminded Felicity a little of Sean Connery as James Bond.

"Hi," Felicity said.

"Are you a student here?"

"Yes."

"I assume first year?"

"Good guess."

"From America."

"Canada."

"Oh. William Nesbitt-Jennings," he said, holding out his hand. "But call me Will. Second year. Pianist. Accompanying."

"Felicity Alexander. Singing."

"Are you auditioning today?"

"I just did."

"You — wait, that was you I just heard? 'L'ho perduta' and 'Tornami'?"

"Yes," Felicity said, embarrassed he had heard her underwhelming performance.

Will rocked back on his heels and looked her up and down. "First year, you said? Who's your teacher?"

"Philip Cook," Felicity replied, wondering if she could get kicked out of Philip's studio for poor performance. Miss Fisher had told her that Philip was by far the Guildhall's best teacher. He was legendary for having studied at Guildhall and almost immediately afterward, at only twenty-two, landing significant roles with major opera houses. He enjoyed a career as one of the world's leading baritones and then, when he turned forty, announced that this would be his last season performing as he wanted to devote the rest of his career to vocal pedagogy, reviving what he saw as the dying art of bel canto singing. He had been teaching at his alma mater for seven years now and hand-picked his students. Felicity always had a vague sense of panic at her lessons with him, expecting him to see through her lack of talent at any moment.

"So you're the one," said Will.

"Sorry?"

"We heard last year," said Will. "They'd found this brilliant soprano in America. Someone so good that Philip was willing to take her on in first year. So, it's you. I can see why. Or I should say, I can hear why."

A voice rang out over the courtyard. Will closed his eyes and said, "Ah, 'Letzte Rose.' Nice. That will be Margot, of course."

"Who?" Felicity asked.

"Margot Laird. She's in her last year here. She's in Philip's studio too."

Felicity listened to the sound raining through the window and sighed at the creamy fullness of it. "She sounds so good."

"She does, but you're going to be better very soon," said Will.

"Me? But I was terrible in there!" Felicity gasped.

"You were not," Will said. "'L'ho perduta' is a silly little aria. It's not the same material Margot has. But it's still Mozart, and you sang it like it was Mozart. Longing and beauty all at once. And that Handel was glorious. The rumour is they want to do the show."

"What show?"

"*Alcina.*"

"What's that?"

"Oh, young innocent, do you not know the opera your aria is from?"

Felicity shook her head, feeling stupider by the second.

"That's all right. It's not the type of opera you're likely to see performed. Not like *Nozze* — I can presume you've seen that one?"

"I've never seen an opera," Felicity muttered.

Will struck a pose of exaggerated shock. "Never seen — Why on earth not?"

"I'm from Winnipeg," Felicity said. "That's in Canada, by the way. There's no opera company there. They're getting one soon. Maybe by the time I graduate, I'll be able to sing there."

Will laughed. "That's your ambition? To sing in some two-bit house in some outpost of the empire?"

Felicity's eyes smarted. "I didn't say it was my ambition."

"So what is, then?"

Felicity had only the stories Miss Fisher had told her from her own career. "To sing in New York," Felicity said. "The Metropolitan Opera. Have you heard of it?"

"Of course I've heard of it," said Will. "The Met is one of the world's great houses."

Felicity imagined New York as she had seen it in pictures with its mighty bridges, its tall buildings vanishing into the clouds, and people of all colours walking the streets, just like in London.

"Sic parvis magna," said Will.

"What?"

"It's Latin. Don't you know Latin?" Seeing her expression, he said, "God, we are provincial, aren't we? It means 'great things come from small beginnings.'"

Felicity heard a piano begin the introduction for "Tornami a vagghegiar" and saw Will playing along on his thigh. He said, "This year, they're going to let me be a rehearsal pianist, so I've been practicing."

"And you came out here to listen?"

"That and to partake." He reached into his pocket and pulled out a joint. Felicity felt pulled to it as if it were a magnet. "Do you want to share?" Will asked, seeing her hand already out. Just as she took her first puff, Margot botched a run.

"Ouch!" Will said. A few seconds later, she stumbled again.

"You see," Will said. "She can't move her voice like you. That's always been her weakness. They need singers for *Alcina* who can."

"But they didn't even let me finish the aria." Felicity exhaled.

"Look," Will said, snatching the joint from her hands. "You've got a lot to learn about auditions. They rarely let you finish a piece, and if they don't, it doesn't mean anything. It could mean they've heard enough to visualize you in the role. Or what you did, it was just so perfect — I would have stopped you too just so I wouldn't lose my mind." They listened as Margot sang the repeat. "You see?" Will said. "They let her finish because she's the favourite and they wanted to give her a chance to redeem herself. Not because it was good."

A male voice filled the courtyard next. Will said, "That's Franz."

"He's in first year too," Felicity said. "From Switzerland."

"He is that. And I've got my eye on him for other reasons."

"What reasons?"

Will looked at Felicity and held her gaze. "You may as well know now, Felicity Alexander. I'm a poofter. A fairy."

"What?"

"Dear girl from the hinterland, I am attracted to men. *Similia similibus*. I like what is like me."

"Oh!" Felicity tried not to show her surprise. She had never actually met a man who had admitted an interest in other men. She thought of what her mother would say. *It is an abomination for a man to lust after a man. God destroyed Sodom for its sin.* But Felicity had had sex outside of marriage. Who was she to judge?

"Well, you're not running screaming," said Will.

"No, why should I? I'm a different colour. That's just about as bad to most people."

"Ssh, I want to listen."

Franz's voice poured from the windows. Felicity thought his high notes sounded strained and thin, and Will apparently thought so too, because he shook his head in disappointment. "He'll get better," he said, after the first piece ended and no second piece was forthcoming.

"Where are you living?" asked Will.

"The YWCA," said Felicity.

"What on earth for?" Will let out a long, thin stream of smoke.

"I'm still looking for a room," she said.

"Looking? There are rooms all over London, girl from the outpost."

"Not if you're Black." Felicity looked down at her shoes.

"Oh," Will said. "Oh, bugger. Sorry." He handed the joint to Felicity. "Find a Jew," he said.

"What?" Felicity bit down on the joint.

"Jewish people. They'll rent to you. At least, that's what I've heard."

A drop of rain plopped onto Felicity's hand, and she instinctively put both hands up to try to protect the remnants of her straightened hair. Will stubbed out the last of the joint. "We should get inside," he said. As they walked through the door, he said, "Let's check the bulletin board and see what operas are coming up for us to see."

"See an opera?"

"Of course. They offer student tickets to Covent Garden all the time." He walked over to the bulletin board that had held the announcement about the West Indian students. "Here we are," Will said. "*La Bohème,* next Saturday. Now that's perfect. It's the quintessential opera. Couldn't choose a better one for your first."

CHAPTER 14.

London, England, September 12, 1965

FELICITY WOKE UP in her damp and drafty bedroom, only partially heated by a gas meter that ran on shillings.. The room faced west. The mornings were dark, which was just as well since it was harder to see the brown water spots on the sagging ceiling. She could still feel the damp patches on the lumpy mattress. Will had been right. A widow named Mrs. Dinnerstein, who said she had come to London as a war refugee from Austria, was willing to rent to her, but she lived in Golders Green, a long Tube ride to the Guildhall.

Getting ready for school, Felicity practiced sneering into the mirror. When a man smiled at her on the Tube, she wanted to snarl back, wishing she could punch him into the poster behind his head of Dirk Bogarde in *Darling*.

Entering through the front doors of the Guildhall, she saw a large group clustered around the bulletin board. A few heads turned to look at her, and then Will separated from the crowd and approached her.

"Felicity, aren't you going to look at the cast lists?"

"Later."

"What's wrong?"

"Nothing." Unaccountably, she wanted to strangle him.

"Well, you need to come and look."

"I don't want to."

"Come here, you silly girl." He grabbed her wrist and pulled her through the crowd. "Look!" he said.

Felicity looked. She was cast as Morgana in *Alcina* and Linda in *Linda di Chamounix*. "Are those big roles?"

"Are those big roles?" He exaggerated his slack jaw and bulging eyes. "Felicity, they're leads! Two leads for a singer in first year! It's unprecedented!"

Felicity gaped back at him.

"Ad meliora," Will said.

"What?"

"Towards better things. You're on your way."

A voice piped up from the crowd. "It's probably not a good idea to give such big parts to first years," said a soprano in Felicity's cohort, Sarah Stilwell. "My teacher says it ruins your voice to sing opera too soon."

By the afternoon, when she had her voice lesson, Felicity was exhausted. The euphoria was beginning to wear off. She wished she could call Claude Buckingham and tell him about her triumph, but he had her phone number and she didn't have his.

"Miss Alexander," said Philip Cook, getting up from the piano as she walked in. "I assume you have seen the cast lists." She nodded, feeling intimidated before her teacher's greatness.

"Those are two big roles, especially the Donizetti. The school was in need of a coloratura, so they have chosen to elevate you. I would not normally recommend a developing singer of your age to embark on such repertoire, but I believe you have the technique. With appropriate support, you can manage it, but we will have to work hard together." Felicity stood mute. "Come on, child, not a word from you?"

"I'm glad I have you to help me, Mr. Cook," she said.

"Philip," he said. "And I wasn't looking for — Never mind. Shall we warm up?"

Felicity felt her vocal cords creaking to life, her sound not quite as clear and easy to produce as normal. It was Claude. He was stealing her voice from her.

Philip put a score in front of her. "This is the big aria from the Donizetti," he said. "'O luce di quest'anima.' That means, roughly, *light of my soul.* I know you haven't had much language study yet, so let's work through the translation, shall we?"

Together, using a dictionary, they determined that the aria translated as:

Oh, you are the radiance of my soul,
Delight, love, and life;
On earth and in heaven,
We will be united.

Claude, Felicity thought. *Claude, Claude, Claude*. The radiance of her soul.

Philip looked at her and raised an eyebrow. "It's actually a nice aria for someone your age if you can manage the technical demands," he said. "First love and all that? Those blue eyes you dream of, eh?"

"Brown," said Felicity before she could stop herself.

"Brown?" he said and laughed. "Ah, so that's what's eating Felicity today. Pining after someone, are you? Never mind, you must put that aside and focus on your work. This is a significant opportunity you've been given. Let's try the first line on an *ah* vowel, shall we."

Felicity opened her mouth to sing, but instead, a big sob came out. She turned away, covering her face with her hands.

"Oh, good God," said Philip. "Well, come on, we can't learn like that, can we? Sit down." He stood from the piano stool and made his way to a stuffed armchair. "Come on," he said, clapping his hands.

Trying to stop crying, Felicity trailed over to the other armchair. Philip plunked a box of tissues in her lap. Then, he said, "Exactly when is your menstrual period due?"

Felicity was so shocked, she almost choked on her next sob. She hadn't connected the way she felt to her cycle, blaming only Claude for her misery, but now that she thought of it, she calculated quickly in her head. "S-s-soon."

"Well, you mustn't look so surprised," Philip said. "And you mustn't be embarrassed. It's my business to know such things. Our body is our instrument, and anything that affects the body affects the instrument. I've had many young women in this room in your condition."

Felicity blew her nose. Now that she knew what the problem was, she felt a little better.

"Some of the girls say the pill helps," Philip went on.

"The pill?"

"Oh God, you are an innocent. Contraception. Birth control. It's been around for a few years now. Don't the mothers in Canada do their job? See a doctor and ask for a prescription. Make sure you tell them you're married, or they won't give it to you. It will help with Mr. Brown Eyes too. I have seen many a promising career ended because the singer became a mother too soon."

Felicity wished Mr. Brown Eyes would put her in danger of being a mother; but only in danger of it. She didn't want a baby, not even Claude's. But it didn't matter, because she would probably never hear from Claude again.

"Now, let me make you a nice cup of tea, and we can talk through this role. How about it?"

BY THE EVENING of the opera, Felicity had given up on ever hearing from Claude. She was thankful for the clothes Aunt Rose had bought or made her as she slipped into a burgundy velvet dress she had worn to Miss Fisher's Christmas studio recital. She glanced at several unopened letters from Brian sitting on her dresser.

"That dress looks nice on you," Will greeted her, "but it's three years behind the times." Felicity ignored him as she looked up at the vast marble pillars of the Royal Opera House. "Wait until you see inside," Will said. "Now listen. *Bohème* is a perfect opera. It's a treasure. It's about the love affair between Mimi and Rodolfo. They fall in love at first sight on Christmas Eve, but you see, they're both poor, and Mimi's sick, she has TB, so she goes off to be the mistress of some rich guy so she won't burden Rodolfo, and they have this terribly sad parting where she says '*Addio, senza rancor.*' That means *goodbye without bitterness*, it's so sweet, but then she comes back when she's about to die, and she says, '*I know I'm dying, but I want to die with him,*' and she dies."

"You spoiled the ending!" said Felicity.

Will laughed. "Everyone knows the ending when they go to the opera."

Inside the theatre, Felicity looked around at the gilded balconies and chandeliers, trying to contain her awe. When they were seated, Will said, "The music for this opera is sexy. Like Franz. I'm going to picture him singing Rodolfo someday." Felicity looked skeptical. "Okay, a long time away," he conceded. "But Felicity, that man is beautiful."

The woman sitting in front of them turned around and glared. Felicity smiled as sweetly as she could, and when the woman had turned around, she asked, "Have you had any luck with Franz?"

Will sighed. "I've been bumping into him a lot by chance, and I finally worked the conversation around to offering him some coaching help. Next stop, the bedroom." The woman turned around again and glared more pointedly. Felicity smiled at her again and asked, "So what else do I need to know about the opera?"

Will continued, "There's this character, Musetta, and she's a sexy bitch. Kind of like you, Felicity."

Now the woman's husband turned around fiercely and said, "There's really no call for that kind of talk, is there?"

"Sorry," Felicity said, as Will said, "Stuff it." He went on, "Musetta is with Marcello, but they fight and break up, fight and break up. But at the end she tries to help Mimi, and we see she actually has a heart."

Felicity said, "It would be better not to have a heart."

"Still pining for Claude, are you?" asked Will. He patted her hand. "He'll ring soon."

The lights dimmed, and they fell silent as the conductor strode into the orchestra pit in his tails and stood on the small podium. He raised his hands. As the opera began, Felicity was mesmerized. Though she didn't understand the words being sung, no translation was needed when Rodolfo and Mimi met. Felicity held her breath as they walked slowly off stage together, the lights dimming to black, and Mimi sang a chilling high note from offstage on a word Felicity knew. *L'amor.* Love. Will gripped Felicity's hand. Waves of longing and hope washed over her. She was watching Rodolfo and Mimi but seeing herself and Claude. Whatever his reason for ignoring her now, she had felt them drawn together in the excitement of the march. She knew she had not imagined it.

Before Felicity could fully absorb the first act, the second began, with singers rushing all over the stage, and children's voices pealing out above the din. Felicity saw immediately which character must be Musetta. Gorgeously dressed in a mink fur over her enormous dress, screaming and fussing and drawing attention. But over it all rang Mimi's voice, shining its light, pouring out its beauty.

Felicity cried when Mimi and Rodolfo broke up. She cried when Mimi came back, and she sobbed as Mimi died. Will slung his arm around her. She leaned in close. His cheek was wet as well. When the lights came up, she was dazed, her head swimming, her eyes heavy. She sat fixed in her seat, the many different melodies in the opera colliding in her brain. Will was talking, giving his opinion of the tenor, but she couldn't really hear him or focus on the words he was saying. Finally, he yanked her to her feet. "Come on, you prima donna."

"I want to do that," Felicity said. "I need to do that." All thoughts of anything else, even Claude, had been driven out of her head by the opera. How a world had been created on stage, that, even though it was of a time and place long past, with the pageantry of costumes and wigs, seemed more real to her than anything she had ever known.

She recovered over a pint in a pub with Will before taking the Tube home. When she let herself in, she saw a note on the table by the telephone. Moonlight spilled over it as she read "*Miss Alexander, Mr. Buckingham rang. Will ring back tomorrow.*"

THE FOLLOWING SATURDAY afternoon, Felicity met Claude in Trafalgar Square, under Nelson's Column. Claude loped towards her, face animated by a grin. They cleared a path through the pigeons to sit on a bench, where they talked about their childhoods, their families, their hopes and dreams. Claude gave Felicity a primer on the history of the Caribbean and the Black struggle in America, and she talked to him about opera.

As the last few rays of sunlight dropped behind the bronzed lions, Claude said, "My father used to take me to the beach for a swim every day before school."

"I wish I had gone to the beach in Grenada," Felicity said. "We usually stayed in the house. I think the beach was pretty far away."

Claude laughed. "Grenada is twenty-one miles by twelve miles. Nothing is far away. You're never more than about six miles from the sea," he said, "Even more than the water, what I liked the best was talking to my dad. Sometimes after we swam, he'd show me hidden parts of the island. Once he showed me an old slave mill and said to never forget the hard work that previous generations did for me. That is how we can be worthy of their suffering."

"Your dad sounds great," Felicity said, as an ache began to spread within her.

"I would be nothing without him," Claude said. "He worked hard for my uniform and my schoolbooks. My mother, too. I had a scholarship, but it didn't cover everything."

"By the time my cousin was twelve," Felicity said, "he already knew he couldn't go to secondary school."

"After the Revo — that's what Neville and I call the Revolution, a smaller version of the word for a small island — we will provide everything to pupils. A scholarship will mean a scholarship. Uniform and books." He touched Felicity's hand. "But you haven't told me anything about your father."

"That's because there's nothing to tell."

"He was never around?"

"No." She wanted to tell him what her father had done to her mother. She opened her mouth, but the words wouldn't come. They were too monstrous. She waited for the rush of tears, determined to head them off rather than cry on their first date, but it didn't come. She willed him to hold her. She needed to be held more than she needed to breathe. And then he opened his arms, and she was nestling against his chest. The urge to cry dissipated at the thrill of being close. Claude didn't wear the cologne and aftershave Brian did, nor did he smell of tobacco like Jack. He had his own musky, salty scent that banished all thoughts of other men.

Claude's voice rumbled, "That's why I hesitated to ring you, you know. I thought, if a girl who looks like you was raised by a white man, how loyal could you really be to our cause? But now I know he didn't raise you, he abandoned you. So you have just as much reason to hate the white devil as anyone. You can tell him to fuck off, you don't need him. Fuck white men. Fuck them." He spoke the ugly, jarring words as if they were poetry, turning their starkness to honey, and not the crisp bluntness when Jack said it.

Felicity listened to Claude's heartbeat, a distant drum pounding only for her through flesh, bone, and blood. He stroked her arm, and said, "You have a lovely colour, Felicity. It reminds me of all the spices back home. You're the colour of nutmeg." Felicity smiled and pressed closer to him. "Nutmeg is sweet," said Claude. "I could call you that, you know."

"Call me what?"

"Nutmeg," said Claude, but then a moment later, he exploded, "Shrimps, man, what am I saying? Tibbs's secret police are called the Nutmeg Squad. I can't name you after them." He thought for a moment, and then he said, "Cinnamon. That's a nice brown too, and it's sweet, but it has some spice. A little zing. Like you." She heard him smiling as he said, "That's you, Felicity. Cinnamon."

CHAPTER 15.

London, England, October 25, 1965

EVERY MUSIC STUDENT at the Guildhall was required to perform in a few recitals a year, and every other music student was required to sit in the audience, comparing themselves to their peers, glorying in their slips, cheering on their friends, and half-heartedly clapping for rivals. Felicity's turn came after many of her classmates had already had their baptisms.

She wanted to perform "O luce," but Philip said, "No opera in recital. Not yet. You'll sing enough of that in rehearsals. For now, we'll start with song repertoire. Your German needs the most work, so you will sing three Schubert lieder," he told her. "And then, as a treat, I'll give you a big girl song. Something by Strauss. 'Im Abendrot,' one you will grow into." Felicity tried to wipe the disappointment from her face, but Philip said, "Cheer up. There'll be plenty of time for opera later."

"How about Brahms? 'Wie Melodien'?" Will was practicing it to perform with a second-year at the next recital, and Felicity loved how lush it sounded.

"Oh, no," Philip said. "That's for a low voice."

"Couldn't I sing the high voice transposition?"

"My dear." Philip wore a pained expression. "The composer writes the music for a certain vocal weight and timbre. I don't hold with this idea that you can change the key willy-nilly and nothing will be lost. Stick to the music written for your voice type. Schubert and Strauss." Felicity looked away, chastened. She should have kept her mouth shut.

"Have you thought of a pianist?" Philip didn't seem to notice her change of mood.

"Will. I mean, William Nesbitt-Jennings."

"Ah, yes. I've noticed you chumming around with that young man. Not flashy, keeps things steady." Felicity knew that this was Philip's mark of approval. Will would be ecstatic when she told him. "'Rastlose Liebe' is a bit of work for a pianist, so you'd better get the music to him and have him come to your next lesson."

Felicity had grown increasingly frustrated, preparing four songs in a language that knotted her tongue at the very sight of it. One afternoon, in a practice room with Will, she threw the Schubert book against the wall.

"Now, now, that's not any way to treat an old master," said Will. "One more time, and then we'll go round the back, shall we?" That meant smoking weed in the courtyard. *"Ad meliora,"* he added. When she shrugged her lack of comprehension, he said, "Remember? 'To better things.'"

She complained to Claude about Schubert so much when she saw him that he began every conversation with, "How's the German?" They studied together almost every evening at the law library with Neville, who waited for Claude to brief the cases and then copied his conclusions. On the night before her recital, as Felicity reviewed vocabulary for German class, Claude looked up from a volume of contracts cases. "How's it coming, Cinnamon?"

She pushed the book away. "I hate German," she whined.

"German?" Claude grinned. "Do I have to watch out for flying books?"

"My back hurts," she complained.

Claude came around the table to sit beside her. "Aw, poor Felicity." He probed it with his fingers. "Where is it the worst? Here?"

She pointed, and he began to massage the area, his knuckles moving rhythmically up and down. He looked down at her German book. "What is that, parts of the body?"

"Yes," she said. "It's a song the teacher taught us, like we're little kids. You know 'Head, Shoulders, Knees, and Toes'?"

"I remember it."

"Well, in German it's Kopf und Schultern, Knie und Zeh, Augen, Ohren, Nase und Mund."

"Oh, I see," said Claude. He took one hand away from Felicity's back and touched his head. "This is Kopf?" He pronounced it perfectly. She nodded. "And Schultern? Knie? Zeh?" He pointed to each part, pronouncing them correctly.

"I've been studying this language for weeks, and it takes you a minute?" Felicity pouted.

"Sorry. I like languages. I was just trying to help," said Claude.

"Well, don't."

"Come on, Cinnamon, it's just your back hurting," Claude said. "Let me finish this case brief and then I'll rub it again." He went back to his side of the table.

"If you two lovebirds are finished, I'm wondering if you have the *ratio decidendi* for *High Trees* anywhere, Claude," said Neville.

IN THE MORNING, Felicity put on another of the dresses Aunt Rose had packed for her. She now knew from Will that all her clothes were terribly dated and out-of-style in London, but she didn't have the money for anything new. She was saving her grant money for a gown to wear at the hurricane relief concert being organized by the West Indian students. She woke up without enough time to touch up her hair with the hot comb, so she pulled it back into a tight bun. Perhaps too tight, because her scalp felt achy and tender for the rest of the morning. The ache burrowed into her spine during Italian diction class where, instead of open vowels, Felicity's head was filled with Claude. As soon as class was dismissed, she hurried to the front door of the school, where he was waiting. "Hi, Cinnamon," he said, moving to kiss her, but she ducked.

"Lipstick."

"Your hair is up," he said. "I haven't seen it like that before." He traced the shape of her jaw with his finger. "It shows off this lovely face."

From behind her, Will grumped, "Oh, will you two stop it?" He held out a hand to Claude. "I'm Will. I've heard more than enough about your big brown eyes, so it's past time we met."

Claude, prepared by Felicity, simply smiled and said, "Nice to meet you, Will."

When it was her turn to sing, Felicity climbed the stairs to the stage and settled herself into the piano's curve as Will spread out his music, cupped his hands, and blew into them. The first piece was "An die Musik," an ode to music. The holy art that in so many painful moments had transported the singer to a better world.

She knew what to do. Her breath was steady, her sound was even, she pronounced the words more-or-less correctly. But it felt stodgy. Her emotions felt contrived. She plodded through the songs, arriving at "Im Abendrot." Felicity had puzzled over the words for hours; "Wenn das Rot, das in der Wolke blinkt, In mein stilles Fenster sinkt." *When the red light that flashes in the cloud sinks into my quiet window.* As she sang them now, she thought, *the red light.* The way the Grenadian skies had illuminated as she stood in the brush, her face turned to the spreading flames. And Claude had seen that too, years before they met.

The applause was enthusiastic, but Felicity found it hard not to scowl as she bowed. They were being polite. She knew she could sing better. Philip would know that too. Her chest burned as she walked off stage. Will was beaming, having played flawlessly. "That was great, Felicity," he whispered. Claude looked at her as she approached, his eyes soft, his tongue poking out to wet his lips. But Felicity could not bear to return to that hard seat. She walked down the aisle and out through the auditorium doors.

She sat down on a bench and let the tears start. A moment later, Claude and Will were sitting, one on either side of her.

"Felicity? Cinnamon?" Claude held out his arms, but she turned away.

"Jesus Christ," Will said, "don't be such a prima donna, Felicity. You sang splendidly. Your German is becoming quite passable."

"I was terrible.

"You were not terrible," Will scolded, "you've just got your bloody period coming and you want to suffer."

Of course. But the knowledge made her feel worse, not better, and she began to sob harder.

"What?" she heard Will say to Claude. "You didn't know?"

Claude bent his head close to Felicity's. "Are you not feeling well, Cinnamon?" he asked.

"My back hurts."

She felt Claude's hands probing. "Here? Here?" She nodded when he found the spot, then turned and buried her head against his chest.

A minute later, she heard Philip's voice. "Dear me. What a hullabaloo on a Thursday afternoon." She couldn't look at him. "Ah. This must be Mr. Brown Eyes," Philip said next. Philip knelt before Felicity and Claude. "Haven't you seen your doctor yet?"

She shook her head inside the fence of Claude's arms.

"Why on earth not? There is absolutely no reason for you to carry on like this, when there is a medical solution."

Claude asked, "What kind of doctor?"

"One who will prescribe contraceptives," Philip said. "Which I imagine is in your best interest, too. The law is that the woman must be married, and some doctors are stricter than others in verifying that, you understand."

Claude said, "I know someone."

"Good," Philip said. "I suggest you make her an appointment immediately. And take her home," he added. "She's no good to anyone like that."

"I have keyboard harmony —" Felicity said.

"I will speak to Lewis about that. Just go home," Philip said. Then he added, "I suppose it's my fault really, for not checking the blasted calendar before suggesting you sing today."

"I've got to get to a coaching," Will said. "Good luck, Claude."

Claude led Felicity out of the building to the Tube station. "Are you really the only Black student in this entire school, Felicity?" he asked as they walked.

Felicity shrugged. She was used to being the only one.

"That doesn't bother you? I got a funny feeling just walking in there."

"Not many Black people study classical music, Claude."

"Because they don't have the opportunity. They don't come from money."

"Do you think I grew up rich?" Felicity asked. "You do, don't you? My mother raised me on her own. Some days, she didn't eat so that I could. She saw that I had potential, and she made sacrifices to get me music lessons. I wish more of our people had the same chances. Maybe if I make it big, it will encourage others."

"That's nice," Claude said, slipping his hand into hers, and she felt him relax.

"What is?"

"What you said about your mother. The first really nice thing you've said about her."

The train was full, the air laced with the smoke of countless cigarettes. Felicity and Claude were separated and had to stand. As Felicity gripped the metal pole, her back began to spasm. She put her purse down on the ground and tried to massage the ache, reaching behind her as the train swung her from side to side. Giving up, she bent over, trying to relieve the pressure.

"Cinnamon." Claude shoved his way through the crowds to get to her. "It's hurting again?" He addressed the women sitting in a row against the window. "Can you let my girlfriend sit down, please? She isn't feeling well."

"Young girl like that can stand," one of the women muttered.

"No, she really can't," said Claude.

"Looks all right to me," said another woman, her shopping bag tucked between her stout legs.

"I can't believe this!" said Claude.

Felicity pulled on his coat. "Forget it."

"You English!" he said. "Treat dogs better than people."

"Rather dogs than wogs!" shouted a male voice behind them. Claude's shoulders tensed and he backed away.

"I'm sorry, Cinnamon," he said. "You'll have to stand, since these prejudiced pigs won't give up their seats. Can you manage? I'll try to rub your back at the stops."

"What does *wog* mean?" she asked.

His pupils constricted and his eyes grew dark and glittering. "Short for *golliwog*. Stupid colonialist dolls made to look like Black people with these big fat red lips. It's like calling someone a ... you know."

When the train emptied out, Felicity was able to sit. Claude sat beside her and rubbed her back. As the pain eased, Felicity said, "You didn't say anything about my performance."

"It was beautiful," he said. "I've never heard anyone sing like that."

She saw his Adam's apple jump and patted him on the crotch. He started. "Felicity!"

"You felt it here," she said.

"Felicity, you're killing me."

"So you liked it. You felt love."

"I did," he said. "But ..."

She twisted her head to look at him. "But what?"

She saw him measuring what to say, not wanting to set her off again. "It was all in German, and I couldn't understand any of it."

"Well, I only understand it because I studied it. But I told you, the first one's thanking music for being a comfort, and the second one —"

"I meant, what does it have to do with us?" Claude asked. "Our struggle. Black people."

"We love, too!" Felicity shouted. "We have the same hearts, the same feelings as anyone else!"

"You're right. You're right." Claude reached for the spot on her back again, but she batted his hand away. Heads were turning to look at them. "Did I tell you how pretty you looked on stage?"

"Shut up, Claude!"

"I say, that's not how we behave in England," said a white-haired man with a cane hooked over the opposite seat.

"Mind your own business," Felicity told him. Claude's hand came down over hers in warning, and she fell silent.

He spoke into her ear, "Never mind. I don't know what I'm saying. Watching you made me" — he stopped and then whispered — "gooey inside." Her anger faded as she remembered the revelation she'd had on stage.

"Claude," she said. "When I sang my last song, I realized that it could be talking about the Red Sky Revolution." She repeated the translation, right to the last line: *And this heart, before it breaks, still drinks in the embers and revels in, savours the light.*

"Yes," Claude said. "The red light. Bon jay, that was a beautiful night, Cinnamon." He put an arm around her. "I bet no one has sung those German things and made them about Grenada before." He pressed his lips to her cheek. "You're right, Cinnamon. You will make our little island great. To the Revo."

"To the Revo." She rested her head on his shoulder, drinking in the fire and savouring the light. The world needed art as much as it needed revolution.

CHAPTER 16.

St. George's, Grenada, October 14, 1983

FELICITY REACHED FOR her purse and felt inside it until her fingers closed around the hardness of the plastic disc. She swallowed the small pill without water; after another long night of little sleep on the unyielding frame of the couch, she was too weary to get up and go into the kitchen. She was grateful that she always carried a three-month supply of contraceptives when she travelled, just in case, and that she always kept them in her purse.

She had first been prescribed the pill when Claude took her to see Dr. Taylor, who was from Jamaica. He entered the examination room after she had changed into a scratchy paper gown, pressed Claude's hand in a complex handshake, and said, "Well, my young friend, this is a surprise. It is usually young Mr. Carpenter who seeks these things. And he doesn't come in with the girls."

"One girl," said Claude. "I have one girl. This is Felicity."

Dr. Taylor was all smiles. "Of course, of course, wonderful." He turned to Felicity. "Sit on the table there. Come on. Now, Claude says you are in need of contraceptives? For cyclical discomforts, or birth control?"

"Her back hurts a lot," said Claude, just as Felicity said, "Both." She looked at Claude to see how he would react and saw his lips twitching.

"I see." Dr. Taylor grinned. "I shall have to examine you first, young lady."

"Examine?"

"Yes, have a look internally, just to be sure all is in order." Something about his smile unsettled Felicity.

"Mr. Buckingham, you can wait for her outside."

"No," Felicity said, her voice quavering. "No, I want him to stay."

"Of course, Cinnamon." Claude rushed to the examination table and took her hand. "I can stay if she wants me to, can't I?"

Dr. Taylor's smile dropped. "Well, yes, of course."

"Please," Felicity said. She didn't want to be alone with this man.

"It's all right," Claude said, squeezing her hand.

"Open your legs," Dr. Taylor directed, and the instant Felicity did, his gloved hand was inside her, probing, rough. Felicity bit her lip and inhaled sharply at the pain, gripping Claude's hand tighter.

"You're doing well, Cinnamon," Claude encouraged.

At a further twinge, Felicity shouted, "Ow!"

Claude addressed Dr. Taylor. "Can you be a bit gentler?" he asked. "She isn't used to this."

"No one is used to it," Dr. Taylor said. "At least, you wouldn't want her if she was, would you?" He poked around a bit more before he withdrew his hand, with more rubbing and scratching. "All seems fine," he said. "I'll write a prescription." He didn't look at either of them.

Outside the clinic, Claude rubbed the hand she had squeezed and asked, "Cinnamon, was it that terrible?"

Felicity was amazed at the things men didn't know. Claude had no idea that Dr. Taylor had been rough on purpose, that he viewed Felicity as damaged goods and therefore available for the taking, and so he had taken personal pleasure from what should have been a professional interaction. An opera of looks and touch had taken place right under Claude's nose, and Felicity had endured it to get this precious prescription.

SHE HAD NEVER desired children, and yet here she was with two daughters, half-sisters whose unrelated halves divided them far more than their shared ancestry connected them. Mara had just turned fourteen, and each year increased her otherworldly beauty. She had long, wavy, almost white-blond hair, a pale, elfin face and large eyes, lighter than blue, transparent and colourless like river ice. At eleven, Adele was a carbon copy of Felicity, a couple of shades darker and with tighter, denser curls, but the same blocky body and the same prominent nose.

Mara was the favourite of her grandmother, and there was a lot of Dolores in Mara's tall, slender frame and sculpted cheekbones, as well as the imperious, slightly judgmental way she took in her surroundings. Adele wanted to be just like Felicity. She loved singing, though it was obvious to Felicity that she had no particular talent for it. On the few occasions that Felicity was home, Adele followed her around, asking questions about her performances, trying to dress and do her hair the same way as her mother. Felicity found it exhausting. She knew that mothers were supposed to miss their children when they were apart from them, but she found only relief in being able to leave them with her own mother and escape to her next engagement. An opera was a world in itself; not just the one created onstage by the director, but the tight circle built by the participants — the friendships, the rivalries, the flirtations and affairs — all-consuming for a few weeks before they dispersed and jetted off elsewhere, uncertain as to when they would meet again. Such intensity admitted no one else, not even her offspring.

It was Adele who wanted to be a singer, but it was Mara who had inherited Felicity's musical ability. When Felicity was home last spring, both girls were preparing to compete in the Winnipeg Music Festival. Adele yapped on at dinner about her selections until Felicity asked, "Mara, what are you singing?"

Mara shrugged. "A bunch of stuff. I have this German one."

"Which one?" Felicity asked.

"Lachen und Weinen."

"That's for a high, light voice," Felicity said. While Adele sang soprano, Mara's voice emerged from her throat in a low, dark growl incongruous in a girl of her appearance. It was a rare and beautiful thing, but Mara thought high notes were the only important part of singing, and Felicity didn't have the energy to convince her otherwise.

Mara stabbed the casserole Dolores had made. "I'm singing it transposed, down a fourth."

Felicity repeated what Philip Cook had told her. "The composer writes for a particular heft and timbre for a reason." Mara shrugged and took a swig of juice.

Later, when Felicity went upstairs, she heard "Lachen und Weinen" with piano accompaniment seeping under Mara's bedroom door. It was an astounding rendition — slower than Felicity had ever sung it, less playful, more knowing. Felicity knocked. The music stopped. Mara opened the door. Fine wisps of hair had come loose from her ponytail and plastered her temples.

"What recording is that?" Felicity asked.

Mara looked at Felicity with the baleful, wounded expression with which she generally regarded her mother. "That was me practicing with a tape," she said.

Felicity had been too amazed to say anything, but hearing her daughter made her question her long-held belief. Philip's insistence on voices staying within a narrow *fach* was similar to the constraints of race. It felt like the way colonial rulers barged into countries not their own and imposed arbitrary rules. There was no reason an alto couldn't sing Schubert in a low key, or why she couldn't sing Brahms in a high key.

Felicity's next return to Winnipeg coincided with the Festival, and she went with her mother to see the girls compete. Adele was eliminated, but Mara was recommended to the finals. When the singer before Mara was announced and Mara stood up to take her place backstage, Adele crumpled against Felicity's shoulder in tears. Felicity supposed that the reality had hit her younger daughter that her older sister had been chosen and she had not. Felicity hesitated. She wanted to spare Adele the humiliation of being seen sobbing with jealousy, but she didn't want to miss Mara's performance. As the other girl began climbing the stairs to the stage, she decided. She put her arm around Adele, dragged her out in the hallway, and pushed her down onto a bench. "Sit here and get yourself together," she said, and turned back towards the auditorium.

"I'm sorry, ma'am," said the usher. "We don't allow people to leave and come back in."

"You've got to be kidding me," Felicity said. She restrained herself from adding, *Do you know who I am?* Instead, she said, "My daughter's singing next."

"I'm sorry, the rules are the rules."

Now she did say it. "I'm Felicity Alexander. I just sang at the Royal Opera House and I'm going to the Houston Grand Opera next week."

The usher looked at her blankly. "That's nice, but I can't let you in."

"So you don't allow bathroom breaks?" Felicity asked. "You force people to sit there and piss their pants or leave bloodstains all over their seats?"

"Don't be vulgar," said the usher.

Felicity waited in the hall until the competition was over and her mother informed her that Mara had been announced as the runner-up. Both Dolores and Mara glared at Felicity with unconcealed animosity. Felicity was used to her own mother's disappointment, and she knew she was an inadequate parent, but she was unprepared for the look her eldest daughter gave her. It was Brian's angry eyes that stared at Felicity.

Mara had barely spoken to Felicity in the seven months since. Felicity wondered if any of them, her daughters or her mother, were thinking of her now. Her mother never seemed to miss her when she was in London. Perhaps her absence was a relief, or just what her family had grown accustomed to.

CHAPTER 17.

London, England, December 24, 1965

FELICITY LACED HER fingers into Claude's and shivered as rain pelted the umbrella he held in his other hand. She pulled Claude into the phone booth with her and pressed her back against his chest. His arms went around her as she fed coins into the slot, dialed the operator, and waited to be connected.

Her mother answered after five rings. "Felicity, what are you calling for?"

"I just wanted to wish you a merry Christmas."

"You could have called tomorrow."

"I'm going to be busy."

"Doing what?" Mom's voice sounded suspicious, ungiving, even beyond the notes of sleepiness.

"I'm singing for a church service tonight, and then tomorrow, I'm having Christmas lunch with some of my friends from the West Indian Students' Association."

"A Catholic church?"

"Anglican." From the silence, Felicity knew that that was almost as bad.

"Is there someone there you're involved with?" Mom asked. "Brian called me the other day. He wants to know why you aren't answering his letters. He's waiting for you, Felicity. You don't have time to have a relationship over there. You're there for your studies."

"I know that." Hearing the operator's warning, Felicity held out her hand. Claude placed a coin in her palm and she fed it into the slot.

"I mean it, Felicity! No boys."

"I just have friends, Mom." Any hope of introducing the subject of Claude, of thinking that Mom might be happy for her, that she might understand love, that she would ever let it soften her, dripped to the floor with the rain from the umbrella.

"Friends. I don't know why you have male friends, like that awful Jack. It looks bad."

"Josiah's a boy."

"That's different and you know it. So what about Brian? Are you going to write to him?"

"Mom, I have to go. I have to get to the church."

Felicity waited, but all Mom said was, "Bye then. Have a nice Christmas." She was glad Claude couldn't hear her.

Felicity hung up. "I wasted money I could have used on the meter," she said. "I didn't tell her about you." Claude pulled her closer and stroked her hair. He stretched a curl and let it snap back.

"You don't need to tell her yet," he said. "There's lots of time for that. I haven't told my parents either. Maybe it's best if we just let this be our time, Cinnamon."

Felicity burrowed her head deeper into his chest. "But, Claude, she hates me."

"Of course she doesn't."

"She never shows it."

Claude said, "She's from a country that survived slavery, which broke the original family structures of Africans, and still lives under harsh colonial rule. Bon jay, you don't show love if everything you love has been taken from you."

Felicity wriggled free so that she could look up at him. "Aren't you're from that country too?"

"And I told you, I was fortunate. My father learned to love himself, and love his land, and only then could he love others. And that's why my mission is to teach everyone in Grenada to do the same." He brushed his lips against Felicity's. "And to love you, Cinnamon. Your mother may not know how to show it, but I do."

There came a rapping on the door of the phone box. "I say," shouted a man, "it isn't enough that you wogs are here in our country, but now you're tying up a phone box with your filth on Christmas Eve?"

Claude squared his shoulders and clenched his fists.

"Let's just go." Felicity pulled Claude out of the box and said "Sorry" to the man who pushed past them. Claude started after him, but Felicity begged, "Claude. My performance. I can't be late," and Claude relented, took her hand and began walking with her again.

"White people," he said. "Most miserable people to ever walk the earth."

EVEN THOUGH IT was Christmas Eve, even though they could see glowing fireplaces and twinkling trees through almost every window they passed, after the service, Claude and Felicity went to the law library. On the way in, they met Neville.

"Brother!" he said. "I was looking for you, to borrow your case briefs. Hello, Felicity." The three of them headed to their usual corner. Stacks of leather-bound volumes stretched to the ceiling, covered by a thin veneer of dust. Neville slumped in an a chair, hanging his legs over an armrest. "I met a woman yesterday who was complaining about how she can't get a job as a teacher, even though she has a better degree than anyone they hired," Neville said. "I'm going to see if I can write some letters to the City Council, get other people to write some too. You in, brother?"

"I have to get this exam under my belt first," said Claude. "I'll have to study for the rest of the holidays."

"Admiralty law," scoffed Neville. "These whites think they own the sea. What use is that to us?"

Claude looked up from his book. "Bon jay, Neville. Have you forgotten that we come from an island?"

Felicity pulled out her German textbook, but the unfamiliar words stuck together before her eyes. Singing, even though it was only some simple carols, usually filled her with energy, but tonight it had exhausted her, wrung all emotion from her. Shivering in the drafty room, she stuck her hands into the pocket of her coat and felt the cold glass of her pill bottle, almost empty. Dr. Taylor had said that it would take two to three months to become effective, either as a contraceptive or to ease her monthly symptoms. Almost two months later, she and Claude had not had sex.

Claude looked over at her. "How's the German going?"

"Okay."

"Okay?" Claude smiled. "That's better than 'I hate German'."

He didn't want her. He really was only a friend, like she had told her mother. He said he loved her, but it was only the brotherly kind of love, because she was unlovable in any other way.

"That woman, that teacher?" said Neville. "Brother, the backside on her. You should see it. If I give her some help, I hope she gives me some loving."

"Neville!" said Claude. "Sleeping with clients isn't ethical."

"We're not lawyers yet," said Neville. "So those rules don't apply."

Felicity bent her head over her German book.

"Cinnamon?" Claude slipped out of his seat and spoke into her ear. "Are you all right? Back hurting again?"

"I'm just tired, Claude." It was up to him to let her know he was interested. She wasn't going to embarrass herself.

"Well, let's get you home, then." Claude went back to his seat and began packing up. "See you tomorrow, Neville."

"Have fun taking her home," Neville said with a wink. "Before you leave, can I copy the *ratio decidendi* for *Armory and Delamirie*?"

IT WAS RAINING on Christmas morning when Claude rang Felicity's doorbell. As they waited in the Tube station, she reached into her pocket for the wrapped box she had placed there when she woke and passed it to him. "Merry Christmas," she said. Her eyes ached from lack of sleep. She had lain awake all night lamenting Claude's lack of interest.

"Thank you, Cinnamon." Claude eased off the wrapping paper and opened the box to look at the cufflinks she had picked out. "Oh, these are lovely. I can wear them when I'm called to the Bar." He gave her a quick kiss on the lips and reached into the inside pocket of his coat. "I got you something too." He handed over something that was clearly a book wrapped in brown paper. Disappointment rose in Felicity, but she smiled and took it from him. A book. Something you gave a friend. She unwrapped it and opened it to read the title *The Autobiography of Malcolm X*.

Hope rushed in. They had discussed Malcolm X on the day they met. That day must be special to Claude, too.

"It just came out," Claude said. "I got a copy too, so we can read it together." She turned it over in her hands. "Open it," he said. She opened the cover to read, *To Cinnamon, my love, that you may always remember the fighter that is within you.*

"Check the back cover," he said, grinning. She did, and found a silver chain taped there, with a heart-shaped pendant dangling from it. She had miscalculated. He must feel something for her after all.

She thought that absolutely nothing could dampen her mood, but when they arrived at Alison's place, things began to go downhill. The afternoon started well enough, with Alison greeting them warmly and seating them at the long table with glasses of champagne.

"So, Felicity," said Gerald. "Did Claude get you anything nice for Christmas?"

"He did," Felicity said proudly. "*The Autobiography of Malcolm X* and a necklace."

"Do you even read?" Marlene looked up from her plate, her eyes malevolent slits.

"Of course she does," said Claude. "We're going to read it together and then talk about it."

"Oh," said Marlene. "I didn't know you two did any talking." She and Alison snickered. Claude put his hand over Felicity's. Felicity took a big gulp of champagne.

The conversation around the table turned to hair. Alison announced that going natural had been a big challenge, but she was now loving the change.

"It's not too bad for me," Felicity said, eager to join the conversation. "I just put gel in and let it dry on its own. I've worn it curly before."

Marlene turned on her. "Oh, have you?" she said. Then she looked at Claude. "Claude, get your child out of my sight or I will not be responsible for what I do, so help me, God."

Claude stood. "Marlene," he said, "Felicity is my guest, and you will be civil." He turned to Alison. "Alison, Felicity and I will eat in the kitchen." He put a hand on Felicity's back and steered her to the door before picking up both of their plates.

"I'll join you, brother." Neville picked up his plate. "Can we smoke in there, Alison?"

Claude closed the door to the kitchen before addressing Felicity. "Sorry about that. Marlene and I were together before I met you. I think she's still upset about how it ended."

"You were together?" All the conversations Felicity had had with Claude and this had never come up. Felicity sensed that Marlene had feelings for Claude, but she could not have guessed that he had ever reciprocated.

Neville fumbled in his pocket for a joint. "Marlene and Claude were glued together just like you and Claude."

"Shut up," Claude said. "We never were, and you know it, Neville. Felicity, come here." She shook her head and stood where she was. Claude sank down into a chair as Neville lit the joint.

Claude sighed. "We met through the Association, just like you and me, and we were together about a year, but when my classes started again this autumn, I ended it, and she was really upset."

"Why didn't you tell me?"

Claude sighed again. "What's the point of dwelling on the past, Felicity? I ended it because we weren't compatible. You see how vicious her tongue is. She isn't sweet like you."

"I get mad too," Felicity said, the champagne rising to her head.

"Yes, but not like her." Claude implored, "Please, Cinnamon, come."

Felicity couldn't stand to be so far from his liquid brown eyes. She moved closer. "Eat some more," Claude said. "The food is delicious." When Felicity shook her head, he said, "All right. Enough." He put his plate down on the table and stood up, grasped her around the waist and pulled her back to sit on his lap. Felicity thrilled at the marvel of his closeness. Claude shoveled a heaping forkful of rice into his mouth, then prepared another one. "Open up," he said, nudging her lips with the fork. Felicity did, and he pushed the rice in.

Neville laughed. "She's like your baby," he said, blowing out a stream of smoke.

"She is my baby." Claude squeezed Felicity's shoulder. "Save some of that for us," he said, nodding towards the joint.

Alison came out of the dining room. "Everything all right in here?" she asked. "Anyone need anything?"

"Everything's fine," they chorused, and she withdrew.

Neville said, "What about what Felicity said? About her hair?"

"What about it?" Claude asked.

"Haven't you done any teaching?" Neville shook his head, put out the joint on the side of his plate, and took a bite of chicken. "Felicity, you know you have lighter skin than us?"

"She's not blind, Neville."

"There are lots of divisions amongst Black people," Neville said. "It started during slavery. The white men raped our woman and the people that resulted were treated better than the darker ones. Sometimes their fathers freed them. Or they got more prestigious jobs — they got to work in the domestic sphere while the darker ones did manual labour. So, some darker-skinned people resent lighter-skinned people like you."

"But why is that my fault?" Felicity said. A burst of laughter came from the dining room. "I'm not a slave. And I grew up in Canada. I was dark-skinned, compared to everyone else. I got picked on for being dark, not light." She looked at Claude for validation, but he frowned. And then she thought of Salvation Baptist. How when she got all the solos in the church choir, some of the other girls would whisper furiously to each other and Felicity would hear snatches ... *thinks she's cute ... Just because she has good hair*. Her church friend Abby holding her arm out alongside Felicity's and saying, *My mom says if I stay out of the sun, I might look closer to how you look*. Aunt Rose's mother telling Mom, *The way that one looks, you're going to have to lock her up*. And then the kids in Grenada. *Your father must be white because you're red. Red almost dead."* Laughing as she cried.

Neville said, "Don't you notice how all the men look at you, Felicity? No one except for Claude has looked at Marlene."

"What do you mean, all the men?" Felicity asked, swallowing the piece of curried goat Claude fed her.

"Look at how Gerald looks at you," Neville said. "Or Lester."

It had never occurred to Felicity before that darker women, women like Marlene, saw her the same way she saw blondes like Sheila. The thought of being preferred, of being someone's ideal, stopped her world for a moment.

Claude jumped in, "You have to learn to shake off your Western imperialist thinking, Felicity."

Neville said, "That's going to be hard, when you spend your time singing opera. What are you doing for our movement? For the revolution?"

Claude retreated. "That's not fair, Neville. She's going to sing for the hurricane relief concert."

Neville retorted, "You know that's not enough."

Felicity could think of nothing to say. Her eyes watered. Then Claude said, "Fuck, Neville, it's Christmas. We can worry about that another time. Gimme that." He reached for the joint, lit it, took a drag, and passed it to Felicity's waiting hand. He sighed. "I'm going to have to hide away for a few days after Christmas to study for that exam and write those essays."

"What essays?" Neville asked as he took the joint from Felicity.

"Remedies and jurisprudence."

"Did you do any research? We could meet up and compare what we have," said Neville.

The door opened again, and Alison said, "You want to come back in here now? We need Neville to explain something. How does Marx's theory of the lumpen interact with race? What do we do about all the lumpen when the revolution comes?"

Neville looked at Claude, and Claude said, "They are vulnerable to counter-revolutionary forces. So we educate them."

Neville strode towards the dining room, his hands and lips already moving in anticipation of the lecture he would deliver.

"I don't want to go back in there if Marlene's staying," Felicity said to Claude. It was a test of his loyalty.

"Anything you want, Cinnamon," Claude said, squeezing her fingers. "I can take you home now." Felicity thrilled to his touch. He had passed the test.

CHAPTER 18.

St. George's, Grenada, October 15, 1983

THE CAR CAME up the driveway too fast, squealing its brakes at the curb and throwing the painted gravel into the air behind it. Neville went to the window and said, "Shrimps." In a second, Claude was beside him.

"Felicity," he said. "Go upstairs. Quickly. Don't come down till we come and get you."

She understood now was not the time to ask questions, and she went. The first door she opened appeared to be Neville's bedroom. It had large sash windows that overlooked the driveway. The immense four-poster bed, hung with sheets of gauzy white fabric and a mosquito net, looked like one where a king would repose. The walls were cluttered with artwork, likely gifts Neville had received, much of it depicting Black people. There were portraits of Malcolm X and Martin Luther King as well as traditional West African paintings and scenes in jazz clubs. There was one of a mother and a little girl, and she waited to see if she felt a maternal pang, but as usual, the thought of her children was painless.

She stopped in front of a painting that appeared to depict a naked man and woman, both with immense Afros, in bed together, and she appreciated the contours of their bodies for a moment. Her full enjoyment of the scene was marred by the fact that the pictures had been hung haphazardly, so that they crowded each other and much of their individual impact was lost. The bed was unmade. A bra and panties Felicity assumed were Alison's lay on top of one of the pillows.

Felicity looked out of the window as the car door slammed and three men in suits with briefcases strode to the front door. She heard voices but couldn't make out what they were saying. She roamed the room, examining the paintings. Then she flopped down on the end of the bed. There was a pile of books on the nightstand. She recognized *The Autobiography of Malcolm X*. She still had the copy Claude had given her for their first Christmas together. The rest were a jumble of titles: *The Wealth of Nations, Das Kapital, Soul on Ice, Africa Must Unite*. Thick dust had settled on the covers.

While the living room where Felicity slept and spent most of the day overlooked the courtyard behind the house, Neville's bedroom had a view of the harbour, ringed with pink, orange, and yellow houses, sandwiched between the blue of sky and sea. The beauty of Grenada never failed to constrict Felicity's heart. She recalled Neville saying at dinner last night that the Americans had already invaded Grenada's waters, and she squinted, trying to see if their warships were indeed patrolling the coast. The only things reflected back to her were the white fringe of the waves and the clouds drifting above. She placed her head on the underwear-free pillow and gasped aloud at the feel of a soft, welcoming place to sleep after over a week on a hard, cramped couch. She pulled the covers over herself and drifted off.

Felicity awoke to the ecstasy of opening her eyes a crack to see Claude's face inches from hers.

"I can't wake her," said Neville's voice. "Could she be on something? There's nothing in here. She must have brought it with her."

"Take it easy," said Claude. "She sleeps that hard sometimes, if she's really tired. She used to do it after she sang."

Felicity opened her eyes wider. Claude's eyes were dark and solemn as he bent over her. He still smelled musky. A faint aroma of cocoa emanated from him. "She's awake," he said.

During her sleep, the T-shirt Felicity wore had ridden up to reveal the ampleness of her flank. She left it that way and stretched and yawned in a cat-like, sultry manner. "You can come downstairs now," said Claude, and the spell broke.

"What happened?" Felicity asked. "Who were those men?"

"Never you mind," said Neville.

"Neville, I'm in this as much as you are," Felicity said.

Neville looked over at Claude, who shrugged and spread his arms in a gesture absolving himself of responsibility.

"Fine," Neville said, "if you must know, those were negotiators, sent by Mark Henry."

"What did they want?"

"To discuss a power-sharing arrangement."

"And what did you tell them?" asked Felicity. She wasn't sure how she felt about the crisis ending. On one hand, she could return to her career and her social life, but on the other, she would lose contact with Claude. She had spent the past week refamiliarizing herself with the rhythms of his body, how his moods lodged in his eyes, his jaw, the movements of his hands. He demonstrated exasperation now as he stuck them into his towering hedge of hair.

"Neville's going to think about it," said Claude. "Certain concessions were requested and will be considered."

"And if he agrees, we're out of here?" Felicity asked.

"That's right," said Claude. The beseeching look he gave Neville was drenched with his concern for Pat.

"Mark Henry thinks we can fight the Americans. He says draft everyone, and if anyone complains, that's what jail is for," said Neville. "He says we're not following doctrine. But my government has slashed unemployment, reduced poverty, raised literacy, improved industry. Isn't that more important than some words in a book?"

Felicity looked at the dust-covered volumes beside the bed. "Yeah," she said, "like religion. It's better to just live your life than worry about what someone wrote thousands of years ago."

"Felicity, that's brilliant!" Neville said. "They do sound religious. They're fucking Bible-thumping zealots using politics as their new church."

Claude scowled at Felicity. "But remember what you're supposed to be doing, Neville. You're in favour of modernizing and opening up. We said we'd accept Henry on the condition that he agrees with us that we need to release all political prisoners. America will like that."

"When are they going to release theirs?" said Neville. "Who made them the world's policeman?"

"We can't do anything about that," Claude said. "Our message to America is live and let live."

Alison stepped into the room. "What are you all doing? The food's ready."

"What did you make?" asked Neville.

"There wasn't much today. They brought some flour and fish. I made hotcakes. There's fruit, and some pear from the garden." Felicity remembered that *pear* was what Grenadians called avocado.

Neville shook his head. "I'm all right."

"Neville, you have to eat!" Alison's voice fractured into a wail Felicity had never heard from her.

"I'm a dead man if I eat their food," said Neville. "I'm a dead man if I don't." Felicity looked at Neville again and saw how the whites of his eyes had yellowed, how the edges of his fingernails had frayed. How the parts of him that had chased women and danced until sunrise had been rubbed away.

Claude tried to get Neville's attention, shook his head at him, but Neville said, "They won't stop till I'm dead."

"Neville." Alison pressed her hand to her mouth and moved her head slowly back and forth.

"I have an idea," Claude said to Alison. He went over to her and put his arm around her shoulders. "Come," he said, and led her away.

Neville dropped onto the bed beside Felicity. "Do you remember London?" he asked her.

"Of course I do."

"I thought I was in some colonial hell at the time," Neville said, "but it turned out to be the best time of my life. Everything was possible. When we marched, it felt like there was only one way things could end, and it was with us on top. Do you remember that feeling?"

"Yes," said Felicity. She hadn't cared much about the politics. She had just wanted to be with Claude.

"And the anti-apartheid concerts," said Neville. "That's why I wanted to do this showcase, you know. To bring back that feeling."

"Me, too," said Felicity. Neville knew nothing of her memories. The best time of her life was private.

CHAPTER 19.

London, England, March 18, 1966

JACK DUG IN his backpack for a joint and passed it to Felicity, who lay beside him on his hostel bed. Her high school friend from Winnipeg was visiting her in London before beginning his travels across Europe.

"So did Brian ever stop writing to you?" he asked.

"Oh yeah, around Christmas," Felicity said.

"What was in his letters?"

Felicity shrugged. "Dunno. Never opened them."

"Ohhhh," Jack teased. "That's mean." He rolled closer to Felicity and nuzzled her cheek.

Felicity had turned this scenario over in her mind hundreds of times since she and Jack had made plans to meet. She had imagined succumbing more often than not, but now, she knew that she was going to refuse.

She gently pushed Jack away. "Jack, I can't anymore."

He sat up. "Sure, Fizzy, of course. Is it something I said?"

"No," Felicity said. "No." She burst out, "I'm in love!"

"Who is it, Fizzy?"

"His name's Claude," Felicity said. "He's from Grenada. We've been together for almost six months."

"Grenada," Jack said. "Like your mom."

"Yeah."

"She must be happy."

"She doesn't know." Felicity had given up on telling her. Every letter ended with an exhortation to focus on her studies and keep walking in the ways of the Lord. Felicity was so content with Claude, so grounded in bliss, that she couldn't risk letting anyone into their circle who might disrupt it.

"You never mentioned him in your letters."

"I guess not. I was just trying to figure things out."

"You're happy with him?"

"Very."

"Is he a good lover?"

Felicity paused for a moment. She told him the truth. "We still haven't."

"In six months? Is that what you want?"

"No!" Felicity elbowed him hard.

"Are you sure he likes women?"

"Positive! My best friend at the college is homosexual, and he's met Claude, and he says he's definitely not interested in men."

"Well, have you asked him if he wants to?"

Felicity looked at her hands. "Not outright."

"Come on, Fizzy, that isn't like you. Just ask him."

Felicity said, "I want it to be special, Jack. I'm scared."

"Wow." Jack exhaled a curl of smoke. "You really are in love, Fizzy."

THE NEXT DAY, Felicity zippered into a garment bag the gown Claude had gone with her to choose. When he said he liked purple because it was the colour for a queen, she had tried on a lilac satin number with flowers etched on the skirt in darker purple sequins. Claude had whistled when she modelled it for him. "I'm the luckiest man alive, darling," he said.

She was the last act of the hurricane relief concert. The hall was full, the audience restless after a long program. They were still whispering and chuckling as Will began to play the sparse accompaniment. Then she sang:

Tis the gift to be simple, tis the gift to be free
Tis the gift to come down where we ought to be,
And when we find ourselves in the place just right
It will be in the valley of love and delight.

The hall fell silent. Felicity could sense that she had the audience's full attention. "O luce" was next, and she sent it out to Claude, delight of her soul, her light and life. She wanted everyone in the audience to see how much she loved Claude. She wanted Claude to see it. She wanted him to know that she wanted his body to touch hers, enter hers, and she couldn't wait any longer. All this she poured out, and she was rewarded with a swell of applause. Then Neville came on stage, exhorting people to donate one more time for the rebuilding of the islands damaged by the storms, and volunteers passed baskets around.

Afterwards, at the reception, Felicity found Claude, who was with his usual group of friends. Alison said to Neville, "After Felicity sang, we took in over three times more than after anyone else performed."

"Still think I'm not doing enough for our people, Neville?" Felicity asked.

Neville gave her a rueful smile before returning to his argument with Clayton about whether an African country could be first to reach the moon if their resources hadn't been stolen.

Felicity wasn't in the mood to hear it. "I'm going to get a drink."

"I'll get it for you in a minute," Claude said, but Felicity turned and pushed her way through the crowds, past the tables of grapefruit hedgehogs bristling with toothpicks of cheese and pineapple cubes alongside Caribbean snacks such as patties and fish cakes. She almost collided with a white man in a suit and dark-rimmed spectacles.

"Ah, the star of the evening," he said, and clinked his glass to hers. "I didn't catch your name"

"Felicity Alexander."

"What a poetic name. I'm Lindsay Fletcher. Your performance was outstanding. Where else do you sing?"

"I'm a student. At the Guildhall."

He whistled. "Top-notch school. Who's your teacher?"

"Philip Cook. Do you like opera, Mr. Fletcher?"

"I love opera, Miss Alexander. I love the States, too. I sometimes do business there."

"I'm not from the States," Felicity said. "I'm from Canada."

"Oh." He blinked. "Would you perhaps like to have dinner some time?"

Felicity looked over her shoulder for Claude. "I have a boyfriend."

"Ah." Lindsay said. "Well, I won't keep you, but just in case, here's a card."

"Barrister in criminal defence," she read. "Dean, Fletcher and Simpson. Fletcher, that's you?"

"No, that's my father. I'm not a partner yet."

"Do you want to be?"

He laughed. "All in good time. Now, you'd better go and find your boyfriend. Give me a ring, if things change."

Felicity was so consumed by her feelings for Claude that she had forgotten she might be attractive to other men. That she could enjoy conversation with other men, who appreciated the same things she did. She tucked the card into her purse. Just in case.

Felicity found Jack, and introduced him to Will, and to Neville, Claude, Clayton, Lester, Gerald, and Alison. They talked and laughed together while eating copious amounts of rice and peas and curried chicken. They tramped in and out of the hall to smoke weed outside. Several people gushed to Felicity about her singing. When Jack said he had to get back to his hostel before the doors were locked, Felicity walked him out.

"I like him, Fizzy," said Jack. "And he definitely likes women, and he's nuts about you. Try him tonight. You sounded beautiful, you look beautiful, you have him in the palm of your hand."

When Felicity returned to the reception, Marlene was talking to Claude and Neville. She had her hand on Claude's arm. As Felicity got closer, she heard Marlene laughing, "Oh, that's what the petite bourgeoisie are for, darling, never mind about the means of production."

Felicity slid in beside Claude and he immediately lifted the arm Marlene was clutching and put it around Felicity. "My dear one," he said, bending his head low to nuzzle her cheek.

A steel grille fell over Marlene's face. She looked Felicity over, and said to Claude, "I see she's still wearing her hair according to the white man's standard."

"Nah," Claude said, "Felicity is her own woman. She does her own hair for her own reasons."

Marlene turned her back on both of them, and said to Neville, "Now, what about the patriarchy?"

"Ready to go?" Claude asked Felicity.

Neville said, "Taking her home, eh?" He gave his usual wink, and everyone but Marlene laughed.

They went down to Felicity's dressing room so that she could gather her belongings and change out of the gown. Claude said, "Hold on a minute," and pressed her up against the wall, where they began kissing and pawing at each other. They were so engrossed that they didn't notice the dressing room door bang open. Alison and Marlene stood there, holding garbage bags. "Oh!" said Alison. "Sorry, Claude, thought you were taking her home."

"We're leaving now," said Claude, scooping up Felicity's flowers and not seeming troubled in the least. Felicity wiped her lipstick off his chin as Marlene stared at them.

They crossed Trafalgar Square. Although it was dark, there were still a few tourists and pigeons wandering around. Claude led Felicity to Nelson's Column and sat down on the top step, patting the one below him. Felicity settled herself between his legs, shivering with the nearness of him.

"Are you cold, Cinnamon?" He took off his overcoat and wrapped her in it. Felicity breathed in his smell from the lapel and tilted her head back against his knees to look up at the stars, barely visible amid the city lights.

Claude said, "We're in the shadow of the South African embassy. That building is evil. I can't rest as long as our brothers and sisters struggle, Cinnamon. We must all use our skills and talents for the Revo. I was so happy to see what you did tonight. Bon jay, I must admit, we overlooked the effect of inspiring people to revolt through music." He squeezed her shoulder, and went on, "My father always said that no one is going to give you anything, son. Anything you want, you will have to fight for. And, Felicity, the fight is just beginning."

Felicity snuggled closer. After a moment, she heard a loud groan from Claude. Turning to look at him, she asked, "What's wrong?"

"Nothing." He grimaced as if gripped by a strong pain.

"Tell me."

The words rushed out. "I'm sorry. You might hate me, but I want you so much."

A waterfall crashed through Felicity. "Want me how?"

"Want all of you. Your body and my body. I'm sorry, I know I shouldn't —"

Now was her chance. Felicity laid her head in his lap. "I want that too."

"You do?" he asked. She twisted her neck back to look at his eyes, sparks in the dark. "I've longed to for so long. But I didn't think you would."

"Why not?" How could he have missed the signals of her desire?

Claude let out a gusting sigh. "When I was with Marlene, we didn't make love to each other for over a year and then one day, she was upset and crying because she felt like she was ugly and worthless because of her skin and hair. Her whole life she was taught that women like you are beautiful, and women like her are not. I'd never seen her cry the whole time we were together. So I suppose I was trying to show her she wasn't ugly, and it just happened. But after we, you know, she was crying even more, saying we shouldn't have done it, she wanted to wait till marriage. That's what nice girls do. Then she worried and worried that she might be pregnant. And then she started hounding me to get engaged so it wouldn't be as wrong, and I knew that wasn't what I wanted, so I had to end it. Sex ruined our relationship."

"It won't ruin ours." Felicity reached back to Claude's crotch and gave it a quick squeeze. She could feel how hard and swollen he was and thrilled to the realization that she was doing that to him.

"Oh Felicity, don't," Claude said. "It hurts so much."

"Well, let's go and get rid of that pain."

"Are you sure, Cinnamon? Once you cross that bridge, you can't cross back," Claude said, and Felicity realized he thought that she was still a virgin.

Felicity stood up, taking charge. "Where can we go? My landlady doesn't allow me to have men over."

"Nor does mine allow women to visit," Claude said. "But I don't care. I'll sneak you in."

As they began walking, Claude asked, "That Jack you introduced me to. Was he ever your boyfriend?"

"No," Felicity said. "Just a friend from school."

"Good," Claude said. "Bon jay, I don't like the idea of you and a white man together."

It wasn't a lie, Felicity told herself. It was just a small omission. "I don't like the idea of you and Marlene together," she said, and Claude laughed.

"What I felt for her is nothing compared to what I feel for you."

When they got to Claude's place, they took off their shoes and crept up the stairs. In the dark, they fell onto his bed and undressed each other. The sex itself was fast and unremarkable, born of urgency and need. "I'm sorry it was so quick," Claude said. "Was it awful for you? I'll be better next time."

"It was great," Felicity said. The moments he had been inside her had reduced her to water absorbing the full warmth of the sun. Claude's haste wasn't like Brian's ineffectual quick releases. It had had power and passion behind it, even as it was over too soon.

"Doesn't it hurt?" he asked, and she realized that she was supposed to have been a virgin.

"A bit," she lied. "I'll be all right."

"Poor Cinnamon," he said, reaching down and gently touching her between the legs. "Let me look at you." He switched on a lamp. "Bon jay, you are beautiful." He flattened his palm against her head. "I love your Kopf." He kissed her shoulder. "I love your Schultern." Wriggling downward, he said, "And your Knie. And your Zeh." He raised himself back to face her. "Augen. Ohren. Nase. Mund." Each word was pronounced perfectly, months after he had last spoken them. He covered her mouth with his and began kissing her again. When he came up for air, he whispered, "Next time, I want your hair to be curly."

INTERMEZZO
CHAPTER 20.

London, England, March 20, 1966

FELICITY'S BATHROOM AT Mrs. Dinnerstein's was even chillier than the rest of the house, with barely enough room to maneuver between the toilet, sink, and tub. To wash her hair, she had to plug the meter so that the water ran hot, which in actuality meant lukewarm, and then either sit in the tub and bend her head underneath the tap or stand over the sink and do the same. In preparation for this adventure, she had visited a beauty shop in Lewisham after class. Claude had recommended the salon, which was at such a distance from the Guildhall that it involved changes at two Tube stations. He had offered to go with her the next weekend, and she had agreed, but then invented a rehearsal and gone by herself as a surprise.

Faye's Place smelled of spices simmering in a pot, the sizzle of coconut oil evaporating through the teeth of a hot comb, and the sweet chemical mix of shampoo suds. Calypso music blared through a radio, just as it had done in Grenada when Felicity had visited eight years ago. Customers sat in leather chairs with their heads streaked white with lye or bristling with rollers and topped with hooded dryers. Mannequin busts topped with wigs lined every wall except for one, which held shelves of endless rows of bottles and pots. Felicity stood in front of them, trying to decide what to buy.

"Hello, love," said a stylist to Felicity. She was dressed stylishly in a patterned mini, her own hair straight and shiny. "Do you need a relaxer?"

"No," Felicity said. "I just need to buy some hair pomade."

"Oh," the stylist said. "You're one of those girls who does her own hair at home? No wonder your edges are so frizzy. Pretty hair like yours, I could nice that up for you quick-quick. Come in once a week and I'll have you sorted."

"I don't want to wear it straight anymore," Felicity said.

The stylist stepped back and sucked her teeth. "You're one of those Americans, talking about Black is beautiful, then. Easy for you to say."

Felicity remembered Marlene's outburst at Christmas, but this time, she would not be cowed. "I can go somewhere else and buy what I need," she told the stylist.

The stylist pointed. "Get that one and that one," she said. "Put the lotion on when the hair is wet and comb it through good-good. Twist up the curls around your fingers, understand? Then use the gel to harden them, and when it's almost dry, use this pomade for shine."

"Thanks," said Felicity.

"Oh, and get this." The stylist lifted a wide-toothed comb. "Never use a brush." Having lost the opportunity to regularly straighten Felicity's hair, she pressed merchandise on her instead. As Felicity waited at the register for the stylist to ring up her purchases, the woman said, "When you get tired of it, come back here, you hear?"

Felicity would find another salon next time. She chose the sink and stuck her head into the flow from the tap. Tepid water ran through the strands of her hair, changing their shape into bends and squiggles. She coated them with the products, shaped them into ringlets, and waited hours for them to dry while she studied her scores. When she eventually looked in the mirror, her curls were back, vibrant and full, but more sculpted than they had been the last time she wore them out. She shook her head from side to side and watched them bounce up and then settle back down. She had forgotten how in its natural state, the twists and turns of her hair brought out its multiple shades, reddish brown with gold and tawny streaks catching the light. It was a miracle, this hair. It could do anything. It claimed space for itself; it announced itself. And it was hers.

CHAPTER 21.

London, England, August 20, 1966

IT RARELY GREW hot in London, but when it did, the air was almost as heavy and sticky as Felicity remembered it being in Grenada, though when she said this to Claude, he laughed and said, "Grenada is much more humid than this, Cinnamon. The sea is all around."

They sat down on a bench in Trafalgar Square, and Claude reached in his satchel to produce a thermos of lemonade and ice and two Cornish pasties, which the pigeons eyed. "Mandela said 'I am prepared to die,' but we must be prepared to fight. He says he is left no other choice, but what about those of us who have a choice?"

Felicity said, "That should be in the speech."

"What speech?"

"The one for the anti-apartheid march. You should do the speech, not Neville."

Claude shook his head. "Neville always does the speeches, Cinnamon. He's the face of the protests. I'll write that line in there for him."

"But why can't you deliver it?"

"That's not how we do it," Claude said. "Why, are you wishing you could be with the leader, Felicity?" He said it with a smile, but she sensed the seriousness behind the question.

"I am with the leader." She put her hand on his knee and pressed her body against his. "I'd follow you anywhere."

"Bon jay, you are beautiful," Claude said. "How'd I get so lucky?"

Felicity said, "I wish we didn't have to wait till it got dark to sneak into your house. To be together." Claude swallowed his mouthful, and she said, "When you find me a place closer to the college, it will be easier." Claude had explained that the best way to find suitable housing, better even than renting from Jewish people, was to send a white friend to answer the ad and sign the lease with your name on it. Claude had a law school classmate currently looking for new digs for Felicity.

"I was going to surprise you later," Claude said, "but now is as good a time as any." He fumbled in his satchel and brought out a rose, crushed from its confinement. Tied to its stem was a plain gold ring. He handed it to Felicity. "My love," he said, "you can say no of course, but Bill found something incredible. An entire house! It's in Shepherd's Bush, so it's farther than you wanted, but that's where many of our people are settling. Where our work is. And it's big enough that we can live there together. You and me." He paused. "If you want to, that is." When she didn't respond, he said, "I'm sorry, Felicity. I only asked because it's so hard living so far apart. And I want to be with you all the time."

Felicity watched a toddler running around the fountain, kicking at the sparkling jets, giggles bubbling up like the water. She could not remember ever being that happy as a child. But she felt that way now, with joy welling up from her hips along her spine to her sternum. Her cheeks ached from smiling. "Of course I want to," she said. "I want to be with you all the time, too." She looked down at the ring attached to the rose. "Is this —?"

"It's not a real wedding ring. Not yet," said Claude. "I can't afford to marry you properly right now. This is to make you look respectable."

Respectable. His choice of word conjured Felicity's mother, brought her into the square with them. Her mother would be horrified if she knew what Felicity had just agreed to do. In her mother's eyes, she was now a loose woman, no better than a whore. Even Aunt Rose would be disappointed. Making the decision to live with Claude would cut the last string connecting Felicity to her home.

"My mother —" she began.

"She doesn't need to know," Claude said. "I'm not telling my parents." He pulled her to him, and she pressed her face into his chest. "It will be our secret, until we're ready. Until we have our careers." Felicity listened to his heartbeat thud through his cotton shirt and inhaled his scent. Musk, salt, and a hint of marijuana.

LATER THAT AFTERNOON, Claude accompanied Felicity to the small auditorium where she was auditioning to sing Vivaldi's "Gloria" with orchestra. She wished she had been able to shower and change. Her underwear was soaked through with sweat and need from being close to Claude in the heat all day. At least she had had the foresight to pull her hair into a bun, at Philip's suggestion. "As lively as your hair is," he said, "for an audition, you really should —" and Felicity had agreed. Despite these efforts, curly tendrils had escaped from the sides and were plastered to her flushed face. She did her best to clean up in the ladies' room, but she complained to Claude, "I look wilted. Messy."

"You look gorgeous," he said, and bent to kiss her.

"Miss Alexander?" A grey-bearded man stood frowning in front of them.

Felicity pulled herself away from Claude, feeling her face warm even further. "Yes, sir," she said.

"You're late."

Felicity looked at her watch. "It's five after six!" she said. Her audition was at six fifteen.

"I like people to be at least fifteen minutes early for an audition," said the man. "Surely Philip Cook told you that."

Philip hadn't given Felicity a specific time, but she did know it was important to be early for auditions. She had spent longer in the ladies' room than planned, trying to freshen up. She shouldn't have spent the day with Claude. She should have stayed home and prepared.

"We'll be with you soon," the man said. He turned and strode down the hallway. Felicity felt her confidence fading.

"It's okay, sweetheart," Claude said. "Don't worry." He put his arm around her and squeezed her shoulders. "You practiced. You're ready."

They waited several more minutes. "Are you nervous?" Claude asked.

Felicity leaned against him, fiddling with the buttons on his shirt. "No," she said. "I just want to get in there and sing."

At that moment, someone came walking down the hall towards them, high heels clicking against the parquet. Felicity started towards the person, and then stopped. It was Margot Laird, looking unbothered by the heat in a gauzy beige dress, her hair shellacked into place, her makeup fresh. She stopped and smiled at Felicity before continuing on her way. Felicity's hopes sank further. She had no hope of succeeding if Margot was also in the running. Claude squeezed her hand and held it until, ten minutes after the audition was supposed to start, a younger man, blond and blue-eyed and reminding Felicity vaguely of Brian, burst out of the doors behind her.

"Felicity Alexander?" he asked, his tie askew, glasses slipping.

She dropped Claude's hand. "Yes, sir."

"Come this way." He almost ran down the hall and Felicity in her high heels struggled to keep up. She looked over her shoulder at Claude. He raised his thumbs and smiled.

The blond man pushed his way through swinging doors into a room with a black and white tiled floor. The bearded man sat at a table and a third man at an upright piano.

"Well, come on, then," said the blond man. "Have you prepared 'Domine Deus'?"

Of course she had. Felicity swallowed a rush of irritation and smiled. "Yes, sir."

"Well, then, let's start."

Felicity willed him away as she centred herself. She breathed deeply, down in her pelvis, allowing air to fill the places where Claude touched her. She let the breath fill her whole body slowly, gently, like smoke. Then she began to sing "Domine Deus, Rex coelestis, Deus pater omnipotens." *Lord God, heavenly King, God the Father Almighty*. An entity for whom Felicity had no use, but her task over the next few minutes was to sing as if she believed in the majesty and power of God with all her being. As if she were her mother. Felicity had dismissed her mother's words and advice as being irrelevant to her life, but now they flooded back to her. She had always seen her mother's faith as a hammer with which to beat her preferred moral choices into others. The purity of this melody was crafted from that same faith.

When she finished, the blond man smiled at her, but the smile seemed forced. No one had introduced themselves, she realized. "Well!" he said. "I wondered why Philip sent you, but —" He stroked his chin. "What's your dress size?" he asked, and then, before Felicity answered, he addressed the bearded man. "I want to go and look at some options with her. We'll be back in a jiffy." He walked out of the room, beckoning Felicity to follow.

Felicity felt her insides yawning, opening into a warning. But she wanted this opportunity, and that meant that she had to follow the man. He took her into a rehearsal room with a piano and a metal rack from which hung several dresses. "You'll need to wear something black," he said.

"I have a black dress," Felicity said. She had worn it for her Winnipeg recital, which now seemed too distant to properly recall.

"But we'd like you to match the alto soloist," he said. He flipped through the rack. "Hmmm," he said. "Turn around for a second. Let's see what size you are."

Felicity turned, knowing what would happen. His fingers brushed across her buttocks and down one thigh. She stood for a moment as if she were on the auction block, ready to endure the poking and squeezing. But then she remembered Claude. And she remembered her mother, too. A white man had taken what Felicity's mother did not want to give. She walked to the door.

The man reached out and grabbed her elbow. "Don't you want the job?" he asked.

She shook her head. *No, not this much.*

He said, "You know, I could easily have refused to hear you."

She grabbed the door, twisted the knob, and ran down the hall, searching for the place where she had left Claude. The man didn't follow, and after doubling back, she saw Claude waiting by the doors.

"How did it go, Cinnamon?" he asked. "Not good?" He slung an arm around her shoulders as he turned her around, took her through the swinging doors into the evening air.

Felicity couldn't speak. There was a rock in her throat that would shatter if she did.

"Come on, my darling, talk to me," said Claude. She shivered and tried to pull away. Then he said, "Surely you didn't sing that badly." She shook her head. "Then what...?" he paused. "They weren't nice to you? Were they ..." Claude stopped walking and spun her around so he could see her face. "That's it, isn't it?" he said. "They said something. They —"

"Touched." Claude pulled the word from her, all his love and concern and focus pooling into his miraculous eyes trained upon hers.

"What?" Bystanders turned to stare. "He touched you?"

She nodded, almost blinded by the orange light of the setting sun.

"I'll kill him." Claude began heading towards the auditorium, but Felicity grabbed his arm, shaking her head and feeling it flop like a demented rag doll. "How dare he!"

Felicity didn't want Claude avenging her. She wanted nothing more to do with that room or those men. Perhaps, later, she would tell Philip about it over a cup of tea in his studio, but now, she just wanted to cry herself to sleep.

"Cinnamon." Claude stopped walking and wrapped his arms around her. "All right. I won't go in there. It's all right, my love. Let me show you our house instead."

The neon glare of the lights on the Tube hurt Felicity's eyes, her head, her tongue. She was struggling not to cry, not under the gaze of the sweaty, irritated passengers. Their compartment was crowded. She and Claude were quick to stand and offer their seats to elderly people. Felicity knew Claude was also remembering the day when no one had given her a seat when she was unwell, and she knew that as Black passengers, they would be criticized with lifted eyebrows, frowns, and bodies shuffling away if they remained sitting a moment longer than anyone else. Felicity's clammy palms clung to the metal pole as the train bumped over the tracks and Claude stood behind her, one arm clamped around her waist.

She barely noticed as Claude led her off the train at the Shepherd's Bush station, down a street, up an alley, past gardens and shops. He fumbled for the keys. Then he ushered her through the door of a small two-storey house. He walked her from room to room, pointing out the embossed wallpaper, the carved banisters, the bathroom with the frosted window. "What do you think, should this be our bedroom?" He pointed. Felicity began to cry.

"Oh, Cinnamon," Claude said. "You shouldn't have to put up with those kinds of things." He put his arms around her again, but Felicity's legs were tired. She slid down to the carpet in the empty room. Amid the promise of days to come and the ruin of the day just spent, she abandoned herself to her tears. Claude lay next to her, folded his body around hers, rocked with her against his chest.

When Felicity's tears slowed, Claude handed her his handkerchief. She dabbed her cheeks and blew her nose, staining the white cloth with her lipstick and powder. "How many of these have I wrecked?" she asked.

"I keep one specially for you," Claude said, stroking the hair that had escaped from her bun. "My father taught me that. Always have one handkerchief for her, and one for yourself." He ran a finger along Felicity's cheek. Sparks exploded in her stomach. "Better?" She nodded. "Forget about that bastard," Claude said. "You're already the best singer in London."

Felicity gave a waterlogged laugh. "Not even close." She looked up at the ceiling. There were fine cracks in the plaster. "But eventually, I want to be. I want to sing in the best houses in London, New York, Milan, everywhere."

"You will," said Claude. "You're going to be one of the greatest singers in the world, Cinnamon. And I'll be there cheering you on."

"What are you talking about?" said Felicity. "You'll be the famous revolutionary, leading a march somewhere." She hooked one of her legs over his. "I'll find you after the opera and show you how much I missed you. Like this." She pressed her lips against his, knowing he would taste the salt there. She ground her hips into his, feeling him groan, feeling him stir, feeling herself open. Letting the anger, the helplessness, the sadness dissolve before the wonder of being with Claude in their own home.

"To the Revo," Claude said, and Felicity rubbed her fist against his.

"To the Revo."

CHAPTER 22.

St. George's, Grenada, October 16, 1983

NEVILLE AND HIS associates — *the cast of characters*, as Felicity thought of them — began the day clustered around the radio awaiting the next illicit broadcast. It began with the news that Grenada's neighbours had reached out, offering to negotiate with Mark Henry, but he had refused.

"Of course he did," Claude said. "Miserable son of a bitch."

"Why is he so angry?" Felicity asked from the couch, where a blanket was still twisted around her legs from her efforts to get comfortable throughout the night. She was light-headed and disoriented.

"None of your business," said Lee.

It was Pat who explained. "The Revo is tired," she said. "You wouldn't think it takes so much work to run a place this small, but it's never-ending. The people put so much trust in the Revo. But they want everything, and they want it now. Their roads fixed, their roofs fixed. Not enough of we to do it all."

"It's not unreasonable to want their roofs fixed," Felicity said. Her thoughts went back to her arrival on the island over a week ago. She had flown with her mother and daughters from Winnipeg to Toronto, Toronto to Barbados, Barbados to Grenada. For most of the time, Felicity studied her music. "O luce" was Claude's aria, and she had been sure she was going to perform it at the showcase. But strapped into her airline seat, her folder lit by the thin yellow beam of the overhead bulb, she recalled that she had sung it for their parting, and that feeling of immense grief had imbued the way she interpreted it ever since. Did she want to bring that melancholy to their reunion? She had flipped through her music, wishing Adele was not beside her watching everything she did, conscious of Mara and her mother across the aisle.

Nobody spoke much through the long flight into the night with the dark ocean stretching out beneath them. Mara worked her Rubik's cube, the colours flashing in her hands and the squares clicking a quiet rhythm as she turned it over and over in her palms. Adele huddled against the window cradling her Walkman and reading the liner notes from her Michael Jackson and Lionel Richie cassettes as intently as if she had never seen them before. They ordered a taxi at the airport and, as it sped down the almost deserted highway, Felicity pointed to the large billboards lit from above with hanging lanterns. They held posters proclaiming slogans such as "Black is Beautiful," "Education is the future for the Black race," "Cooperative socialism for all," "March forward together."

Felicity looked up at these illustrations of Claude's dream and felt a need to share it with the girls. She pointed their attention to the billboards. "The only things up there used to be ads for foreign products," she said, "but Neville Carpenter's government banned roadside advertising and changed the billboards to positive sayings to inspire people." Mom sucked her teeth in disgust. Felicity said, louder, "The Revolutionary Government is fixing things. Building new schools and houses, making sure people have enough."

"That's right," said the taxi driver. "March forward together."

"To the Revo," said Felicity. Mom gave her teeth a longer, harder suck.

The taxi creaked up the hill and disgorged them and their luggage in front of Aunt Beulah's. Even in the darkness, Felicity could not miss that the house was lopsided. Long cracks ran down its walls, and clumps of leaves poked through them. A jagged hole was visible in the roof, also filled with foliage, and tangles of overgrown bush erupted from the paving stones in the yard.

"I thought you said Neville Carpenter's government was fixing homes," said Adele.

"It looks like shit," Felicity said. "Aunt Beulah let it run to shit." The next thought was even more bleak. *And the Revolutionary Socialist Government is letting it stay shit.*

"Language, Felicity," said Mom, but with no real bite. She pushed open the rotting gate and they proceeded to the side door. Felicity noticed the girls exchanging dismayed glances.

Aunt Beulah appeared, wearing a loose cotton caftan-type garment and a headscarf knotted around her head.

"So you back," she grunted.

"Hello, Beulah," said Mom.

"You sleep upstairs and don't make no marse, you hear me?" She turned and walked away, leaving the four of them to somehow push and pull the suitcases up the ladder into the tiny room, where two mattresses awaited them on the floor.

"We'll go to a hotel," Felicity said, once they were in the room. "Tomorrow. We'll go after my first rehearsal."

She hadn't had the chance to move her family to a hotel, because she had gone looking for Claude. She should have gotten her mother and daughters registered in rooms with phones, helpful staff, and the means to evacuate. Perhaps they would be safely back in Winnipeg, watching events on television. She could have been there with them. But now her mother and daughters were high above the capital, trapped by a curfew and relatives who resented their presence, and Felicity was down here, surrounded by soldiers.

"We're going to fix everything," Claude said. "We just need time."

Felicity didn't say that they didn't have time. Time had been seized by Mark Henry. He controlled it now.

"Shhh," said Neville.

"... contacts abroad are saying that Percy Tibbs is preparing for a return to the island," said the announcer.

The room filled with jeers and shouts.

"He wouldn't dare!" said Neville. "He ran like a scared little mouse to America. Let him stay there."

Claude said, "We should have put him in jail, under heavy manners."

Felicity remembered the moustached face of the man who had led the workers' strike, and a decade later, his callous smirk.

"Percy Tibbs let us down," she said. No one replied. They were consumed with thoughts of the return of their enemy.

CHAPTER 23.

London, England, February 9, 1967

PROFESSOR FINLEY DREW yet another chord progression on the chalkboard. Felicity struggled to keep up, her manuscript paper already rubbed grey with repeated erasing.

"And what is this chord?" Professor Finley asked. Scanning the room, he called out, "Miss Alexander?"

Felicity jerked forward. She had been doodling in the corner of her page. "Um ... the dominant?" she guessed.

"We just left the dominant. Do try to keep up. Anyone else?" Sarah Stilwell raised her hand. "Miss Stilwell?"

"First inversion of the subdominant."

"Very good," said Professor Finley. "I'm glad someone is paying attention. Miss Alexander, a lovely voice does you no good if it comes from an empty head."

Sarah snickered loudly. Felicity slumped in her seat. This class didn't matter; she would be going home to Claude afterwards.

As soon as her key turned in the door of their house, he ran to meet her. "Guess what, Cinnamon?" he said. "Tibbs is here."

"You mean Percy Tibbs? From Grenada? The chief minister?"

"The Devil himself," said Claude. "He's in London. Judging the Miss World pageant. Miss Grenada is in the running, and there are already National Front out there protesting because they say Tibbs is marking up all the Black girls above the white girls." He smiled. "If true, that's the first good thing Tibbs has done in years.

And a whole pile of feminists are there too, protesting the whole idea of beauty pageants. Bon jay, it's the place to be tonight! I've already written Neville's speech. I worked on it while I was waiting in magistrate's court. But we have to hurry, Cinnamon. And," he said, "wear comfortable shoes. We could be walking for a while." Coming from a voice lesson, she had worn heels at the last march she had been to, one against nuclear disarmament, and by the end, she was hobbling in pain. Claude had sat on a park bench holding her feet in his lap, massaging them for an hour before she could walk well enough to get home and soak them in the bathtub.

The pageant was at the Royal Albert Hall, where Felicity had heard a number of recitals with Will. They exited at the High St. Kensington station, and as they got closer to the hall, Felicity heard chanting. Security guards hauled women one by one out of the building. They clutched tattered bags of flour and several of them were coated in it. "They must have been flinging that around inside," said Claude. "I wonder why?"

One section of the pavement was occupied by the black-clad National Front, waving signs reading "DEFEND WHITE BEAUTY" and "SEND THE BLACKS BACK" and "BRITAIN FOR THE BRITISH." A smaller group of Black faces stood opposite, yelling "Go away, Nazi scum," and "We belong here too."

"There's Neville," said Claude, pulling Felicity along with him. Neville was with Alison, Marlene, Clayton, Gerald, and a few others from the West Indian Students Association.

"Brother!" Neville's face was glowing with uncontained joy. "They've just crowned her! Miss Grenada is Miss World! Just think, little Patricia Jack, the most beautiful woman in the world."

Claude squeezed Felicity's hand. "Not the most beautiful. I've got that one right here." Felicity pressed closer to him.

"Yes, yes," Neville said. "We all know how in love you are. But remember Patricia? When she was at St. Anne's, and never let anyone feel her up at the Emporium? Bon jay, look at her now."

A door opened near them and security came out, sweeping the crowd back. Two more security guards escorted a woman towards a limousine. Flashbulbs began popping from the cluster of reporters who had also gathered in the area. The woman was wearing a crown and she was brown; the colour of maple syrup, a warm, treacly shade. Her hair hung past her shoulders, beneath the crown, curving in deep glossy waves. Her face wore an expression of terror. Felicity looked at Claude and saw, with a pang, that he was watching the woman too.

Marlene patted her short kinks. "Her hair isn't natural," she said in a smug tone. "Probably a wig."

Though Felicity's skin was still lighter than hers, Patricia Jack was not as dark as Marlene or Alison or most of the other West Indian women present. Her coronation was supposed to be an elevation of the beauty of Black women, but Felicity understood that it still left many Black women out.

Marlene seemed to read Felicity's mind as she stared at Claude. "It's always the fair-skinned ones, isn't it?" she said. "But no one is protesting that. How can you, when you've fallen for it yourself?"

Resentment replaced understanding. "Maybe he just doesn't want to be with a miserable bitch," Felicity said.

Marlene threw her head back and gave a hard laugh, like the crack of a whip. "That's always what they say, isn't it? Us darkies are the bitches, the leftovers no one wants. You think you're so much better, don't you? You just wait, he'll get tired of you too. He isn't going to want to babysit you forever because you don't know the simplest things about your own history. And he's right, these white people still think you're a nigger, just like me. See that sign, 'NIGGERS OUT'? That's for you too."

Felicity jerked backwards at the force of her vitriol. It was as if Marlene had vomited a year and a half of resentment down the front of Felicity's coat. After the incident at Felicity's first Christmas dinner in London, Felicity had given Marlene as wide a berth as she could and Marlene, in return, had ignored her. It seemed that the hostilities had faded to a mutual dislike. But all this time, Marlene had been honing her hatred, clasping it close to her, polishing and refining it like a diamond.

Claude put his arm around Felicity. "Marlene," he said, "that's uncalled for." The chants of the crowd had swelled and he had to shout over them. "I've told you before —"

The shouts of the crowd swelled. Neville ran back and forth, testing the barricades for signs of weakness. He ran up to Claude. "They're coming!" Neville shouted.

Claude turned from Marlene and pointed. "His car will have to pass there."

Neville said, "We'll block it from passing. Then he'll have to speak to us!"

Neville distributed signs. "TIBBS CALL AN ELECTION." "TYRANT TIBBS STEP DOWN." "FREE GRENADA." It was drizzling and cold. Claude kept Felicity nestled against him, his body heat radiating through the damp, as they drifted away from the rest of the group. She was still stunned by Marlene's outburst, but she knew it was not the time to complain to Claude. Something bigger was happening. The crowd began to grow restless, chanting and singing. Alison and Marlene approached Claude. Marlene stood silent behind Alison, looking away from Claude and Felicity. "Claude," Alison said, "Neville wants you to come and stand with him, so you can help lead the march."

"We're all right here," Claude said. "We can see everything." He squeezed Felicity closer to him and she took heart that he was keeping her away from Marlene. That he still chose her.

Then someone shouted, "They're coming! The cars!" People spilled into the road, shouting and waving their signs. The first car stopped, unable to back up because many other cars stretched behind it.

Neville ran along the row, searching for the car with Tibbs in it, shouting when he found it. Lifting the megaphone, he began the speech Claude had written. "Percy Tibbs, we the people of Grenada, exiled by your actions, demand that you bring democracy to our country. We demand fair elections. We demand that you return property stolen from the people of Grenada." Felicity roared her agreement — not too loudly, as she didn't want to ruin her voice for her coaching appointment the next day — and raised her sign, caught up in the exhilaration of the moment. She had just stopped an official government motorcade. She was standing up against injustice. For all the moments when she had said nothing in the face of unfair treatment — Brian's parents, people shouting at her on the street, men thinking they had the right to touch her — now she was fighting back. It was the Red Sky Revolution, but instead of watching it from afar, she was challenging its very architect.

Claude pulled Felicity with him as he elbowed his way through the crowd to stand beside Neville. The window to the back seat of the limousine slid down just as police arrived on horseback. One of them held a megaphone and directed, "Leave this area immediately!"

Neville shouted Claude's words, "You have betrayed our trust. You have turned your back on the workers who brought you to power."

A face looked out through the window of the car. A dark face, very dark, with a trimmed mustache and big eyes. A handsome face, Felicity thought, not the grotesque visage of a monster she had envisioned. "Well, well, well," said Percy Tibbs. "Young Neville Carpenter, is it? Family from St. Andrew's. And Claude Buckingham. Son of Albert Buckingham. A man of many business interests, if I am correct. You should stick to protesting apartheid." His gaze landed upon Felicity. "I don't know this half-caste," he said, "but I see you have excellent taste, Mr. Buckingham. A pity she doesn't hold your attention as much as she should." He smiled at Felicity. "I assure you my dear, I would have far more interesting ways to spend an evening with you." Felicity laughed to herself that he had not connected her to the dark-skinned Alexander family from Vincennes.

Percy Tibbs scanned the rest of the group. "Marlene Francis and Alison Greaves. Forever unlucky in love, aren't you? My people have been watching you all. No Grenadian studies abroad that Uncle Percy doesn't know about them. Let me tell you, I appreciate the ebony sisters amongst us even if the rest of our men do not. Charles Davies. From a fishing family. What do you think they will catch in the future?" Percy Tibbs licked his lips. "I shall be sure to say hello to the folks back home. You don't even have to ask."

The window whirred back up. "Call an election!" shrieked the crowd. Fists hammered against the window.

"Disperse at once!" bellowed a voice through the police megaphone. In the next moment, a blast of water, colder and stronger than the drizzle of rain, swept into the crowd. Felicity was knocked sideways, her hand wrenched from Claude's. The crowd screamed and scattered as the water cannon continued to gush. Felicity was sure she heard the high laugh of Percy Tibbs as his limousine rolled past.

"Claude!" she shouted, getting to her feet. Water poured from her shoulders and her hair. She slipped in a puddle as she tried to stand. She broke her fall by grabbing a fence post. "Claude!" The police herded the protestors into a corner. She craned her neck, trying to see if Claude was among them.

"Move along, miss." A police officer on a horse blocked Felicity's way back to the area where most of the protestors were. She needed to find Claude. But at the insistence of the police officer, she retreated a block before sinking down onto the curb. She was soaked, and so cold her teeth were chattering. Her hair clung to her scalp and cheeks in dripping worms. She realized that she had no money, no house keys. She hadn't brought her purse, knowing it was better to be as unencumbered as possible at a protest. Claude had her things in his pockets. Neville had laughed at Claude the first time Claude dug in his pocket for change and emerged with a tampon and eyebrow pencil in his fist, but Claude just replaced the items and said, "Nothing I won't do for her, Neville."

What could he do for her now, cold and wet on a curb with no way home? And even in the lowest heels she had, her feet ached. She hugged her knees to her chest, shuddering, attempting to keep the tears and panic at bay, trying to think of a solution. She sat for half an hour, trying to gather the courage to go back and demand that the police help her. Or to knock on someone's door and request assistance.

"Felicity, oh my God." She looked up to see Claude running up to her, followed by Neville, Alison, and Marlene. "Oh, Cinnamon." He sank down beside her and pulled her close, cradling her body to his. His wet shirt stuck to her face. She could feel his heart thudding. "I was worried sick." She felt the tension release as Claude smoothed her wet hair from her face.

"How touching," snickered Neville. Marlene muttered something to Alison.

"We need to get the women home," Claude said to Neville, over Felicity's head. "We don't want anyone catching a cold. Let's get a taxi."

Seeing their wet clothes, the driver didn't want to let them in, but when he realized what the fare would be to four separate residences, he grunted his assent. Claude helped Felicity in and draped his damp coat over her shoulders. She buried her face in his chest as the taxi began to move. Neville said, "After we drop them off, we should get down to Heathrow and see if we can find Tibbs there."

Claude said, "Neville, we have to be careful. He knows who we are. He threatened our families. He's been watching us."

"Nah," Neville said, "that's just talk."

"Neville," said Claude. "You know it isn't just talk. He has his Nutmeg Squad all over the island, hunting people. He locks them up in Richmond Hill prison."

Felicity heard Neville blow his cheeks out in frustration. "You're letting him win."

"Neville." Claude's voice was plaintive, stripped of its usual warmth. "He threatened my father. His businesses. He could ruin us. Or what if he ..." His voice trailed off in a squeak, and Felicity recognized the precursor to tears. She felt for Claude's hand and held it. Stroked calm into it. Burrowed closer to him, she registered the panicked clanging of his heart. It began to slow as she traced circles into his palm.

"Fine," Neville said. "We'll wait."

"Just until we're strong enough," said Claude.

CHAPTER 24.

London, England, April 8, 1968

IF YOU ARE *fatally shot the night before you lead your people in a great triumphal march for freedom*, wondered Felicity, *what does it feel like? As you watch your own blood seeping, pump by excruciating pump, do you try in vain to squeeze your arteries shut against the tide? Or is it your breath you try to control, each drop of oxygen granting you another few seconds of life, but costing you agony as your tattered lungs heave against the weight of the air pressing down on them? In that moment, do you wish yourself back to a time when you could have chosen another life, an ordinary one, a quieter one? Was there ever such a time, or were you always marked, both for greatness and for suffering?*

Felicity carried the last pile of files into the back room of the law office where Claude waited with a box. "This is everything from this week, Claude," she said.

Claude clapped his hands. "Good. Good."

"Three more housing complaints."

"And a criminal case. Black boy caught shoplifting with two white friends who never got charged."

The building, an abandoned grocer in Shepherd's Bush, had slowly taken shape to become the Black London Legal Help Society. Neville and Claude had drawn on their vast network to receive help with painting, sanding, knocking down walls, and installing lights. There was no lack of need, and no client was turned away if they could not pay. Whenever Felicity was not in class or a rehearsal, she was at the office performing secretarial and receptionist duties.

Claude described the cases without his usual enthusiasm. He had hummed at a lower frequency since Friday, when their alarm clock had trilled them awake. Claude turned on the radio and Felicity headed to the bathroom, stumbling as she walked. She had been to Cambridge on the train the day before to rehearse Beethoven's Ninth with her Counterpoint professor, Dr. Wells, who was the guest conductor. They had had a few pints together afterward, and Felicity's head felt heavy and her tongue dry.

Felicity was supposed to receive her diploma next month, but her marks in Counterpoint were atrocious and had placed her graduation in jeopardy. Her mother had booked a ticket to come to London for the occasion, and Felicity had toyed with the idea of introducing her to Claude. Failing Counterpoint would ruin everything, but Dr. Wells had given her to understand that he could see to it that she didn't fail. She sat on the edge of the claw-footed bathtub, looking away from the rust spots inside it, and weighed the decision. Mechanical, meaningless sex in exchange for a passing mark, versus an ugly, baying secret lying between herself and Claude.

She went back to the bedroom to find Claude pacing the room, hands on his head, a wild look on his face she hadn't seen before. For a moment, she thought he had read her thoughts, but then he whirled and said, "Cinnamon, oh my God, come here," and opened his arms to her. She walked into them, and he said, "Dr. King's dead!"

At his words, the stars came tumbling out of the sky all at once to fall in a smouldering heap at her feet. Claude's voice seemed to come from afar. "Shot in Memphis. Oh my God."

Felicity pulled away to look up at him. "I can't believe it."

"This is what they do to us, Felicity. Any Black man who speaks up and tries to make a difference gets killed." He put his arms around her again. "Someday, that might happen to me."

Claude organized signs and supplies for the next protest at South Africa House. He had thrown himself into the preparation with grim determination. "We're protesting them killing King as well as apartheid."

Felicity's singing at the protests had led to several newspapers dubbing her the "Nightingale of Trafalgar Square." One day before Movement class when the instructor was late, Sarah Stilwell said, "So Felicity, you're singing at anti-apartheid protests now?" Without waiting for a response, she went on, "My uncle lives in South Africa. He says most of the natives like apartheid, apart from the silly ones going abroad and protesting."

Felicity said, "Pearls of wisdom coming from the chorus?" She was rewarded with a small swell of laughter, as Sarah in four years had not landed even a small role in any of the operas.

On the train, Felicity snuggled close to Claude, but he was far away, on the hotel balcony in Memphis, imagining Dr. King shot and silenced. As they walked across Trafalgar Square, she saw Neville and Gerald standing by the fountain with handfuls of handcuffs and chains cascading through their fingers in a metallic parody of the jetting waters. Claude's face broke into a broad smile for the first time since hearing the news of the assassination. "Bon jay, Neville, you got them," he said.

"Are you in, Felicity?" asked Gerald.

"In for what?"

Gerald looked at Claude. "You didn't tell her?"

Claude shook his head slightly, a secret warning. But Marlene, standing nearby, said, "Felicity wouldn't want to mess up her hair. Even she can't flirt her way out of getting arrested."

"Arrested?" Felicity word casually, but the word struck her like a slap. How could Claude have shut her out of his plans?

Claude said, "We're going to chain ourselves to the embassy gates, and we're not leaving voluntarily."

Felicity gasped. "But you could be there a long time! Won't it get cold?" An even more dreadful thought seized her. "What if you have to go to the bathroom?"

Marlene looked contemptuously at Felicity. "Soft," she said.

A tornado of anger rose inside Felicity, sweeping her up in its funnel. She thought of grabbing a chain and being the first one to attach herself to the gates, but then she remembered her audition on Tuesday for the junior company at the Royal Opera House. Philip had told her several times that it was an opportunity that could launch her career.

Claude began helping Neville to untangle the chains and distribute the ominous, clanking lengths. Felicity watched the group head to the embassy gates, as if through a misty window, wrapping the links around their wrists and the iron bars. "Felicity, can you lock us in?" Claude tossed her a big ring of keys.

Figures came rushing out of the building, and Neville said, "Quick, Felicity!" Her mouth dry and her fingers damp, Felicity scrabbled at the hard, cold metal. Each pair of handcuffs clicked like a punctuation point as the wind picked up, tossing a pile of their flyers into the air and launching them across the square. "Put the keys in your bag," Neville said.

A minute later, the running figures arrived panting at the other side of the gate. "What's going on here?" demanded a burly blond man with a South African accent.

"Let my people go, you pig!" responded Neville, as the others chanted and rattled their chains against the gate. The man took out a radio and began speaking urgently into it.

"Free Mandela!" shouted Claude, and everyone took up the chant. "Free Mandela! Free Mandela!"

The security guards shook the embassy gates, but they were barricaded on the other side by the weight of the bodies chained to them. Claude motioned with his head for Felicity to come closer, and he begged, "Felicity, do it. Join us. Put on chains to shake off our chains."

"I can't, Claude," she said. "My audition."

A hood fell across Claude's eyes. "Is your audition more important than protesting the degradation of your people?" A shining path stretched between him and Felicity, transporting them both back two and a half years to that moment when Claude had chosen to leap into the blazing fire of her desire for him. But the give-and-take between them was no longer enough.

She said, "I do care about it, Claude, but this is my career. What you're asking isn't fair."

"Dr. King gave his life, and you can't give up one audition?"

"This is my life!" she retorted. She knew as soon as the words flew out of her mouth that they would fall on harsh shores. She watched him turn his head away.

A police siren wailed ever closer, and then police officers swarmed the square. One of the officers shouted into a megaphone as he ran, "Attention! You are trespassing on embassy property. Remove yourselves at once!"

Neville, affixed to the gate, with his arms stretched out like Jesus on the cross, shouted, "Free Mandela! Boycott the South African regime!" His companions shouted and rattled their chains. "We are in chains because they are in chains!"

Two police officers produced bolt cutters. "You are trespassing! Remove yourselves or you will be arrested!"

Felicity saw the light in Claude's eyes. He wanted to be arrested. He saw glory awaiting him through those prison bars. If the police had any sense, they would ignore the protestors, leave them there until it got dark and at some point, bodily needs and lack of attention would force them to unchain themselves. But in this theatre, this dance, roles must be played and lines spoken.

The police began to cut through the chains, removing handcuffs only to replace them with new ones. As Claude was grabbed, his arms bent behind his back for the ritualistic march to the police vans, Felicity ran behind him, but he wouldn't look at her. Marlene, stumbling along beside him, wore a grin befitting someone who had just won a trophy. The protestors were loaded into the vans as Neville shouted at everyone to remain silent. The vans pulled away. Felicity was alone. She gathered all the belongings the group had left behind and put them in the cardboard box that had held the flyers. Loose flyers skidded across the concrete and the pigeons pecked at them as they blew up against the fountain. She stepped around the links of chain strewn beside the gate and watched a lone plastic bag attempt, and fail, and try again to rise with the wind.

She lugged the cardboard box home on the Underground, put her key in the lock, and trudged up the stairs alone. She took out the folder with her audition arias for Tuesday and tried to read through them, but she couldn't focus. She got up and paced back and forth for a while before an idea occurred to her. She ran to her purse and dug through the detritus — old concert programs, lipstick stubs, loose pennies, mints encrusted with lint — until she found the business card she was looking for, its edges grey and blunted. The card she had taken, never thinking this would be the reason she would use it.

He answered on the third ring. "Lindsay Fletcher."

"Mr. Fletcher!" Felicity said. "I didn't really think you'd be there on a Sunday!"

"Then why did you phone?" he asked. "And to whom am I speaking?"

"Felicity Alexander. I met you at a hurricane relief concert a couple of years ago." It was ridiculous. He wouldn't remember her.

"Ah, yes," he said. "The Canadian opera singer. To what do I owe the pleasure?"

Felicity stumbled through the events of the afternoon, coaxed along by Lindsay. Once the time and place of arrest, Claude's full name and date of birth had been provided, Lindsay said, "Leave it with me. I'll find the magistrate on duty and discuss release."

"Can I pay you next Monday? I'm singing in Cambridge on the weekend. They'll probably give me a cheque then," Felicity said.

"Pay me? You don't have to pay me, Miss Alexander. You're doing me a favour."

"How?"

Lindsay gave a short, high laugh. "You're handing me a client arrested for civil disobedience. Conscientious objectors. The attention my firm will gain from this is worth more than anything you could afford. No offence meant." His voice grew serious. "But tell me, what are you performing in Cambridge? How is the singing going?"

Felicity would have spoken to Lindsay much longer, just to keep the silence in the house at bay, but he had to go to the police station to free Claude. Talking on the phone had lessened the burning in Felicity's chest. She rarely made social phone calls as they were outside her budget, but this was an emergency, so she dialled the operator and asked for Will.

"Felicity, how's practicing?" Will's phone was on the table by his piano, and she heard him playing chords with his left hand. He didn't express any surprise at her call.

"Will. Claude got arrested."

"Arrested? What the hell for?"

"Protesting, at the South African Embassy."

An arpeggio pinged down the line. "You weren't there, were you?"

"Yes, but I —"

"Felicity, you have an audition on Tuesday. The most important one of your career. Whatever stupidity your boyfriend's got himself into is for him to sort out himself. You know what Beethoven said? 'Sacrifice all the trivialities of social life to your art.' The great man never lied." One finger picked out the opening motif of Beethoven's Fifth in a mocking da-da-da-dum.

There would be no help forthcoming here. "All right, thank you, Will." She put down the receiver. All her friends were Claude's friends, and they had all been arrested with him. She had acquaintances at the Guildhall, but no one she was close to besides Will. Aunt Rose, Josiah, and Jack were too far away to be any help, and she had never been able to confide in her mother. She had sacrificed her social life to her relationship with Claude.

CHAPTER 25.

London, England, April 9, 1968

IN THE MORNING, Claude had still not returned. Felicity dressed and went to class, an aching band of weariness tight around her forehead. Between classes, the students relaxed in the lounge over cups of tea. Waiting for the kettle to boil, Sarah Stilwell, a large diamond adorning her left hand, inquired, "So who's auditioning for the Royal Opera House tomorrow?" Several hands went up. "What are you all singing?" Sarah asked. "This is what I have." She rattled off the names of several arias and others followed suit.

"Felicity, aren't you auditioning too? You haven't said what you're doing," said Sarah.

"I have a headache," Felicity said.

"Do you need an aspirin?" asked Elsie, a contralto from Dublin.

Felicity didn't want to feel better, so she lied and said, "I took one, thanks."

"So? What are you singing?" asked Sarah, undaunted.

Felicity couldn't remember why she had thought that this audition was so important. "'Chacun le sait.' 'O luce di quest'anima.' 'Mein Herr Marquis.' 'Laurie's Song.' 'Casta Diva.'"

Sarah asked, "What's 'Laurie's Song'? And you're really doing 'Casta Diva'?"

"'Laurie's Song' is from an American opera called *The Tender Land*," Felicity said, as she had explained dozens of times.

"American?" Sarah said. "I don't think they're going to like American. Americans don't know anything about opera."

Felicity rubbed her forehead as Sarah went on, "And isn't 'Casta Diva' a little advanced for college?"

Elsie said, "Sarah, she studies with Philip Cook. I'm sure he knows what he's doing."

Sarah retorted, "He can't know as much as you think if he gave her 'Casta Diva.' That's one of the most glorious, beautiful arias there is."

Felicity roused herself to say, "He calls it a stretch aria."

"A what?"

"An aria that's a bit of a stretch, that shows where you might be headed vocally in a few years, that they can ask for if they want to hear it, if they're curious."

Sarah said, "It's one of the most divine arias ever written! It's not for a student."

Franz cut in, "I would like to hear Felicity sing it." Of Felicity, he asked, "Shall I get your tea?" Besides the scene work they did for the operas, Felicity had never talked much to Franz. Will, now in receipt of his diploma and back at the college as an apprentice pianist working on the operas, still spoke longingly of Franz, but years of the same had turned his words to white noise.

Franz brought the tea to Felicity and said, "I hope your headache goes away soon." Felicity was almost relishing the miserable feeling. Maybe Claude would be there to tuck her into bed and rub her temples when she got home, all forgiven. She traipsed after the others to class, which might as well have been in Russian for all she made of it.

After class, Franz approached her again. "I'd like to hear 'Casta Diva' now," he said. "If your headache isn't too bad."

"It's a bit better," Felicity fibbed. As upset as she was, she felt a stirring desire to sing. "It might not be so good without piano, though. We should find Will. Maybe he can —"

"I can play," Franz said. "Not very well, but it will give me a sense of how you sing the piece. I just love that aria. I think it would be gorgeous in your voice. A true dramatic coloratura soprano is so rare."

Felicity trailed after Franz to the practice rooms. She picked her favourite, the one on the end of the row with a window that looked out onto a large oak tree. Franz seated himself at the piano and flexed his fingers, then played a few chords. "May I have the music?" he said, his manner suddenly formal. Felicity walked over to the piano and placed her folder there. Franz began to play, without the ease and buoyancy of Will, but more or less the correct notes in the approximate tempo.

Her entrance was approaching, and she summoned her breath, gathered it into a ball right in the middle of her, and began to sing:

Casta diva, che inargenti
Queste sacre antiche pianche
A noi volgi il bel sembiante
Senza nubi e senza vel ...

She was an ancient priestess, singing to the moon: *Pure goddess, who silvers these ancient plains, you turn your beautiful face to us, without cloud or veil.*

Any sighting of the moon was hours away. The skies were their London daytime grey. But Felicity had a vision of the bright beams piercing dark skies to illuminate feeble desires, weakness of the flesh, deeply held dreams, love, and artifice. As she sang, tears gathered in the corners of her eyes at the simplistic beauty of the melody in its silvery wash of sound. Sarah was right; she was not equal to singing something this beautiful. The tears came faster. She had said to Philip once, "Sometimes I get choked up when I'm singing and it's really hard to get through the piece."

He nodded. "Very common in temperamental people like yourself. It's a gift. The trick is, if you feel like crying, just cry. Be vulnerable before your audience. Tears don't hinder your voice. Trying to hold them in does."

Felicity took his advice and let the tears slide out as she sang. Halfway through the aria, she became aware that Franz had stopped thumping his way through the accompaniment. She turned to face him.

"My playing does you no justice," he said. "I see what Philip meant. You will grow into this aria and it will be just right for you someday. You have such a gorgeous sense of line. You —" He cleared his throat, noticing the tears. "Felicity, why are you crying?" he said. She dropped her face into her hands. "Your head is still hurting," he stated. She nodded. He came out from behind the piano and put his arms around her. She at first resisted burying her face in his shoulder, but the closeness of another person, any person, was too much to bear without responding.

"I know something that can help a headache," Franz said. Felicity knew what he had in mind. If only it could help a heartache. She allowed him to lead her into a corner of the room, watched as he opened his pants, and let him to flip her skirt up and pull her panties and nylons down. He wormed his fingers into the warm moistness of her. Felicity bit her lip as she groaned, despite a shadow in the back of her mind that was telling her to push Franz away and run home to Claude. She willed the shadow to leave and nudged her body closer to Franz.

"I've been watching you for a while," Franz whispered in her ear. "You're so beautiful and your voice is so lovely."

She could still tell him. She could still invoke Claude's name, a spell that would repel Franz, would stop this before any harm was done. But the words formed bubbles that fizzed and popped in her head as he began kissing her, his mouth covering hers roughly and sloppily. Felicity felt a flash of anger that this was happening, but whether she was angrier at Franz, Claude, or herself, she didn't know. Franz entered her and she jerked fiercely in rhythm with him. "Oh my God," Franz gasped. His breaths caught at the edge of hers, tearing in an uneven line. Felicity cried out as the circle surrounding them drew her closer to him, a circle within a circle binding them. At the moment of their release, she could see into his soul, past the glass pane of manners and pleasantries that normally separated them, right through to the dark place within him. As she shuddered, the door to the practice room banged open.

"I thought that was you, Felicity." Franz flopped panting against the wall. Felicity turned in a daze to see Will standing in the doorway, his face creased in upon itself. He turned and left the room.

"Will!" Yanking her undergarments back up, she rushed out of the room. "Will, wait!"

Will held up a hand. "Don't," he said.

"Will, please, let me explain!" Doors flew open along the hall and students poked their heads out of the practice rooms, watching the unfolding drama.

"Dear me," Will said. "Are we going to have a scene?" He turned to face Felicity. "Don't bother," he said. "La commedia è finite." Felicity knew what those words meant. It was Italian, not Latin. The last words of the opera *I Pagliacci. The comedy is over.* Her friendship with Will was over. The purity of her relationship with Claude, maybe even the entire relationship, was over. But Franz was right. Her headache was better. She decided to go and see if Dr. Wells was in his office. Having transgressed already, she had nothing to lose, and she might as well pass Counterpoint. Music was all she was going to have left in this new world she had entered, the one where love was no longer enough.

WHEN FELICITY GOT home, sore in body and mind from her encounter with Dr. Wells, she found Claude in the living room reading *Why We Can't Wait,* one of Dr. King's books that they had read together. He closed the book, unsmiling. "Felicity, you look exhausted. Did you sleep last night?"

She raised one shoulder and he went on, "A lawyer found us, I don't know how, and we got bail this morning. We kept the office closed and I slept all day. Have you eaten?"

"I'm not hungry."

"You have to eat. I'll run down and get some takeaway. Fish and chips or Chinese? Or go round the corner for curry?"

"Fish and chips," said Felicity. Sending Claude out would give her a chance to wash away the smell of recent sex. When he returned, he put the newspaper package on the table and brought plates and cutlery from the kitchen. "Claude, tell me what you're thinking," Felicity begged, but he motioned to her to sit. She tried to force a few chips down her throat as Claude attacked a big piece of cod.

After he finished, he said, "All right. I've been thinking of this for a while, but everything that just happened sped it up for me. It's time for me to go back to Grenada and start preparing for the Revo. Neville thinks so too."

"Of course he does," Felicity said. The introduction to "Casta Diva" began playing in her head, not flowing the way Will played it, but choppy and heavy under Franz's fingers.

Claude leaned across the table, the fire in his expression once again stoked as it had been when he was shackled to the Embassy gate. "Brother King died for what he believed in. I got arrested for what I believe in, but I'm not doing it where it matters most. There are lots of people who can stand outside South Africa House, but little Grenada has been forgotten. Bon jay, our people are suffering. My father says it's getting worse with Tibbs. He's killing anyone who opposes him. Neville has a plan to help Grenada, and he needs me. He has another friend, Mark Henry — I know him too, but he's more Neville's friend — and he's been studying in the United States, getting a PhD in Economics, which we can really use. He's almost finished, and he's planning to go back to Grenada. So is Neville. That leaves me."

"So Neville comes first." The notes were louder, more insistent, drowning out Claude's words. She shook her head, feeling the ache return, blinked as Claude's face wavered before her eyes.

Claude pounded the table, and the knives and forks jumped.

"Grenada comes first." If an orchestra were playing "Casta Diva," a flute would enter now. But instead of a patina of sweetness, the notes spiking through Felicity's ears were fractured. Claude's words spun after them, dropping into the great pool of darkness in her chest. Her fingers twitched in time with the phantom pianist. Sound squeaked out of her mouth, as plaintive as the notes of the flute.

"But what about us, Claude? I can't move to Grenada."

"No, you can't," Claude agreed. "You don't belong there. You belong in a big city like London, where you can become a famous prima donna, just like you're meant to be."

Felicity hugged herself. "So then —" Her head ached. Her chest ached. Her ears ached. The moon was inside her, stretching, burning.

Claude said, "Truly, Felicity, I have adored my time with you. I love you dearly. But maybe this was something for us both to learn from before we fulfil our true destinies. I'm going to be part of the Revo that brings to power the greatest leader Grenada will ever have, and you're going to be one of the best singers in the world."

Felicity lowered her head to the table. A rush of fatigue battered her. "Tell me something. Is Marlene going back to Grenada too?"

"She wants to."

Something had to break. Felicity didn't want it to be her. She seized her plate from the table and flung it to the floor. As it shattered, Claude shouted, "Felicity!" She threw herself after it and landed shivering in a heap on the ground, moaning as a dark curtain trembled across her gaze. Her heart began pounding in her chest, too quickly for her breathing to catch up. She thrashed around, a fish out of water, certain that the world was ending.

"Felicity," Claude said more quietly. He dropped to his belly and wriggled over to her, then put an arm around her waist. "My love. Cinnamon. It's all right. It's all right."

Gasping for air, she lifted her head and turned towards him. Claude said, "You're in the way of everything I've ever hoped for." He rubbed slow circles on her back. "I'm not saying I'm leaving

London right away. I was just trying to prepare you for the future. We've got some momentum at South Africa House and with the tourist season coming, we need to keep that up. I am going to go to Grenada, but not yet." As his words soaked in, Felicity's breathing slowed and she felt her trembling ease. "I'm not leaving yet, my love, I'm with you a while longer," he repeated. "Come on. You have an audition tomorrow. I'll run you a nice hot bath and then you need to go to bed."

"I'm sorry, Claude." Felicity couldn't say why, but she could at least speak the words.

He wrapped his arms about her. "It's all right," he said, and she felt her blood squelch within her, thick with the knowledge that he would not forgive so quickly if he knew why she was really apologizing.

CHAPTER 26.

St. George's, Grenada, October 17, 1983

THE SOLDIERS BROUGHT a sack of flour, one of pigeon peas, and a basket of shrimp on ice to the back door. They picked a few handfuls of greens from the Government House garden. Alison said she would stew the peas and shrimp and make dumplings, and Felicity made another effort to recapture the brief moment of connection the two women had shared while cooking.

"Can I help?" she asked from the kitchen doorway.

"Devein the shrimp," said Alison, not looking at her.

"What do you mean?" Felicity asked.

Alison sucked her teeth, drawing out the sound into a dragging squeak. "Your mother never taught you that?"

"She tried," said Felicity.

"Well, you should have listened. You're useless, eh? Probably don't know how to shell peas either."

Felicity said, "I can wash and chop those." She pointed to the greens.

"So could a baby," said Alison, but she pushed a knife over to Felicity.

"Did I do something wrong?" Felicity asked.

"You're still here, aren't you?" Alison banged a large pot onto the counter. "One more mouth to feed. One more person getting in the way."

"Is that what Neville said?" If he had, it would have come from Claude.

"Of course he didn't. Neville wouldn't. He has more to think about than you." Alison used a smaller knife to slit the shrimp shells one by one. Click, click, click. They fell effortlessly to the cutting board.

Felicity looked down at the blade she was holding. For a moment, she fantasized about using it to cut Alison's throat. Or her own. She didn't know whose blood she would rather see dripping onto the tiled floor.

Alison said, "Neville loves shrimp."

"He probably loves anything you make," Felicity said, shameless in her pandering.

"He has to eat." Alison's voice was laden with worry that hung like a rotting fruit.

Felicity said, "Feed him in bed."

"What do you mean?" Alison's voice turned as sharp as the knife point.

"I mean, when you're in bed, distract him with your body, and then slip food into his mouth. Shrimp, a piece of fruit, a chunk of bread. Just slide it right in there. Or put it on your body. You're the plate. If he wants to play, he has to eat first."

The knife fell from Alison's hand and clanged into the sink. "You're serious, aren't you?"

"Why wouldn't I be?"

"You think I would do something so sluttish?" Alison asked. "Would you?"

"I have," Felicity said. "Just don't use chocolate sauce or syrup. It's so sticky and it's hard to get it off after."

Alison stared for a minute, and then she laughed. "Is that what living in the western world does to people?"

Felicity said, "You think it's western to like sex? I bet they liked it a lot more in Africa before white people got there with all their missionaries and rules. I know for a fact Neville likes sex."

"You know for a fact?" The smile disappeared from Alison's face.

"Oh, no, no, I never," Felicity said. "I can just tell."

"Hmph." Alison rummaged in the cupboard for nutmeg, mace, and allspice and slapped the jars down onto the stovetop. "You really think it will work?" she asked.

AFTER DINNER, OF which Neville did not swallow a mouthful, Alison hustled him up the stairs as soon as the dishes were done. Felicity lay on the couch scratching her mosquito bites, redder and bigger than anyone else's in the house. Unlike her, they were used to these insects. The faint sound of laughter rolled through the ceiling. Felicity hoped that Neville was eating.

"Lydia," Elrick called from outside, and she sat up and went to the window. The young soldier held up a bottle of rum. Felicity craved the warmth and comfort contained in the amber liquid. She reached for the bottle and tipped it upward.

"How's it going with Brother Buck?" he asked.

Felicity took another gulp of rum. "It isn't," she said. "And you can't tell anyone I told you about that." She should have known better than to discuss her matters of the heart with a child.

"Of course I won't," he said. "They go shoot me if they see me talk to anyone in the house." He pointed to the bottle, and she passed it back.

An arc of light swept across the room and the distant sound of wheels on gravel reached Felicity.

"Shrimps!" said Elrick. He ran across the courtyard seconds before a Jeep rolled up to the house and three bearded men jumped out, holding rifles. The soldiers formed a silent row, their own weapons raised. "We only want talk them," said one of the new arrivals in heavy-accented English. *Cubans,* Felicity thought.

The standoff lasted only a minute or two before the Commander shouted, "Stand down!" The row of soldiers parted and they stepped back. The Cubans marched to the porch and rang the doorbell.

Felicity heard footsteps moving down the stairs and knew they were Claude's. She could picture how he would lope from step to step, easily skipping one each time. Voices filled the hall, indistinct to Felicity. They grew closer. Someone rattled the doorknob. She heard Claude's voice, speaking Spanish. More footsteps on the stairs, and then the group moved into the kitchen.

Felicity tiptoed to the living room door and opened it a crack. The kitchen door was open. Claude spoke in Spanish, listened, and then translated what he heard back to English.

"The American medical students," Claude relayed. "They are a liability. The Americans will use them as an excuse to invade."

Neville said, "They've been looking for excuses for years."

There was a flurry of Spanish words, and then Neville said, "It's not so easy to get rid of the medical students. They bring in money."

More Spanish. Claude translated, "You are in the Americans' pockets. You let them own you. You betrayed our revolutionary values. You should have got what you needed from us. Now they can invade and say they are protecting their citizens."

Neville said, "Our Revo is pragmatic. We do business with anyone because we're trying to get money to help our people."

Felicity's head nodded vigorously as Claude delivered a Spanish sentence. Then he said, "We don't want Cuba or America telling us what to do." A response came that ended with the word, *amigos*.

Claude translated the response as, "You are too small a country to decide on your own what you will do. It's a big world out there. Be careful, my friends."

CHAPTER 27.

London, England, October 13, 1968

FELICITY SLUMPED IN her chair. Like everything else in the rehearsal room assigned to the junior company at the Royal Opera House, it was grey. Grey carpets, grey walls, and no windows. The light was grey. She tried to focus on the director, Sir Thomas Maxwell. He had just informed the members of the company that they were to prepare an opera for presentation to school groups, and they could choose the piece they wanted to do, subject to his approval, as long as it was in English. The ideas flowed through the room.

Felicity waited for last before suggesting, "*The Tender Land*? Aaron Copeland?"

Erin Kelly, a bombastic tenor from Dublin, made a face. "No American opera, thank you."

Felicity persisted. "It has lots of good roles for everyone," she said.

Sir Thomas peered at Felicity and said, "That's an intriguing suggestion. I know the show well. Miss Humphries would make a lovely Laurie."

Felicity gulped as Diana Humphries preened. "I'd love to sing Laurie," Felicity ventured. "I've worked on the part."

"No, no, no," Sir Thomas said. "Look at how busty you are. And your complexion! Laurie is a fresh-faced farm girl. She's not dusky."

The vocal coach, who found infinite reasons to put his hand on Felicity's bust and her backside during private sessions, interjected,

"Miss Alexander did sing 'Laurie's Song' in her audition for us, and as I recall, it was a big reason for her acceptance."

"Hmmm," Sir Thomas said. "I would have thought her voice insufficiently lyric for it. Miss Humphries, on the other hand, would make a splendid Laurie. Well, we'll continue this discussion later, shall we? I believe you are all sitting in on the *Butterfly* rehearsal this afternoon?"

The thought of Felicity's beloved role going to Diana Humphries, a pert, condescending blonde from Australia, legs constantly on display beneath an endless parade of miniskirts, who reminded Felicity of Sarah Stilwell, only with a better voice, made her blood thrum dangerously in her veins. She would go for a walk over the lunch hour and hope that the fresh air would calm her. As she reached the front door, a man strode through it and held it open for her. She looked up to thank him and realized she knew him. It was Lindsay Fletcher, the lawyer who had secured Claude's bail.

"Miss Alexander?" he said.

"What are you doing here?" she asked.

"I've been asked to join the board of directors and I'm here to pick up my board manual. They also suggested I stay for the rehearsal this afternoon."

"Oh," she said, ready to move past him, but he said, "I had forgotten that Claude mentioned you work here now. I'm just going to lunch, if you'd care to join me?"

"Sure," said Felicity. She could use a distraction.

Outside, on the street, Lindsay asked, "Do you like blues music, Felicity?"

Felicity said, "My Aunt Rose does. I learned to like it from her."

Lindsay said, "There's a lovely blues café at the next corner, Blue Waters. They have a guest singer from America there today."

When they were seated, Lindsay said, "Something tells me things aren't going so well for you today. Same here. I lost in court this morning." He exhaled loudly.

Felicity said, "Don't tell me that. That's not going to help Claude."

Lindsay laughed. "Even the best lawyers lose sometimes. But Claude will be all right. So, what's bothering you?"

Felicity explained the *Tender Land* situation to Lindsay, interrupted only by the waitress taking their order. He listened with his hands clasped under his chin. Then he said, "That's always been the good thing about opera. It doesn't discriminate. Size, age, skin colour, none of that matters as much as the quality of a singer's voice. It will be unfortunate if Sir Thomas doesn't respect that."

A thought burst upon Felicity. "Well, maybe I can make it matter, but to my advantage. There aren't many Black opera singers out there. I've never met another one or worked with one. Sir Thomas made it into a liability that I am one. What if I make it into an asset?" Another idea sparked in her brain. "Bring the blues to opera?"

The singer arrived and seated herself on a stool with a guitar. She was a deep shade of brown with her hair cropped very close to her head like Marlene's, and she wore a long black cotton skirt that draped over the bottom of the stool. She had a compelling presence before she opened her mouth. Her voice billowed towards Felicity like a morning mist. It opened up chambers of her heart that she hadn't known existed, revealing a wound in the shape of every indignity, every slur, every rejection she had ever felt. Felicity was still earning the right to sing opera, to belong in the places where it was sung. But the blues were her inheritance; they required only years of suffering.

FELICITY AND LINDSAY returned to the Royal Opera House and sat in the balcony, away from the other junior company members who were seated on the main level. This was the cast members' first rehearsal in the theatre, and from time to time, they were stopped by Sir Thomas to make minor corrections.

When they reached *Butterfly*'s big aria, "Un bel di, vedremo," no one dared interrupt the great Kristine Roeder as she performed her signature piece. At fifty-one, Kristine was at the peak of her powers, both beloved and feared by conductors, whom she had been known to reduce to shivering wrecks with one raised eyebrow if she disliked their tempi. In the darkness, Felicity drank in the aria's sense of longing for someone who would never come back. She wished Claude would return — the old Claude, the one who looked at her with eyes that saw no world without her. Tears threatened, but she sucked them in.

Lindsay took her hand in his, and she squeezed it back. After a moment, he put an arm around her, and she leaned against him. She couldn't say how it happened, but her lips and his met, and the rain of notes melded with the pull of his kiss. She was tempted to fall into the void, but knowledge knocked at her brain. If she did this, if she allowed herself to spiral into the hurt of letting another person in, it could destroy the little that was left of her and Claude. As "Un bel di" ended, she wrenched herself away from Lindsay and left the theatre. Lindsay followed her into the hallway.

"Claude," was all Felicity could say.

Lindsay put his head in his hands. "You're quite right," he said, "Claude is a client. This is inexcusable of me. I'm sorry."

"Please don't tell him!"

"I don't think that will be necessary," Lindsay said. "I think we were both reduced to temporary insanity and have now thought better of it." He pushed his hands into his pockets. His nonchalance steadied Felicity. He said, "Shall we go back and watch the rest? Such a shame to miss it."

THAT EVENING, FELICITY told Claude what Sir Thomas had said about her being too dusky to play Laurie. Claude slammed his hand, still holding a joint, onto the table. "What the hell?" he said. "The old bastard really said that? How dare he?"

"I'm going to get the last laugh," she said. "I'll get the role. I'm not sure how yet, but I will."

"We should protest that place where you work," said Claude. "That opera house." Felicity marvelled that even now, one of the world's greatest artistic centres was to him only "that place where you work."

"Protest? You mean signs and megaphones?"

"The lot," said Claude, grinning. "I'll get Neville in on it."

"No, Claude! You can't!"

"Why not? They're being prejudiced, and everyone should know it."

"I'm going to get them to change their minds, Claude."

"A protest can do that faster."

"Claude, please don't."

Claude stood up. "I'm tired of you telling me what I can and can't do, Felicity!" His voice thundered into the room, a lion calling across the veldt. "Are you letting me in or shutting me out?" They had of course bickered and argued through the years together, and Claude had raised his voice before, but never like this. Never as if he wanted to eviscerate her with the blast of his words.

Claude blinked and rubbed his eyes. "Sorry, I'm tired," he said. "It was a long day. I should go to bed. I have to meet my lawyer early tomorrow."

"Your lawyer is on the board of the Royal Opera House now," said Felicity. "I saw him there today. I bet he'll tell you not to protest there. Ask him."

"Felicity, I'm going to bed. We'll discuss this later." As he left the room, Felicity picked up the remnants of the joint and lit it. There was a time when Claude would never dream of going to bed without her. She had given up a chance of intimacy with Lindsay for this empty room and the continual unsatisfied ache within.

SIR THOMAS CHOSE *The Tender Land* for the junior company show, and he held auditions for the roles. When it was Felicity's turn, she set about the task of drawing Sir Thomas in with "Laurie's Song," her old friend. She could not sing the words with the bitterness she now felt. She had to capture that teenage sense of optimism and invincibility as surely as if she had bottled it back then, if only that were possible.

When she had finished, Sir Thomas took his glasses off and busied himself cleaning them. Felicity peered at him. Had she made the great man cry?

He cleared his throat. "This aria suits you like a glove," he said. "There are some Negroid qualities to it. The wistfulness. The simplicity." He sighed. "Dvorak was right. You cannot have American music without Negroes. And you do sing so beautifully." Felicity held her breath. "I still don't think Laurie is so dusky," he said. "But there is no question that you should sing the role, my dear. We'll see if wigs and makeup can help." He turned to Lorenzo, one of the assistant directors. "Do you think you could look into that?"

Felicity wanted to tell him that the score did not state Laurie's race. That Felicity could sing Laurie looking just the way she looked, and make the audience believe she was the character. That music was for everyone, that it transcended colour. She could give him a speech worthy of Neville. But if she spoke, her emotions would get the better of her. She would yell, she would cry, and she might lose the role. So she nodded, shame at her silence splattering mud over her joy.

As soon as Felicity got home, Claude came to meet her at the door, which so rarely happened these days. "I spoke to Neville and everything is ready to go," he said. The zeal of the cause was upon him. Felicity could see it now, in the tremble of his hands, the blackness of his pupils. She stood and waited as he said, "We've got the signs. 'Opera is for everyone.' 'Cast on merit.' 'Shame on you, Sir Thomas.'"

"No, Claude. You don't need to do that."

"It's too late, Felicity. We can be there tomorrow. If you're not going to help, stay out of our way."

"No, Claude," Felicity said. "You're too late. I got it. I got the part. He cast me on merit. Stay out of my way."

She thought she saw a flash of dismay cross Claude's face before he said, "Well, that's wonderful, Cinnamon. Let's celebrate."

CHAPTER 28.

London, England, February 11, 1969

FELICITY GOT OFF the bus and gulped the damp London air. It tasted grey as it slid through her lungs. It did nothing to ease the nausea that had its firm grip on her body. She already knew the answer that she was going to get, and the only question she had was what to do about it. She pushed her way through the door to the doctor's office and sat waiting, her head swimming and her stomach lurching.

Dr. Swift entered and went straight to the sink. He washed his hands and snapped on gloves without smiling or acknowledging Felicity. Then he turned around and said, "The test results show that you are about nine weeks pregnant."

Even though Felicity had expected the words, they felt like a set of bars dropping across a window. She heard her own voice as if it was rushing down a tunnel, asking, "So when did it happen?"

Dr. Swift walked to his desk and rummaged around, picking up a little cardboard wheel. Peering at it, he said "It would have been at the end of December."

Any faint hope was gone. But still she asked the question. "Could it have been on December eighth?" The last time she had been with Claude before leaving for Winnipeg.

"If you conceived on December eighth, you would be more than twelve weeks pregnant now, and your hCG levels are certainly not that high, nor is your fundus height indicating that timeframe.

When was your last menstrual period?"

Felicity said, "When my pills ran out. Around December ninth."

Dr. Swift's gaze grew colder and narrower. "You conceived while taking oral contraceptives?"

Heat and nausea raged. "I went home for Christmas. I was confused by the time zones. I missed three days and didn't realize it at first. But I've been trying to catch up."

"Stop taking them!" Dr. Swift said. "You don't know the effect they could have on your unborn child. You are pregnant. You don't need them now."

Felicity plucked at her shirt, trying to pull it away from her aching breasts. A trickle of sweat ran down her neck and collected in her bra. It was so hot in this room. Hope had pricked a pinpoint through the shroud of the knowledge that Brian was the father, but Dr. Swift had just sealed the hole.

She forced herself to speak again. "I want to get rid of it."

Dr. Swift's brow creased in an unpleasant frown. His eyes narrowed. "I beg your pardon?"

Felicity spoke louder. "When can I get rid of it?"

"Are you speaking of terminating this pregnancy?" He paused, seemingly more for dramatic effect than to search for words. "Well, young lady, you have come to the wrong place, because I absolutely will not do such a thing."

"I thought you could —" Felicity remembered hearing Claude and Neville discussing with approval a year or two ago the relaxation of English laws prohibiting abortion.

"Well, you thought wrong. There has to be a mental or physical reason, not just regret that you opened your legs to an unsuitable boy and now it's inconvenient. Two doctors have to approve this course of action, and as one doctor, I will not do that, let alone find another."

"But I can't have this baby," Felicity said.

"Then you shall give the child up for adoption. I'll schedule another appointment for the end of the first trimester to check on your progress. Nurse will come and talk to you now." Felicity was unable to bear the thoughts that were entering her brain too quickly to keep up. She couldn't get an abortion. She would have to suffer through seven more months of pregnancy. She was having Brian's baby. She would lose Claude.

She asked Dr. Swift, "Isn't there anything you can do at least to help me stop feeling so sick?"

Dr. Swift said, "It's normal. It will pass in a few weeks. Maybe it will remind you to be more careful next time. Nurse, would you book an appointment for this young lady about three weeks from now?" He picked up his stethoscope and whisked out of the room.

The nurse cocked her head and said to Felicity, "Are you vomiting a lot, love?"

"No," Felicity said, "I've only vomited about three times. I'm mostly just nauseous. In the morning, I have my head in the toilet for half an hour but nothing comes up."

"That can be worse than the vomiting. The important thing is not to let your stomach get too empty. You think you don't feel like eating, but you'll feel better if you get something in that tummy regularly. A lot of the girls like dry toast. Potato crisps, chips, greasy things. You could carry some bread or a bag of crisps with you. Don't worry about fruits and vegetables yet. Drink ginger beer or Coca-Cola, very cold. And get more rest than usual. It will help."

She handed Felicity some glossy brochures. The top one said, "Making the right decision for your baby." Felicity wondered why there was nothing about making the right decision for herself.

"What about your mother, love?" the nurse asked. "Could you ring her?"

Felicity shook her head, shoved the brochures into her bag, and rushed out of the office to catch the bus back to the Royal Opera House. Her mother could never know about this; it would destroy her. A couple of stops before hers, Felicity was seized with an attack of nausea so strong she was convinced this time she would surely vomit. She hurried to get off the bus. Once she was standing in the street, she retched a few times, bent over the gutter, but nothing came up. Passersby screwed up their faces and hurried past.

Traffic was heavy, and Felicity wondered what would happen if she simply threw herself into the path of the next bus. She would die. Everyone would mourn her, and no one would be any the wiser as to what she was carrying inside her. She walked faster. She could do it right now. She would leave Claude believing she had always been faithful to him. She stopped and watched for a while as buses, taxis, and cars flashed past her. After the next one, she would jump. Or the next one. She began walking again. Maybe when she got to the corner.

Tears formed and the wind pulled them to the corners of her eyes, the salt stinging her skin. The baby was Brian's. He had come backstage after her final *Messiah*. She was alone; her mother, Aunt Rose, Josiah, Jack, and everyone from Salvation Baptist had come to the earlier performances. He said he was there to see Sheila McLean, his fiancée and Felicity's childhood tormentor, who was singing in the chorus, but then he confessed to missing Felicity. A wild sense of competition had sprung up in Felicity. Rich, blond, beautiful, pampered Sheila had not been enough for him, and though an ocean had lain between Felicity and Brian for three and a half years, he still longed for her. She cared nothing for Brian, but she wanted to make Sheila hurt. It was revenge for the way Sheila had bullied Felicity in elementary school.

She had left the concert hall with Brian, in the same car he had driven in high school. She had thought she would flirt a bit, maybe kiss him, make Sheila jealous, and then go home. But Brian had had other ideas. He had taken what she did not want to give, and now he had given her something she didn't want to receive. She had been so stupid to forget to take her pills and then not to leave well alone with Brian. Her mother was right. Everyone was right. She was a slut, a cheap whore. She had no standards for herself, and this thing inside her was her punishment.

She walked faster down Bow Street as the tears flowed in time with her steps. Had Brian been Black, she could have pretended that this child was Claude's, but it was probable that Felicity's white heritage would blend with Brian's to create a child who looked more white than Black. Could she pass that off as just an aberration of genetics, or would Claude realize what she must have done?

She could never explain to Claude what had happened with Brian. Claude was from Grenada, from a loving family and a community of people who looked like him. He didn't know what it was like to be the only Black girl in the school, to have girls like Sheila looking down on her, making fun of her hair and her skin colour, and then to be miraculously chosen by a boy like Brian, who turned the intensity of his blue eyes upon Felicity as if she was finally worth seeing. He would not understand how, even on the night of a professional triumph, after singing a glorious *Messiah,* being once more in the city of her birth could bring back all those feelings of shame and despair, so intense that they precluded any exercise of judgment.

She was crying so hard, she walked straight into another body. "Steady on," said a familiar voice. Felicity blinked through her tears and looked up to see Lindsay.

"Sorry," she said and tried to push past him, but he held her by the shoulders.

"Oh, my goodness," he said. "Oh, dear. This won't do." He steered her past crowds of shoppers to a bench and gently eased her onto it. Then he reached into his pocket and handed her a handkerchief, seating himself at a respectful distance as she dabbed at her tears. She wished he were closer so that she could bury her face in his neck and have him hold her as she sobbed. When she was finally finished crying and was blowing her nose, he said, "This might be frightfully English of me, but I think a nice cup of tea might help."

"I have rehearsal," Felicity said.

Lindsay looked at his watch and said, "No, you don't. It's lunch time. I was just going to Blue Waters. Come on, you can get that cup of tea."

She allowed him to lead her through the lunch hour crowds. As soon as they arrived at Blue Waters, another shock of nausea jolted her. "I need to wash my face," she said, and hurried to the ladies' room where she again expected to vomit, but only heaved twice before the feeling subsided. She breathed deeply for a moment, then splashed water onto her cheeks and forehead. In the mirror, she looked haggard, years older than she had appeared yesterday. Her eyes were red, their lids swollen like bug larvae. She shuddered and reapplied lipstick and powder before returning to Lindsay, who was perusing the menu. Her stomach roiled again. Remembering the nurse's advice, when their waiter arrived, she asked for two pieces of toast, a plate of chips, and a ginger beer. Lindsay raised his eyebrows but ordered a steak and kidney pie with chips for himself, and a pot of tea.

Felicity comforted herself with the knowledge that Lindsay had no wife or children and had no reason to understand her strange meal order, but just in case, she said, "I'm dieting to fit my *Tender Land* costume." She swallowed as she realized that she would now be expanding regardless of what she ate. "I'm cutting out meat."

"I see," Lindsay said. "I think you look lovely as you are."

"Sir Thomas doesn't."

"Oh, Sir Thomas. Who's he?"

Felicity giggled. Then she turned her attention to the group onstage. There was a guitar player with a microphone, a bass player, a drummer, and a keyboard player.

"They're from St. Louis," said Lindsay. He pronounced it the French way, and Felicity laughed again. "You say it Lew-is."

"Ah," he said. "Thank you for enlightening me."

Lindsay's meal smelled strong, and Felicity turned her head away from it, fighting the urge to gag. She took a tentative sip of the ginger beer and after a minute, the cold bubbles did seem to lay a protective coating on her stomach. She took another and bit into her toast. To her surprise, the toast went down easily, and she felt herself hungering for more. She took a bigger bite and sipped more ginger beer.

Lindsay poured some tea. "If you want something hotter, try this," he said. She took a sip, but it was bitter on her tongue.

"Nothing like tea after a good cry," Lindsay approved. A moment later, he asked, "Are you feeling better?" She nodded. "You look better."

Felicity ached to tell him the whole sordid story of Claude, Brian, and the baby, but it seemed an insurmountable task. And what if Lindsay let it slip at a board meeting and Sir Thomas found out? She would be branded a whore by all at the Royal Opera House. And Claude was Lindsay's client. What if Lindsay told him before she could?

The group had just finished its first number, and now a woman was strolling up to join them. Something about her cheekbones reminded Felicity of her mother. When she began to sing, Felicity recognized the song as one of Aunt Rose's favourites, her crying music. "Stormy Weather."

Lindsay put his fork down. "That sounds like London, doesn't it? Raining all the time."

It was raining all the time, Felicity thought, not just outside, but within her, too. She had learned a song by Debussy in her first year with Philip: "Il pleure dans mon coeur." *It rains in my heart.* That was exactly what she was feeling now: rain in her heart. It was too hard to sit there and listen to someone else's pain and not shout her own to the room. Felicity stood. "Thank you for lunch, Lindsay, but I really need to get back to rehearsal." She pushed her chair in so hard, it skidded across the linoleum. Heads turned as she dashed for the door. She thought she heard Lindsay calling her name, but didn't look back.

When she got home that evening, Claude was watching television in the living room. "Look at this, Cinnamon," he said, without taking his eyes from the screen. "The Americans are getting closer to landing on the moon. Can you imagine that? They've destroyed everything here on earth and now they want to wreck the moon. If they find any aliens there, they'll impose their ridiculous racial categories on them too." Felicity sat down slowly and drank in the sight of Claude relaxed and comfortable in the home they shared, wondering how much longer it would last. Claude went on, "Typical imperialists. They'll spend millions on millions going into space but nothing to help the countries they ruined." Felicity opened her mouth to agree, but a surge of bile rose, and she jumped up and sprinted to the bathroom. She gagged and choked over the toilet as a thin stream of saliva hung from her lips.

"Felicity?" Claude had followed her, and he stood in the doorway. "What's wrong, Cinnamon? Are you ill?" He knelt down beside her, brushing her hair out of the way with his hand. "Is it the flu?" he asked. She heaved again, and then he said, "Wait, sweetheart. You've been ill in the mornings, too, haven't you?"

She could lie. But that would only prolong the inevitable, so she nodded, still bent over the toilet bowl as tears plopped into it.

Claude said, "So what do you want to do about it? I'll support you in whatever you want."

It was tempting, but she wouldn't do that to him, so she said, "It's not yours."

"Not mine? What do you mean? How do you know? Then whose?" She heard his voice splintering. She couldn't look at him.

"My high school boyfriend. From when I went home."

Claude got up and began pacing. "You mean when you were back in Winnipeg for Christmas, you went and slept with someone? Is that what you planned to do all along?"

"No," Felicity said, "It wasn't like that."

Claude asked, "Is this man white?" Felicity nodded again. He slammed his fist into his palm and began to pace. "I knew it!" he raged. "I told you. I told you to tell all those white men to fuck off. But that's half of you, isn't it? Everyone told me, and I didn't listen.

They said you'd choose the white man's ways. And you did. You opened your legs and let one in."

"I didn't let him," Felicity said.

Claude stopped moving. "He forced you? Like your father?"

Felicity clasped her hands, almost as if in prayer. "He did." This was the way out.

"Well, you had to have gone willingly with him! How did you end up alone with him?"

She should have known it wouldn't be that easy. There was no answer she could give that would assist her. She stayed quiet. Claude dropped to his knees in front of her and grabbed her shoulders. "Is there any chance, Felicity, any chance at all, that it's mine?" She shook her head, tears carving a path into her cheeks that would remain forever.

Claude stood up. "Then that's that. You and I are over. You can stay here. I'll go to Neville's until it's time to go back to Grenada. I'll sort out a way to get my things later."

"Claude, no!" Felicity launched herself forward but missed Claude and fell to the tiled floor.

"Felicity, don't be so extreme," Claude said. "You're not going to change my mind this time. You've betrayed everything I thought you were, everything you learned. I'm building up Black people and raising their consciousness, and you're busy running off with white men."

"Claude, don't go," Felicity wailed, crawling after him on her hands and knees, the tears falling thickly now. Claude went to the bedroom to pack an overnight bag. He ignored her as she lay weeping on the ground. He stepped over her and walked to the door, then turned.

"I really loved you, Felicity. I was prepared to turn my life inside out for you. I would have done anything for you." His voice wavered. He opened the door. A minute later, it reopened. Felicity lifted her head, hope lightening her tears, but he simply walked to the bedroom, took the quilt off their bed and placed it over Felicity where she lay, then left. His key scraped in the lock for the last time. Felicity sobbed without restraint on the floor of the home Claude had chosen for the two of them.

ENTR'ACTE CHAPTER 29.

St. George's, Grenada, October 18, 1983

THE BUSH TEA smelled like the jungle, rain-soaked leaves and overripe fruit and life and decay. Felicity breathed in the steam, sitting in Neville's study, to which Alison had banished her while she cleaned the living room. Felicity had offered to help, but whatever brief bond she had shared with Alison had been severed. Alison looked at her with drooping eyes and said, "No, thanks. You can help by staying out of the way."

The car arrived quietly this time. It slid through the gates like a creature of prey. Before Felicity knew it, there were voices coming down the hall. She dived behind the couch and pressed herself to the wall. Her heart pulsed like a wound. Neville and Claude had impressed upon her that calamity would ensue if her presence in the house became known. It would spark an international incident. It would provide the United States with the pretext they needed to invade: the rescue of the hapless Canadian opera star.

"But they know there's an American here," Felicity said. "When they showed up to start all this, remember?"

"They've probably forgotten about that, in all the confusion," said Claude. "And if they do check, there's not going to be an American citizen named Lydia Felix staying in Grenada at the time who is unaccounted for."

"But I'm unaccounted for," Felicity said.

"You're supposed to be in Vincennes. They're under curfew. There's no phones up there, no communications." He spoke casually, as if it meant nothing that Felicity had stepped out her front door and disappeared, as if she would not be mourned. Perhaps he was right, and she would not be.

"Yes, we must discuss that," she heard Claude say very loudly outside the door, giving her time to conceal herself. The door popped open and several pairs of footsteps trod through the room. The couch in front of her buckled as bodies settled themselves.

"Is everyone in the house in good health?" asked one of the visitors, a strained-sounding tenor.

Claude said, "Yes, for now, but Patricia is late in her term. She needs rest. Can't you release her to her mother's care?"

"You know we can't do that. She is too close to sensitive information."

"What are you trying to achieve, Henry?" asked Neville, and Felicity was annoyed on Claude's behalf that Neville had chimed in before Claude had finished his point.

"The people don't care for Sister Pat. You know that," said a baritone with a voice that buzzed like a circling fly, that echoed with the hint of an American accent. "They prefer Sister Marlene." It was the only time in her life that Felicity would root for Marlene to come out on top. "Sister Pat is a bourgeois threat with her beauty pageant ways."

"Mark, she hasn't done that for years!" Claude said. "She competed for Grenada, to put us on the map, to bring attention to the abuses Tibbs was committing."

If Claude truly believed that it was for Grenada that Pat had entered Miss World and won and let herself be photographed at fancy parties around the world, baring her pampered skin in one sexy dress after another, then why had he been so conflicted about Felicity's profession? Had he changed so much?

"All of you are bourgeois," continued the baritone. "That's why we had to act. You have betrayed the Revo. Working with banks and business when they are enemies of the people."

"We need an economic infrastructure to feed our people," said Claude. "You think they don't have commerce in Russia? We nationalized the banks, so they belong to the people. They share profits with the people. That's how we've been able to pay for our initiatives."

The tenor said, "You're kissing up to the USA. You will sell our country to them for tourist dollars."

"Well, what would you do better?" asked Claude.

"Deal with the counter-revolutionary forces. Do something about the American propaganda. Seek closer relations with our African brothers and sisters. Nationalize the land. There is still too much private ownership. You have done well in many of the parishes, I agree, but too many of our poorest brothers and sisters, those up in the hills, they still don't have electricity or phones. Their housing is inadequate." Felicity thought of her aunt's house, already half-swallowed by the jungle.

"We are working towards all that," said Neville, "but it has to be a gradual transition."

Someone sucked his teeth as if popping the skin off a mango and spoke in a basso profundo. "That sounds like Brother Buck," he said. "He has too much influence."

Claude said, "That's why we've considered the offer of Mark and Neville sharing the prime ministership and me continuing as deputy. I'm willing to give it a try. It's more important to unify the country against the foreign threat and save the Revo."

"I'm glad you think so," the basso profundo said, "but it is Brother Carp who has to agree."

The air in the room condensed with expectation.

"I am the leader," Neville said. "The people love me. They will never accept any limit on my powers."

"There are no limits," said the tenor. "There is strength in numbers, look at it that way."

"Think of the country." The baritone. "Things are at a standstill. People are suffering." *Whose fault is that?* Felicity wondered, but no one said it. Another silence dragged on.

"The Cubans want me as leader," said Neville. This, then, must be why they had come last night.

"They are not our people," the tenor replied. His voice was agitated. "The Cubans have too much say in our affairs."

The baritone spoke again. "You remember, Brother Carp, how we used to organize? Those student strikes where it was you and me at the front of the march." Felicity swallowed a bubble of satisfaction. She was right. Mark felt replaced by Claude. "We used to talk about getting rid of Tibbs. Remember how we found it so difficult to believe that Tibbs, the one who stood up for our people against the white man, had turned corrupt?"

Neville made a sound from somewhere deep in his throat.

The baritone continued, "You know what Tibbs did wrong? He started putting what he wanted ahead of what was best for the country. And that's what you're doing now, brother."

"Do not compare me to that man!" Neville's voice shook the hot, close air in the room. "How dare you, you horse's ass. You're the one destroying the country for your own need for power."

"Remember, I was the one trying to get you to call an election," said the baritone.

"And I will. But we didn't want to assume the European model of what they call *democracy*. We wanted to make it truly representative. We were doing consultations. It was Claude's idea."

"But you haven't called one yet. And without an election, there is only one way to change the government. The same way you did. By force."

"We didn't kill anyone when we took power from Tibbs." Claude spoke with a quiet authority.

"And we don't want to kill anyone either. If Brother Carp agrees to share power, we will order the army to stand down."

"Neville." The rest of what Claude said was spoken so quietly, Felicity could not hear it. Their conversation went on for several minutes. Felicity looked down at her chest, moving up and down under Neville's T-shirt. She no longer took breathing for granted.

"Okay!" Neville said. "Shrimps, man. I'll do it. Joint prime ministership, on the condition that we take it to the people for an election once the crisis is over."

"But the Party must endorse the slate."

"Yes, yes, of course," said Claude.

"You and me, working together, like old times," said the buzzing baritone. "You'll see, it will only be for the good of everyone."

Cigar smoke rose to the ceiling. No one spoke. Then Claude broke the uncomfortable silence. "Will you announce this to the public?"

"Yes. Tomorrow. We'll do a radio broadcast. I'll direct the army to return to Headquarters, and you'll all be free to go. I'll write the speech tonight. Someone will bring it to you in the morning."

Tomorrow, thought Felicity. *This will all be over tomorrow.* In the morning, she would be leaving this house. Relief and regret blended and settled in her like the herbs in the tea.

ACT II
CHAPTER 30.

London, England, June 28, 1969

FELICITY FROWNED AT her reflection, examining how the new purple gown she had bought, in a deep, penitential shade, was draped over the large lump in her middle. Dr. Swift said that she was approximately twenty-nine weeks pregnant. The despised thing kicked and tumbled inside her when she sang, and it would soon be impossible to hide this mound that insisted on rising higher and higher. She had run into Alison when she went to the hospital last week for bloodwork, and as Felicity talked to her, plucking her hospital gown away from the telltale curve in her middle, Alison's eyes had drifted there with a knowing smile.

When Felicity met with the adoption counselor, the woman flinched at the sight of her. "I'm afraid it may be hard to place a child who is ..." Felicity almost laughed at the ridiculousness of this woman being unable to voice a word describing Felicity's skin colour, in the face of the much greater indelicacy that she was here as an unwed mother to discuss giving her baby away to strangers.

"You mean, because I'm Black," Felicity said. When the woman was silent, she offered, "I'm only half-Black. My father is white." This inconvenient fact, generally not of use to her, could serve her now. "And the baby's father is white. So it will probably look mostly white."

"But we'll have no way of knowing that ahead of time," said the counsellor. "And don't they sometimes get more colour as they get older?"

Felicity understood. The sorrowful truth was that Black blood was a taint that no one wanted, even people desperate for a child. "What can I do then?"

The woman shrugged. "We will try to find a family of your race, but if we cannot, the baby will go to an orphanage." She asked, "What about the baby's father? Have you tried to talk to him?"

Brian was not an option.

Today, she would see Claude. Before their split, she had agreed to sing for an Apartheid Awareness concert, sponsored in part by the West Indian Students Association. She had assumed that her appearance had been cancelled after Claude left, but three weeks ago, she had received a call from a member of the committee asking for the names of her selections. She was going to sing for Claude again, wearing a new gown that fit her new body in his favourite colour, the colour of a queen. A fallen queen.

Hand on her aching back, she lumbered out into the hallway and saw Marlene carrying a jug of water to another performer's room. She had a bright cloth flower pinned to her hair, and when she turned around, Felicity saw glittery eyeshadow spread over her eyelids and up to her brow bone. Marlene smiled insincerely. "Hello, Felicity." She looked straight at Felicity's stomach. She knew.

"Hi, Marlene," Felicity said. They looked at each other, saying nothing. Marlene had the subtle air of someone cared for, and the smile of someone who had come out on top. Felicity knew what would happen next, and it did. Claude appeared.

"Felicity, how are you?" His mouth barely moved. His eyes barely moved. An eternity passed.

"I'm all right," Felicity said. They all stared at each other some more, and then Claude asked Marlene, "Could you give us a minute, please, darling?" Marlene's body jerked, and Claude pecked her on the cheek. "Just a minute," he said. Marlene sauntered away. Claude's eyes cleared. In them, Felicity saw their first date, felt the beat of his heart as he held her against him with the autumn sun warm on their heads.

Claude asked, "Are you really all right?" She nodded. Of course she wasn't. How could she be all right, without him? He cleared his throat. "You look well." She shrugged. He rubbed a hand over his forehead and then asked, "Is there still no possibility that it's mine?"

Felicity had gone over and over it. She shook her head. Her hands formed fists. She would not cry.

"But you don't know definitely. You can't know." He looked over his shoulder and then looked back at Felicity. "When you have it, if you think it could be mine, write to me at the office." He passed her a business card, as if the address wasn't blazed onto her brain.

Felicity blurted, "How could you go back to Marlene?"

Claude shuffled his feet, looked behind him. "Felicity." He dropped his voice further. "It's not like us, if you must know." Her heart pumped harder. The creature in her belly began moving. "She's loyal. She's hard-working. She's good company. Neville is the playboy. I have to be the settled one." He closed his eyes. "I've got to go. It was nice to see you." He turned and strode away She heard Marlene's voice in the distance. The thing inside Felicity uncurled and thudded a rhythm against her kidneys that sent her rushing to the bathroom.

A knock came on her door, and she opened it to see Gerald. "We're ready for you, Felicity," he said.

"Okay," she acknowledged, humming under her breath to keep her voice warm. Since she and Will no longer spoke, one of the apprentice pianists from the Royal Opera House was playing for her, and she saw him lurking in a corner, curling and uncurling his fingers.

As she and Gerald began walking up the stairs, the pianist trailing them, Gerald said, "I'm sorry about you and Claude."

"So am I," she agreed. The enormity of the loss of Claude made her stumble.

Gerald put out his hand to steady her. "Felicity, do you remember when we met?"

"You were the first person who talked to me at my first march. You introduced me to Claude. And Neville."

"I lived to regret that. I only did it to show you I knew people."

"Claude always said you were interested in me." It had been a joke between Felicity and Claude, when they were both so sure of the eternal love they shared, when their hearts were fastened tight against all intruders.

"He was right," Gerald said; then, leaning in close to Felicity, "I still am."

She jerked back in shock. "Gerald, don't you know I'm —" She couldn't say the word *pregnant*. Pregnant meant unloveable. Fat, blubbery, heavy breasts, stretch marks, and the fruit of another man's seed within her.

"I know," he said. "You're expecting."

"Claude told you?" She tried not to imagine how he must have thrown the proof of her betrayal around her former circle of friends, the better to cast her out.

"No, he didn't," Gerald said, lowering his voice as they entered the backstage area. "It was Alison. She saw you at the hospital. Before, I didn't know what had happened. I just thought Claude was cutting ties before he went home." Gerald paused. "I don't need to know the story, Felicity. Obviously, Claude is not the father. I know things happen to a woman sometimes. My own sister —" He pulled out a handkerchief and wiped his forehead. "I am not like these crazy Grenadians. I am a Bajan. We are practical people. I'm staying in London. I just got a good job as an accountant with Cox Devereux Waters. I'm giving up all this protesting."

When she didn't respond, Gerald gave an embarrassed laugh.

"Felicity, I'm asking you to marry me. It's not romantic, but as I said, I'm a practical person. I'll take care of you and the baby, and you can carry on singing."

She summoned a smile. "Gerald, I'm so flattered, and I'm so moved —"

"But you love Claude, and you want to marry for love and love alone." He was smiling too. "I understand. I didn't mean you had to accept today, but the offer is open as long as I stay single."

"Thank you." She kissed him briefly on the lips. Gerald was a way out, an instant solution to her problem. She could marry him, announce her pregnancy, let him raise the child who took after its long-departed white grandfather. But Gerald would remind her every day of his absent friend, Claude. Their marriage would be defined by what was missing, not what was present. And over time, despite what he said, Gerald would grow resentful and expect from her what she could not give. She would not be able to promise faithfulness. Look how easily she had weakened even when she was in love with Claude. Marriage was not for her.

Gerald nudged her. "Your turn, Felicity." She realized that she had been called to the stage. She walked out, concentrating on not waddling, not allowing her belly to dictate how she moved. She had chosen to sing "Laurie's Song" and "O luce." "Laurie's Song" was a mechanical exercise, now that she had performed the full role at the Royal Opera House, in costume and with staging. It was no longer a piece she had to work to characterize. It had grown with her along with the treacherous baby, and without any effort, she could recreate the mood she had projected onstage; a sense of the world opening up to consume her innocence.

But "O luce" was different. It was still a piece that sang to her of Claude, only of Claude. The aria had turned from sweet to bitter in her mouth overnight. Now it was the way that she would be singing goodbye to Claude forever.

She let the words of the recitativo linger in her mouth like a dissolving candy. She was waiting for Claude to call. She believed he would. She believed he wouldn't. She hoped. She feared. Then the aria started, and she sang the words that were inscribed on her heart.

Light of my soul,
Delight, love and life,
Our fates shall be united,
On earth and in heaven.

No matter where the rest of her life took her, no matter who else she might meet, no love would ever be as pure and abiding as the one she had for Claude. It was his face she would see when she died. He would be there, touching her gently, saying "Kopf, Schultern, Knie, Zeh," in his perfect German accent. She sang to him, sometimes so softly she could see the audience leaning in, trying to catch what she was doing. The fast scales of the piece that she had sung with such joy and exuberance at the hurricane relief concert were now sorrowful rippling sighs. She pulled back, forcing the piano to slow. As she sang, tears rose with the music, and she allowed them to spill out, following Philip's advice to let herself be vulnerable before the audience. As soon as the aria was over and the applause started, she dipped her head to acknowledge it and fled the stage. She bolted past Gerald, past everyone, to her dressing room, gathered her belongings as quickly as she could and ran, still in the purple gown, still crying, to the Underground.

She let herself into the home where she had lived with Claude and burrowed into his side of the bed, imagining that she could still smell him. She fell asleep twisted around his absence and woke to a knocking on the door. Rising from a dream of Claude, she thought joyfully that he had come back to her. She ran to the door, wrenched it open, and came face to face with her mother. Only belatedly did she realize how she must look with makeup smeared all over her face, black mascara tears dried on her cheeks, her eyes red and puffy, indentations of the pillow on her face, her hair matted and clumpy, wearing her wrinkled gown, and her stomach sticking out.

Her mother stood rigid on the doorstep, her face a carnival mask of horror. At last, she stepped into the hallway, lifting a large suitcase, and slammed the door. The sound of a taxi driving away served as punctuation. "Sweet Lord Jesus, Felicity!" she exclaimed.

"Yes, Mom. I'm pregnant."

"When were you going to tell me?"

"Hello to you too," Felicity said. "What are you doing here?"

"I had to use up the ticket I never used for your graduation, and Rose thought it would be nice to surprise you."

"Well, are you surprised?"

"Who's the father?"

"I can't tell you."

"You can't, or you don't know?"

"Of course I know!" Felicity said. "I'm not a whore!"

"Well, I don't know about that," Mom said, lips a thin line. Felicity wanted to fly at her and scratch her prim, self-righteous face, but instead, she said, "This is my problem to deal with. I'm sorry you had to see me like this."

"You can't marry the father?"

"No, I can't," Felicity said, steeling her mind against the abhorrent image.

"He said no?"

"I never asked him. That's not what I want. I'm going to give this child up for adoption." Performing at the Apartheid Awareness concert, even in a small hall with a rickety piano and an unsophisticated audience, had given her fresh determination to keep singing. She was not one of those women who could settle for raising a child and tell herself it was what she had always wanted, more than whatever else she was doing before the child came along. She would not throw away her dreams.

"You're not going to do that, Felicity," said Mom. "A Black child would be almost impossible to adopt. I'm not having my grandchild grow up unloved."

"Why not?" Felicity said. "I did."

"You did what?"

"Grew up unloved."

"Are you out of your mind?" Mom shouted. "You were loved every second of your life. And you were taught to fear God."

Felicity raised her head to look at her mother. "Love and fear don't go together, Mom. Doesn't the Bible say something about that?"

"Perfect love drives out fear. 1 John 4:18." Mom's voice softened. "We're going to get you packed up, and you're going to come home to have your baby."

"No," Felicity wailed, her hand over her mouth. Her life was in London. The Royal Opera House. Claude. Lindsay and their trips to Blue Waters. Will, if she could ever get him to speak to her again. The Underground. The fish and chip shop. Hyde Park. The Thames river. Trafalgar Square. Trafalgar Square, conjuring the full spectrum of joy and pain. The feeling of anonymity on the crowded streets, swimming in a river of people of all races and colours.

If she left London, she wanted to go somewhere else where she could be an anonymous brown face, somewhere like New York. She couldn't go back to Winnipeg and the curious stares on the streets, the judgmental ones at Salvation Baptist. But then Winnipeg also had Jack, and Josiah, and Aunt Rose — people to whom she could pour out her sorrows. People who knew her as she really was, not just the facade of confidence that she presented. She could go home, have the baby, leave it with her mother, and come back to London, or go to New York. The relief of having made a decision slid down her throat like cool water and, as if sensing that its future had just been decided, the baby stretched itself out to receive the blessing it had been given.

CHAPTER 31.

Winnipeg, Manitoba, September 15, 1969

FELICITY WAS SPLITTING in two, a slow, torturous tearing. She lay on the couch groaning and clutching her stomach. Aunt Rose knelt beside her, rubbing her back. She had moved in with Aunt Rose when she came home, not wanting to see Mom's anguished face everywhere she turned. Aunt Rose had called Mom when Felicity's labour started.

"I'm trying to figure out how often the contractions are coming," Aunt Rose said to Mom, "but she's so agitated I can't tell when one starts and the other one stops. We're starting to calm down though, aren't we, flower?"

"Aunt Rose, it hurts, it hurts. I hate it," Felicity wailed.

"I know, flower. It will be over soon, and then you'll have your beautiful baby."

She didn't want the baby. She wanted to get it out of her and move on with her life.

"It may be a bit soon, but we'd better get to the hospital just in case," Aunt Rose suggested.

Mom said, "Felicity, get up and brush your hair and put on something reasonable."

"I can't, Mom."

"Rose, help her. There are still standards around here. I'll get the hospital bag."

At the hospital, a nurse took Felicity behind a curtain for an examination. "I don't want anyone to touch me," she said. Pain curled through every part of her, throbbing even behind her toenails.

"It's too bad you didn't feel that way nine months ago," said Mom. Felicity reared up from the stretcher, palm open to slap her, but Aunt Rose laid her back down and formed a barrier between her and Mom.

"We'll give you something soon," said the nurse. "Takes all the pain away and you won't feel a thing."

"No!" said Aunt Rose. "Don't give her anything! Those drugs are awful!"

The nurse flapped her hand at Aunt Rose. "And how would you know? You couldn't have received an epidural. They're new."

"I got knocked out when I had my baby," Aunt Rose said. "I couldn't remember anything. I woke up tied to a board, all scratched and bruised."

"That was twilight sleep. This is different. She'll be awake the whole time."

It was true. When the needle went in, there was an agonizing moment of coldness, but then Felicity really couldn't feel a thing. Not being able to feel a thing physically helped her mind to go numb as well. Not being able to feel a thing also meant that she couldn't feel how to push the baby out, and so the doctor pulled it out with forceps. Then there was a bustle of testing and bathing and wrapping the baby while Mom and Aunt Rose sat exhausted in the hard orange plastic chairs.

A nurse approached with a swaddled bundle, the edges of the blanket hanging down beneath her elbows, and Mom asked, "Is it a boy or a girl?"

A sudden hope beamed its rays into Felicity's heart. Maybe the doctor had been wrong. What if the baby was Claude's after all?

"A girl!" the nurse said, peeling away the blanket from the

baby's face, and Felicity stared down at the blue eyes, chiselled nose, and rounded chin of Brian.

ONCE SHE WAS sewn up, Felicity fell asleep. An hour later, a nurse woke her. "How are your breasts feeling?" she asked.

Felicity touched them and winced. "They're sore."

"Your milk is going to start coming in. But you aren't planning to breastfeed, are you? They make some very good formulas now."

Felicity looked at Mom and Aunt Rose who were still seated at her bedside. "Feed it from my breasts? No way."

"It might be nice to try," said Aunt Rose.

Felicity recoiled. "Ugh! No!"

Later that day, Jack and Josiah arrived, bearing a large bouquet of flowers. Felicity couldn't say much to them in front of Mom. When they left, taking Aunt Rose with them, Mom said to Felicity, "What are you calling the baby?" Felicity was surprised at how calm Mom was. How the disapproving fire of her glare had cooled at the first sight of the infant.

Felicity said, "I thought of Mara." *Wait!* she thought. She wasn't keeping the baby. She wanted to get back to normal life.

"That's a pretty name," Mom said. "It's Biblical. I dreaded you picking some of the silly hippy names that are so popular these days. Children named River and Rain and things like that. Why Mara?"

"Robert Schumann. He's a composer who was married to Clara. He really loved her, and they were both talented musicians. And it's also the name of a character in *Porgy and Bess* that I learned in case I ever have the chance to audition. But Clara's a little bit old-fashioned, so I thought I'd change it to Mara. I'd like my baby to have that kind of love and that kind of talent in her life. Since I don't."

Mom pounced. "Well, why don't you? Why don't you call the baby's father?" She hesitated. "It's Brian, isn't it?"

"I can't, Mom. Just understand, I can't."

Aunt Rose came back the next day, and as Felicity snoozed, she heard Mom ask her, "Should I call Brian?"

"Oh, honey," said Aunt Rose. "Not if Felicity doesn't want that."

"But why doesn't she?"

"Maybe the way it happened with Brian wasn't nice."

"No!" Mom said. "Brian wouldn't."

Felicity screamed soundlessly into her pillow. She wondered what Mom would say if she knew that she and Felicity were now linked not just by blood, but by forced motherhood.

FELICITY AND MARA went home to Mom's house. She had last slept in her childhood bedroom when she came home to sing *Messiah*. Then, professional triumph in what she knew had been a spectacular performance had mingled with the loathing that followed her night with Brian, and her fears for her relationship with Claude, which had now come true. She curled under the blankets and got up only to use the bathroom, or to scrounge for food. Food was her only comfort, but eating the way she did meant that her stomach remained swollen, lifting the blankets in a mound as if she were still pregnant. All the more reason not to show the world how disgusting she was.

Mom got a Moses basket for Mara and placed it beside Felicity's bed, but Felicity ignored Mara's cries. It was Mom who came into Felicity's room at night to give Mara her bottles. Jack came by as often as he could to help. When Mom realized that no amount of nagging or yelling would get Felicity out of bed, she started coming home from work at lunch to feed and change Mara. Felicity covered her head with blankets when Mara cried and, soon enough, Mara stopped bothering. She lay on her back staring at the ceiling until her grandmother or Jack showed up.

After a month of this, the phone rang while Felicity was making a snack. She answered without thinking. It was Lindsay. "We haven't spoken since you left the Royal Opera," he said. "It was very difficult to track you down, Felicity. Sir Thomas spoke to Philip Cook, and he remembered you'd studied with an Eileen Fisher, and he contacted her and she gave him your mother's telephone number."

Felicity felt a rush of embarrassment. "I wasn't planning to leave, Lindsay. But the truth is —" She tried to decide what to share.

"You were pregnant."

"You knew?"

"Of course I knew. I knew for months," he said. He laughed. "It was rather obvious, Felicity. But don't worry, I've kept that piece of knowledge to myself."

"Why didn't you say anything?"

"I didn't feel it was my place. Anyway, the reason I'm ringing you has to do with *The Tender Land*." Every muscle, every nerve, every drop of blood in Felicity's body began to sing out loud.

"Sir Thomas was extremely impressed with your work on Laurie. And he's had an inquiry from the Vancouver Opera Association. It's in Canada. Where Joan Sutherland made her North American debut. Is that anywhere near you?"

Now Felicity laughed, an unfamiliar feeling in her throat. "It's days away, unless you fly."

"Oh," said Lindsay. "They're doing *Tender Land* in a couple of weeks. Bit of a gamble, but they had Jane Masters singing the role. It was a huge coup for them. But she's fallen ill, rumour is cancer. Keep that to yourself."

"Jane Masters?" The name was an incantation. Jane was one of the foremost singers of contemporary music in the world.

"They need someone who knows the role. And nobody but you seems to know it."

Mom would have to watch Mara while Felicity was in Vancouver, and that might take some convincing.

THE NEXT DAY, when Mom was at work, Felicity spent a couple of hours with her *Tender Land* score. She needed to pack, but she struggled to find clothing that fit. She tried on outfit after outfit, whipping them off in disgust when they wouldn't zip or button or clung too tightly to her rolls of fat. Finally, she let out a howl that tore at her throat. Mara made a sympathetic squawk. Felicity went downstairs and dialled. When he answered, she wasted no time, "I need you, Jack."

"Why?" he asked. "What's wrong?"

"I just got a call from the Vancouver Opera Association. They have an emergency, and they need me there tomorrow to do a show."

"That's great! That's fantastic, Fizzy! So what's the problem?"

"I just need you."

"I'll be right there."

Minutes later, he surveyed the scene in Felicity's bedroom. Mara lay in the Moses basket. Clothes were draped everywhere.

"Packing, I see."

Felicity sank down on the bed and put her head in her hands. Jack sat next to her and waited.

"Jack," she said, "I feel ugly, and fat, and disgusting. I have to go play Laurie, an innocent, beautiful girl, and I'm so gross." The idea had formed subconsciously and now it felt like a stone on her tongue. She raised her eyes to him, summoning all the longing and pleading she could from the wells inside her.

"Oh," Jack said. "Fizzy. You want —"

She didn't want, she needed to feel life stir within her again. Not the life of a treacherous baby, insisting on moving and kicking no matter how hard she wished it still, but the life of a man, growing and swelling, filling the space inside her, if only just for a few minutes.

Jack cleared his throat, opened his mouth, and then closed it again. Felicity pushed a pile of dresses to the floor, making space on the bed. "Come on, Jack."

Jack's fingers unfolded. "Felicity," he said, "I was going to tell you." The air in the room grew heavy. He plunged ahead. "Remember I told you I've been spending time with Abby? Your friend from church?"

"Yes," Felicity said. "I remember." She had only pretended to support Jack in this endeavour. He had always been hers, and she didn't want to share him with Abby. And although Abby had been her friend longer than Felicity could remember, the closer Abby got to Jack, the less Felicity wanted to spend time with her.

"I'm thinking of making it more serious."

"You mean making Abby the only one."

"I mean maybe marriage. I mean maybe kids."

Felicity doubled over, feeling like her labour pains had returned. The idea of Abby in the condition Felicity had just been in, but with Jack's baby inside her, was like carrying a boulder where Mara had been. Jack would be a fantastic partner to Abby during pregnancy, and after she pushed out their child. The baby might have Felicity's colour. She tried to keep her voice casual as she said, "I didn't think you wanted kids."

"I don't. I didn't. But Abby does, and, well, I guess helping out with Mara changed my mind."

By leaning on Jack, Felicity had driven him closer to the thing she least wanted him to have. She knew Abby would make a perfect wife and mother, something Felicity could never be. Music and her own emotional life left no room for nurturing.

"It's not only that, Fizzy. When I finish my degree, I'm thinking of going to the Lutheran seminary in Saskatoon."

The block of ice inside Felicity hardened and crusted over with snow. She hugged herself around the middle as another contraction of grief bent her over again. "You want to be a pastor?"

"I think so," Jack said. "I think I can do some good that way. People need to understand that following Christ is so much more than a bunch of rules. Churches need modernizing, or they will die."

"So let them die!" Felicity shouted. She grabbed her pillow and threw it at him. "Aren't you making rules now, Jack Mueller, you hypocrite? You always liked sex before. You've never had a problem with it! God gave us sex! He gave us a way to feel close to each other and heal, and people decided to turn it into this thing that only certain people get to do in certain ways."

Jack put a hand on her knee. "That's actually excellent theology, Felicity. You're right." He began lifting his sweater over his head. "Okay. We'll do it this one time, but it has to be the last, understood?"

As Felicity took her own clothes off, she looked through the window and saw a flock of geese slicing through the smoky grey sky. She lay back on the bed as Jack took in the dark red stretch marks across her stomach and hips, the sagging layer of flesh hanging from her lower abdomen, her now-deflated breasts. She said, "I'm hideous, Jack. None of my clothes fit. What am I going to do?"

Jack traced one of the stretch marks with his little finger. "Borrow some from Rose. She's a bigger lady, and she's a good dresser. I'm sure she can spare a few outfits. Just until you get back to yourself, and you will. Be easy on yourself, it's only been a month." He looked at the Moses basket. "Should we do this with her here?"

Felicity shrugged. "Why not?"

"Well, okay then," Jack said, as he took one of Felicity's breasts in his hand. He felt his way around her new contours, providing sex like it was medicine, and Felicity blossomed as she recovered. When they were finished, Jack said, "I really need a smoke."

"We have to go outside," Felicity said. "My mom will go nuts if she smells it in her house." She looked out of the window. "Is it cold out?"

"A bit. Wear a sweater." As Felicity rummaged through the pile of clothes on the floor, Jack said, "Wait. We have to bring Mara."

"Can't we just leave her inside?"

"No, we can't, Felicity. What if she chokes?" Felicity looked away as he stood up. "Where's her stuff?" She indicated the drawer, and watched as Jack wrapped her daughter in a blanket, the way he had once done for her when she lay on his couch. No one would take care of her now. It was her job to take care of another person. The edges of her heart curled inward.

"When does she have to eat?" he asked. Felicity shrugged again. "Come on, Fizzy, you can't punish her because of who her father is."

Felicity knew that she was supposed to feel a rush of love for this tiny human being, but whenever she looked at her child, a dull feeling came over her. It was more than just Brian being Mara's father and Mara having his face. It was the realization that Felicity had made a chain for herself, forged of blood rather than steel; that she had put a rope around her own neck and tightened the noose, and for what? To win a contest with Sheila that the winner actually lost.

They went out to the patio through the glass sliding doors and Jack placed the Moses basket on the ground between their two wicker chairs. Felicity propped a bottle up with the nipple in Mara's mouth as Jack rolled a joint on the wicker table.

As she blew the sacred smoke up to the graphite sky, listening to the fading cries of the geese, a shriveled, brown leaf gusted across the lawn. "Snow's in the air," Jack said.

CHAPTER 32.

Vancouver, British Columbia, November 2, 1969

AFTER THE OPENING performance of *The Tender Land,* there was a reception in the lobby of the Queen Elizabeth Theatre. Felicity was eager to unleash two weeks' worth of nervous energy. Although she knew the music, she had lived with the tension of learning new blocking and getting to know castmates she had never worked with, all far more experienced than she was, and none of them particularly welcoming. She knew that her performance at the dress rehearsal had been lacklustre; she was exhausted and frustrated. She sensed her big opportunity slipping away, and that had galvanized her. At her first entrance on opening night, she had stepped onto the stage and commanded it. She had channelled all her insecurities into the character. Laurie was insecure too. She felt small. She felt scared. Felicity stood in the spotlight and trembled for the audience to see.

At intermission, the tenor who played Martin, her love interest, nodded at her and said, "Nice singing." It was the first compliment she had received; the first sign that anyone in the cast felt anything other than resentment that this upstart had replaced their beloved Jane Masters. She was so grateful for those two words, and yet she couldn't allow the slights to pass; the lunches and coffee breaks she had spent alone. Allowing hurt like this to make its home with her had sent her into Brian's arms, and he had taken advantage of her vulnerability and devastated her life. She would never allow that to happen again. The only possible response to the cruelty of others was to put up defences so tall and strong that no one would try to scale them.

"Of course it was," she said, and walked past the tenor.

For the reception, she wore one of Aunt Rose's dresses, as suggested by Jack. She had already slimmed down a bit with all the anxiety of rehearsals, but her size no longer bothered her. Opera singers were supposed to be big, and she was a real opera singer now. The dress was burgundy and dotted with sparkling beads, and Aunt Rose had also given her a fur stole to wear with it.

The tenor was standing by the bar, and as she passed, he said her name.

"What?" she replied, intentionally rude.

"You really did sing well today," he said. His face was red, and he held another beer as he swayed on his feet.

"You said that already." She turned to go.

"Hey," he said. "Don't be like that, okay?"

"Be like what?"

"Like you're mad at me."

"I'm not mad," Felicity said. "I just don't think we have much to say to one another." This man reminded her of Brian; not with his looks, for Brian was far more attractive, but with his indignant air. Like Brian, he would spend his life having things handed to him and still manage to portray himself as the aggrieved one.

"Your performance," he said. "I'm curious. Where did that come from? I mean, you're young, you haven't lived yet, you don't have children. So is your character, but you gave her so much wisdom and strength. It has to come from somewhere."

"I have a child," Felicity said, and it was the first time she had thought of Mara in days. As soon as she had stepped on the plane to Vancouver, a string loosened at the bottom of her heart, allowing it to float upwards. No more bottles, no more soiled diapers, no more quiet cries, all of it behind her. She would not look back.

"Oh," the tenor said. "You're married already?"

"No," Felicity said. "I'm not."

He took a step backwards. She had only invoked Mara to repel him, but now that it had worked, she felt the lash of rejection.

"Your people do like to do that, don't they?" the tenor said.

"Do what?"

"Have children without a man around."

"My daughter's father is white," said Felicity. Let the blame for bad behaviour be placed where it is deserved.

"Yes, but you are not," said the tenor.

As if she wasn't aware of that. Never for a second did anyone let her forget that she was not white. She looked around the party, at all the pale faces, all the pink hands gripping their glasses, the wispy white hair combed over peach domed heads, the blond hair contrasting with the black clothing most people wore. After the wandelprobe, when the cast rehearsed with the full set for the first time, the director had asked Felicity to stay after everyone else was dismissed. "Your skin," he said. "It looks washed-out on stage. It looks sickly." He turned to the lighting designer. "Can't you do something?"

Felicity looked down at her hand, bleached to a jaundiced shade in the intensity of the beam in which she stood.

"We're losing the shape of her face too," the lighting designer said. He had Felicity move in and out of the spotlight as he swore and conferred with the director and flashed blasts of different coloured lamps at her until her eyes and her head began to ache. "I'm going to have to take all the yellows out of the designs," he said. "Make a different plot for you."

The director asked accusingly, "How much overtime will that be?"

Felicity was tired, and hungry. She stood in a pool of brightness watching her hand change colour and feeling her forehead throb. She felt as exposed as when the head of wardrobe had not bothered to conceal her dismay at how much bigger Felicity was than Jane Masters, how the costumes would have to be let out, how many corsets and girdles would have to be purchased to try to press Felicity's flesh back into a girlish shape.

It should all have been humiliating. It was all humiliating. And yet, when the orchestra started to play, when the blend of strings, woodwinds, and brass rose up to the lip of the stage, when she felt herself breathing in tandem with the motions of the conductor, all of them — conductor, singers, and instruments — one symbiotic being, it raised a wave of emotion in Felicity so strong that for a moment, she could not move. She forgot the blocking she had paced into her muscle memory late at night in her hotel room. And then it all rushed back. She sang, she acted, she was Laurie, and the applause came and came and came. There was no other world for her, not one other thing that mattered. There was no race, no skin colour, no baby, no men, there had never been any love as great as the one created on the stage. There was no room for any other feeling.

This was the life Felicity wanted. She had to do this, again and again, or she did not want to exist. It was that simple. As she took her curtain call, she sent a wish out into the cheering crowd. *Please*, she thought, *give me more chances to do this. Let me do this for my whole life, this and nothing else.*

Doing this again meant not making enemies unnecessarily, so she smiled at the flushed-faced tenor while she tried to figure out a way to extricate herself from the conversation. It was the director who saved her. "Miss Alexander!" he swooped in. "That was a remarkable performance. Remarkable."

"Thank you." Felicity opened her eyes wide and cocked her head. "I loved working with you." *Hire me again*, she chanted to herself.

"I wonder, do you sing traditional repertoire as well?" the director asked. "Mozart, bel canto?"

"I do. I covered a lot of the standard repertoire at the Royal Opera House."

"The Royal Opera House!" The director put out his hand and touched her shoulder, just for a microsecond. A flash of energy. "I must have missed that you've worked there."

"I was a young artist," said Felicity.

"I see," said the director. "Now, I can't promise, but I believe that there's a small company in Toronto looking for someone for a concert version of *I Puritani.* I think you'd be perfect. I can put you in touch, if you'd like?"

Felicity had manifested her future, and now it was coming to pass. She placed her palm on the same arm with which the director had touched her. "I would like that," she said. "Very much."

CHAPTER 33.

Winnipeg, Manitoba, June 5, 1970

FELICITY WOULD HAVE liked to wear a big, puffy white wedding gown, like an operatic character would wear on her wedding day, but her mother vetoed the idea. "Your child is going to be present at the wedding," Mom said. "It wouldn't be right, Felicity. What would people say?" She looked to Aunt Rose for support, but Aunt Rose said, "Oh, I don't know, Dolores. Times are changing, isn't that what they say?"

Mom sucked her teeth impatiently. "You should be happy Anthony is willing to take you on. Choose a nice simple dress in a dark cream."

"I should be happy he's willing to take me on?" Felicity demanded. "Like I'm some reject?"

"Oh no, flower, that's not what she's saying," Aunt Rose hastened. "It's just that when you're a woman alone with a child, a lot of men aren't interested, and Anthony loves you enough to accept you and your child." She looked wistful. "I would have given my right arm for someone to marry me after I had Josiah."

"Brian might have married her," Mom said. "He probably still would, but she won't have him."

"He's married to Sheila, Mom."

Aunt Rose soothed them both. "She's following her heart. Brian wasn't the one, but Anthony is, isn't that right, flower?"

"At least she chose someone with a good job," Mom said.

"Anthony drives a taxi," said Felicity.

Mom pleated the beige fabric of a dress between her fingers. "It's good, honest, stable work. Which at least one of you needs to have. Goodness knows you don't."

Felicity drew herself up as if she were about to emit a piercing high note. "I got hired by the Calgary Philharmonic to sing Haydn's *Creation*. You should like that, Mom, it's about the Bible. And I'm doing *Messiah* this December in London, which is also about the Bible, and then I'm going to do Clara in *Porgy and Bess* there in the spring. That's a lot of work for someone only out of school two years."

"Do you think you should be travelling to all those different places once you're a married woman?"

"This is what I do, Mom. I'm a singer. I sing. I go where the work is."

Aunt Rose interjected. "And we're very proud of you, flower. Now what do you think of this pretty dress?" She handed over a beige lace creation with sequined flowers sewn into it.

Felicity said, "I guess it's fine. But this veil I like doesn't go with it."

"No," Mom said. "You are not wearing a veil. There are enough strange things happening with this wedding. Men being in the wedding party. I never heard of such a thing."

"Josiah and Jack are my best friends," Felicity said. "I can't do this without them."

Aunt Rose said, "I think it's nice."

Jack still came by the house to visit, but Mom didn't like that. "Jack," she had said a few months ago, "do you think it's wise for you to be spending so much time over here with Felicity when you're Abigail's beau, and Felicity is engaged?"

Jack had shrugged. "I'm Felicity's friend, Dolores, that's all." But Abby didn't like the visits either, and they tapered off, or became double dates with Anthony. However, one evening when

Abby was working the night shift, Felicity went over to Jack's apartment uninvited.

"Jack, do you think I'm doing the right thing, getting married?" she asked.

"Do you think you are?" he countered, putting his Bible aside and marking the page with a bookmark.

Felicity laughed. "It's still so weird to see you reading that thing."

"It's part of my Synoptic Gospels course. So, your thoughts on your engagement, Fizzy."

"Anthony's nice. I mean, really nice. He's always bringing me flowers, or chocolates, and he's really great with Mara."

"That's promising," said Jack. "Acts of love."

"Mom likes him, because he's part of the Grenadian League she started." When immigrants from the Caribbean began arriving in Winnipeg in a steady flow, Mom, as one who had arrived two decades earlier, coordinated the newer arrivals into an organization that assisted those who needed it and hosted events to preserve and share their cultural heritage. Anthony was one of the members and that was how he and Felicity had met.

Jack ushered her into the kitchen, placed a beer in front of her, and said, "What do you think the purpose of marriage is, Fizzy?"

Felicity took a swig. "Respectability."

"What do you mean by that?"

"Well, when a woman has a child out of wedlock, Jack, there are people who think she's a whore. Never mind that the father can go on and do what he wants. The scarlet letter is on the mother. I remember how people looked at me, when they figured out my mom was a slut and I was a bastard. And if it were just small-town idiots who thought that, I wouldn't much care. But I've seen the way artistic directors and stage directors look at me when they find out about Mara. Women always get asked 'Do you have kids?' 'Are you married?' With every person I talk to when I'm working, I have to decide whether to lie or tell the truth."

"I see."

"So if I marry Anthony, I'm a married woman with a child, and that sounds okay. That's respectable. My mom wants me to be respectable, even though she has the scarlet letter too. And Anthony can watch Mara when I work, instead of my mom. He drives a taxi, he can work when he wants. Maybe if things really take off for me, he can stay home with her. Why not? Women have done that for centuries."

"What does Anthony want?"

"Me, Jack. He wants me."

"Does he know about Claude?"

"Of course he doesn't. That's private. He knows I was seeing someone in London, but not who he is. Anthony is from Grenada, Jack. Claude is well-known in Grenada, and he's married now." Her heart twisted. "I can't mess things up for him."

Jack got up and came back with a second beer each. "Do you remember when you were with Brian in high school? And you used to tell me you loved him?"

"I was seventeen. What did I know about love?"

"You're not seventeen now. You know about love. Is this it?"

Felicity wanted to see him squirm with the same discomfort she was feeling. Then they could be allies. "Do you love Abby, Jack?"

Jack said, "We might need something stronger for that." He got up again and returned with two more beers and a bag of weed. As he rolled, he said, "I don't know where things are going with Abby yet, Felicity. She's a really interesting person to talk to. She's cute. She's funny. But I don't know if I'm the settling down type." He lit the joint and passed it to Felicity. "And I'm not sure you are either."

"Jack," Felicity said. She could feel herself being drawn to the energy that crackled between their bodies.

"We can't let it happen again, Fizzy. I told you it was the last time."

She inhaled.

Jack begged, "If we do, people will get hurt, Felicity."

She exhaled. She had already been hurt. Let others fend for themselves.

THE NIGHT BEFORE the wedding, the bridesmaids hosted a dinner for the wedding party and a few of Felicity's other friends. When Abby was in the bathroom, Jack leaned into Felicity.

"It's still not too late," he said. "You don't have to do this if you don't want."

"I know that."

"If it's really that important to you to be married —" Jack said, then stopped. She waited. He swallowed and looked around. "Maybe we should just do it."

"Do what?"

"Get married. And agree we can still each live our own lives, and no one is going to get upset about it."

Hope began beating its wings in her chest, but then she remembered. "What about Abby?"

"I haven't promised her anything yet."

"But she's my friend," said Felicity. "I've known her all my life." It was a test. Felicity would turn her back on Abby in a heartbeat, but she wanted to see what Jack would do.

"You're right," he said. "I've been drinking too much. I'm a selfish asshole, Fizzy. That was a disgusting thing to say. Forget I ever said it."

"Forget what?" asked Abby, appearing at Jack's side.

"He's just teasing me about stupid high school stuff," Felicity said. "I should get some sleep. I'll see you guys tomorrow."

She got dressed for the wedding at her mother's house, knowing it was the last day she would live there before moving to Anthony's apartment, and also knowing that she would be having sex with Anthony for the first time that night. Though neither of them was a virgin, Anthony thought that they should do things Biblically now that he had joined the church, and Felicity had agreed reluctantly.

When she presented herself, Aunt Rose's eyes filled with tears. "Oh flower, how beautiful you are!" she cried. "Dolores, look!"

"Yes, she is beautiful," Mom said. Her voice shook.

Felicity wasn't sure if she had heard right. "You mean that, Mom?"

"Of course I do. Now, don't let it go to your head."

The bridesmaids, Abby and Lena from church and Janet from high school, were full of praise as well, and Jack gave Felicity a little smile and a nod of approval. Josiah had not arrived, and Aunt Rose was fretting as his son Malcolm ran around the house and his daughter Olayinka screamed from where she lay in Mara's crib. Mara was quiet, looking around the room, sitting in her baby chair, dressed in a frilly satin dress that matched her blue eyes, the bridesmaids' dresses, and Jack's tie.

"Where could Josiah be? He knew the time he was supposed to be here," Aunt Rose said, over and over.

"I'm sure he'll come soon," Jack said. "I talked to him this morning."

A minute later, Felicity said, "I'm going out for some air," and stepped out into the yard. Shortly after that, Jack slid out. "What is it? Where is he?" she asked.

Jack's face was grim. "He's having a hard time, Fizzy."

"Why?" she asked, but she thought she knew.

"Because you're getting married."

"So he's not going to come?" She hugged herself. "He's my brother, Jack. I know our mothers always hoped we would marry, but we're too close. We have a stronger bond than any marriage."

"I'm sure he'll come." Jack lowered his voice, even though no one else was around. "He went to make a delivery, Fizz."

"Oh, shit. Where?"

"Not sure, but I got the impression it was somewhere rough," Jack said. Then he slammed his fist into his palm. "Fuck! I'm just saying the wrong thing all the time. Forget I said that, Fizzy, I don't really know."

"He shouldn't have dropped out of university, Jack. He was doing so well with football."

"Don't worry about him right now. This is your wedding day."

When Josiah did not arrive, the rest of the party decided to head to the church. "But Josiah's supposed to walk me down the aisle!" Felicity said.

"Jack can do it," Aunt Rose said. "Can't he, Abby?"

Josiah did arrive, however, panting and in disarray, five minutes before the ceremony was to start. "Sorry, Felicity," he said as he fell in beside her. "You look like an angel."

"I'm so glad you came, Jo," Felicity said. "I can barely breathe. I don't know if I can do this."

"Yes, you can," Josiah said. His pupils were dilated, and he was breathing hard. "If you only knew what I went through to be here for you. We are walking down that aisle right now, together." He swayed slightly, and Felicity grabbed his arm. "I'm not gonna let you down."

As Felicity began to walk down the aisle, the waves of an ocean of dread washed against her insides. But they subsided as she held Josiah up, leaning against him to make it look as if he were the one supporting her. Josiah, her brother. She kept her eyes fixed on him as they reached the altar. Even as Anthony stood with wide eyes taking in the sight of Felicity in her dress, Felicity looked at Josiah, making sure he stood tall and solid, making sure he didn't stumble.

AFTER THE SERVICE and dinner at Salvation Baptist, a limousine took Felicity and Anthony to the house he had rented for them, with Mara in tow. It was a small wooden bungalow with an impeccable lawn, Anthony's taxi parked in the driveway.

"Home sweet home," said Anthony. Felicity, still wearing her beige wedding dress, waited for him to carry her over the threshold, but he just said, "Well, come in, then."

Later, when Mara was asleep in her new bedroom, Felicity changed into the white satin negligee she had picked out for her first night with Anthony. She couldn't have a white wedding dress, but she was going to wear white now. She slid in behind Anthony as he sat on the couch watching TV. "Hi, handsome," she said. Her new husband did look nice with his shave and haircut, his skin as smooth as a stone worn by the sea. Felicity had married to please her mother and the people who ran opera companies, but there was no reason she couldn't enjoy the benefits of marriage too.

Anthony turned from the television to look at her. "Hello," he said, and looked back at the screen. A beer sat open beside him.

"Can I have some?" Without waiting for his answer, Felicity picked it up and took a swig.

Anthony frowned. "You drink beer?"

"Sometimes."

"In Grenada, the women drink shandy."

"Oh," Felicity said. "Well, I prefer beer." She went to the fridge, helped herself to her own bottle, and sat down next to him. "Cheers," she said, clinking her bottle against his. She took a sip and swallowed the disappointment that it was not Claude who was her husband. Claude would have taken one look at her in the white negligee and groaned quietly, then led her to the bedroom where he would have peeled it off her. But Anthony continued to stare at the TV. She reached out to stroke his neck. He jerked back, then relaxed against her hand.

"We should go to the bedroom, handsome," she said. Maybe he was nervous.

"You go. I'll come when the show's finished."

Felicity walked down the hall to the bedroom, digging her fingernails into her wrist to prevent any tears. She didn't want her new husband to see her with red swollen eyes and a blotchy face on their wedding night. There was no point thinking of Claude. Claude was married to Marlene. She had to make her marriage work. She sprayed perfume on and sat up in bed awaiting her husband. After half an hour, he had still not arrived. Felicity, worn out from the long day, began to feel sleepy.

She awoke to see Anthony in bed beside her, snoring. She slipped out of bed and checked on Mara, who was sleeping soundly. She went to the bathroom, brushed her teeth, tidied her hair, sprayed on more perfume, and slipped back into bed. She nudged Anthony awake. He started when he saw her, then his features settled into a smile. "My beautiful wife," he said. Felicity's heart lifted on springs of hope.

"You didn't come last night, Anthony," she said, shaping her lips into a pout.

"I did, but you were sleeping, and I was tired too. I'm sorry."

"We can make up for lost time now." She began sliding out of the negligee. Anthony watched for a moment, and then wriggled his pyjama bottoms off and slid on top of her. Felicity closed her eyes. She could almost believe it was Claude's weight she lay under. After a moment, Anthony moaned, "Shrimps, man."

Felicity looked down. His soft penis wagged at her, folded in half, flapping like a leaf in the wind.

"Maybe I'm still tired."

"It's all right," Felicity said, trying to control her rising panic. "Leave it to me."

She slid down the bed and rolled the flaccid organ between her palms before putting it to her lips.

"What are you doing?" Anthony asked.

"Pleasuring you, darling."

"Stop it!" he said. "That is what a whore does! You are my wife!"

"But —" As Felicity looked up at him, Mara began to cry next door.

"I'll go see," Anthony said. He stood up, pulled his pyjama bottoms back on, and returned a moment later with Mara clinging to his neck. He placed her next to Felicity in the bed. "I'll get her a bottle."

CHAPTER 34.

London, England, March 20, 1971

GEORGE GERSHWIN HAD specified that no company could perform his opera *Porgy and Bess* unless it had an all-Black cast, and Felicity sent a message of gratitude to his spirit. She had imagined this for months — how it would feel to laugh and joke with a large group of Black people, in a way she hadn't since she and Claude had parted. In this show, she wouldn't have to worry about the people working in lighting or hair and makeup being stymied by her skin tone.

As always before the first rehearsal of a show, Felicity twanged with nerves, a string tuned too tight. She walked through the car park of Sadler's Wells in a light rain, thinking of Claude. She had traced this same path with him when she had brought him to a performance of *Madama Butterfly*, sung in English. She put her hand in her pocket and felt her wedding ring rub against the fabric. She stopped to pull it off and tuck it away in a pocket of her purse. Anthony had been angry with her before she left, and they had argued. She couldn't remember why, but the bad feelings lingered, and she didn't want the ring dredging up bitterness while she was working.

She had thought she was early, but most of the cast were already in the rehearsal room, giggling and shrieking like old friends. The room went briefly silent as Felicity came through the door, then everyone returned to their conversations. It was like being a newcomer walking for the first time down Catfish Row, the fictional slum where the opera took place.

Felicity had a stage agent now, and this was the first gig he, Robin, had booked for her. It was thrilling, the idea of having someone take away the stress of walking into casting calls cold, of seeking out artistic directors and conductors at parties and simpering insincere praise, of combing through audition notices in the newsletter periodically sent to her home. To attract the interest of a talent agency, she had had to prove herself, mailing out copy after copy of her resume and headshot and receiving a stack of rejection letters in reply, until finally, Jennings Artists Management in Toronto had taken a chance on her.

In addition to booking work for her, Robin dispensed unsolicited career advice. "Clara in *Porgy* is for a young, pretty singer," he said. "You come on near the beginning, sing 'Summertime' and steal everyone's heart, and then they love you for the rest of the show. If you do it justice. You have the best tune, but it has to be just right — wistful, soulful, a bit jazzy. Everyone has performed or recorded it. You sing a good Clara in Europe, it opens ingenue roles for you in a lot of places." The show was rehearsing and opening in London, but was then touring to Bonn, Munich, Vienna, Zurich, Brussels, and Amsterdam.

Most of the other singers seemed to know each other, and, as Robin had said they would be, they were older than Felicity, and mostly from the United States. He had also warned her that she would have the lightest voice. "In rehearsal, they'll all be competing with each other. You'll hear this great honking sound and think you won't measure up. Don't try to. You're there for sweetness. Innocence. Purity." No one said anything to Felicity when she found a chair, sat, and began looking through her score, although she could sing her role "upside down, sideways, or asleep," as Philip put it. The room didn't hush again until the conductor entered. He was a tall white man, with long arms and a long nose and a long face. He rapped his baton gently against his music stand in the universal rehearsal room signal to shut up. Everyone sat up straight and stopped speaking. Felicity felt like she was back in school.

"Good afternoon, all," he said. "I am Hans Vogel, your conductor. Obviously." He had a light German accent and a melodious tenor voice. *Sexy,* Felicity thought, and then, *Where did that come from?* Claude would be appalled. In a room of Black people, she was drawn to the only white man, one who Claude would say had just breezed in like a colonial ruler.

"Let us go around the room and introduce ourselves and what part we are singing in the opera and where we are from," the conductor continued. "I am from Bonn, but I conduct in Vienna and Lucerne." He pointed his baton at the singer furthest to his left. "You. Next."

"Robert Bradley. From Memphis, Tennessee, based in New York now. I'm singing Crown."

Other introductions followed, with singers from Mississippi, Alabama, Georgia, Chicago, Detroit, working in New York or Boston or San Francisco. The singer playing Jake, Felicity's husband in the show, was Wilson Walker, from Chattahoochee, Florida, based in Philadelphia. Felicity was glad to see that he was reasonably attractive. She had not realized there were so many Black opera singers, and she wondered why she had never performed with any until now.

When Hans pointed at Felicity, she said, "Felicity Alexander, from Winnipeg, Canada. I'm singing Clara." She hoped her voice didn't shake too much.

"Canada!" said Hans. "Nice to have some variety. Canada makes beautiful people, I see." He had not commented on anyone else's introduction, and the woman sitting next to Felicity narrowed her eyes at her and let out a hissing breath.

"Carolyn Grant," she said. "I'm from Gary, Indiana, based in New York, and I'm singing Annie."

The pianist, also white, entered the room, and they began the first sing-through. The sound in the room was so live that the bigger voices bounced off the walls, magnified by the extreme resonance. Felicity remembered her agent's advice, and also Philip's coaching when he had given her "Summertime," correctly assuming that she would sing it someday. She stood and let her voice fall into the swooping, swaying lines of the aria. "Summertime" was a lullaby, and she knew that onstage, she would be given a baby doll to hold. She thought of her real baby, a toddler now, at home with her husband and her mother, but she had never sung "Summertime" to Mara, and she couldn't imagine doing so. Mara was Brian's blue-eyed child. She didn't look like any baby would look that came from two inhabitants of Catfish Row.

Felicity could hear the smallness of her voice, even with the additional sound of the room. But she listened for the ring at the core of her sound, for the piercing clarity a lighter voice possessed, which enabled it to travel as well as the larger voices in the room. When she reached the final slide from high B, she took her time, holding the note before letting it tumble, slowly at first, then faster. When she finished, the silence in the room buzzed. Then Wilson, her show husband, clapped slowly, and others joined in. Carolyn didn't; she tightened her lips.

Hans laid his baton on the stand. "Well," he said, "Canada makes beautiful singers, too."

For the rest of the run-through, Carolyn kept her body turned away from Felicity. Felicity thought it was just jealousy. She had a bigger part than Carolyn, with a show-stealing aria. As a mezzo, Carolyn was doomed to a life of playing second-fiddle to young ingenue sopranos. It was only natural she would be resentful. But at the end of the rehearsal, Hans said, "It is my pleasure to go out on tour with a cast of Negro — Black — singers."

"Most of us are Black," Carolyn said under her breath. Felicity registered that it was *this* again. Whatever other reasons Carolyn had to resent Felicity, her skin colour seemed to be the biggest one. She searched for a comeback; but, as always, comments about her complexion flustered her and made her think of her father, filling her with sadness and shame instead of fight and fire.

She noticed Hans watching her. After rehearsal, she lingered, taking her time putting her music into her bag and doing up her raincoat until they were the last two in the room.

"Miss Alexander," said Hans.

"Maestro."

"That performance. It was incredible."

"Thank you, Maestro." She knew he didn't want to talk about her singing.

"Did you have plans for supper? Are you joining your castmates?"

"They didn't invite me."

"Oh, my dear," Hans said, with real compassion in his voice. "You are young and beautiful and talented. They don't trust you. Not yet, but they will come to respect you."

Felicity looked at the floor. She couldn't explain to this white man that it was more than that.

"Come now," Hans said. "This won't do. You and I will dine together, *ja*?"

She had thought she might call Lindsay, but that could wait. They had spent most of her free time together when she was in London for *Messiah;* he wouldn't begrudge her one night with Hans.

IT WAS MORE than one night. By the time the tour reached the continent, Felicity was in Hans's hotel room, or he in hers, almost every night. As when she was with Lindsay, she had no qualms about Anthony at home. They had already agreed that Anthony would provide her with the respectability she needed, and Felicity would provide him with Canadian citizenship and the means to bring his family to Canada. Anthony talked about having a child together, a prospect which Felicity dreaded, but she permitted his often-ineffectual lovemaking while continuing to take the pill without his knowledge.

Hans was married too. He had told her so, on the first night. "I have a wife," he said. "In Lucerne. That shouldn't matter to you, except that, you understand, when the tour is over, this ends." She had stamped her assent onto his lips with hers, but she had not mentioned Anthony, or Mara.

Lindsay was also married. His parents and his wife's had wanted the union for business reasons. He was miserable. *All marriages were unhappy*, Felicity thought, and she was thankful for music, which always brought her joy. The morning after *Porgy* opened, as she lay in bed with Lindsay, he opened the morning newspaper. "Felicity," he said, "you are a triumph. It says here that your rendition of 'Summertime' stole the show."

Felicity yawned and stretched. "It always does."

"It says so, but it also says this. 'Even making allowances for the show-stopping nature of this gem of an aria, Miss Alexander's performance was a force of nature, both with respect to the ease and colour abundant in her singularly beautiful voice, and in her remarkable stage presence."

Felicity batted his hand away. "Philip said not to read reviews during a run."

"Why ever not?" Lindsay pushed his reading glasses down the bridge of his nose.

"Because I'll become complacent and stop listening to my inner critic, which is the most important one."

Despite Philip's words, Felicity was delighted to hear what Lindsay had shared. She was tempted by every newsstand she passed, and she was glad when they left England and she couldn't understand the headlines anymore.

In Vienna, Hans took her to a skeet shooting range and stood behind her as she held a gun for the first time. As he showed her the scope, the trigger, the barrel, electricity travelled between their bodies and she pressed closer to him. He pointed to the target. "In the middle, there," he said. "Imagine the face of someone you hate. And put a bullet right between their eyes."

That was easy. Felicity pictured her father at first, but she didn't know what he had looked like. As he was already dead, she replaced him with Brian. And Hans himself, because Felicity was spending so much time with him. She had drawn a line between herself and her castmates by running off with this white man, but being with him was better than being alone. And she hoped he might hire her to work with one of his companies in the future. Of course, despite their efforts to be discreet, the other singers had taken note of their liaison. It further emphasized her alienation.

"Did you sleep well, Felicity?" Carolyn asked her every morning, to snickers from the rest of the cast.

Carolyn talked often about how much she missed her boyfriend, the first violinist with the Cleveland Orchestra, and the first and only Black player there. Felicity hadn't told her that her agent had got her a gig singing "Knoxville: Summer of 1915," Samuel Barber's concert scene for voice and orchestra, in July at the Blossom Festival, the Cleveland Orchestra's summer home. She imagined Carolyn's face on the target along with Brian's.

Her first bullet landed dead centre. She followed it up with several more shots, reloaded, and hit the same spot with another fast round.

Hans walked over to her from the next target where he had placed a few of his own shots. "Enough, enough," he said. He loosened her fingers from the gun. "You will destroy the target."

Felicity breathed hard, remembering Claude saying "Fuck white men. Fuck them." Where was Claude now? What was he doing?

"My dear," said Hans. He put his arm around her. It was warm and solid, and she leaned against him, letting her breathing slow. "I think that is enough for today," he said. "I didn't take you for such a — what do they say? — crack shot. Let's go back to the hotel."

In his bed, he ran his finger along Felicity's jaw. "Are you back to yourself now?" Before she could answer, he asked another question. "Was it your husband you were shooting at?"

She sat up so fast, she cracked her skull against the headboard.

"Felicity, Felicity." Hans's blurred face hovered above hers. "Lie down. Let me fetch some ice." He felt inside her hair and held it to the spot where her head was tender. "Did you think I didn't know?"

"I never told you about him," Felicity said.

"You didn't have to. I can tell someone is making you upset, and who else but a husband?"

It was enough to loosen her tears. Hans held her and passed her tissues. After a few minutes, he withdrew one arm to look at his watch. "We have a wandelprobe in the theatre."

"Shit. Shit." Felicity looked across the room into his mirror. Her face was swollen from crying. "I look like crap."

"It can't be helped," said Hans.

She tried to avoid the rest of the cast, but as they stood backstage, listening to the stage manager instruct them on the theatre's quirks, Wilson Walker, Felicity's stage husband, tapped her on the shoulder. "Are you okay?" he asked. "Did he do something to you?"

"Of course not," Felicity said. "I'm having a bad day. Homesick."

It was a lie, but it caused sympathy to bloom in Wilson's eyes. "I'm sorry," he said. "I wish I could tell you it gets easier, but it never really does."

Their interactions on stage were a lot more tender than they had ever been. After rehearsal, Wilson asked her if she wanted to get a coffee. "Or maybe you want to try a Wiener *schokolade*? Vienna is famous for its hot chocolate."

She would see Hans later, she reasoned. He would want her to bond with Wilson.

They walked along the Ringstrasse, the famous road encircling the Palace of Justice, the Parliament Building, and the Vienna State Opera, looking for a café. The air carried a strong, sweet scent. "The lilacs are in bloom," Wilson said. "Chestnuts, too."

"You've been here before?"

"I studied here," Wilson said.

The hot chocolate was like nothing Felicity had ever tasted. It was so thick, so strong that she used the spoon provided, itself dipped in a chocolate coating, to scoop it from the glass.

Across the table, Wilson said, "I don't want you to get the wrong idea, you know. I have a wife and I'm happily married."

Felicity felt a faint disappointment.

"I've been married twice," Wilson said. "I met my first wife here. She's Viennese. White," he added. "We were happy, but when we went back to Florida, it didn't work. Interracial marriage being illegal at the time and all. But then I met my second wife. She's Black, like me. It felt like coming home. We have a daughter. I can't help but wonder what it would have been like if Annika and I had had a child. They would have looked like you. I wonder how the world would see them. How they would fit into it."

Felicity licked the back of her spoon. "I fit into the world just fine," she said. "I know who I am. It's not my fault if other people have forgotten who they are." On a good day, this was true. She stirred her hot chocolate. "What's it like, being back here? Does it make you think of your first wife?" She was thinking of London, and Claude, hoping that Wilson could show the way through her labyrinth of grief.

Wilson picked up his mug. "My wife is the only one for me now," he said. He inhaled. "But Vienna. It smells like lilacs — and regret."

WHEN FELICITY KNOCKED on Hans's door, he opened it only a crack. "I have work to do," he said. His face was grey with stubble.

"I was just coming in to say good night," said Felicity.

"Well, now you have said it. Good night." He closed the door.

He's jealous, thought Felicity. He thinks something happened with Wilson. His rejection tormented her as she tried to sleep, alone for the first time since the tour began. In the morning, she went back down the hall to his room and knocked again. He didn't answer, and she banged harder. The opposite door, Carolyn's, flew open. "Will you stop making that noise!" said Carolyn.

Hans opened his own door. "Come in," he said.

His blinds were open, and the early morning sun blessed the rooftops of the Innere Stadt, the ancient heart of Vienna, as Wilson had explained it. A newspaper was open on the table.

"Why are you mad at me?" Felicity asked. She could feel her tears gathering like raindrops in a storm cloud.

He sat down at the table and lifted his coffee cup. "I am not angry," he said. "It's nothing to me who you spend your time with."

"It's not like that," Felicity said. "Wilson is married."

"So are you. So am I."

"But he actually loves his wife," Felicity said, and then the tears rolled down her face faster than she could dash them away. She had thought all marriages were doomed, but Wilson had a good one. She envied him.

"Oh, not more tears," said Hans. "I'm so tired of them."

She would go then. She turned and headed for the door. Her toe caught a corner of the rug and she went down, hard. She yelped as her cheekbone hit the floor and began stinging. Hans leaped over the couch to get to her.

"*Scheisse*," he swore. He knelt beside Felicity and lifted her head into his lap. She sobbed into his crotch. Her face throbbed.

"You're okay," Hans said. "You're okay." He patted her back, rubbed circles on it, and she began to reassert control over her emotions. "Maybe this is the wrong time to tell you,"he said. "But there's an article in the Viennese newspaper, about the performance tonight. It says that you are the singer to watch tonight, out of all the cast. The star of the show, the most beautiful voice." The surprise of it stopped her tears. He turned her over to look at her face. Before she could tell him she didn't want to read the papers, he said, "Good God. We need more ice." Felicity's face felt stiff. Hans scooped her into his arms and staggered with her to the bed. She wanted to look in the mirror, but he wouldn't let her. He brought her ice cubes wrapped in a towel and pressed them to her injury. He lay down beside her. "I'm sorry," he said. "I assumed. Now you have hurt yourself again, because of me."

Felicity tried for more sympathy. "I was up all night, wondering what I did wrong."

"Nothing," Hans said. "You did nothing wrong. But you were up all night? There is a dress rehearsal this evening. You must get some rest now."

There was another knock on the door. "*Scheisse*," Hans said again. He spoke in German to whoever it was, and then he said to Felicity, "I must go to the lobby for a phone call. Stay and rest."

It was his wife, Felicity thought. He would return guilt-ridden and kick her out again. She should go. But the bed was irresistibly warm, and she had begun drifting to sleep when Hans came back and got under the duvet with her. "You won't believe this," Hans said. "You know I told you I'm conducting *Elisir* in Lucerne after the tour? Well, my Adina has broken both legs in a car accident and will have to withdraw."

Felicity's cheekbone pulsed. "I've learned Adina."

Hans lifted her hair from the pillow and twisted a chunk of it around his finger. "You would be lovely in the role. I will telephone them, later. Now, rest. You'll have to go to the theatre early so makeup can fix this." He touched her cheekbone with one finger and she yelped. "There I go again," he said. "Hurting you."

THEY LEFT VIENNA early by minibus. Felicity plastered the bruise on her face, still a deep purple, with her own makeup, and hoped her hair would cover it. She planned to sit by herself on the bus, but Wilson squeezed into the seat next to her. "You're not fooling me, covering that bruise with makeup," he said.

"He didn't hit me. I fell." Felicity fiddled with the buttons on her raincoat. Hans climbed up and sat with the rehearsal pianist. She looked away from the smile he cast in her direction.

"Everyone says that."

"No, really. It's true."

Carolyn got on the bus and looked around for somewhere to sit. There was nowhere left except the seat in front of Felicity; she made a show of rolling her eyes before stomping down the aisle.

"You're getting great reviews," Wilson said to Felicity. "Can you read German?"

"I don't read reviews during a run," Felicity said. "My old teacher told me not to."

"The Viennese press adored you," Wilson said.

"Don't tell me."

Carolyn turned around. "The princess doesn't need you adding to her admirers, Wilson." The sun caught the creases around her eyes and mouth. She looked tired. Her straightened hair, pulled into a hasty ponytail, was dry and brittle.

Felicity looked out the window. A café owner was setting up tables and chairs. A man rode by on a bicycle with a front basket stuffed with flowers.

"Are you too good to talk to me, princess?" Carolyn taunted.

"Carolyn," said Wilson.

"What, Wilson? Don't tell me it doesn't bother you. Because it bothers the hell out of me."

It would end faster if Carolyn said what she needed to say.

"What bothers you?" Felicity asked.

"I'm forty-five," Carolyn said. "I've been at this probably longer than you've been alive. I've performed at regional houses and small theatres all over America; I've sung at companies in Europe. No one has ever said that I have "*eine Stimme, die so schön ist, dass sie Tränen in die Augen treibt.*"

Felicity tried to figure out what Carolyn had said. She had caught the word *Augen* — eyes.

"You see? So ignorant, you don't even know," said Carolyn. "The rest of us worked at our languages."

"A voice that is so beautiful it brings tears to the eyes," Wilson translated.

Felicity knew she should keep her tongue curled over the words that were begging for release. "Maybe you should sing better, then."

Carolyn spoke to Wilson over Felicity's head. "Listen to this infant. Sie hat keinen Respekt."

"When you show me something worth respecting, I will." Felicity was thrilled to hear what the journalist had written, realizing why Philip had said to ignore reviews during a run. She had thought of it as a quirk that made her look artistic, but in fact it had a very real benefit. Every time she went on stage, Felicity took a moment to empty her mind. When she sang tomorrow night, she would forget everything else, she would erase this upsetting conversation, and she would make herself small. She would create space for the music to fill, for the notes she had practiced so intensely to reach the audience as if it was her first time singing them. Always new, always fresh, not influenced by anything that had gone before. She could only bring tears to the audience's eyes if she approached them from a place of humility.

"I was singing before Civil Rights," said Carolyn. "I grew up in the Deep South. My father was a sharecropper. I learned to perform in the church. There was no chance of an education for me. I learned languages by studying dictionaries, going to libraries, and reading newspapers, begging native speakers to talk to me. I had to do everything the hard way."

"I thought you said you're from Indiana," said Felicity.

"We moved up there, so I could have a voice teacher. My mother and I cleaned houses and scrubbed toilets to pay for those lessons."

"My mother sacrificed for me too," said Felicity.

"I'm sure she did." Carolyn dipped her head in acknowledgement. "But you don't look like me, and the world you're starting in isn't the world I started in."

"So you're mad because of things I can't control?" Wilson put a hand on Felicity's knee. She pushed it off.

"I'm mad because you have no gratitude. No modesty. Running around with the conductor, acting like you're white."

"Oh, that's what your problem is?" Felicity said, raising her voice for the whole bus to hear. Claude would have approved of Carolyn's speech. He would have urged Felicity to consider the historical context and her place in it, to show understanding and tolerance to Carolyn. But Claude was not here, and he never would be again. Felicity played sweet little ingenues on stage, but she did not have to be one in real life. She had already been marked, judged, and proclaimed guilty, and she might as well embrace who she really was. "You think I only like white men?' she said. "Don't worry, Carolyn, I'm integrated. I'm singing at the Blossom Festival this summer, and I'll be sure to find the only Black violin player and fuck him hard."

CHAPTER 35.

Winnipeg, Manitoba, August 13, 1971

FELICITY WAS AWAKENED by the doorbell. She had fallen asleep on the couch with the score of *Die Fledermaus*. Looking at her watch, she saw it was after one thirty in the morning. She supposed it must be Anthony, having forgotten his key. She had thought he would at least stay out working until the bars let out at two. Well, he would have to wait while she used the bathroom. As she was washing her hands, it rang again. Irritated now, she stomped down the hall and yanked open the door to see two police officers. She knew what was going to happen when they asked, "Are you Mrs. Felix?"

"I'm Felicity Alexander."

"But your husband is Anthony Felix?"

"Yes, he is."

"May we come in?" She stepped aside and the police officers entered and seated themselves on the couch. "Ma'am," one officer began, "we know this will come as a terrible shock. Your husband's taxi was hit on the driver's side. Your husband had the right of way. The other car ran a stop sign. We believe the other driver was intoxicated. We have located him, and he is in custody. Your husband was rushed to hospital, but he sustained massive injuries and couldn't be saved. He passed away less than an hour ago. He had his wallet in his pocket. We were able to have his identity confirmed by his colleague who happened to be nearby."

Felicity drew a deep breath. "You're saying my husband is dead?"

"Yes, ma'am."

She stood up. "Thank you very much for telling me. Have a good night."

"Are you sure you're all right, ma'am? Are you here alone?"

"My daughter is upstairs."

"How old is your daughter?"

"She's almost two."

"I don't think you should be alone," the officer said.

"I'm fine," Felicity said. "I'll call my mother in the morning."

As they vacillated, the radio in their car, parked in front of the house, crackled with a message, "Ten four in progress. Units requested." They looked at Felicity, unsure what to do.

One of them said, "Well, good night, ma'am. Sorry for your loss."

Felicity returned to the couch. She was no longer sleepy. Deciding that she might as well get some work done, she picked up her score. She studied until the score fell from her drooping hand for the second time and awoke to the sound of the telephone. It was Anthony, she thought. He sometimes called when he woke from sleeping by the side of the road in his cab. Then she remembered Anthony was dead. "Felicity!" Mom shouted down the phone. "I made a pot of oil down for Anthony and he hasn't picked it up!" She spoke as if this were an emergency. Felicity kept her own voice even and calm. "Mom, Anthony's dead."

"What? Don't be silly, Felicity. That's not funny."

"No, really, he is. The police came to see me last night. A drunk driver hit his taxi."

"Lord Jesus! You're serious, Felicity?" Mom's voice rose. "The police came last night, and you're just telling me now, when I called you? Have you done anything?"

"I just woke up," Felicity said. "What is there to do? He's dead."

"I'm coming over now." Mom slammed down the phone.

When Mom entered the house, her eyes were snapping. "There's so much that has to be done when someone dies, Felicity. How could you be sitting there lazing around? You need to phone his parents, phone the pastor. Where's the body? You have to go and see it. Someone has to wash it."

Mara toddled up to Dolores. "G'amma," she said, holding out her arms. Mom picked her up and ruffled her soft blond hair.

"Hello, my darling," she said. "Felicity! Put that stupid music down and make yourself useful. Call Anthony's family."

Felicity picked up the phone, feeling dread coalesce in her stomach as she flicked through her address book for the nursing station's phone number.

"Has Mara had breakfast yet?" asked her mother. Her voice sounded like an exceptionally irritating mosquito.

"Not yet."

"Not yet? It's almost ten o'clock."

Felicity turned her back.

"Come on, darling," Mom said to Mara. "Let's see what we can make you. Do you want oatmeal and fruit?"

"Yeth," said Mara. They disappeared into the kitchen.

"Felicity, is this all the fruit you have? These canned peaches? You didn't buy anything fresh?" Mom called.

"Whatever's there is what there is," Felicity called back, then muttered "fuck off" under her breath. Reluctantly, she let go of the vision in her brain of *Die Fledermaus*, where she twirled across the stage in a beautiful gown, a champagne glass in her hand. She would rather immerse herself in that world than this one. She did not want the miserable task of telling a mother her son had died. She dialled the operator, who connected her to the nursing station, and the phone rang so many times that she was about to hang up.

A distorted voice said, "Good morning, Perdmontemps nursing station."

The line crackled. "Hello," Felicity said.

"Can't hear you!"

"Hello!" she bellowed. "Can I please talk to Joan Felix?"

"Who?"

"*JOAN FELIX.*"

"Oh, is you. The light-skinned one from foreign," the voice said. Then it perked up. "You need any nurses there in Canada? You think I could —"

"It's an emergency," Felicity cut in.

"All right, all right. We send someone to get her. Phone back in ten."

Mom returned, plopped Mara in her high chair, and brandished a spoon. "She can feed herself," Felicity said.

"Is this milk still good, Felicity?"

Felicity wanted to scream. The date on the milk, the fruit she bought, the timing of breakfast. None of it mattered. "I don't know."

"It expired yesterday."

"I'm sure it's fine." She watched the second hand tick by on her watch. She gave three extra minutes before calling again. The same woman answered.

"Is Joan Felix there?" Felicity asked again.

"Well, hello to you too. People in foreign. Too sociable to say hello."

"I need to talk to Joan Felix. It's urgent."

"What did you say?"

"*JOAN FELIX.*"

"All right, all right. I heard you. She just walking up the road now. I see her."

An awkward silence sparked between them, there were some muffled voices she couldn't hear, and then, "This is Mrs. Felix."

"Um, this is Felicity."

"Oh, you." Joan sniffed. "Why you calling, rushing me out me house? Where my son?"

Felicity said, "I'm sorry, but he's dead." The line arced with static.

"What's that? Speak up."

"I'm sorry, he's dead."

"What?"

"HE'S DEAD."

"Dead? Oh, Lord. Oh, shrimps. Oh, no. No, no, no ..." Felicity heard a thud and loud wailing. Then the nurse she had spoken to previously picked up the phone.

"Why you go and give her shock like that? Why not tell me first? You beh-beh or what?" It was hard to hear anything else over Joan's loud, high sobbing. The nurse raised her voice and said, "She wants you to send the body home."

Felicity listened to the wailing a minute more, then shouted "Bad connection! Sorry!" and hung up.

"So," called Mom from the kitchen. "What did she have to say?"

"She wants me to bring the body home."

"Yes, that is your duty."

ONE WEEK LATER, Felicity left Mara with her mother and went to Grenada. Anthony's parents allowed her to stay in their home, but they made their dislike plain. The funeral was as dreary as she had feared. The next day, as his family members sat in the living room drinking themselves into yet another stupor, Felicity slipped out and caught the bus into St. George's. She walked along the Carenage, the seawall, admiring the beauty of the Grenadian capital, with its pink, green, and orange houses rising from the hills ringing the harbour. She didn't notice the two people coming towards her until one of them said, "Felicity? Felicity Alexander?" He had a British accent. Something about it plucked at Felicity's heart. She looked up. Will, his eyes shielded by sunglasses with round lenses, stood in front of a towering white cruise ship, beside an older man in plaid Bermuda shorts.

Will turned to the man. "This is the woman from college I was telling you about, the singer with Grenadian heritage." He turned back to Felicity. "Felicity, come and meet Donald."

"I've heard so much about you," Donald said, grasping her hand.

Felicity looked intently at Will. The sun was blazing behind him.

"Oh, for crying out loud, Felicity," Will said. "It was a little spat. *Ad astra per aspera* and all that. For our little philistine here, that means through adversity to the stars." He cleared his throat. "All right, I admit it, I was awfully annoyed for a while. But then I got hired as a rehearsal pianist at the Royal Opera House and I said, brilliant, I'm going to be working with this girl, so may as well make peace with her. I wasn't expecting to get there and find you gone. So tell me, where did you go? Are you based in New York? I know you don't live here. I saw your *Messiah* in London, hung around the stage door to try to catch you, but you were otherwise occupied." Felicity remembered she had left after each performance with Lindsay. "You sounded glorious, by the way." Will took a breath. "Are you here with Claude, or is that over?"

Felicity said, "It's a long story, Will."

Will looked up at the cruise ship. "We've all day in port," he said. "Shall we find a place to sit down, and you can tell me this long story?"

They found a restaurant that overlooked the water. As they sipped rum cocktails, Felicity told Will the tale of her reunion with Brian, her pregnancy with Mara, her breakup with Claude, the arrival of her mother, her marriage to Anthony, and now his death. She found she could talk to him just the way she had in college. The way she still talked to Jack and Josiah.

"Hang on," Will said. "Are you telling me that you are a mother, and you're based in Winnipeg?"

"How delightful," Donald hooted.

"And what about Claude?" asked Will. "Are you going to see him while you're here?"

Felicity took a swig of her drink. "I was thinking of it." The casual way she said it concealed the fact that, since Anthony's death, the possibility had consumed her thoughts. She had sat through her husband's funeral thinking only of seeing Claude.

"But you must!" Will said. He turned to Donald. "Those two were so frightfully in love, you wouldn't believe." Felicity felt a veil of tears form over her vision. "Oh, now she's crying," Will teased, and Felicity lowered her head.

"Don't, Will," said Donald.

Will said, "Go and see him, Felicity. Just go."

"He's married now," Felicity said, wiping her eyes. "To Marlene. His girlfriend before me."

"You mean the one who took a year to shag him and then almost died of the shame?" Will said. "You see, I'm a good listener, Donald."

After Will and Donald left on an island-wide taxi tour, Felicity walked back to the Carenage. The thought thudded around in her brain: if she and Will could reconcile, why not she and Claude?

She called Claude's law office from one of the few public phones in town. She recognized Alison's voice when she answered, and, deepening her voice, Felicity asked for Claude. When he came to the phone, the sound of his greeting almost undid her, but she managed to say, "Claude, it's Felicity. I'm in Grenada."

"What?" She heard the phone clatter to the floor. A moment later, he whispered, "Where are you?"

"Right now? I'm at the Carenage, beside a fruit stand. Frank's Fresh Fruit."

"You're just around the corner," Claude said. "I'm coming there, all right? Alison," she heard him call, "I have to go out to meet a client."

She strained for the first sight of him, and then there he was, striding down the hill in a dark suit and tie. When he saw her, he ran across the street, glancing left and right, and then stopped in front of her. "Not here," he said. "If I give you an address, can you meet me there in two hours?"

She drank him in. He was every bit as handsome as she remembered. More. Being in Grenada had relaxed and elongated him. He was the Claude of her dreams.

"I'll get a car," he said. "We'll go up north. Meet me at this shop, here" — he pulled a notebook from his pocket and wrote directions. He beamed. "Bon jay, Cinnamon. I always hoped you'd come back."

CHAPTER 36.

Sauteurs, Grenada, August 27, 1971

CLAUDE WAS LATE. Felicity was almost ready to give up and go back to Anthony's family home when a horn beeped, and Claude pulled up in an old brown Bel Air.

They drove for a minute before he asked, "What are you doing in Grenada?" She told him the reason for her visit.

"You married a Grenadian." Claude's smile was as broad as she had ever seen it.

"I did." She stuck her hand out of the car to feel the warmth of the afternoon sun.

"I've missed you, Cinnamon," Claude said.

"I miss you all the time," Felicity said. "I only married him because I had to."

"You didn't marry the baby's father."

"Why would I? I hate him. I told you. He forced me."

"You did tell me that," Claude said. "I didn't listen." He put his hand on Felicity's knee. She noticed the hollows in his cheeks, and said, "Aren't things going well with Marlene?"

Claude sighed and said, "Not particularly, no. I had hoped she would get pregnant quickly, but it seems we'll have to be patient. She's very intense. She —"

"She still doesn't like sex."

"Only for getting pregnant."

"I see," said Felicity. She rejoiced. She wanted to whoop her praises to the sky. She reached over and cupped the front of Claude's pants in her hand. His eyes seemed fractured by the sun.

"All right, all right." He pulled the car over to the side of the road, under the overhang of a large banana tree, and started to undo his fly. Then he looked at Felicity. "What about you? I don't want any accidents."

Felicity said, "I'm on the pill, Claude." Sexless as her marriage was, she had continued to take it to alleviate her cyclic discomforts. She didn't want to mention the liaisons with Lindsay and Hans.

"Weren't you on the pill before?"

"I was, but I mixed up the days and times when I was travelling. I'm far more careful now."

"All right," Claude said. "If you're sure."

"I don't want another child. I didn't want this one. Labour was awful. I felt like I was being ripped apart. I work a lot. The last thing I need is another baby messing things up."

Claude pulled her close, began kissing her neck, while undoing the zipper on her dress. They made love under the banana tree, and farther up the road, and when they got to Sauteurs, one of the northernmost points of the island. "We've been doing a lot of organization for the election," Claude said. "A lot of people know me, but we haven't done Sauteurs yet, so I'm a little less known here. Still have to be careful. It's a small island." He drove her back to Perdmontemps and dropped her at the bottom of the hill. She climbed up alone to retrieve her suitcases from Anthony's family home. Her time with Anthony was over; it was time to be with Claude.

Abel, Anthony's brother, confronted her as soon as she stepped inside the door. "Where were you?" Of all of Anthony's family members, he was the coldest towards her, and Felicity wondered what Anthony had told him.

"I have a friend here from London," she said.

"Would that be the white man you were seen with in St. George's?"

Felicity said, "It's not what you think. He likes men."

"You were with a buggerman!" Abel's mouth twisted. "You'll bring the police here!"

"Police?"

"Is illegal to be buggerman!"

Felicity said, "It's been lovely staying here, Abel, and I'm so sorry for the loss of your brother, but I'm going to go and stay with my family now."

Abel didn't help her lug her suitcase back down the hill to where Claude waited. Claude drove back to Sauteurs and set Felicity up in a bed and breakfast.

"I'll be back tomorrow, Cinnamon," he said, looking at his watch. Felicity lay on the bed under her mosquito net, watching the ceiling fan spin, picturing Claude speeding back to Marlene, telling her about his long day seeing clients.

CLAUDE AND FELICITY stood on a large cliff overlooking the sea. "You see here?" said Claude. "This is where every Indian on the island —"

"You mean Indians from India?" asked Felicity.

"No, I mean the first people of this island. The Caribs. They all ran and jumped off those cliffs and died, rather than be conquered by Europeans." Felicity nestled her palm against his and looked up at the steepness of the cliff and the certain death that it posed; on one side, rocks, on the other, the sea.

In the car, Felicity pressed against Claude before he could start the engine. They had made love at the bed and breakfast an hour ago and it had already been too long. There was so much time to make up for.

"I know it sounds strange, after seeing such a sad place," said Claude, "but I'm so happy, Cinnamon. I haven't been this happy in so long."

Felicity was happy too. "You are the radiance of my soul, delightful life and love," she said, speaking the translation of "O luce," but there were no words, not even any music, to convey the overwhelming joy of being with him again. Her body would have to do the talking.

ONE MORNING, FELICITY woke up, tried to get out of bed, and crumpled to the floor, her legs too weak to hold her up. A sharp pain started in her forehead. She lurched to the bathroom to splash cold water on her face. Her stomach heaved. She crawled to the toilet and retched, spitting up bile and saliva. When Claude arrived, she was shivering in bed under the thin cotton blanket. "Could it be food poisoning?" he asked as he paced with his hands on his head.

"We ate the same things yesterday," she said. "Can you bring me some water?" He went to the kitchen and came back with a glass, which she drank and promptly vomited over herself.

"Oh, Cinnamon. Oh, my love." Disregarding the germs she could be shedding, Claude crawled into the narrow bed with her. "Try to rest."

"It hurts," she said. "Everything hurts."

He got up. "I'll go to the pharmacy and see what I can find to make you feel better." He returned with aspirin, ice, orange juice, powdered soup, but everything she swallowed came up. Throughout the day, she sweated, shivered, and slept intermittently. Claude dabbed at her forehead with a damp cloth. When it was time for him to leave, he asked, "Sweetheart, what will you do on your own tonight?"

"I'll be okay," she said. She would not guilt him into staying with her when he was on the verge of coming to her freely.

When he returned in the morning, her chills were worse, and she still could not hold water down.

"Enough," Claude said. "I'm taking you to the nursing station."

"But what if someone sees?"

"Let me worry about that. You need medical attention."

In the car, Claude said, "We shouldn't give them our real names. What do you want to call yourself?"

Felicity said, "I'm Lydia Felix." Her middle name and Anthony's last name. "I'm American."

"I'll be Gerald Mason." Claude smiled. "He introduced us, do you remember?"

"He asked me to marry him," Felicity said, through chattering teeth. "After you left."

"He did?" Claude wrapped his arm around Felicity's shaking body as he navigated through the hills. "Bastard. I hope you told him where to stuff it." She pulled on his sleeve, indicating that he should open the door so she could vomit again.

Outside the nursing station, Felicity felt faint and almost collapsed. Claude staggered inside, carrying her in his arms.

"She is not from here," the nurse said. "Could be malaria. Or dengue."

"I thought we didn't have those in Grenada," Claude said. "Isn't that what the English say?"

"What do they know? Her fever is very high. She should stay here tonight. We can put her on an IV, get some strong antibiotics into her."

Felicity saw Claude's worried face wavering above her before she closed her eyes, too dizzy to look at anything, even him. The walls of the room felt like they were squeezing the life out of her, and she wondered if she was going to die, a second before the world turned black.

The rehydration and antibiotics did their work. When Claude came back the next day, she was stronger, sitting up and holding juice down. She leaned on him as he led her to the car, clutching her cylinder of antibiotics in his other hand.

When they got back to the bed and breakfast, Claude brought Felicity water and the pills. After she drank, he said, "Rest, Cinnamon."

"I want you, Claude."

"Now? Cinnamon, you're too weak. Maybe in a few days."

Felicity had been given her life back, and the rush of blood in her veins reminded her that she was a breathing, needing woman. She drew on the argument she had been reluctant to use. "Claude, you're going to leave me tonight, to be with her. I need all of you while you're here." She conjured a tear.

"All right, my love, all right," Claude said. "If you're sure." He squeezed himself into the narrow bed and Felicity reached for his belt.

WHEN SHE HAD recovered, after they had lain together through the worst of the afternoon heat, he took her to an abandoned sugar mill in Vincennes. "This is almost certainly where your ancestors were slaves," Claude said. After pushing through the brush, beating off mosquitos and scanning the ground for snakes, they made love against the rotten walls, beside the rusted buckets and pumps, abandoned for almost one hundred and fifty years, now slowly reclaimed by the jungle.

Afterwards, they sat on a crumbling brick wall and Claude talked politics with the Grenadian sun slanting through the trees and striking his eyes like arrows. Tibbs was on the brink of being overthrown, he said. He and Neville were planning a general strike. All work would come to a standstill and the demonstrators would march to the jail and free the political prisoners.

"To the Revo," he said.

Felicity touched her fist to his. "To the Revo." She tried to smile, but talk of revolution only reminded her that she and Claude had separate destinies. They had been together every day for two weeks, but soon he would go on to protest in the streets of St. George's, while she would have to get back to her preparations for her *Fledermaus* rehearsals.

"What is it, Cinnamon?" Claude asked. He had always been aware of her moods.

"This won't last," said Felicity. She regretted ever calling Claude. She had rekindled all the feelings from which she had freed herself, after soul-draining months of sobbing into her pillow, into Jack's arms, onto the piano keys as she practiced. Now she would have to go through that wrenching again.

"You mean, you and me?" Claude asked. She shivered at the understanding in his voice, the closeness of him.

He put his arm over her shoulder. "It can last," he said. "We can make it work. You travel now, don't you?"

"Sometimes."

"I do too," Claude said. "Officially, as far as Tibbs knows, I'm teaching courses in the law to West Indians abroad. But really, I'll be meeting with Grenadian expats to shore up international support and raise funds for the Revo. Do you ever go back to London?"

"I might sing the *Messiah* there next Christmas," said Felicity. "And I'm thinking of doing some auditions there, if I can afford it."

"How about New York?"

"I haven't been hired there yet, but I'm singing Beethoven's *Ninth* in Providence in the spring. Rhode Island. Not far from New York."

"I can plan my trips to match up with your schedule."

Felicity's melancholy was wiped away by the exultation that rippled through her body. He had been thinking about a future for them. She was no longer married. She was free to be with him. But, she remembered, Claude wasn't.

"When will you tell Marlene?" Felicity asked. The name felt stiff on her tongue.

"Tell her?" Claude scrunched up his eyes against the light. "Why would I tell her?"

"Don't you want to leave her and be with me —" Felicity's mouth dried at the look of horror on his face.

"Felicity, I didn't say I was going to leave her. She's my wife."

"But you don't love her. You love me." Felicity contemplated flinging herself off the wall. She would welcome the pain of impact. Maybe a snake would get to her before Claude could react.

"It's not about love. She's a good political wife. She'll be a good mother."

"You don't have children."

"I will father a son soon. There's no reason I can't." Claude blinked and looked away. "You are not made for marriage, Felicity. You said it yourself."

Felicity tried to swallow around the hard ball of anger at having told him that.

"I want you to be my mistress," Claude said. "The one I confide in. The one I can look forward to seeing. The one I can be passionate with, just like in the old days."

"Mistress," Felicity said. The word flew from her mouth and dropped like a tarnished penny to the ground. She didn't want to share him with anyone, least of all Marlene. Marlene was better behaved and more respectable than Felicity, and Blacker. Felicity would always be less in Claude's eyes, the light-skinned outsider whore to play with when he got bored. "I don't want to be your mistress, Claude," she said. "And I want to go back to the bed and breakfast." She didn't wait for the tears to well up before she told herself that there could be no crying.

Claude pressed his head close to hers. "I'm sorry, Cinnamon," he said.

"I want to go back to the bed and breakfast," she said again. She could not let him think that she was hungry for whatever crumbs he chose to scatter at her feet.

"All right. All right." Claude leaped off the wall and extended a hand to help her down. She ignored it and jumped hard, pain jolting through her heels and calves. The sunlight pooled on a clump of leaves. She stared at it, opening her eyes as wide as she could. She didn't cry.

CRYING CAME LATER, in the bathtub at the bed and breakfast after Claude left. When he tried to come into the room with her, she had scratched his face, leaving a track of red welts. He slammed the door shut and she laughed to herself, imagining him trying to explain her claw marks to Marlene, before the tears exploded from her. At first, they were tears of outrage, of insult. But, as they tapered off, they became tears of self-pity, and then of loss. She lay in the cooling water and tried to see what he had seen; a vision of the two of them in London and New York, stealing away from meeting halls and opera houses to meet each other in the shadowy places of the world's greatest cities. Her body softened as she imagined opening it to him.

She had been too hasty. Claude was right. They could never marry. They had their separate paths, and it was true that marriage wasn't for her. Her singing career was just starting, and she couldn't afford to have it be derailed by a Grenadian revolutionary with big brown eyes. But Claude could draw feelings from her that no one else could. He fuelled her art. She would be a fool to throw that away out of pride. She would let him stew for the rest of her time in Grenada, but when she was back in Winnipeg, she would write to him at the law office to arrange a meeting. It would scandalize her mother if she knew — and the thought made Felicity happy — but all the best operatic characters, with the most beautiful love affairs, were mistresses.

CHAPTER 37.

Winnipeg, Manitoba, September 13, 1971

TO LOSE CLAUDE a second time was worse than the first. This time, Felicity didn't realize at first that she had lost him. She took a taxi home from the airport. Her mother was at her house with Mara, and Aunt Rose was there. Mara was already in bed. "Hello, Felicity," her mother said. "How was the funeral?"

Felicity tried to remember, and settled on, "It was fine."

"Was it in a Catholic church?"

"Yes."

"You know Catholics don't believe in —"

"Salvation by grace, I know. You know I'm not interested in any kind of religion."

"Did you bring back a prayer card?"

She had forgotten to take one. "Maybe in my suitcase."

Aunt Rose said, "It's so good to have you home, flower. It's going to be difficult, but you know we're here for you."

It was convenient that they thought she was grieving. She was, but not for Anthony. The sadness was exhausting. She went to bed thinking of Claude, certain she would lie awake all night remembering his touch, but she slept so heavily that Mara had to jump on her, diaper dragging almost to her knees, before she woke. She sat with a score at the piano Anthony had bought before she moved in, practicing for *Fledermaus* and learning roles her agent suggested she get into her voice. She wondered when she would work again once this show was over. After only a few minutes, she had to get up and lie on the couch. One evening, she woke to find her mother standing over her, holding Mara. "Felicity, I've been knocking and knocking!" she said.

"Sorry." Felicity yawned and stretched. Her head felt heavy, as if she hadn't slept at all.

"You're sleeping at this time? You haven't made supper? Take Mara." She passed Mara over and she brushed against Felicity's chest. A sharp pain caused Felicity to yelp.

"Felicity, I know you miss your husband," Mom said. "But you have a child to take care of."

Mara put her hand on Felicity's face and Felicity batted it away.

"I'll make something to eat," said Mom.

On the weekend, Mom took Mara to her house, and Felicity picked her up at Salvation Baptist after the service. They had agreed on this arrangement: Mara got the religious education her grandmother felt she should, and Felicity got to avoid attending services. When Felicity arrived at the church, Aunt Rose offered her a plate of food as usual, but Felicity looked down at the ham shining with oil and stifled a retch. "No, thank you," she said.

"Oh, flower, are you dieting again for that show you have coming up? I made meatloaf. Just have a little. I know you can't resist my meatloaf."

"No, I can't," Felicity said. "But I will have some bread, if you have any." Aunt Rose placed a basket of buns on the table. Felicity saw Aunt Rose exchange a look with Mom as she stuffed one into her mouth.

"Flower, is it possible that you're pregnant?" Aunt Rose asked.

Of course she was. She knew she was. Her mouth was full of bread, so she nodded her answer.

"But that's wonderful!" Aunt Rose said. "You'll have a piece of Anthony to keep with you forever."

A piece of Anthony was the last thing she wanted. A piece of Anthony would be a wedge between her and Claude. It would keep Anthony's name from fading from her tongue; she would have to say it again and again to her child. Aunt Rose went over to her and gathered her into an embrace. "I know it will be hard without your husband, but we're all here for you. We'll make sure both your children are loved."

AUNT ROSE URGED Mom to help Felicity more in the house for the time being. "It isn't easy, in that early part of pregnancy, you remember," she said. "It's so tiring. We were lucky, we lived with my parents, but Felicity has to do it all on her own and look after a little one too."

"I worked double shifts at the hospital when I was pregnant," Mom said. "I mopped floors and cleaned toilets." This was the first Felicity had heard of her origins. She listened for more, but Mom's lips were pursed.

Aunt Rose said, "Because we worked so hard, our children don't have to. Isn't that right? I'll help you too, flower."

With Mom and Aunt Rose doing her housework and Mara spending most of her nights with her grandmother, Felicity was free to work on *Fledermaus*. Rehearsals were starting in Calgary in a couple of weeks. She was glad she would not be showing much, but she hoped she would have enough energy to get through the run. She had worked at the Royal Opera House in early pregnancy after Claude had left, but this time, her fatigue and her sorrow were insatiable, demanding ever more of her. "You're pregnant, not ill!" her mother reminded her. But she was sick with the absence of Claude.

When Mom was over one evening, she turned on the news. Mara toddled around with a toy. Felicity lay on the couch in her housecoat, eating toast, heedless of the crumbs dropping to the floor. She paid no attention to the commentary on events in the House of Commons and the Vietnam draft, but then the announcer said, "And now to St. George's, Grenada."

Mom stopped dusting. Felicity stopped chewing and sat up straight. There was the seawall, the Carenage, and the familiar intersection of Church Street and Market Hill, just past the cathedral. She could not walk in the capital with Claude by day as people might see them, but one night, he had driven her through the city, pointing out the major landmarks.

"As Independence from Great Britain looms, the island is faced with growing unrest from those who oppose the formation of an independent nation with Percy Tibbs as leader, most notably the trade union movement known as the Black Pearls, led by Neville Carpenter. Today, a general strike turned violent, and five people were killed."

Felicity must have made a noise, because Mom said. "What is it, Felicity?"

"I know Neville Carpenter," Felicity said. "And some of the others."

"How would you know them?" Mom asked.

"From London. The West Indian student group."

"I didn't send you there to associate with hoodlums," Mom snapped. Mom's voice barely registered. Felicity's eyes were fixed on the screen, where she was sure she had seen Claude walking away from a gurney draped with a sheet. She would recognize his stride anywhere.

"... the security forces of Premier Tibbs, known as the Nutmeg Squad. One of the fatalities has been identified as local businessman, Albert Buckingham, whose son Claude —"

The announcer's words broke into a cloud of static that whooshed through Felicity's brain as a great wind. Her blood rose up to meet it and the television screen turned grey and then black.

"Felicity. Felicity." Mom was tapping on her cheek. She opened her eyes. She was lying on the couch. The TV was still on, but it no longer showed Grenada. "You fainted," Mom said. "Don't sit up yet. I'll get you a glass of water."

Claude's father was dead, killed by his mortal enemy, Tibbs.

Claude loved his father. The loss would only strengthen his resolve. His sole focus now would be to see that Percy Tibbs was removed from office, whatever the cost. Felicity could imagine the look in his eyes, the conviction in his voice. She ached with the desire to hold him, to let him weep in her arms. She recoiled at the thought that he might be doing that now, with Marlene.

Mom returned with water, and a sandwich stuffed nauseatingly with cheese and tinned meat. "You're not eating enough for the baby," Mom said. "No wonder you fainted. I don't know how you think you're going to Calgary to sing in a silly opera."

Felicity didn't know how she was going to do it either. Her mother was right. *Die Fledermaus* was a silly opera. It was a comedy. Her character, the chambermaid Adele, was an aspiring actress who got dressed up in her mistress's clothes and snuck out to a fancy party and showed off her high notes to all the guests. She would have to flirt and giggle while Claude and four other Grenadian families mourned. She heard Neville asking, "What are you doing for our people? How are you helping the Revo?" She had no reply.

THE NIGHT BEFORE Felicity left for Calgary, Josiah and Jack came over for a visit. Jack brought his guitar. As his fingers moved up and down the strings, Felicity said, "You're getting it. That's the blues scale. That slide from the flat three to three." She had studied the blues by listening to recordings on an old record player she had borrowed from Aunt Rose's parents. When she should have been working on *Die Fledermaus,* she had laid on the floor — the couch was not hard or punishing enough — and let the music work on her soul. Jack had studied it too; music was an easier means of communication than words.

"Want to sing something?" Jack asked.

Felicity began to improvise, "Missing you, feeling blue, oo-oo." Jack twanged on the lowest string, and the notes marched onward in their despair. Felicity went on "Without you here, I shed a tear, you're nowhere. Oo-oo, I got the lonely heart blues." It was the strength and sadness of Black music that she needed, from places opera could never go.

They were interrupted by a piercing, ethereal sound, like a tiny gust of wind boring into the room. Felicity turned to see Mara, humming the blues scale exactly as Felicity had just sung it, note for perfect note.

INTERMEZZO
CHAPTER 38.

Winnipeg, Manitoba, June 18, 1972

AUNT ROSE ACCOMPANIED Felicity to the hospital when she went into labour for the second time. This baby was much more eager than Mara to leave the safety of the womb; the delivery lasted five hours and not the eighteen Mara had taken. Despite the epidural, after several pushes, Felicity could feel a burning. She cried out and put her hand down to feel something smooth, the edge of a pebble warmed by the sun, and her fingers came away streaked with blood. "I see the head, flower!" Aunt Rose exclaimed as the doctor shoved her out of the way.

"Just one more push, Mommy," he said. Felicity pushed and screamed as her body opened to the sky and something slippery rushed through her and out to the world.

"Aww, it's another girl," said Aunt Rose. "Congratulations, flower."

Felicity sank back onto the pillow. Another girl. She had so hoped for a boy. Boys seemed so simple, so impervious to the troubles of life. But then she thought of Josiah and how Aunt Rose's nurturing and love had not been enough for him in the absence of a father. Perhaps it was best she have daughters. "Can I see her?" she asked. The nurse turned the bundle towards her, and both she and Aunt Rose gasped. There was a little form in a warm, cocoa colour with tufts of black hair sticking up around her head, matted with blood. Tears began leaking from Felicity's eyes and she sniffled and looked around for a tissue. Aunt Rose was at her side in seconds offering one. "Oh, flower," she said. "How I wish her daddy could be here to see her."

Felicity leaned against the solid, warm comfort of Aunt Rose. She still could not picture herself as a mother. But with the birth of her second child, she was able to see through the lens of one who had sheltered life in her body and brought it into the world, however reluctantly. "Me too, Aunt Rose," she said.

When the baby was handed to her, Aunt Rose said, "So what is this one's name?"

Felicity had thought only of boys' names. Josiah had already used Malcolm. She had contemplated Martin. Julian, after the Grenadian slave revolutionary Julien Fédon, whom she had learned about from Claude. Felicity had wanted her son to have the name of a fighter. But here was a girl with a fierce, challenging expression in her deep brown eyes. She would have to fight too, as she grew into a Black woman. She would be growing up with an unusually beautiful older sister who turned heads wherever she went. A girl could be called Martina or Juliana, but the only name that came to Felicity's mind was the name of the role she had been preparing when she realized this child was on her way. Adele, the feisty chambermaid in *Die Fledermaus*, who saw what she wanted and went after it and got it. "Adele," she said. "Her name is Adele. Adele Juliana."

"That's pretty, flower," said Aunt Rose. "Mara and Adele. Those sound nice together."

The nurse interrupted, "Have you thought about feeding plans, Mommy?"

A desire stirred in Felicity to have this baby remain a part of her, connected to her, for as long as possible. "I think I might want to try breastfeeding," she said.

"Ain't no harm in trying," Aunt Rose said. "There won't be any milk yet, but you could try to get her to latch on."

The nurse said, "We usually give them a bottle to start, till the milk comes in."

"Nonsense, dear." Aunt Rose folded a blanket and placed it on the table. "Before there was formula, we all fed our babies ourselves from the beginning. They have to suck to bring the milk in."

The nurse said, "Well, since you seem to know everything about it already —"

Aunt Rose and Felicity didn't notice the huffiness in her voice. Their attention was completely upon Adele, who had opened her mouth like a fish and turned her face towards Felicity's nipple. Her tiny hand, the colour of the trunks of the trees in the Grenadian hills, reached out to stroke her mother's breast. Her eyes were wide open, drinking in all the world had to offer.

CHAPTER 39.

Lucerne, Switzerland, April 28, 1973

FELICITY HAD NEVER been entirely comfortable with Philip Cook. She had spent three years of college in his studio. In the end, while she was less awed by him than in first year, she remained intimidated, never quite assured of his good opinion of her. She was not surprised when her agent informed her that Hans Vogel had requested her return to Lucerne, this time to sing Zerlina in *Don Giovanni.* Though they had differed artistically, her performance in *L'elisir d'amore* had been a hit with the audiences and critics. She was, however, shocked that Philip was to sing the lead role.

"It's the strangest thing," Robin said to Felicity on the phone. "Apparently, last year he called up his agent and said that turning sixty isn't far off and he wants to return to the stage before it's too late."

Felicity would have to let Philip seduce her. She would have to appear with him in the famous duet, "La ci darem la mano," that they had sung together in lessons when they talked about character. She would have to blend her voice with his in the ensemble passages.

"Just think of him as another colleague," said Robin. "He'll be nervous too. He's been away from the stage for fifteen years. He's aging. He'll be wondering if he can still perform. And he has to do all that under the watchful eye of one of his star students who is on the rise. It's just as hard for him, Felicity."

Jack agreed. "Fizzy, you're thinking about it all wrong," he said. "He has more to lose than you do."

She longed to talk to Claude. But Claude thought that the way she described her lessons was colonial, and he called Philip "that white man you're always listening to." She was again reminded of how her talent always led her to a place where Claude and the West Indian students could not follow. On the walk from her hotel room to the first rehearsal, she worried she would vomit, and her muscles were tense and tight.

As she approached the stage door, she heard footsteps hurrying behind her. She turned and saw Philip. He was gaunter than she remembered, but his smile was the same. "Felicity," he said. "I was trying to catch up with you. Didn't you hear me calling you?"

"Sorry," she said. "I was a bit preoccupied." She already felt herself shrinking, blushing, stammering.

"Well, what a thing this is," Philip said. "I never expected to share the stage with you."

"Neither did I," said Felicity.

Philip held the door for her. "You are having an impressive start to your career. It is what I expected."

Felicity tried to think of a response beyond thanking him. Before one came to her, Philip said, "You've sung here before, haven't you? How are the acoustics?"

He was nervous too. "It's a bit dead," Felicity said. How could it be that she had sung somewhere he hadn't?

The pianist was practicing scale passages, warming up for the sing-through. Felicity surveyed the other singers as they arrived. Some of them seemed to know each other, but they were all strangers to her. Hans appeared and winked at her. They had to be careful in Lucerne, because Hans lived here with his wife; he would not have a hotel room. Felicity could not waste thoughts on what might take place. She had to concentrate on the music. Like all her operatic performances so far, this role was a debut; she wanted to get it right. She sat patiently through Act 1, Scenes 1 and 2, where Donna Anna and Donna Elvira had music, but Zerlina had yet to appear. She listened to their bigger, more luscious voices and worried about the dead acoustics. In *Elisir,* she had been the only female lead; there were no other voices to compare hers to. She stopped worrying about that at the end of Scene 2 and enjoyed Leporello's famous list aria, where he recounted all the conquests of his employer, and Donna Elvira's vow of revenge.

Felicity forgot her insecurities in her pleasure at the performance of her colleagues. She and Philip applauded with the rest of the cast. Then it was her turn. Scene 3 began with the music for her onstage wedding. She stood up and thought of Zerlina, young, naive, knowing she was supposed to be happy, but already doubting that she was — exactly how Felicity had felt at her own wedding. She made her voice as attractive and sweet as she could. Innocent as Zerlina was, surely she realized she was on display, and anyone could take a liking to her. It was not too late yet. Anything could happen. "Giovinette, che fate all'amore," she sang. "Non lasciate che passi l'età." *Young girls who make love, do not let this age pass you by.* Then she had a section of recitativo, the speech-singing that moved quickly through blocks of text, the orchestra temporarily silent and the voices accompanied only by the tinny ring of a harpsichord.

Philip had said, "Don't be perfunctory with recit, but don't be too precious with it, either. Use it as a vehicle to convey the character to the audience." Now here was Philip, standing beside her, proposing to seduce her. Her voice shook, but that was in service of the drama of Zerlina, the peasant girl, trying to resist the nobleman. They moved into the duet, and Felicity imagined that she and Philip were back in his studio at the Guildhall, Claude waiting for her at their home in Shepherd's Bush. When Philip sang "Vieni, mio bel diletto!" urging her to come with him, he had always extended a hand to her. He did so today. Felicity took his hand as she sang her reply and was surprised when Philip squeezed it. At the end of their duet, someone in the cast whistled, a low, slow pitch that rose swiftly to a shrill blast. Then everyone clapped.

Scene 4 was easier, because most of Zerlina's interactions were with her stage husband, Masetto. Felicity had her first aria, "Batti, batti," which she had learned under Philip. When she finished, and Philip stood for his next entrance, he whispered, "Nicely done." With this test over, she began to feel more centred.

At the end of Scene 5, the entire cast ganged up on Don Giovanni. Felicity's job was to scream from offstage and scream again as everyone rushed to rescue her. Leporello and the Don had the last word. As Felicity sang her part of the ensemble scene, she watched Philip. His voice seemed unchanged by time, as crisp and clear as always, the diction still precise. He embodied everything Felicity strove for in her own art. As he sang "Se cadesse ancora il mondo, nulla mai temer mi fa," his hand shook, and then his voice did too. *If the world should fall apart, nothing could ever make me afraid.* Felicity heard the fear in his voice. Something was wrong.

The act ended. Hans called for a break. Felicity remained seated, the music and her new knowledge of Philip swirling in her brain. Hans came over to her, holding out his score as if he wanted to discuss her performance. "Well!" he said. "I knew you would make a fine Zerlina. We'll have to talk about your tempo in 'Batti,' of course." He sat beside her. "The chemistry you had with Philip Cook. Were you and he ever —"

"He was my teacher," Felicity said. *He is still my teacher*, she thought. He would always be her teacher.

Hans's face cleared. "Naturally," he said. "You must have been the darling of his studio. That relationship will play very well on stage." He touched Felicity's hand. "Listen, I can't see you tonight. Obligations."

"It's fine," Felicity said. She wanted to talk to Philip anyway. She was tiring of Hans.

ON THE MORNING of the piano dress rehearsal, a notice slid under the door of Felicity's hotel room stating that the director urgently needed everyone at the theatre. Walking over with Philip, Felicity asked him, "What do you think this is?"

Philip said, "Could be anything with this director. He's so particular. A new safety hazard, a fire code, something added to the set."

"It's interfering with my routine," Felicity said.

Philip laughed. "My dear, you're sounding like a seasoned diva already." Since those brief tremors at the sing-through, he had not betrayed any further distress, and Felicity had given up trying to discern what might be going on.

The director stood at the front of the rehearsal room with a stranger. After they all filed in, he made the announcement. "Maestro Vogel has taken ill," he said, and Felicity gasped before she could restrain herself. Hans had visited her hotel room the previous evening, and he had seemed fine. All eyes in the room swung towards her. She lowered her head, feeling the blood rush to her cheeks. She wondered what they knew of her relationship with Hans. Philip had never mentioned it. She had had dinner with him a few times, and he had only asked about her personal life once.

"So tell me, Felicity," Philip had said. "I heard that you had a child."

"I have two," Felicity said.

Philip tucked his napkin into his shirt. "So, you did not take my advice," he said. "But I am pleased it hasn't held you back."

"I did take your advice," Felicity said. "But it wasn't foolproof."

"I see," Philip said. "So, the young man who was always around when you were a student. Mr. Brown Eyes?"

Felicity looked away. "We broke up. Then I got married, but my husband died."

Philip reached across the table and took one of her hands between both of his. "I'm sorry," he said. "You must have help, to be able to be here singing if you're on your own with two children."

"My mother," said Felicity.

"That's good of her," Philip said. Felicity supposed it was. She had just assumed her mother didn't mind.

"As to Mr. Brown Eyes," Philip said, "I always knew it wasn't meant to be. It's better this way, isn't it?"

It could never be better without Claude, but she gave a traitorous nod. Philip released her hand, made a comment about rehearsal, and never mentioned Claude again.

The director's voice cut through Felicity's thoughts. "Maestro Enzo Romano, the cover conductor, will be filling in until further notice." Felicity looked at the other man again. He was not a stranger after all. He had sat at the back of the rehearsal hall, day after day, perusing his score of the opera and Hans's movements in equal measure, pale and quiet as a ghost. "We are not going to make you all sing the opera twice in one day," said the director, "but we will play through some of the major parts, just to set the tempi for Maestro."

It didn't matter to Felicity who waved the stick. She paid minimal attention to Hans when he conducted, and she would pay even less to Enzo.

That evening, she arrived at the wig department with her hair freshly washed and detangled. She expected the wig mistress who had coiffed her for *Elisir,* but someone new stood by the mirror wearing an apron with a pocket laden with clips and combs. "*Wer bist du*?" asked the new wig mistress.

"I'm singing Zerlina," Felicity said. She wasn't up to attempting to respond in German.

"You are Zerlina? They expect me to work with that?" The wig mistress pointed at Felicity's hair, on which she lavished her time and money to keep it healthy and bouncy, which she lovingly combed and oiled.

"I'm sorry, I know there's a lot of it," Felicity said, then questioned why she was apologizing for what grew naturally out of her head.

"Well, sit down, then." The wig mistress pointed to the chair. Felicity sat, and the wig mistress began parting her hair and rubbing sections between her fingers. "How am I going to get the wig on?" she asked.

"Which wig?"

The wig mistress lifted it from the stand. It was blond, with long twisted sections like a milkmaid. The absurdity of the moment pressed the air from Felicity's lungs.

"It is a small wig. This will not fit." The wig mistress replaced the wig and lifted another chunk of Felicity's hair. "It has to be straight."

"You can straighten it," Felicity said, trying not to think of herself onstage with hair so blond it was almost white. How had the director allowed this? He had nitpicked over every inch of the rake of the stage, every shadow cast by the set, but ignored the utter unsuitability of this wig, which undoubtedly would create headaches for the lighting crew due to the unexpected contrast between it and her skin tone. This opera company lacked the sophistication of the Royal Opera House, where even as a student cover, Felicity had had wig and costume fittings well ahead of showtime. There was no point protesting now, the decision had been made without her. She would only look difficult.

"How do you straighten this?" The wig mistress dropped the handful of Felicity's hair she had been holding. It sprung upward.

Felicity sat on her hands, which were itching to smack this woman. "Do you have a hot comb?" she asked.

"*Was ist das?*"

"Okay, then you have to wash it and blow-dry it straight."

The wig mistress shook her head as she led Felicity to a sink in the corner. Felicity tried not to look at the clock and the precious minutes of warm-up time being swallowed by this charade. She sat, dripping in a stylist's chair, as the wig mistress raked a brush through her hair so violently — even more so than her mother ever had — that Felicity cried out at the stinging pull on her scalp.

Felicity's hair had been abused enough when she used to straighten it; she was gentle with it now. She combed it slowly and carefully in small sections and moisturized it as she went. The wig mistress, however, attacked it with a comb whose teeth were too close together, while holding the blow-dryer so close to Felicity's head that it burned. "It's not going straight," she said.

Felicity said, "You have to hold it like this." She pantomimed the motion of using a brush to create tension in the hair.

The wig mistress switched the blow dryer off. "Is impossible."

Felicity held out her hand. "Give me the blow-dryer," she said. "I'll do it myself."

The singers who played Donna Anna and Donna Elvira sat in stylist chairs, having their own hair pinned and readied for their wigs by hair department assistants as they hummed their warm-ups. They cast the occasional glance at Felicity as she did her best to reshape her curls, a job that was extraordinarily difficult to do alone. Little by little, her hair began, unwillingly, to unspool into longer threads. "That's better," said the wig mistress. Her assistants left their posts to watch, and chattered to each other in German, pointing at the contrast in textures on Felicity's head. She was an exhibit on display: *Black woman's unruly hair becomes acceptable.* Tears formed in her eyes, and she watched in the mirror as they fell into her lap while she brushed and pulled her hair until it was straight enough to put on a blond wig.

FELICITY HAD DISCOVERED the stagehands' gathering place when the sets arrived and were being assembled. They clustered around a small door to the rear of the theatre where they joked and laughed and, most crucially, smoked; sometimes cigarettes, and sometimes weed. The smell of marijuana reminded her of home, of sitting with Jack on his patio or hers with a joint, a conversation and a history burning between them. Or it took her further back, to her university days when she, Claude, Neville, and the other West

Indian students sprawled on the floor of someone's bedsit, the windows open no matter the temperature to dispel the odour, passing hastily rolled cylinders back and forth as they discussed apartheid, colonialism, and revolution. They would have been furious at the scene she had just endured in the wig room. They would jump to her defence with posters and placards. But Felicity was almost on her own here; alone, except for Karl.

Karl was a Black stagehand, who spoke a little English. From the couple of conversations they had had at the stage door, she had learned that his father was an American serviceman who had been posted in Germany at the end of the war. Karl did not know him but had grown up with his white German mother: an inversion of Felicity. She had shared a joint with him before and hoped she could get another one. Theatres had strict rules against performers going outside, even for a minute, in wig and costume, but no one would think to look outside an obscure service door. Another rule of the theatre, unwritten but no less strict, was that artists with the company did not fraternize with the working grunts.

The stagehands looked startled when Felicity appeared. Karl was not among them. "*Wo ist Karl?*" she asked.

"*Nicht hier*," someone responded.

"*Grünes?*" Felicity asked, using their word for weed.

"*Karl hat es.*"

She searched for the German words for what she wanted to say next, but she had reached the limits of her linguistic ability. "Can you tell him I'm looking for him, when you see him?"

They nodded. "*Ja, ja.*"

"You hear what happen Maestro Vogel?" someone asked her. She wasn't sure if it was an idle question, or if even the working stiffs of the theatre knew of her relationship with the conductor.

"Him wife try kill herself," her informant said.

Felicity gripped the door handle she had been reaching for. The blood drained from her hand, and hanks of blond hair brushed against the veins. "When?" She managed to make the word casual.

"Yesterday night."

Hans was with her last night. She pulled on the doorknob and the service door popped open, almost smacking her in the face. She ran up the stairs to the makeup department, but the spectre of Hans's wife attempting suicide because of her, Felicity, was overwhelming. She could not sit before another mirror, this time having her skin scrutinized, analyzed, and deemed inferior. She realized that she needed to use the bathroom, a constant sensation before performances when the extra water she consumed to lubricate her vocal cords passed through her. Her dressing room was on the floor below, but there was a public ladies' room to her left. She dove inside and threw herself into a stall where her head began to spin. She thought she might faint.

She had never intended harm with their affair. She had assumed that Hans' wife was as dissatisfied with the marriage as Hans. If one partner was unfaithful, the other was too, whether sexually or by neglect of other aspects of their vows. A relationship with the conductor added a little sizzle to her performances and made coming to rehearsals fun, and it was a bonus to be on the conductor's good side when it came to seeking future work. She had been so sure she was not hurting anyone. She sat on the toilet, lifted the wide skirts of her costume carefully out of the way, and gripped her knees as her world reconfigured itself.

Someone hurried into the bathroom and began vomiting in the next stall, gasping and straining as the contents of their stomach splattered into the toilet. Perhaps Felicity could help this person instead of being a liability. She knocked on the door. "Are you all right in there?" she asked. There was a groan, from a voice far too deep to belong to a woman. "Do you need help?" she asked.

The door opened, and Enzo Romano stood there, wiping his mouth with a wad of toilet paper. His eyes were red and his face paler than normal. "I am sorry," he said. "I was just walking past, and —"

"Are you sick?" Felicity asked.

He rubbed his forehead. "No, it is just, what do you call it, the nerves. Excuse me." He pivoted back into the stall and retched again.

Felicity said to his heaving back, "If it makes you feel any better, we singers never look at the conductor anyway."

He flushed the toilet and turned around. She expected a light-hearted response to her joke that wasn't really a joke, but he said, "I have been looking at you."

His admission could not have come at a worse time. One conductor looking at her had led to tragedy, and now here was another. "Don't you have a wife to look at?" said Felicity.

"No wife," he said. He held out his left hand. "No ring." There was no band of lighter skin.

"Oh," Felicity said. Enzo did not have Hans's magnetism. He was a lowly assistant conductor. But tonight, he would harness the power of an entire orchestra and cast with a few gestures. Perhaps he was more attractive than she had thought. He had been looking at her. He had appreciated her skin colour and her natural hair texture.

"You might feel better if I gave you a massage," Felicity said to Enzo. "Actually, I could use one, too."

She chided herself for her impulsivity, but her decision made sense. Enzo needed to be taken in hand, or the entire performance would suffer. And she needed something to steady her, after multiple blows to her confidence. Since she hadn't obtained any marijuana, sex would have to do.

Enzo turned his back to her. "I would like that."

"Not here in the bathroom," Felicity said. "We have to go to your dressing room, and quickly, because I need my makeup done." She could warm up during Acts I and II.

She had never made love in costume, and the skirts were a nuisance, but also exciting as they rustled and puffed around Enzo's face. "Is this how Zerlina would have done it with the Don?" Felicity asked Enzo. She wanted to make it clear that this was mutual release of tension, not a commitment.

Enzo reached over to the table beside her and picked up his baton. He used it to trace an oval around her face — the shape of her jawline, cheekbones and forehead. "You will sing your best for me," he said. Her magic had worked; he was already transforming from a scared student to a suave, urbane conductor.

She lowered his hand and jumped off the couch. "I will sing my best for me," she said.

When she opened the door of Enzo's dressing room, Philip was in the hallway. She tried to hurry past him, hoping he would think she had been reviewing music with Enzo, but he looked straight at her and gave a slow, small shake of his head, his lips compressed. As they stood there, Karl came into view. Sauntering past Felicity, he opened his palm and Felicity's hand found it and closed around a joint. She squeezed for a second to indicate that she would pay him after the show.

Philip said to Felicity, "I can't imagine what you think you're playing at. Curtain is in fifteen minutes, and you aren't made up."

"I'm on my way," Felicity said.

"There's no time now, but the teacher in me says I should talk to you about your behaviour after the show."

Guilt and shame coalesced into defiance. "You're not my teacher anymore," said Felicity. She had lied; he would always be her teacher.

"All the same, it would be in your best interest to meet me later," Philip said. His face was remote, closed to her as it had never been.

Felicity choked back a wave of remorse so thick, for a moment, it felt as if she would vomit as forcefully as Enzo had. She sought to explain herself. "Look at this wig," she said. "And they didn't know how to do my hair."

Philip's disapproving expression dissolved like a misty window wiped clear. "Oh," he said. He cleared his throat. "Your hair, Felicity," he said, and she remembered how he had always told her to wear it up or otherwise control it before an audition. She had used the wrong angle to seek sympathy. "Your hair is mighty," Philip said. "As mighty as you. Go to makeup, and we will speak later."

Felicity gripped the joint as she made her way up the stairs.

"I SAW YOUR determination from the beginning," Philip said. "But not your vulnerability." He sipped from his steaming cup. "Have you had Swiss hot chocolate before?"

"No," Felicity said, "but I like the Viennese version." She was relaxed and calm now that the piano dress rehearsal had gone well. After a few hiccups, Enzo had risen to the occasion, and the orchestra had accepted him. Felicity had put her ridiculous wig out of her mind and had given a successful performance.

Philip smiled as he stirred his drink. "Vienna," he said. "A lovely city." He sipped again. "It cannot be easy for you, being away from home when your children are young. And I understand that the opera is mired in traditions, often detrimentally so. But the way you are carrying yourself will not do, Felicity. A young woman should not be going into the conductor's dressing room, for any reason. There is a rehearsal room for reviewing music."

Felicity looked down at the whipped cream melting into her drink.

"I'm sure you know that marijuana is illegal," said Philip. "If you are caught with it, you can go to jail. Abroad. Away from your family. It is imperative that you behave yourself."

Felicity shrugged, feeling rebellious again in the face of his chastisement.

"I don't want you to have a breakdown," said Philip. "You have far too much talent for that."

Felicity looked over the rim of her cup. "Is that what happened to you?" she asked. "Is that why you quit singing?" She didn't care if she sounded rude.

Philip said, "I'm sorry, I hope you don't take this as a judgment on your situation, but I left the stage because I wanted a normal family life."

"I thought you didn't have children," said Felicity.

"I don't. We don't. But we hoped, for a long time. And it was upsetting for my wife. She needed me at home." His mouth snapped shut, as if he had said too much, and there would be no more information forthcoming.

"I appreciate the advice," Felicity said, "but I'm fine."

"Are you? Because everything I'm seeing is someone headed for a breakdown. And before that, if you ruin your reputation, you may find it harder to get work. Do you have anything scheduled after this?"

She didn't. She had been hoping that Hans would offer her another opera, but she didn't know where she stood with him now. Robin, her agent, hadn't been able to persuade any other companies to hire her.

She avoided the knowing glint in Philip's eyes. "I'm going to keep moving upward, and guess why?" She leaned over the table. "I can manifest the things I want to happen. Like singing at the Met. I can see it happening to me. I can feel it." She let the sensation fill her body as she visualized herself stepping onto the world's biggest stages, winning over the most sophisticated audiences with her voice and her stage persona, but keeping everything else inside, allowing them to see only what she wanted them to see.

CHAPTER 40.

London, England, January 19, 1974

THE BRITISH HAD grudgingly accepted what they saw as the defection of their colonies and, after decades of watching nations leave the fold, the London newspapers were resigned in their reporting on the latest loss, Grenada. Felicity spread the newspaper, wet with January rain, on her hotel room bed. She read with an idle curiosity until she came to a passage stating that Grenada's premier, Percy Tibbs, would be coming to London this week to sign the documents to facilitate independence, set to take effect in fewer than three weeks. He was bringing with him the leader of the Opposition, Neville Carpenter, and deputy leader of the Opposition, Claude Buckingham. The journalist implied that this was a cynical move, designed to reassure Britain, and the international community, that Tibbs was willing to work with his detractors, and that all was well in Grenada after recent violence.

Felicity didn't care about the intentions or the reasons. Claude was going to be in London at the same time she was. It was especially miraculous, given that this was her first engagement abroad in some time. After *Giovanni* in Lucerne, the work had dried up. Hans's wife had died, and he had not been in touch. The guilt was unbearable, but worse was the knowledge that perhaps Philip had been right, that news of her offstage behaviour had reached the ears of artistic directors and general managers, and they had collectively decided that she was more trouble than she was worth.

Was her mother right too? Living in an immoral way had caught up with her, and the vengeful God who made marks in His book had added so many to her column that she could no longer be redeemed. She'd had the odd oratorio performance in Regina or Calgary but no major role since. She was stuck in Winnipeg, with a mother who didn't know her and two daughters who looked at her with big eyes, hungry for what she didn't know how to give.

"Be patient," Robin had said in a phone call. "This is not unusual at the beginning of a career. You had a strong start, but then it will take a while for the offers to become steady. I can tell you that the Met is interested. They've been asking about you. I think they want your Met debut to be in an unexpected role. Something spectacular. It takes time on their end to work that out."

Felicity had hoped and imagined and sent out visions of herself singing at the Met, but all that came back was a noon hour recital for a Winnipeg chamber music society, and a *Creation* in Saskatoon. "Singing is singing," said Jack, but this was something else he didn't understand. Opera was different from other singing. Not only did it have the most glorious music, undergirded by the sweep and breadth of orchestra and chorus, but the characters embodied the purest forms of love and loss, jealousy and reconciliation. She had come to this conclusion when she sang *Fledermaus* in Calgary; she had begun rehearsals sure that this ridiculous, meaningless show was not worth separation from Claude, that it had nothing to say about the serious struggle in which he was involved, fighting for the right to nationhood and self-determination.

Then, at the sing-through, she heard the soprano, Alesya Kravchenko, sing Rosalinde's big aria, "Klänge der Heimat," *Sounds of my homeland*. Philip had always said that it was important to learn the literal translation of every line in the opera, even the roles she wasn't cast in, even if she wasn't on stage. She generally did that, but struggled so much with languages, German in particular. Between going to Grenada, the loss of Claude, the news of his father, and her pregnancy, she had skipped that crucial step of learning every line in *Fledermaus*. But there was something so wistful, and yet so powerful, in the way Alesya sang the aria that Felicity hauled her German dictionary from her suitcase and went to work that evening in her hotel room.

Sounds of my homeland, You fill me with longing, Bring tears to my eyes when I hear your native songs, Felicity translated. *O homeland, so wonderful, The sun shines so brightly. How green your forests, how laughing your fields. O land, where I was so happy!* The aria was about Hungary, but it could be describing Grenada. *Yes, your beloved image, So completely fills my soul, And though I am far from you, so far, I am with you for eternity. My soul, ever there, Consecrated to you alone!* Felicity wasn't sure if she had the right to call Grenada her homeland, as one who had been raised entirely outside it. But Alesya described herself as a proud Ukrainian, and no doubt the depth of emotion with which she had sung the aria came from her feelings for Ukraine, oppressed under Soviet rule. She wasn't born in Ukraine, nor were her parents or grandparents, from what Felicity knew. If Alesya called herself Ukrainian, Felicity could be Grenadian — and *Fledermaus* could speak to Grenada's aspirations the same as Ukraine's or Hungary's.

It was not opera, but Felicity had nonetheless been grateful when the invitation to perform in London came through Robin, her agent. He had called when she was in bed with a particularly vicious flu, glad that she did not have to try to struggle through an engagement. Philip Cook's return to the stage had been short-lived. He was retiring again. Felicity was to be one of the singers for his retirement gala at Wigmore Hall. He had requested that they sing "La ci darem la mano" together. She and Philip had parted somewhat abruptly in Lucerne, and Felicity was going to tell him that he had been right. From now on, she was going to behave. She would do anything if it would help her stalled career. She was dedicated to the concert and nothing but, until she read that Claude was to be in London.

The article said that the Tibbs delegation would be received at the prime minister's residence at 10 Downing Street on the afternoon of January 22, which was the evening of the show. Though Felicity had just committed to behaving herself, and she didn't think that that included throwing herself in Claude's path hours before a concert, fate had sent him here and, like a good operatic character, she must obey.

At the dress rehearsal, the night before the concert, Felicity secreted herself in a quiet corner of the backstage area to soak up the energy of the performance space before it became busy and loud. She flipped through her folder of music, searching for insights that might have eluded her. She was singing "O luce di quest'anima" along with "La ci darem" with Philip, and the glorious sextet from *Lucia di Lammermoor.* Two pairs of men's shoes moved past on the other side of the curtain and stopped right in front of her.

"This isn't too much for you?" asked a voice with a Scottish accent.

"No, it's giving me renewed hope and energy, if anything," said Philip's distinctive, warm, deep, kind voice. Always kind.

"They haven't said how long you have left?"

"We're not at that stage yet," said Philip. "The doctors still believe there are treatments. They are sending me to a clinic in Switzerland after this."

"No," said Felicity, to the darkness in which she sat.

"Who's that?" said the first voice.

"Felicity?" Philip parted the curtain, and he and a man in a suit poked their heads through.

"Felicity, what are you doing back here?" Philip sounded more curious than annoyed.

"Trying to focus." Felicity's heart pounded. *Philip is sick*, it cried. *Philip is sick. Philip is sick.*

"You have a dressing room for that."

"I like to come backstage when it's quiet." *Philip is sick.*

"Ah, I see."

"A true artiste," the Scottish man approved.

Philip knelt down beside her and took one of her hands between his, just as he did in the Giovanni duet. "Listen, Felicity," he said. "You weren't supposed to hear that."

"I know." *Philip is sick.*

"I'd appreciate if you kept it to yourself," Philip said. "I don't want it hanging over the concert. As you know, I've always valued my privacy. There is still cause for optimism. I've known for a while. That's why I returned to the stage. But now it seems more intense treatment is needed."

"I won't say anything." *Philip is sick.*

"Where are my manners?" said Philip, standing up. "Felicity, this is an old classmate of mine from the Royal Northern College of Music, Luke Christie, who is now the artistic director of the Scottish National Opera. He was just having a gander at the set-up on stage because he's got a tour coming here. Luke, I don't believe Felicity needs an introduction."

Felicity felt a tingling as she shook Luke Christie's hand. "One of your top students," Luke Christie said. "The young Zerlina who took Lucerne by storm. Is this perchance who you had in mind for my Adele?"

He looked at Philip and back to Felicity. "We are moving into a new facility in the next year or two, and we have decided to christen it with *Fledermaus*. It's a crowd-pleaser, but it's got all this symbolism of disguise and reinvention. Do you sing Adele?"

Felicity said, "You'll have to talk to my agent about that."

Philip and Luke Christie laughed. "I see you taught her well," said Luke.

SHE HAD TRIED her best to put Philip's illness out of her mind during the rehearsal, but it nagged at her. She had gone five years without seeing him after completing her studies at the Guildhall and before singing with him in Lucerne. It wasn't as if she couldn't live without him, but during those five years, she had known where he was. She thought of his advice all the time, and if she needed a refresher, she could write to him, or incur the expense of a call, or drop in on him if she was in London. The thought of that lifeline disappearing made her feel frail and alone. She remembered Philip trembling when he sang of death and judgment in the *Giovanni* sing-through, and she trembled too, with anger that he had kept it to himself.

The next day her thoughts were all for Claude. The newspaper article had said that Tibbs would meet the prime minister in the afternoon, so Felicity set out before noon. She made sure her hair and makeup were just right and brought an umbrella to protect them should it start to rain, as it probably would. She packed her gown and shoes for the performance into a small suitcase and brought it with her.

There were crowds outside Number Ten when Felicity arrived. Many of them were Black people waving signs: "TIBBS STEP ASIDE." "NO INDEPENCE WITH PERCY THE KILLER." "FREE ELECTIONS FOR GRENADA." Felicity scanned the crowd for familiar faces, but she saw no one from the protests she had once attended. They had all gone home or moved on, and this was a new generation of students, young and firm in their zeal as she and Claude had once been. She attached herself to the edge of their group and waited. It began to rain, a light, cold drizzle. She opened her umbrella. She had underestimated the cold of a London January — even with no snow, it was biting. She waited and waited. People came and went. Tourists posed for pictures in front of Number Ten. A line of bobbies kept the protestors from getting too close.

It was almost three o'clock. Felicity was shaking with cold. This was terrible for her voice. She should leave. She should be hydrating, relaxing, gently warming up. She began talking herself into turning around and making the walk back to the Tube station. She had just decided to go when a black car drew up. A valet came out of Number Ten and opened the back door of the limousine. Percy Tibbs stepped out, then a woman who must be Tibbs's wife, judging by the way she clung to his arm, then a man she didn't know, then Neville, then Claude. He was no more than an arm's length away.

"Claude," she said. His head turned towards her. His eyes widened, just a little. She thought a smile was coming, but he turned back to the car and bent his elbow, positioning his body between her and one more person still getting out. Despite his efforts, Felicity could see Marlene, the expanse of her stomach straining against the buttons of her coat, her nose wide, her face greasy and dotted with acne. Pregnancy did not suit her, but it made no difference to Claude, who helped her onto the pavement and into the house without another glance at Felicity. She would almost have doubted that he had seen her, except she knew he had. While the protestors roared and shook their placards, Felicity trudged back to the Tube station, cold and shaken.

He no longer wanted her. It was over. He would not be coming to see her tonight. Marlene had finally become pregnant with his child — his son, if Claude got his wish — and Claude was devoted to them. It was early, but the theatre was the only place she could think to go. She could not cry; it would dry out her nasal tissues and affect her voice. Singing was the only thing she had left, and she was not going to sacrifice it to Claude.

She was the first to arrive at the concert hall and had to wait for a caretaker to let her in to the backstage area and open her dressing room. She collapsed onto the couch, rubbing her hands and feet, trying to dispel the chill. She wiped off her makeup and applied a fresh face. It was more insurance against crying — tears would make a melted clown of her. She warmed up. She was singing "O luce," which had been her song for Claude, but now she tried to reimagine it. Perhaps it was about Grenada? Perhaps it was about Philip, the man who had taught it to her? No, that wasn't any better, because Philip was sick.

She kept herself busy until it was time to perform. "O luce" was first. The master of ceremonies had talked to her about how Philip had taught her the aria in her first year in his studio, but she had not expected him to give Philip's side of the story. "Mr. Cook said that it was, and is, very uncommon for a first-year student to be cast in a lead role in an opera at the Guildhall. Miss Alexander was selected for two leads. He had no doubt she was up to the task vocally, but was concerned that she might not have the mental stamina, that she might not believe in herself enough. All those doubts washed away when he heard her sing "O luce di quest'anima" for the very first time in his studio. He said it was then that he had a vision of Miss Alexander's career as it could be — glittering, exalted. We present that vision to you tonight. Ladies and gentlemen, Miss Felicity Alexander."

Felicity knew then that her resolve would not hold. She was going to cry on stage. The tears were already gathering at the corners of her eyes. The news about Philip and the words just spoken would have been enough, but Claude had shut her out, in the cold, on the steps of 10 Downing Street. She had no choice but to let the tears come, because they were coming. The audience would assume it had something to do with Philip, that there was more to his retirement, that there was more to their relationship. Let them assume.

She sang, and she cried, and she hurried off the stage to her dressing room, and now she could cry as much as she wanted. She lay face-down on the couch in the purple gown she had chosen and wept into the evening where she had imagined herself delirious with the triumph of a successful performance and the anticipation of meeting up with Claude. At the interval, Philip knocked on her dressing room door. He was not so rude as to ask her why she had cried, but he inquired if she was feeling all right. She knew he thought she was upset because of what she had learned about his health, and he felt guilty about it. He didn't stay long, and she didn't invite him in; he would think it was improper. She pulled herself together and got through the ensembles. After the concert, she left the reception as soon as she could, going back to her hotel to begin the rest of her life without Claude.

In the morning, the front desk put forward a phone call to her room. It was Robin, his voice brimming with the kind of elation that could only be found in an agent who discovers they have backed the right horse. He was so excited, he seemed not to notice the dull, dead tone Felicity heard in her own voice.

"Felicity," he said, "I have phenomenal news. Your performance last night has reaped dividends. Many companies who were considering hiring you are now reaching out. I'll save the best for last, shall I?" Without waiting for her response, he went on, "I had a call from Scottish National Opera about *Fledermaus*."

"I know about that already," Felicity said.

"Lucerne wants you back. They're thinking *La fille du régiment*. Perfect role for you. The Royal Opera House, remember we've been talking, well, they have an opening in the '75-'76 season for a Papagena, and then the next season they want something more substantive, an *Elisir*. The Royal Concertgebouw in Amsterdam wants you to do a recital, with piano, open to suggestions for a pianist."

"Will," said Felicity.

"Who?"

"William Nesbitt-Jennings."

"And then." Robin took a big breath. This was it. Felicity's destiny. She already knew what he was going to say. "The Met. In winter '76-'77. You've sung a Handel opera before as a student, haven't you?"

"I was in *Alcina*."

"The Met has decided that Handel isn't just for students anymore. They're mounting a production of *Giulio Cesare*. And they want a beautiful Black woman to play the role of Cleopatra. It's a phenomenal debut, Felicity. The world will be watching."

She had manifested this, and in her lowest hour, at the time of her deepest need, her dream had come to be.

"The rest of the cast is not confirmed, but they have Katherine Woods as Cesare, and they'd like to hire another Black singer or two, preferably also in Met debuts."

"Which roles?" Felicity asked.

"Cornelia, Tolomeo, Sesto ..." No doubt he was already considering which of his other clients might be a fit.

"Are any of those roles for a mezzo?"

"Cornelia, the widow. Why, is there someone you'd like to work with? I'm sure they'd consider that."

"Carolyn Grant," said Felicity.

"Who?"

"I did the *Porgy* tour with her." I must be crazy, Felicity thought, though she knew why she was making the suggestion. Claude thought she was a drag on the movement, that she had no revolutionary spirit. That was why he had turned away from her. But here she was, proving her commitment to the Black struggle in her own way, even if Carolyn would never appreciate it.

"Isn't she a bit older? I think they want a young person at the beginning of their career, like you."

"She's earned it," Felicity said. "She was singing before the civil rights movement when it was really hard for Black singers. If they want to support us, they need to acknowledge the people who paved the way for us."

"I can make the suggestion," Robin said.

CHAPTER 41.

New York City, March 12, 1977

FELICITY WAS SUFFOCATING. Every breath felt like her last. Each time she drew air, she sucked it through a pipe stoppered with ice. The lightbulbs rimming the mirror of her dressing room fractured into jagged chips of brightness that scattered onto the black and white tiles. When she stood, the floor sloped upwards and the walls squeezed inward. The flowers on her makeup table wavered as they bent their heads in her direction. The petals detached from their stems and floated upward, forming new bouquets behind her vibrating eyeballs. She was suffocating, and she had waited too long to save herself.

She took the back staircase, her crinoline-lined skirts in one hand, her score in the other. The air backstage trilled with the energy of the final moments before curtain. Stagehands hurried about adjusting ropes and wires, and from the orchestra pit beneath the front lip of the stage, the steady whine of the oboe cut through the dissonance of string players perfecting competing scale passages. Careful not to disturb the intricate loops that the hair department had spent hours pinning into her wig, Felicity opened the stage door a crack and stuck her head through. She fumbled inside the corset of her silk ball gown to retrieve the precious package that she had stowed against her left breast. She lit the joint with the matches that nestled under her right breast and tried not to smear her lipstick as she savoured the sweet smoke.

The stage manager's voice crackled through her headset above the din from the orchestra. "Miss Alexander, curtain in fifteen."

The pay phone was right there on the corner of Broadway. She didn't like to think of what would happen if the general manager ever got a whiff of this, but she ran towards it. It was typical of New York that a woman in full Baroque costume and wig barely received a glance from the crowds thronging the street. Weirdness was to be expected in the theatre district. Dropping a fistful of dimes into the phone and whispering the numbers to herself, she dialled, hoping he would be the one to answer. When he was, she said, "Jack. I'm suffocating." She wanted to let herself cry, but that would ruin her makeup and her voice.

"Fizzy," said Jack. "You're not suffocating. You're doing just fine. Aren't you performing tonight? Where are you calling from?"

"I'm at a pay phone. I'm waiting to go on, but I can't do it."

"What do you mean, you can't do it? You're a born performer. You do this all the time."

She took another puff of the joint. "Right now, it feels too much."

"Fizzy, it's a dress rehearsal, isn't it?" Jack said. "Not the real thing."

She smiled at the confirmation that he knew her schedule. That he understood her world.

"Who even comes to a dress rehearsal?" said Jack.

"Students." Felicity remembered her student days, sitting in the audience at Covent Garden as the world's most celebrated voices floated down to her, dreaming of one day being in their place. She thought of her very first *Bohème* with Will. "They're the harshest critics."

She heard the click of Jack's lighter, the moment he took to fill his own lungs, before he said, "The real critics love you. You know that."

The critics might love her, but the general manager didn't. The story was too much to explain to Jack now, but the trouble had begun as soon as she arrived in New York and learned that Enzo Romano would be conducting the show. Since he took over for Hans in *Don Giovanni,* his star had risen as rapidly as Felicity's: he had covered twice for other conductors at the Met, and *Giulio Cesare* was his third Met show, his first as Music Director. But the terrified, vomiting Enzo Romano of Lucerne had been transformed into a suave, international Maestro who acted as if he had no memory of that night, and who was a tyrant with his tempi.

Three days before, at the sitzprobe, the first rehearsal on stage with orchestra, Felicity had taken the Adagio marking at the end of the B section of "Totto può donna vessoza" as a chance to add some florid ornamentation, as her vocal coach had suggested. Enzo did not attempt to understand what she was doing. He brought the orchestra to a halt. "Let's have none of that," he said. "Just a slight slowing, but sing through."

"I thought —"

"They don't pay you to think," said Enzo. The chorus, spread out in the audience for the moment, snickered. Felicity withered. She was sure she heard Carolyn laughing. When the aria began again, she ignored Enzo and made the Adagio even slower and more ornate. Enzo rapped his music stand with the baton.

"No," he said. "No, no, no, no. Again."

The third time around, Felicity did not slow at all, but made her voice bored and flat and exaggerated the beat in a peasant-like style. Enzo glared, but did not stop.

Felicity knew how she could bring him down a peg. The next day, she called Luigi Bertolli, the opera gossip columnist, whom she had met at a post-show reception the previous season in San Francisco, and she invited him out for a drink.

"So tell me what's going on at the Met," Luigi asked in his breathless, nasal voice. "Who's fucking who, who's not getting along, who had a big fight."

"Off the record."

"Always, hon."

"Enzo Romano," Felicity said. "I've fucked him before."

The column had come out yesterday, and the general manager summoned Felicity to his office before the evening run-through. It was only when she saw him with the newspaper spread out on his desk that she realized this might not have been a good idea. This was her Met debut. She was not taking Philip's advice to behave.

"Miss Alexander." The general manager's eyes were breathtaking in their complete lack of warmth. He tapped the newspaper. "I am reading disturbing rumours."

"About what?" Playing innocent was the only way to go.

His stare grew more pointed. "We like games, do we?"

"No idea what you're talking about." She forced herself to smile, not to shake.

He puffed out his cheeks and pushed the paper aside. "This is your first time here, Miss Alexander. If all goes well, the Metropolitan Opera tends to enjoy long relationships with its principal artists. But if it does not, well —" He drew a line across his neck. "You follow the conductor's tempi, or you will not sing. Do you understand?"

"Miss Alexander," came the stage manager's voice through her headset, still transmitting at this distance, "curtain in five."

"Jack, I have to go." She wasn't on till Scene 5, but they would want her close and accounted for.

"Call me after, Fizzy." He exhaled again, and the familiar sound steadied her. She knew what she was going to do. There was really no question. She didn't want to sing at the Met again if she was just to be a body, not paid to think, expected to follow some puffed-up pretender.

WHEN THEY REACHED the Adagio, she slowed down. She felt Enzo trying to catch her eye, trying to whip the orchestra ahead of her. But the players were professionals, and they melded their lines to hers. Enzo's beat relaxed, his movements matching her breaths.

The audience breathed with her too. At the close of the aria, they gave her a standing ovation, unusual in a dress rehearsal. Enzo laid his baton on the stand and scowled.

Her last aria was the exquisitely slow "Piangero, la sorte mia." Her outfit was skimpier — a beautiful chest piece over a silky tunic — and her wig had been removed to reveal a head of dark-red, waist-length braids with blue glass beads on the ends. Two braiders had been brought in from the Bronx and had spent five hours on Felicity's style. Despite looking stunning, Cleopatra had just lost the war and her lover, and now lamented *I will weep for my cruel, painful fate as long as there is life in my body.* Even Enzo could not find a way to rush this. Felicity thought of the role study she had done with the Met coaching staff. Handel ended the opera with Cleopatra triumphant and ruling over Egypt, but later, according to the acting coach, legend had it that she died of suicide by snake bite rather than face the humiliation of defeat, and "Piangero" foreshadowed her death.

She crossed downstage, travelled upstage left, returned to centre stage. Her body had learned the directions well enough to execute them without thought, leaving her mind free to dwell on Claude, for this aria was all about him. She had lost him but gained a career. Cleopatra got to have love and power, but Felicity was not so lucky. She crooned to Claude, so softly at times that she sensed Enzo hushing the orchestra. It was not a surprise, was almost welcome, when the tears started. And, as Philip had advised her so long ago, Felicity let them flow. The rustling in the audience let her know that this had not gone unnoticed.

Felicity sang, pulling back on the high notes. Cleopatra was already realizing her love affair was doomed. Her seductive powers would not last. Beyond her glorious conquest lay only sorrow. All love, everywhere, turns to grief. Enjoy happiness where you find it, because it will not last. Find comfort in music, because it is all you have left. Felicity sang and cried.

The audience gave her another standing ovation, this one even longer. They wanted her to sing the aria again, in contravention of the Met's policy against encores, but Felicity waved them off, pointing to her throat. She had to save her voice. The audience and the lights were blurred as she stumbled off the stage. The makeup artist met her in the wing. "Let's get you fixed up," he said, with a practiced calm. He had used waterproof products, just in case, but they were no match for the force of Felicity's tears.

CHAPTER 42.

Los Angeles, California, March 9, 1981

AS SHE WAITED for a car to pick her up from the studio, Felicity sipped a mimosa and flipped through the *Los Angeles Times*. She started with the entertainment section and was pleased to see that her latest recording had earned five stars. The blues record she had put out last year had garnered enthusiastic approval from jazz experts but had been less enthusiastically received by the classical world. She was now putting the finishing touches on a recording of *Guilio Cesare* with a full period orchestra, not the modern one that had played at her Met debut. She saw her name in a second article and read: *Felicity Alexander is an overrated opera singer.*

"What?" Felicity lurched forward and half the contents of her glass spilled across her knees and the newspaper. Opera snobs sniping at her blues recording was one thing, but she was almost universally praised for her work in the classical arena.

Let us not forget that while other far more worthy singers toiled in minor European opera houses to hone their craft, read the article, *Felicity Alexander's celebrity came as a result of her last-minute substitution for the incomparable Jane Masters, implausible as that sounds, using her physical difference from Miss Masters to make a political statement, rather than staying true to the composer's vision. That cheapness has never left her. Her recent performance of* Norma *at Covent Garden is a prime example. One of the most divine arias ever written, "Casta Diva," was transformed by Miss*

Alexander into — Felicity put the soggy newspaper down. Her fingers tingled. Something sounded familiar. She looked down at the byline. Sarah Stilwell-Adams, her former classmate.

"That bitch!" Felicity knew she should stop reading. Sarah was jealous. She had always been jealous. She had not achieved the singing career she had longed for when she came to the Guildhall. The one they all longed for, even knowing few would accomplish it. And it must be an especial jab to Sarah that it was Black, foreign, outsider Felicity alone who had reached that goal. Desperate to punish herself, to absorb the malice bleeding from the paper with the sodden ink, she read on: *Felicity Alexander has become a celebrity, a woman known for her outfits and her string of romances more than her music. Her vocal talent has taken a backseat to a personal life that leaves much to be desired.*

Her car arrived. Felicity snapped back to reality. She balled up the newspaper and threw it into the garbage can as she left the building. She was here in Los Angeles not only to make a recording, but to shoot a film version of *La Boheme*. Sarah was watching from afar, a journalist and not a singer. Sarah was the outsider, and Felicity was the insider now.

Felicity had argued with her new agent, Margit, about which role to sing in *Boheme*. Robin was more sanguine about the switch than she had expected; her New York agency represented most of the Met's regulars, and its agents were experts at running interference between the singers, artistic staff, and management. Margit was doing the same thing with the movie production team now. When the film studio first requested Felicity's participation, she had wanted to play Musetta, thinking of how the colourful, scene-stealing character would look brilliant on camera. It was a rare event to have a Hollywood studio interested in filming an opera, and Margit had insisted that Felicity take the director's offer of the lead role of Mimi — which, like Musetta, she would never be asked to play on stage as they both required bigger, fuller voices than Felicity had, which film editing could address in a way live theatre could not. The role of Musetta eventually went to a singer with a genuine big voice: Alesya Kravchenko.

Today they would be filming Musetta's big scene. Alesya came up beside Felicity as she checked her reflection in the mirror hung behind the set.

"Looking good, sweetie!" Alesya said. "But not as good as me!" She struck a pose like a model on a runway. She seemed determined to wear Musetta's big personality off set as well as on. When she and Felicity had worked on *Nozze di Figaro* in Chicago, Alesya had driven cast and crew nuts, mooning about as the spurned countess, even at coffee breaks. Felicity found it endearing; she herself was able to slip in and out of roles like changing costumes, but she enjoyed watching the processes other singers used.

Felicity scowled into the glass. "I'm not feeling so great today." She saw that she looked tired, even under the layers of makeup.

Alesya exaggerated her alarm. "Don't give me whatever you have!" she said, emitting her Musetta scream.

"No, it's nothing you can catch," Felicity said. She felt worn down and unsettled. The weight of this nomadic, competitive, lonely life pressed down on her in a city where people chased perfection.

"Period coming?" Alesya made a sympathetic face.

"Something like that."

"I have Midol, if you need. Always good to be prepared."

"I'm okay for now, but thanks."

"So, I saw an interview you did," Alesya went on. "You said you're half-Ukrainian?"

Felicity wondered what had possessed her to share that fact. The way the interviewer kept saying she looked exactly like the rising soprano Evelyn Grimm had annoyed her; Evelyn was extremely dark-skinned and had delicate features and was very slim, but the interviewer saw none of those differences, and certainly not the contrast between their skin tones. Felicity hadn't realized that her comment, spoken out of irritation, would be published. "Yeah," she allowed.

"I always knew it," Alesya said. "You have the ... you know" — she tapped the middle of her face — "the nose. The Ukie schnozz."

Felicity knew exactly what Alesya was talking about. Her nose, which had always felt mismatched and unbalanced compared to her other features, prevented her from being a real beauty. Alesya had a similar nose, but it fit better with the rest of her. Alesya didn't have competing Black ancestry. The last thing Felicity wanted was a calling card from her father, front and centre on her face.

They were called to the set where, after days of being the constant focus, Felicity, in character as Mimi, was in the background, sitting at her table in the meticulously constructed café commenting bemusedly to Rodolfo about Musetta's attention-seeking behaviour. The chorus members were milling around the square examining the stalls displaying toys for purchase on Christmas Eve.

Over the clamour generated by Musetta, Marcello, Alcindoro, the waiters, and bystanders, Felicity leaned in close to her leading man and sang of love, true love, not the games Musetta was playing, just love. Over the strength of the piano playing the orchestral score, the bigger voices of her co-stars, the antics of Musetta in a flashier, brighter coloured gown, the bustle of the chorus, Felicity's voice rose.

The director called "Cut!" and there was some huddling, some discussion, and then assistant directors began circulating among the groupings of chorus and extras, making minute changes to where they stood and adjusting lighting. Felicity, unused to the ways of film, tried to shake off her feeling of boredom. Once again, the piano started and her voice pealed out across the set. Her mind lingered on what she was singing. "Io t'amo tanto, e sono tutta tua ... Che mi parli di perdono?" As Musetta preened and flirted and commanded attention, Mimi's pure love floated above it all, *I love you so much, and I am all yours. Why speak to me of forgiveness?* Her love for Claude had once been so strong. No one and nothing could penetrate it. Did he remember that?

She could let herself cry, but she couldn't sing with a stone in her heart, with a rope around it pulling and choking. She slid to the floor. The piano kept playing as the tears spilled silently down her cheeks. A minute or two passed, then "Cut!" said the director again. The music stopped. Felicity dropped her head to her knees, shoulders shaking. The director huddled with the rest of his team, and then announced that they would be breaking indefinitely. Timothy Faustino, the singer playing Marcello, helped Felicity up from the floor and slowly walked her off the set, his arm around her. Felicity buried her face in his shoulder, heedless of the smears her makeup would leave on his costume. As they left the stage, she heard one chorus member ask another, "Do you know what's going on?"

She heard the reply, "Didn't you see it in Luigi Bertolli's column on Monday? Her old teacher, Philip Cook, is sick."

Tim took Felicity to her trailer. No words were spoken as they undressed each other. He knew the treatment she needed. Just as they were about to begin, there came a knocking at the door. Timothy swore and wrapped a towel around his waist before going to answer.

She heard him ask, "What do you want?"

A gofer spoke. "To see how long Miss Alexander needs."

"She has a headache," Timothy said. "She's lying down and can't be disturbed."

Felicity felt gratitude for Timothy, that he would be back with her in a moment, that he would take the rock from her chest, and she would not have to be alone. That even if it was only for an hour or two, someone would love her.

FELICITY SAT ON the couch on the set of *Late Night With Z*, opposite the host, Zebediah Miller. She was wearing a bright green silk dress with a very short skirt that continually rode up her crossed bare legs. The show's stylist had left her hair loose and curly in a huge buoyant mass. She knew that to the audience she shone in a way that only a woman with a red-hot career could.

The beginning of the interview was the usual breathless banter and preening commentary on the designer of Felicity's dress, jokes about whether Felicity's halo of curls was prettier than Zebediah's kinks styled into a tall high-top fade. Then the interview took a serious turn.

"You were involved in politics as a student in London, weren't you?" said Zebediah. He pressed a button, and the screen hanging over the set filled with a black and white photo. Felicity didn't remember seeing it before. She was wearing the plaid duffel coat that had seen her through all three of her Guildhall winters. Her hair was frizzy, as it always was in London, and she gripped a large megaphone and held it close to her rounded lips. To her right was Neville, his fist raised in a Black Power salute. To her left was Claude, his hand on her shoulder, smiling down into the soft expanse of her hair. It was a jolt to see herself, almost fifteen years ago, happier than she could remember being.

"You were known as the Nightingale of Trafalgar Square," said Zebediah. "You led the singing at anti-apartheid sit-ins."

"I did." Felicity should look at the person interviewing her, but she couldn't tear her eyes away from the picture of Claude.

"You knew Neville Carpenter, didn't you? You're together, right there in that picture."

"Yes," Felicity said. "We were friends in university."

"It's been just about a year and a half since he took power from Percy Tibbs in an armed coup."

"It was peaceful," said Felicity. "No one died."

"And you've gone from protester to diva."

Felicity uncrossed her legs and smiled into the camera, imagining that Claude was watching this interview. "Well, Z, I'm both. Because at the heart of it all, I'm still a girl from Grenada."

Zebediah Miller looked down at his cue cards. "Grenada has a population of less than one hundred thousand people, and a land mass of one hundred and thirty-three square miles," he said. "And you're here in Hollywood, shooting a movie version of an opera set in Paris about painters and poets. How does that relate to the protest movement you were once so connected to?"

Had Neville and Claude jumped out of the photograph to grill her themselves? Felicity took a moment to breathe calm into her chest before she replied. "I would love to be in Grenada, singing for my people. But thanks to hundreds of years of European rule, that isn't an option. Britain enslaved my people and took their labour for free and then ended slavery but continued to exploit us, and then they said they gave us our independence, though it wasn't theirs to give. They did it with a mad dictator in charge who was killing people, and they refused to tell him to stop because they wanted us to be weak. Neville was able to stop Tibbs, but now he's got the good old U S of A making it more difficult for his government to achieve what it's trying to. Nothing about that is elevated. Nothing about it is beautiful. I have to live outside Grenada to show the potential of Grenadians, but I am telling you, if the rest of the world ever allows it, Grenada will be great." She thought of one of Claude's favourite quotes. "Martin Luther King said that justice —" She couldn't remember the rest.

Zebediah cleared his throat. "I grew up in Tennessee," he said, "In Memphis. Heart of the south, where Dr. King got killed, and I remember every second of that day."

"Me, too," said Felicity. The day that began the end of her life with Claude.

"What were you doing?"

"I was in opera school in London. I woke up and I was getting ready for class. It came over the radio."

"I think I'm a little older than you?"

"I'm not telling," said Felicity.

"I'm forty-two," said Zebediah. "Yeah, I look good, don't I?" He struck a pose, to wolf whistles from the audience. "A bit too old for you, right?"

"I wouldn't say that," flirted Felicity.

"I was twenty-nine when Dr. King died. I was married to my second wife. Don't get me started on that."

The audience laughed at a joke they were a part of.

"I was working as an organizer for the Black vote. My wife and I were actually going to a rally to hear Bobby Kennedy speak in Indianapolis. He announced at the rally that Dr. King had been shot. People fell out screaming, crying. It was crazy. But, back to you. Do you keep in touch with Neville Carpenter?"

Felicity cocked her head. "No, I don't."

"He's a li'l hard to figure out, isn't he? He does these speaking tours and the journalists love him, but how can they love a Communist?"

"He's not a Communist, but so what if he is? Who says Communists are bad? Neville is doing a great job bringing a better standard of living to the people of Grenada, giving them a country they can be proud of." She didn't want to talk about Neville. Neville was too close to Claude, and thinking of Claude was still too distressing. She would have to distract Zebediah Miller. He wasn't bad looking. She'd seen worse. She reached over and put a hand on his knee. "I don't like to dwell on the past," she said. He would never know how much she dwelt on it at night, how she wove a hard pillow of the past that kept her awake into the morning.

Zebediah blinked and covered her hand with his own before recovering. "Well, all right. Let's talk about what it's like to be an opera singer. Lots of hard work, right?"

"That's right," said Felicity.

"And lots of dudes panting after you, I bet," he said. "Especially after a big performance? They all mob you after the show?"

"You got it." Their knees were touching, and she felt herself smiling again.

MARGIT GRABBED FELICITY'S arm as soon as she came off set. "What was that?" she demanded.

Felicity pulled free. "An interview."

"A mad dictator? The USA is making things difficult? Who says Communists are bad?"

"Well, it's all true."

Margit said, "You're here to talk about the movie, not politics."

"The host started with politics right away."

"And you deflect. You should know that by now."

Zebediah stepped off the set. "Commercial break," he said, then, "Is there something wrong?"

"We got too political," Felicity said. *Too Black.*

Zebediah turned his focus onto Margit. "That's my fault," he said. "I should have warned you that my show gets down and dirty."

"Can you do a disclaimer, when you go back on?" Margit asked.

"Sure can." He held out a pen and a notepad. "Why don't you write out what you want me to say?" As she began scribbling, he lowered his voice and said to Felicity, "And would you do me the honour of writing down the phone number of your hotel?"

CHAPTER 43.

Aix-en-Provence, France, August 11, 1981

FELICITY WAS BEGINNING to dare to hope that she could have what she never thought was possible: to be happy with a man who wasn't Claude. She couldn't spend the rest of her life using men to fuel her art or just to fill the space inside her. She had to grow up some time.

"So, princess, this is it. Our home away from home for the next month." Zebediah sat down on one of the loungers, pulling Felicity down with him. She didn't want to know how much a rental like this cost during the summer festival in Aix.

"The photographers —" she started.

He began unbuttoning his shirt. "They can't see over the hedges, and the fence, without getting themselves in serious trouble. We can get in the hot tub if you like."

"My bathing suit is in the house."

"So is mine." He grinned. "I swear, princess, they can't see anything. And if they can, they'll just be jealous."

Zebediah pulled her into the hot tub. She looked across the backyard and noticed for the first time the champagne bucket and glasses on the table. "What's that for?" she asked.

"Celebrating." Zebediah walked his fingers up her spine.

"I thought we just celebrated." Two days before, for the five-month anniversary of their first meeting on his show, Zebediah had met her at the airport and taken her out for dinner.

"That was the anniversary of when we met. This is the anniversary of when you agreed to see me again."

Felicity's stomach clenched, and Zebediah noticed immediately. "Princess, what is it? Aren't you happy?" He lifted her chin to face him.

"Of course I am," she said. "It's just — Happiness doesn't last, Zebediah." She didn't deserve this, she was thinking. To love her was to invite betrayal and misery. Her love was poison.

"Sure it does," he said.

"Really?" Bitterness crowded out everything else with its sick hum. "Have you ever had happiness last, Zebediah?"

His fingers stilled on her back. "Princess, that's not —"

"You had three wives, and where are they now?"

"Felicity." Zebediah had his mouth around her ear. "They don't matter. You matter. Maybe it just took me a while to find what I wanted. What I needed."

His wives had been married to him, Felicity thought. They had his kids. He could move on knowing he'd said everything. Tried everything. A band of envy closed around her heart.

"Oh, baby." Zebediah wrapped his arms around her middle. "One of those moods?"

He had never lived with her. There was so much he didn't know.

"I'm not going anywhere," he said. "I'm here to ride it out with you, whatever it is."

She felt a black sky rise from the horizon in her depths. She shook her head, unable to speak.

"I'm here," Zebediah repeated. "Shh. It's okay, princess."

She breathed in and out. "I ruined the celebration."

"No," he said. "No, you did not. I'm just happy I could go through whatever it was with you." He lifted Felicity onto the side of the hot tub and padded across the yard to retrieve two plush robes. He held Felicity's out for her.

"I'll have some of that champagne now," she said, struggling for brightness. She never should have agreed to date Zebediah. She was a mess. He wouldn't put up with it much longer.

He brought the bucket and the glasses over and poured for her. "Want to talk about it?" he asked.

She shook her head. It was difficult to form thoughts amid the bubbles of the champagne and the churning howl of her emotions. She had to convey to him that she was normal, recovered. Looking down at her toes, she saw the polish chipping. "My toes don't look so hot," she said. "I don't know when I'll have time for a pedicure, with rehearsals starting."

"I'll give you one," said Zebediah.

"You?" Felicity laughed, the sound welcome in her throat.

"Do you have polish and polish remover?"

"In my luggage."

"I'm a pro, princess."

Inside the house, Felicity sat in a recliner as Zebediah knelt at her feet. She watched as he cleaned off her toes with cotton wool. "I think these feet need a massage first, don't you?" he asked, smiling up at her. She closed her eyes as he smoothed lotion over her soles.

"How are your girls doing?" he asked.

She was taken aback by the question. She hadn't thought of her daughters since arriving in France. Men expected women to be maternal, Felicity remembered, and she said, "The girls are fine. I'm missing them, of course." Perhaps that could explain her behaviour.

"Of course," said Zebediah.

She lay on the couch, as the polish dried. Zebediah cooked dinner. She heard him humming as the pots and pans clattered. *He's happy*, she told herself. She had to let herself be happy too.

He prepared beef stroganoff, the latest dining craze, from a recipe he'd been given by the chef from the Russian Tea Room in New York, before coming to France. "So this opera you're doing here, it's by a cat called Donizetti, right?" He pronounced an English "z" rather than an Italian one, but Felicity didn't correct him.

"It is," she said. "How did you know that?"

"I got a book," Zebediah said. "Dude wrote almost seventy operas. They all good?"

"Some are better than others." She was touched almost to the point of speechlessness by the fact that he was reading about opera.

"This one you're doing, it's one of the three queens?"

"That's right. *Maria Stuarda, Anna Bolena,* and *Roberto Devereux,* which is about Queen Elizabeth the First. But I'm doing *Anna Bolena.*"

"They forgot a fourth queen," Zebediah said, nudging his glass with the rest of the champagne against hers. "But I call her a princess." He looked down at her feet. "That colour is perfect."

"My toes look great, Zebediah. And this beef is good too. You're spoiling me."

"Making the most of this time together," Zebediah said. "It's hard, being so far from you. I want to be there for all of it. I want to hear about your rehearsals in person. I want to make you laugh and see you laugh, not just hear it. I want to rub your back and tuck you up in bed when you're not feeling good. I want to have breakfast in bed with you and make you coffee in the morning and surprise you with presents you didn't even know you wanted."

"And —" Felicity was about to say, *And fuck*, but her need to neutralize Zebediah's romantic speech evaporated before she could say the word.

"And make love to you, of course, princess. I'm a man and you're a woman." Zebediah nudged her foot under the table with his.

After dinner, Zebediah tinkered with the television, using the satellite dish to raise American channels. He pulled up a news panel discussing the Cold War in the Third World. Felicity lay with her head in his lap.

"Ooh, Felicity. They're talking about your ex-boyfriend, Neville Carpenter," said Zebediah. He was smiling, but she sensed the real question, the one he kept asking.

Felicity sat up. "He's not," she said.

"Well you were, you know, with him, right? You had to be. He's known for loving beautiful women, and princess, if he was around you —"

"You're assuming I would want to," Felicity said. "The choice wasn't mine?"

"I'm sorry, princess, you're right." Zebediah reached for her, but she scooted away.

"Just because you watch all Neville's speeches and interviews doesn't mean you know him, Zebediah. For all you can tell, he could be a huge jerk."

"Is he?"

Felicity stood up. "I'm going to bed," she said.

It wasn't that she wanted to keep her past relationship with Claude from him. It was just that every time she tried to even dip a toe into that well of memories, they began to pull at her, threatening to submerge her in bitterness, pain, and fear. If she allowed herself to go down, she might never resurface. She would bring the stink of loss and desolation into this relationship and this joyous show she was doing. She might lose them too. She wanted to explain this to Zebediah, but even trying to do that caused her throat and eyes to swell in warning.

Up in the bedroom, she pulled out her folder of music for the French song recital that she was giving on her day off from the opera. When she got to "Si mes vers avaient des ailes," the last verse stopped her short.

Près de vous, purs et fidèles,
Ils accourraient nuit et jour,
Si mes vers avaient des ailes,
Comme l'amour.

In English, that meant, *Near to you, pure and faithful, they would hasten night and day, if my words had wings, like love.* The last time she had performed this song, Claude had been in her head. Wherever he was, she had thought she wanted to be there too. But now, thoughts of Zebediah crowded out all images of Claude. Zebediah was here. Claude was not.

IN SEPTEMBER, THEY moved from Aix to New York. The Met had engaged Felicity to play Linda in *Linda di Chamounix,* the first time it had mounted the opera in forty-six years, and the first time Felicity had performed it since the Guildhall. Once she was settled, Zebediah would go back to work in Los Angeles. The night before his flight, lying in bed, Zebediah said, "I'm so sorry I'm missing your opening, my love, but I'll be back next weekend to see your show." He traced a circle on Felicity's breast as they lay tangled in the sheets.

She snuggled closer. "I'm going to miss you," she said, burrowing her head between his neck and his shoulder, drinking in the smell of him. "You're good for my ego."

"Maybe you can come down to LA this weekend," he said. "I'll send the plane."

Felicity shook her head. "Can't," she said. "You could come here, though."

"I wish I could, but I have meetings. Shouldn't take long. We can still hang out. Come down. Please."

"The show opens Saturday. We'll have notes Monday afternoon."

"I'll have you picked up Saturday night when you're done and fly you back early Monday."

"But there'll be a reception Saturday night." A hot wire was twisting up through her throat through a river of simmering water, and she couldn't look at Zebediah. Her feelings of love for him were dissolving in the steam.

"Can't you skip it?"

The water bubbled, rising ever closer to the boiling line. "Zebediah, going to the reception is part of my responsibility to the show. And it helps me to get future work. There are directors and media at receptions."

"I'll pick you up Sunday morning."

"I'll be sleeping in. That's my chance to rest." There was no valve for the steam to escape. The bubbles sucked at the space between Felicity's ears, lapped at her chest cavity, seeped into her brain.

"You can sleep in LA. With me."

"Zebediah, flights are tiring. Especially across three time zones. And plane air is terrible for the voice." Her head was buzzing. The darkness was threatening. She had to shape the words in her mouth slowly, carefully, as if she were singing them. She wished she could sing, to relieve some of this pressure.

"Funny," he said. "You'd think marijuana would be worse."

"Which is why I mostly smoke it after the show. The most I have before I perform is a puff or two, just to calm me down." Oh, for a puff now. The blessed smoke would dissipate the steam inside her, allow her to breathe. She put a hand to her sternum, pressing on the pain inside, willing it away. "Why am I justifying this to you? I'm the singer, not you."

Zebediah lifted her head from his chest and thrust himself to a sitting position. "Of course. You're the singer and singing comes first. Sorry if I'm trying to make this relationship work."

"Zebediah, we've just spent a month together in France and New York. Now we both need to work." The buzzing further intensified as she turned to face him, trying to blink away the darkness that shivered in the back of her brain. "We'll see each other next weekend."

"Sue me if I want more!" he yelled. "I want more of your time. More of you. But you're wrapped up in the show, the show, the show."

A lump rose in Felicity's throat. "That's so unfair, Zebediah! This is what I do. You knew that when you met me. You're staying in LA for your meeting. Why is my show less important than yours? *Linda di Chamounix* almost never gets performed, and I finally have the chance to do it." It was getting harder and harder to speak. The words had to snarl out around the hot wire turning around her tongue.

Zebediah looked at her, his mouth a stubborn line. "So I need to get out of your way and let you be," he said. She was going to lose him, and the fear would come back, the stink, the dark. She would be alone again.

Felicity grabbed the water jug by the side of the bed and dumped the water over Zebediah, then began hitting him with it.

"Stop it!" He used his body weight to overpower and restrain her without returning a blow. She had no chance against his toned, muscular body, and after the jug fell to the carpet, she stopped spitting and scratching and flopped to the bed. She expected Zebediah to stroke her hair and comfort her, but he got up and began to dress.

"Where are you going?"

"For a run." He slammed the door. She waited up, but he didn't come back until after she had fallen asleep.

There was very little conversation between them in the morning before he left for the airport, and brief, stilted phone calls over the next few days. Felicity did not have time to dwell. She was busy with run-throughs, final costume fittings, and dress rehearsals. The show promised to be a sensation, a standout among the many she had done.

THE DAY BEFORE opening night was Felicity's first off that week. She went to the hotel spa for a massage. She returned to her hotel room to a flashing phone. There were several messages from Zebediah. She dialled him at home.

"Where were you?" he asked.

"The spa," she said. "What's going on?"

"Never mind. It's not important."

She sighed, feeling tension return too quickly after the deep tissue massage. "Zebediah, tell me."

There was a long silence, and then he said, "Maybe we need to take a break from each other, Felicity."

"What?" She was dizzy, nauseous, faint. She sat down on the bed.

"You heard me."

Carefully, gently, she replaced the phone in its cradle. It began ringing again, but she was already gathering her purse, her shoes, to go to the airport, fly to Zebediah, and win him back. Nothing mattered other than making sure she did not have to be alone again, that she would not have another reason to cry at night. She flew economy, shrinking herself into her seat using a baseball cap and blanket to disguise herself. As soon as the seatbelt sign went off, after landing, she leapt into the aisle, pushed past the other passengers, and ran to get a taxi. Looking at her watch, she realized that Zebediah would be in the studio, as it was now evening.

Security recognized Felicity and buzzed Zebediah for her. He came bounding out to meet her in the lobby.

"Felicity!" he said, his face creased with pleasure. "I can't believe it! What are you doing here?"

She had expected a chilly reception. "You said you wanted to take a break," she said, her voice trembling at the strangeness of his excitement to see her. "Please don't. I want this relationship."

"I do too, beautiful," he said, crossing the floor and taking her in his arms. "Of course I do. I'm sorry. I was in a funk when I said that, because I really wanted to talk to you and I couldn't reach you."

Felicity reared back as reality rearranged the events of the past few hours. Slowly, she said, "You didn't mean it, that you wanted to take a break? You let me think that for nothing? I came here for nothing?"

He spread his hands. "I said you could make it here before a show, no problem. You flew commercial? Let's go back to my dressing room and have dinner and some alone time before the show and I'll see if I can get you a charter back."

"You don't get it, do you?" The enormity of what she had done roared at her, its jaws open wide, spraying her face with spittle.

She turned and ran out of the lobby, looking for a taxi to get back to the airport and New York. Zebediah caught up with her on the street.

"Felicity, what the hell?" he said. "You flew all the way here, and now you're walking out on me?"

She expected that she would scream, but her voice was quiet, the words pushing through a thicket of emotion as she spun to face him. "I've been in a lot of great shows, but this is one of the best. It's seriously amazing. It could win awards. I risked throwing all that away for you. But you were only playing some kind of head game with me? Well, I'm the fool. I fell for it. Once, but never again."

His voice rose. "I wasn't playing head games! I was upset, but now I'm over it. I tried calling you but you didn't answer!"

"Because I was begging my way onto a flight here! For nothing!" Now she was yelling, heedless as to who might be watching. "You said we should take a break and you didn't mean it, but I'm saying it now, and I do mean it."

"Come on, princess. You can't be serious."

"I am serious!" she said. "Nothing is more important than this show right now. Nothing."

"Baby." Zebediah moved towards her, holding out his arms. "What brought this on? Did someone hurt you?"

She hugged herself, bent over sobbing, as an arctic wind blew through her in the LA heat. "Don't ask me. I can't tell you."

He flinched as if she had hit him. "After everything we've been through, you still won't tell me?"

"Can't," she managed through her sobs. She bent over further with the force of them. She could not go back to wailing on the floor, like when Claude left. She was strong now, she was in control, she wasn't that person anymore. She would not be that person.

"Aw. Baby. It's okay." Zebediah approached her with his arms out, but she put both hands on his chest and pushed as hard as he could. "I love you, princess," he said, his voice wobbling. Felicity thought of the libretto of *Traviata* that she was studying. Love was described as "croce e delizia al cor" — *cross and ecstasy of the heart*, and she had never felt that so acutely. Zebediah was her cross. He would weigh her down. She had to shed that weight.

"I love you," Zebediah said again.

"It's too late for that, Zebediah. Leave me alone. It's over. I mean it. It's over!"

He stepped back. "Okay, okay, I see you're upset. Let me get you that flight back. I'll come up to New York and see you on the weekend. We'll work it out as soon as we can."

"No. No," she sobbed. "I can't. I can't." The only person she wanted was Claude. His image, so long suppressed, lurched back violently into her mind. But Claude would never be here again. She feared she might vomit from the force of her grief. "Just get me on a plane."

"Sssh, princess," Zebediah said, retreating. "Stay here. I'll call and arrange something." She sank to the curb, hugging her knees, crying into her lap. He returned with a heavy quilt, wrapped her in it, and helped her into a taxi to the private airfield where the plane he'd chartered was fuelling up. She let him put an arm around her on the way there because he was getting her back to New York as quickly as possible. She made no reply when he said he would come to her as soon as he could. She cried the whole way back to New York, mourning every loss she had ever experienced. When she arrived at her hotel, the distortion of her face shocked her. Zebediah had made her ugly. She told herself she would have a hot bath, put a cold cloth on her face, and sleep. But fresh tears fell in the bath. When she lay down, her nightmares assailed her. The phone rang incessantly, no doubt Zebediah calling her.

Longing for comfort, she picked up the phone and dialled. It was the middle of the night and she felt guilty about waking him, but he answered on the first ring. She waited for him to speak first, to make sure it was actually him.

"Hello?" he said.

"Jack." A fresh onslaught of tears began.

"Fizzy, it's past four in the morning! Where are you, New York? Five in the morning for you? What happened?"

As she poured out her story, Jack's lighter clicked and the flame sizzled. The familiar sound grounded her. She had had a life before Zebediah, and she would have one after him. It had been a mistake to think she could outrun her past through a serious relationship. She would get through this, and she would do a better job of protecting herself in the future. When she paused, waiting for a comment from Jack, there was silence. She wondered if he had fallen asleep. Then she remembered he'd been awake in the middle of the night as well. "Jack, what's going on with you?"

He sighed. "I'm sorry, Fizzy. I know I should have something wise to say here, but I can't absorb the end of another person's relationship right now, not when I'm looking at the wreck of my own."

The agony in Jack's voice drew Felicity out of her own pain. In all the years she had known him — more than half a lifetime, now — she had gone through many of her own heartbreaks and griefs with him, but Jack had seemed impervious to the storms of life, calm and controlled, dispensing helpful advice, marijuana, and now, maddeningly, the occasional quote from the Bible. "What happened?" she asked.

"Abby left. Wants a separation."

"Jack, I'm so sorry." She plunged in, "Is it because of not having children?"

Jack's breath shuddered. "I think that's what did it, yes. We can't get past that. She wants to be miserable. She blames me. She thinks because I've had a lot of sex partners — You know."

"Oh, Jack."

"Sorry, Fizzy. I didn't mean to dump that on you. You called me for help."

"You should have called me earlier," Felicity said.

"How could I? You were so happy, Fizzy. Abby showed me some of the pictures in the magazines. You seemed so in love."

Remembering what she had lost, Felicity began to sob again.

"Oh God, Fizzy, I didn't mean to bring it up. I'm not myself."

"I have a show to do, and I don't know how I'm going to get it together."

"You're going to start by getting some sleep. Unplug the phone, draw the blinds, put up the do not disturb sign, and sleep all day. Do you have sleeping pills there?" He was beginning to sound more like the Jack she knew, taking charge of her, directing her.

"You know I always do." She hadn't needed them with Zebediah's warm body to soothe her to sleep, but she had brought them with her just in case.

"Right. Well, crawl under the covers and take some."

"Okay."

Jack gave a mirthless laugh. "Listen to us. A pair of sad sacks." The snap of his fingers travelled down the phone wires. "Want me to come down there?"

"What, New York?"

"Sure. We can be miserable together. I haven't seen you in an opera in a long time, and I've never been to New York. We could have fun, forget our troubles."

"We could." He would be a buffer against any potential attempts at reconciliation by Zebediah. "Sure. It's about time you saw the Big Apple. Why don't you look into flights?"

"I will. All right, bed for you. Call me tomorrow, after you knock them dead in the show."

CHAPTER 44.

New York City, September 28, 1981

THE GENERAL MANAGER spoke in a clipped voice. "A colleague of mine from the Los Angeles Opera telephoned me this afternoon." Felicity's skin grew clammy with a growing sense of doom as he said, "There is a rumour that you were in Los Angeles yesterday evening arguing with your paramour, a Mr. Miller, outside his television studio. A rumour that was picked up by the tabloid newspapers. Which is very strange, since you should have been here in New York, preparing for your media call and performance today."

He was a humourless robot, thought Felicity. He would never understand love, the subject of the operas he oversaw. She looked him in the eye. "You know what they say about rumours."

His jaw tightened. "Given your unexplained absence and the way your face appears, I do not think they are rumours."

Felicity wrapped her arms around herself and rocked forward, the pain shooting through her reminding her of labour. She was bringing forth something, she just didn't know what it was. She lowered her head, wanting to hide her tears from the general manager as the treacherous liquid ignored her direction to remain at bay. She could not believe she still had tears left.

"It is obvious you are very distressed," the general manager said. "I shall have the cover go on for you, and you may go back to your hotel and rest. We will announce that you are indisposed.

I will see how the cover does before I make a decision about the rest of the run."

Felicity's head snapped up. After all this, she was not going to lose the role she had given up Zebediah to sing. "No, sir," she said. "I'm going on tonight."

He gripped the edge of the desk. "You most certainly are not. And given this behaviour, the Metropolitan Opera is going to have to reconsider working with you again. We are tired of your antics, Miss Alexander. They call you 'Alexander the Great,' but inconveniencing others is not so great, hmm? Enough is enough."

Felicity stood up, pulled herself into singing posture, summoned her breath. "This is my role," she said. This was what she had been birthing. "I have lived and breathed this production for weeks. This cast is amazing. We feed off each other's energy. I had a lapse and I'm sorry. I let my personal life temporarily get the better of me, but I assure you, it will never happen again. I am ready to walk on that stage and give everything I have. As I always do."

The general manager frowned. "You are not emotionally stable. You must be tired after flying back and forth. Arguing and crying are bad for the voice. Linda is a demanding role, and a crucial one, and not one you've had in your repertoire in full. I'm sorry, but I don't think we can risk it."

"If it's so demanding, how can you risk it on a cover who doesn't have it in her repertoire either? How do you know she can handle the pressure?" Felicity said. "I have been singing here for six seasons. Have I ever given less than my all?" The general manager flinched under her gaze. "And let me tell you, this is not the first time I have sung here with my heart broken and my personal life in turmoil. I have never let you down and I won't now, because I'm not going to let a man take this from me. Any man, him or you!"

The general manager lifted a shoulder, as if to say, *Go on*. She resorted to a cheaper argument, one she despised, but which was necessary. "You know there are people here to see me. Me, the movie star. They'll want to see me even more now, because of my former relationship. If they've heard about the breakup, they'll be wanting to see how I'm taking it. The thing about me is that I can take what I'm feeling and put it all into my singing. The first time I sang here was not long after my husband died and left me with two little children."

It was six years later, and she had never grieved Anthony the way she was grieving Zebediah, but that was beside the point.

"My voice is in fine shape," she continued. "Listen." She opened her mouth and began to sing "O luce."

Halfway through the aria, the general manager stopped her. "All right," he said. "You can go on, but the cover will be costumed and waiting, and I assure you, at the slightest hint of a waver or a crack in your voice, you come off and she goes on."

"Thank you, sir."

"Miss Alexander," he said as she headed for the door. She turned, hoping he had not changed his mind. "See if makeup can do something about those eyes. Anyone in the front rows with opera glasses will be able to see them."

Outside his office, she ran into Carolyn Grant, who was playing the supporting role of Pieretto, the orphan. "Oh, you decided to show up," she said. "Heading back to your hotel now?"

"I'm headed to put my costume on," Felicity said

"You're singing tonight?" Disappointment distorted Carolyn's haughty features.

"Of course I am," Felicity said. "Maybe someday you'll learn how to sing too." She walked away, aware that several chorus members had heard this and would add it to the list of "Alexander the Great" anecdotes. Felicity already felt better with the besting of two people who were irritants. Her body tingled in anticipation of a spectacular performance.

From the murmurs that came from the audience as soon as the curtain rose on her first entrance, Felicity knew that word of her scene with Zebediah last night had reached the New York press.

Onstage, she stood in an arrow of light, watching the dust swirl through it like snow. She felt the audience watching her, waiting for the magic to begin. Enzo Romano was conducting. She deliberately avoided making eye contact with him as she began to sing the familiar words of the recitativo:

"Ah! tardai troppo, e al nostro favorito convegno io non trovai il mio diletto Carlo"

Ah! I am too late, and my dear Carlo is not at our favourite place.

She would not find Claude at their favourite place either, Trafalgar Square. She didn't know where Claude was or what he was doing now, whether he had a new favourite place with his wife and child.

The recitativo came to an end and the aria started. Picking up a bunch of flowers, Felicity sang:

"O luce di quest'anima,
delizia, amore e vita,
la nostra sorte unita,
in terra, in ciel sarà."

Oh, you are the radiance of my soul
Delightful life and love;
On earth and in heaven,
We will be united.

She took the slower tempo, the one that, predictably, Enzo had rejected at the sitzprobe. "The recit may be slower, but 'O luce' must sparkle. Sparkle!" he had said, shaking his baton at Felicity.

Felicity's stomach had seized. "I am not some naive ingenue, Maestro," she called down to the orchestra pit. She could not allow her beloved role to be reduced to vocal pyrotechnics. "I do not sparkle on demand."

"When I am conducting," he said, "you do whatever I command."

"Maestro, your wish is always my command," Felicity said. "On and off the stage." If he was trying to use their past encounter to blackmail her into submission, she would offer it up for public consumption instead. After the tittering from the orchestra stopped, she had followed his absurdly fast tempi for the rest of the rehearsal. But now, she was going to sing her aria her way. Now it was a game of cat and mouse.

She had expected that she would cry when she sang "O luce," but she really had exhausted every drop of moisture in her body. She felt the performance had been flat, but the audience disagreed. At the end of the aria, they exploded in shouts of "Bravo!" and tossed bouquet after bouquet onto the stage. She had had flowers thrown at her before, but never such a rain as this — roses, tulips, chrysanthemums, lilies coming at her from all directions as she curtsied and smiled and pressed her hands to her heart, in an imitation of the diva they wanted to see. Just when it seemed there could be no more flowers to throw, there was another wave. A man sitting near the front yelled, "Forget about Z! We love you!" and another yelled, "Z who?" Felicity smiled, wondering how Sarah Stilwell would view this breach of propriety, hoping someone would write about it for Zebediah to read.

Each time she left the stage and re-entered for another curtsy, the assistant stage manager told her how long the applause had lasted. At thirteen minutes in, it was still going strong, with shouts of "Encore!" Encores were strictly forbidden at the Met. "This is not a circus," the general manager said when he cautioned singers against reprising their show-stopping arias. Felicity looked down into the pit and met Enzo's gaze, ready to move on. The audience continued to cry "Encore!" as Enzo shrugged and lifted his baton. She almost fainted when the orchestra began playing the recitativo she had just sung. She took her encore, and there were another eleven minutes of applause after it.

There was a duet with Carolyn, now cowed into submission by Felicity's earlier bitchy comment, which received such a rapturous reception, they sang it twice also. Enzo seemed to be making a statement about the Met's encore policy. Or maybe just about himself. *My mastery of the orchestra is so great, it couldn't be helped.* As rude as she was behind the scenes, on stage, Carolyn played her supporting role faithfully, her voice melding and undulating with Felicity's in perfect synchronicity.

In her big love scene, Felicity surrendered herself to the sparks she had always felt with the tenor, the charismatic Donovan O'Donnell. She had made sure to cover her attraction with a layer of stagecraft, out of respect for Zebediah, but there was no need for that now. She allowed her body to press closer to Donovan's, knowing the journalists would catch their chemistry and Zebediah might read about it. At the end of the scene, Felicity walked off stage holding Donovan's hand longer than necessary. The cover's face fell before she pasted on a smile that mingled disappointment with relief.

At the post-show reception, Felicity was mobbed by a long line of admirers. Journalists roamed the room with cameras. Seeing the cover hovering nearby, Felicity decided to take pity on her, and bestow an encounter with the great Felicity Alexander upon her. She said to her, "Thank you for being there for me. Knowing there was someone ready to jump in if I needed it really made things a lot easier."

The girl smiled her surprise and said, "I could tell as soon as you opened your mouth I wasn't needed."

Felicity said, "It's a thankless job, to be the cover. I remember covering Adina at the Royal Opera House, back when dinosaurs roamed the earth, and wanting to sing the role so badly, being so close to it and yet so far from it."

"Not so long ago, I'm sure," the cover said. Then she asked the question Felicity heard incessantly from aspiring singers, "What do I need to do to have an operatic career?" In other words, *How can I be one of the few who get to do what you do?*

Felicity had given many answers to that question, but today, she said, "You put the music first. Ahead of everything. Anything else you have going on, anything. You sacrifice for your art." She smiled, thinking of Will dispensing Beethoven's advice. At the time, she had felt he was dismissing her feelings, but it turned out that he had been right.

The cover said, "I'd like to have a husband and kids someday."

"Bad idea," Felicity said. "Don't do it."

"Don't you have children?"

Felicity said, "Yes, and I'm a terrible mother. No, really, I am. And if I could do it over —" She realized what she was saying, and said, "I'm sorry. I'm tired. It's been a rough couple of days. Ignore me." She laughed, as if she could take the words back. The general manager made his way over to Felicity with a glass of champagne. She grabbed it and he said, as she drained it, "I wasn't sure you'd had a chance to have any. But you will limit yourself, won't you? You'll need to rest up for the next show in three days."

Stop babysitting me, Felicity thought, but she said, "Of course."

He said, "There's someone I'd like you to see, Felicity. Someone you may know?" He turned to the woman behind him and said, "This is Sarah Stilwell-Adams."

Oh, give me strength, Felicity groaned inside, as she stuck her hand out and said, "Nice to meet you."

Sarah, predictably, was extremely thin, her collarbone jutting through her gown, and carried herself as if she were very proud of her thinness, although it aged her considerably. *White women,* Felicity thought, glancing down at her own plumpness. Sarah's eyes widened as she took Felicity's hand. The general manager said, "Forgive me. I thought you two knew each other."

Felicity said, "I'm sorry, I don't remember meeting you. Sarah?"

Sarah opened and closed her mouth as the general manager said, "Ms. Stilwell-Adams told me she studied singing at the Guildhall in the late 1960s. Which, I believe, is when you were there. I asked her about that, and she said you'd done several operas together."

Felicity grinned wider. "I'm terribly sorry, but I don't remember that. But there were many people in the chorus. I suppose you could have been one of them? You must have been a year or two behind me."

"No, we were in the same year." Sarah ground out the words, her eyes searching Felicity's, but Felicity was an accomplished actress, and she had committed to the role.

"Sorry," Felicity said. "Don't remember. What have you been doing since? Where are you singing? I'm surprised we haven't worked together yet."

The general manager said, "Sarah is a journalist, and a reviewer, based in London." Felicity scrutinized him, wondering if he knew Sarah wrote vicious things about her, if he perhaps agreed with them. The general manager was not particularly beloved by singers, and at the closing night party, Felicity planned to regale her castmates with a hilarious send-up of his attempts to fire her.

"Oh, that's interesting," Felicity said. "Who do you write for?"

Sarah began rattling off the publications as Donovan appeared at Felicity's side with another glass of champagne and a plate piled with party food.

"Oh, Donovan, you love," Felicity gushed, then, "Excuse me, Sarah." She took a sip of the champagne, handed the glass back to him, and said, "Donovan, this nice lady is a reviewer all the way from London, and apparently, we went to music college together. Donovan O'Donnell, the most divine tenor, as I'm sure you heard tonight, and Sarah, sorry, what was the last name?"

"Stilwell-Adams."

The general manager said, "These two were magnificent together, weren't they?"

Sarah gritted her teeth and said, "Yes, they were."

"We'll be looking forward to what you write about the production," he said. Felicity decided that he must have somehow missed what Sarah had written before. However annoyed he might be with Felicity, he knew this show was special, and he would want positive publicity, not bitchy comments about the leading lady.

"Oh, reviews," Donovan said. "I can't be bothering with them. I never read them."

Felicity felt a rush of gratitude as she took her glass from him and sipped more champagne. She yawned widely. "I'm sorry," she said. "The show really tired me out. The encores and the flowers made it so much longer."

Donovan murmured in her ear, "If it's comfort ye're looking for tonight, I've got some on offer." It was unworthy of him to make such a cheap advance, and unworthy of her to accept it, but as the cameras clicked, recording her whispering her assent back to him, she knew that the picture of herself and her handsome co-star would go perfectly with the "Z who?" headline and more importantly, she knew she would not be alone tonight.

"If ye'll excuse us," Donovan said to the general manager and Sarah.

The general manager grimaced and said, "Don't keep her up too late. Make sure you both rest tomorrow."

"Okay, Dad," said Donovan as he led Felicity away, giggling. He muttered to her, "I hate that prick." Felicity smiled. This was shaping up to be a fantastic night.

She heard the general manager say to Sarah, "She's temperamental, but her artistry is beyond reproach. She's singing *Norma* with us next season. I await a phenomenal 'Casta Diva.'"

It was a bad day for Sarah. She might have tied her own hands by unwisely bragging to the general manager that she had gone to the Guildhall. If she wrote something panning Felicity's performance now, having admitted she knew her, it might be seen as a conflict, as the manifestation of the envy that it was, and the general manager would be sure to have something else printed that pointed that out.

Sarah had hated Felicity's blues album, but she was already planning on making another. She had not felt ready to record her favourite song, "Good Morning Heartache," because it was too perfect in its chronicling of her missing Claude. But now that she also had Zebediah to miss, she thought she could tackle it. As Donovan led her out of the theatre, she hummed the song to herself. She remembered her childhood and Aunt Rose singing her crying music. Aunt Rose had seemed so old to her then, but she had probably been younger than Felicity was now.

Heartache was always here. It always would be. It was a strange kind of joy, to be happy to wake up each day and sing about pain.

CHAPTER 45.

Winnipeg, Manitoba, October 10, 1982

"IT'S TOO BAD your boyfriend couldn't be here with us, Felicity," said Aunt Rose, as she took a sip of sparkling grape juice. "I shouldn't have any more, but Adele, can you pass me a little more of those mashed potatoes? I just love the way you make them with that nutmeg in there, Dolores."

Felicity shouldn't have any more either, but Aunt Rose was right, her mother's mashed potatoes were delicious — a buttery blend of Canada and the national spice of Grenada. It was always nice to have a home-cooked meal after weeks at a time eating from hotel and restaurant kitchens, no matter how posh. She took the bowl from Aunt Rose as she said, "He's working in Australia at the same time as me. We'll meet up next week in Sydney." She lied, "He would have loved to be here."

Mom said, "Well, I hope he doesn't end up a disappointment like that Zebediah. At least he's only been married once."

"Why isn't Josiah here yet?" Aunt Rose asked.

Uncle Jacob, Aunt Rose's brother and the pastor at Salvation Baptist, snorted with derision. Mrs. Jefferson, ninety-one now, smiled and nodded. When she heard the name *Josiah*, she said "Josiah? Such a lovely boy." Uncle Jacob snorted again and his wife nudged him in the ribs.

Aunt Rose said, "So, Felicity, your boyfriend? What's his name again?"

"Klaus."

"Do you think he's the one?" Aunt Rose clearly hoped for something. Felicity just couldn't tell what. She sensed that Aunt Rose still secretly wanted Felicity and Josiah to end up together. But Josiah had been in and out of jail for the past decade and a half. And Felicity loved him as a brother.

"For marriage?" Felicity laughed. "Aunt Rose, I told you. I don't want to get married again."

"But flower, you're still young. Young enough to have another baby. Maybe a boy."

"Ugh!" Felicity couldn't hide her distaste. "No way would I have another baby. And no way does Klaus want one either."

"Why not?" Aunt Rose said. "Men don't have to do the work, do they? Why wouldn't they want children?"

"Because they have to support them, Rose," Mom said.

"Oh, well, if the women insist on it, I guess they do."

"Klaus is a conductor," Felicity reminded them. "He conducts three orchestras, and he's in huge demand. He's guest conducting in Berlin next year. Most people think that's the best orchestra in the world. He doesn't have time for a wife and kids."

"Well, how does he have time to date you, then?" Mom demanded.

"We met at work," Felicity said. "We see each other if we're working near each other. The music magazines make it seem like more than it is."

Mom said, "The purpose of dating is to determine if a man is suitable for marriage. If you know he is not, then you are being a loose woman."

Felicity was sick of their scrutiny of her personal life. She was thirty-five years old with a successful career, and her mother still treated her like a teenager. In her purse was the latest edition of *Opera Canada;* she was on the cover for the eighteenth time, this time to spotlight her new recording, *Nightingale,* entirely made up of songs about birds, and her upcoming *Candide* in Sydney. She had intended to show it to Aunt Rose; Aunt Rose would appreciate the intricate gown they had dressed her in and the way they had styled her hair, pinning it into 1940s waves. Felicity hadn't read the article yet, but she remembered Klaus had come up in the interview, since he was conducting *Candide*. She didn't want Aunt Rose to see it now. She pushed her plate back. "I'm going to sit outside for a while."

"Can I come too, Mom?" asked Adele.

"No," Felicity said, "I want to be alone." She slammed the screen door as hard as she could and flopped down into a patio chair. The evening was warm for October, which was fortunate since she had left her sweater inside. The questions about Klaus had rattled her. She liked him a lot. His lack of emotionality was refreshing; after a lifetime of men who melted at the sight of her tears, it was a thrill to be with one who said , "Oh, shall we not cry over such a silly remark," or "If you are feeling unwell, Felicity, just say so, and we'll stay in tonight," or "I will leave you by yourself until you are settled, and then we can speak of this calmly."

Klaus wasn't comforting like Zebediah, or like Claude. He was clinical, analytical. In bed, as when he was conducting, he was capable of abandon, but offstage, he was eerily reminiscent of the general manager at the Metropolitan Opera, only sexier. When Felicity had a tantrum and broke a vase in his hotel room, he remained impassive.

"Let us talk about this, Felicity," he had said. "To the world, you are a confident, self-assured woman, *ja*? One of the best singers of our time, and you know it. Alexander the Great, hmm? A raving beauty who eats up men like me? But with a lover, the fears come out. With me, you are like a child."

He helped her to centre herself when she was floundering. But they had not discussed a future. She assumed he didn't want a commitment any more than she did.

She flipped through the magazine, past the pictures of her and Klaus in the production of *Magic Flute* at La Scala, where they had met. A headline caught her eye: *Winnipeg Arts Patron Celebrated.* Felicity was not well tuned-in to the music scene in Winnipeg; she was rarely home and performed at home even less frequently. She read the story with a vague interest.

Local philanthropist and patron of the arts, Bohdan Lysenko, has died at the age of eighty-nine. After a valiant fight, he succumbed to lung cancer three weeks after a Manitoba Opera concert held to honor his contributions to the arts. A lifelong lover of music, Bohdan gave true meaning to the term amateur, lending his strong tenor voice to numerous Winnipeg choirs, including the Manitoba Opera Chorus and the Ukrainian Community Singers. Many chorus masters and conductors noted his fantastic ear for music and the ease of his top register. Said Maestro Roy Nathanson, "It is a real pity he was born to a poor family and did not have the opportunity for a musical education. With training, he might have been one of the great voices of our time."

It was true, Felicity thought. So much of life was about chance. Had she not made her way to Mrs. Hammond when she was eleven, and if her mother hadn't taken on extra shifts to pay for the lessons, she might not be where she was today.

Born in Odessa, he was brought to Winnipeg by his parents at one year of age, part of the earliest waves of Ukrainian immigrants. At a time when Eastern Europeans faced discrimination in Canada, he worked hard to build his fortune. For many years, he was the owner-manager of the New Imperial Hotel in downtown Winnipeg, where he was known for his kindness to immigrants, often providing them with the first roof over their heads in their new country. When the Rest Well hotel chain entered the Canadian market, he sold the building to them for shares. He then used the returns on those shares to start his own hotel chain, Odessa Inns, named after the city of his birth. Over the years, he housed many visiting opera singers free of charge.

Having no wife or children, he has bequeathed his entire fortune to the Manitoba Opera.

Felicity stopped reading. Something had caught her eye. The New Imperial Hotel. Wasn't that mentioned in the letter that she had read on the night of Josiah's graduation? Didn't her mother once live there? Her landlord. Wasn't that who — Felicity's skin crackled with the sense that something dreadful was about to happen. Bohdan Lysenko was Ukrainian. Felicity's father was Ukrainian. There was a picture of Bohdan Lysenko in the centre of the article. With shaking hands, she held the magazine close to her face. She reached down to her purse for a mirror, but there was really no doubt. She would know his nose anywhere. It was the same one that dominated the middle of her own face.

She had found her father. There was the monstrous sight of a white man, wrinkled and smug, reflecting her features back to her. Now she knew where not only her facial structure, but also her singing talent came from. People always assumed that she was musical because she was Black. "Negroes are such good singers," they'd say, or "You people have a natural rhythm." They always found it funny when Felicity said that her mother did not sing, not even in church, nor did any of her Grenadian family. She said maybe she'd picked it up from Aunt Rose and her crying music, or from the church. Now it turned out that it was her father who had a love for opera, and she had inherited his gift. All this time, she had thought him dead, and he had been living, laughing in her throat, pouring out through her to the audience.

How dare her mother keep this from her? How dare she lie to her? Felicity remembered what Claude had said to her on their first date. If she met her father again, she was to tell him to fuck off. Well, Felicity could never meet her father now, and she could never say it to his face, but she could still say it. She held the magazine up and yelled, "Fuck off! Just fuck off!" She began stomping on the magazine, beating it against the floor of her mother's patio with her feet.

"Felicity, what on earth?" The screen door opened, and Mom, Aunt Rose, and Adele came out.

"I know who my father is!" Felicity shouted. "That fucking

disgusting scumbag!"

"Felicity! Language!" said Mom, then, "What are you talking about?"

Her hand trembling, Felicity held out the magazine. No one took it at first, until Aunt Rose plucked it from her, glanced at it, and passed it to Mom. Mom looked at it and then back at Felicity with the expression of a woman who had just seen the pits of hell. "Felicity ..." she began.

"You said he was dead!" Felicity yelled. "You lied to me, you fucking lied!"

Mom said, "Adele, go inside."

Adele pouted, but went.

"Felicity, we are not discussing this if you are going to use such disgraceful language."

Felicity hugged herself. Mom said nothing for a while. A flock of geese passed overhead, honking. Then she said, her voice like a prayer, "He was dead. He was dead to me."

"I thought if he was alive, he would have been there for me. He would have loved me." Felicity rocked back and forth. "When I finally got invited to have dinner with them, I told Brian's parents he was dead, and they looked at me like they knew better. Like I was yesterday's trash."

Mom's voice seemed to fracture in Felicity's ears. "Is that why you didn't want to marry Brian?"

"I didn't want to marry him because he's a piece of shit. Like my father. Like all white men."

"But, hon, your boyfriend is white," said Aunt Rose.

"Language," said Mom again. Then she said, "I told him that I was pregnant with you. I wanted him to marry me. But he wouldn't." She took a great sucking breath. "I wanted you to avoid the mistakes I made. Not to live with the shame."

"But he raped you," Felicity said, hearing the agony in her mother's voice for the first time. "You didn't make a mistake. That's not your fault. I'm just mad you lied to me."

"Raped?" Her mother's mouth hung open in a fleshy circle. "Who told you that?"

Aunt Rose said, "You shouldn't be so hard on your mother, Felicity. I think you know the pain she feels. You do, don't you? I know she would have done anything to protect you from knowing that pain."

Felicity's tears were like rain against her face. "Come inside," Aunt Rose said. "It's chilly out here. Never mind all this digging up the past. Some things are better left buried."

Felicity pushed past Mom and Aunt Rose and ran up the stairs to her childhood bedroom. The room where she had lain in wonder the night she lost her virginity to Brian. The room where she had spent the first days of Mara's life, believing her dreams had been crushed forever. She dropped to the floor. Her head was too heavy, so full of what she had just learned that her body couldn't support it. She needed Claude. She had kept her promise to him and told her father to fuck off. Oh, she needed Claude.

She didn't realize her mother had come into the room until she heard her voice. "Felicity, that was disgusting behaviour, and such language."

Felicity pressed her face to the carpet, feeling its rough weave against her wet cheek, waiting for her mother to leave. After a few minutes, there was a tap on the door, far more tentative than she would expect from her mother. Uncle Jacob entered.

"You have had a shock," he said. "Would you like to pray?"

The last thing she wanted was to pray. Prayer had never accomplished a single thing in this world.

"Then I will sit here and pray a moment in silence," Uncle Jacob said. He lowered himself to the ground and sat a few minutes, listening to Felicity's cries. After a while, he said, "I'll let you be alone now." As he stood, he laid a hand on her head. "God bless you, my dear."

After he left, Aunt Rose came in. It was like Grand Central Station, thought Felicity. All she wanted was to be alone. But Aunt

Rose was crying, too, her eyes red. She stood by the door, her lips quivering. "Oh, flower," she said. "If only you knew what your mother went through."

"She told you?" Felicity forced the words out through sobs.

"She didn't have to. She has blamed herself her entire life for something that wasn't her fault."

"So I was a mistake," Felicity said. She rocked back and forth on the floor. She had never intended to cry on the floor again.

"You were not, flower. God doesn't make mistakes. Having you gave your mother something beautiful after the ugliness she experienced." Felicity remembered the letter Josiah had read to her on the night of his graduation. They had danced to "My Girl" right before that.

Aunt Rose said, "Just remember, you are made in God's image."

Felicity didn't want to hear preaching. She covered her ears and wailed like a child, and didn't hear anything else Aunt Rose said before she left the room. She hadn't cried so hard since her breakup with Zebediah in Los Angeles. As her sobs finally began to taper off, she heard the doorbell ring, and Josiah's voice in the hall.

Uncle Jacob warned, "You had better not pull any nonsense with her. She's very fragile."

"I know that, Uncle."

Josiah came in and lay down next to her on the floor. "I heard," he said simply, his head touching hers. Felicity exhaled, reached for his hand and grabbed it. "He's a fucking asshole." Josiah said. He smelled faintly of marijuana, and more strongly of danger.

"Where were you?" Felicity demanded.

"Making deliveries," he said. "Don't ask."

"Oh, Jo, you're not doing that again, are you?" Felicity said. "You're still on parole."

"Do you have any idea how hard it is to get a job with a criminal record?" The anger in Josiah's voice made Felicity remember all the things he was said to have done to collect his debts. Women wept as they testified in court about his goons holding them and their children at knifepoint until their boyfriends paid. "You wanna get out of here?" he asked.

Felicity followed Josiah out to his car, fitted with flashy tire rims and heavily tinted windows. "Where are we going?" she asked, her voice still thick from crying.

"You'll see." As he drove, his pager went off continuously and he detoured to a few houses, ran up to the door for a minute and came back smiling. As one neighbourhood faded into another, Felicity realized that she knew where he was taking her. They were heading back to their elementary school. The last time she had been here was on the night of Josiah's graduation, the night he had told her about her conception, the story she had revisited tonight, the one she would never shake. She followed Josiah to the swings where seventeen years ago their futures had rolled out before them like a giant carpet. There was no hint then of prison for Josiah — he, the one who had understood the teachings of Malcolm X and explained them to her, the one who glowed on the sports field, dwarfing his rivals with his cocksure leaps into the air to catch the spiralling football.

They sat side by side on the swings. Josiah scrabbled in the dirt with the toe of his Reebok. After a while, he said, "Your dad's a shit, but so am I."

Felicity twisted the chains of her swing around and around. "How so?"

"I'm not a good dad to my kids. Not even sure how many I have now. And I've broken my mom's heart. So I'm probably not the guy for you to talk to about all this. Because as much as your dad's an asshole, I kind of get it, you know?"

"Get what?" Felicity looked up at the greying sky as the chains slowly unwound.

"Why he would just take off. Why he was probably ashamed. Just like my dad. Like me."

Felicity swayed back and forth. Josiah got up suddenly, causing the chains of his swing to jangle. "Come on," he said. "Let's go to the car and call Jack. That's who you should talk to."

CENTURIES OF SLAVERY and brutality and loss raced through Felicity's blood. She lay on Jack's couch, numb. *Claude isn't here* echoed through the room. She had done what Claude asked. She had finally done it. She had told her father to fuck off, just like she had told Brian. She didn't know how much time passed before Jack was at her side asking if she wanted to talk. She shook her head, unable to look at him. Jack had been a faithful friend over many years, but he too was white. She repudiated every treacherous white man who had ever been in her.

Jack said, "I'm going into the bedroom for a while." After he left, Felicity lay drinking in the quiet, then realized that Josiah was sitting at the table looking at her like a starving man surveying a banquet.

"Josiah, come here," she said, and Josiah came. Time began to crawl. Here, poised on the edge of memory, she could make a choice that had always been hers to make. Not making it had been the choice, until now. It was incestuous, it was obscene, it was not the right way to show this kind of love, but that was the point. She drew Josiah's body to hers like a drowning woman pulling close a buoy landing in the water, a lifeline arriving a moment before death. Only it was into death that she plunged, her breath as hot as his, tumbling without ceasing into the final moments of a lifetime of shared confidences and limbs wrestling on the floor, rolling on the grass, and hands clasped in prayer or in arm wrestling, and heads that once pressed together sleeping in backseats and on couches, now coming together in the way all flesh eventually coupled together with Felicity Alexander.

Afterward, Josiah said in a husky voice, "I've wanted that forever, Felicity." He began to hum, and then softly sing "My Girl."

Realizing the enormity of what she had done, Felicity said, "Josiah. It's not —" but she was unable to convey that it had been an act not of love, but of self-loathing. Josiah pressed his head against hers, the way he had done as long as she could remember.

She would know the contours of his skull, the prickle of his tiny, close-cut balls of hair, anywhere.

"I know," Josiah said. "You're far too good for me, and I know you're upset. I'm such a shit that I took advantage of that. I don't expect anything to change. I know you have that boyfriend in Germany."

"Oh, him," Felicity said. Klaus was white, so he would have to go.

ACT III
CHAPTER 46.

St. George's, Grenada, October 18, 1983

THE INHABITANTS OF Government House moved into the dining room for dinner and sat around the large mahogany table, where heads of state had once dined. Claude announced the power-sharing agreement, and Alison served wine in crystal champagne glasses. Felicity held hers up to the light of the setting sun. "These are beautiful," she said. "Where'd you get them?"

"Yes, where, Neville?" asked Lee. "Our foreign friend wants to know." Felicity slumped in her seat in the face of his malice.

"They belonged to Tibbs," Claude said. "We decided to keep them after the Revo because they belong to all Grenadians, and like it or not, we need nice things for state dinners."

"You decided," said Lee.

"The Party decided." Claude lifted his glass into the pink light. "To the Party."

They were still eating when the doorbell rang. They hadn't heard the car, but it sat outside. Felicity slid out of her seat and hurried upstairs without having to be told. Instead of going into Neville's room, she lay on her belly in the landing and looked down through the rails of the stairs. Claude and Neville stood in the hallway, facing off against five men.

"I had the Commander send for you because I thought about it again," Neville said, "and I'm not signing it." Beside him, Claude bit his lip, looking as pained as Neville was pugnacious. Felicity could tell by his expression that he hadn't known about Neville's change of heart until this moment. He wouldn't have announced the deal if he had known.

"But why not, Brother Carp?" asked one of the visitors. "It's a good agreement."

"Good for you, but Cuba won't agree to it. They want a strong leader, and you know he loves me," said Neville.

"If he truly loves you, he will love whatever you agree to."

"I'm not signing it." Neville folded his arms. "How can I work with Henry? He wants me dead. You want me dead," he addressed one of the men.

"No, brother. But we need more discipline. And you need help."

"What I need is for you to get out of my house," said Neville. "I am the only leader of this Revo, and if you want me to step aside, you'll have to kill me." With a sweep of his arm, he indicated the protestors outside the gates. "You hear them. 'No Carp, no Revo.' I am the Revo, and who are you, Mark Henry? A jealous man who wants what I have."

"Neville, wait," said Claude, but the five men turned and began walking to the door.

One of them stopped, turned around and said, "Your house arrest will continue until we decide what to do next." The door closed on the chants of the crowd, the army sergeants calling out drills, and the bark of dogs in the distance.

Felicity didn't wait to be summoned but hurried down the stairs. She asked, "Why did you do that, Neville?"

Neville shrugged. "I needed time to think. I wasn't sure."

"Well, what was there to think about?" Claude asked. "You say yes, or you say no. All this indecision, it gets people killed."

"What are you talking about?" asked Neville

"My father," said Claude.

"Your father?" said Neville. Then, "Oh! Claude, you're still angry about that?"

Claude blinked. "Never mind. I'm tired. Forget I said anything."

Neville snapped his fingers. "I know what we could do!" he said. "Felicity is so good at getting attention out of these soldiers, we could try to send her to Mark Henry to find out what he's up to!"

"Send me to Mark Henry?" Felicity hugged herself to keep her hands from throwing something at Neville. "Listen here, I am not some whore."

"I didn't mean —"

Felicity made a motion as if to slap him. "I may not be a virgin, Neville Carpenter, but I do exactly what you do. I sleep with who I want to sleep with. The same for a man as for a woman. I am not for hire."

"Okay, okay," said Neville.

Claude gave her the biggest smile she'd seen from him since her arrival. "You definitely wouldn't want to sleep with Mark Henry, Felicity," he said. "He's an ugly dog. A real pig."

"What are we going to do?" Felicity asked.

"We're going to fight our way out of here," Neville answered.

"Not yet," Claude said. "Only if we have to. No violence unless necessary, remember? That's how we defeated Tibbs. And there is a pregnant woman here."

Felicity made herself look at Claude. "How far along is she, Claude?" she asked.

"Seven and a half months," he said. "And it's getting tougher every day."

"It does at the end," said Felicity. "Especially in the heat." She shook her head slightly at the absurdity of discussing pregnancy with Claude.

Claude said, more to Neville, "She's scared. She's worried she'll go into labour in this house."

Felicity adopted a tone of sympathy and said, "First pregnancies are terrifying as it is."

"Oh," Claude said. "This isn't our first. Pat and I have a son already. A five-year-old."

Felicity called on all her reserves of acting to keep her face neutral. "Where is he now, if you're both here?" she asked.

"He lives with Pat's mother," said Claude. "And I have a daughter, Olga, with Marlene." He hesitated. "Marlene lives between here and your country, Felicity. She spends a lot of time in Canada. She ended up not being a fan of the Revo after all. So I have a Canadian child."

Now was the time for Felicity to bring up Adele, to say, *Actually, you have two Canadian children.* But Neville was there, and she didn't want a witness. So she said, "How about you, Neville, you must have many children by now."

Neville laughed. "I know how to be careful, Felicity," he said. "Marriage and children are not for me. Not yet. Not until the Revo is complete. That's why the people love me. All Grenadians are my children."

SHE SHOULD HAVE told Claude about Adele years ago. She lay face-down on the couch, reviewing all the opportunities she'd had to break the news. There was the first morning she awoke racked by nausea. As she stumbled to the bathroom, she bumped into a doorframe and her chest area stung, her nipples as hot as if they had been attacked by wasps. A ringing and a buzzing began inside her and she realized that she knew this feeling. *Oh God.* It was Claude's baby. There was no question this time. She had not even attempted to sleep with Anthony for at least two months before he died. After coming back from the *Porgy* tour, she had not been with anyone else. She had taken the pill faithfully, so she didn't know how this could have happened again, but it had. It was only later that she learned that the antibiotics she had been given at the Sauteurs clinic reduced the efficacy of oral contraceptives.

Claude had just buried his father, she reasoned. There would be family obligations. She would wait until he contacted her, until he had an international trip. She was about to give birth when she realized how long it had been without word from him. Well, she would tell him after the baby was born, once she knew the sex. But then she began to fear his reaction. He would be angry. He would think she had become pregnant on purpose. He didn't want to hear from her. She would wait until Adele was older, so it was clear she didn't want anything from him. She wrote him other letters, benign ones, trying to open up the channels of communication so she could ease into the news. He never replied. Then when she saw Claude in London, with a pregnant Marlene, the humiliation she felt at his rejection ended any chance of telling him.

Mom and Aunt Rose assumed Adele was Anthony's baby, of course, and she let them; over time, she almost came to believe it herself, though there was always a part of her that looked at Adele and thought, *this is Claude Buckingham's flesh and blood, his unknown legacy to the world.* Mara's physical appearance, so similar to Brian's, had ended any hope that she could be Claude's, and likewise, there was no question about the identity of Adele's father. Though her features were Felicity's, her mannerisms, her movements, her moods, were all Claude.

Felicity had intended to tell Adele about her true parentage one day. But as the years went by, with only silence from Claude, that day never seemed to come. Keeping the secret began to seem more important than the reason for the secret. Now, Claude was here, and she was more afraid to talk to him about his daughter than to speak of the army encamped beneath her window. They had shown themselves to be largely toothless, but Adele's paternity was a sharp set of incisors that could rip and destroy everything and everyone in their path.

LATE IN THE evening, Neville came to the doorway of the living room and said, "I'm sorry for what I said earlier. It was stupid."

"It's okay, Neville." She heard Claude's voice outside the window, talking to one of the soldiers.

"Just send a message to my wife," Claude pleaded. "That's all I ask."

"You don't care about your wife," the soldier responded. "Not if you're off making Sister Pat's belly big up."

Felicity turned to Neville. "Claude is still married?"

"Of course he is. Didn't you know?"

"But Pat —"

"Marlene is his wife and Pat is his lover," Neville said, as if this were completely normal.

"The public doesn't care? Marlene doesn't care?"

Neville said, "Felicity, this is Grenada, not your Bible belt. Marlene is a good, steady wife for Claude, or at least she was, but Pat is his passion. Marlene spends a lot of the year in Canada, supposedly working on diplomatic relations for us. What do you expect Claude to do if she's not around?"

Pat is his passion, Felicity thought. *Not me.* They listened as Claude came back into the house and clumped upstairs.

Then Neville said, "Did you ever think it was strange that we were never together?"

"We?" said Felicity. "You and me?"

"Yes," said Neville. She could just make his eyes out through the darkness. "You know, when we first met in London? I wanted you right then and there."

"No," said Felicity, "I never thought it was strange. I wanted Claude."

"But," said Neville, "you were unfaithful to him."

"I was," agreed Felicity. "The biggest mistake of my life."

"Well, if that's the biggest, want to make a smaller one?"

Felicity sat up. "Alison —"

"She's sleeping upstairs. And I'm not committed to Alison."

The possibility began to shape itself in Felicity's mind as her plans rearranged. Neville was as handsome and charismatic as he had ever been. Maybe some sparks between the two of them would shake Claude out of his disinterest. Felicity had not had sex in a while. She felt the need to release some tension. "Well, come here, then."

"Wait a minute," Neville said. "Condom."

"Probably a good idea," Felicity agreed. Neville lowered himself onto the couch, his relief evident. Felicity abandoned herself to the idea that she was sleeping with Neville Carpenter at a moment in history when the world knew his name. Her story would be thereafter written into his body. They moved together urgently, at the end of the world.

Felicity whispered to Neville, "We could die, couldn't we?"

"Nah, no one's dying."

She wanted to disengage herself from his arms and beat on his chest. "Neville, we are surrounded by men with machine guns, and to hear you tell it, the American army is waiting for an excuse to bomb this place to shreds."

Neville's words were those of a zealot. "They love me, Felicity. The people here love me. No one in Grenada would ever kill me. The Americans could, I suppose. If they do, then I have died for a righteous cause. I have always known that was a possibility. It is for all revolutionaries." Felicity made a small cry, and Neville said, "You can leave, you know. Any time you want, you just ask your soldier friend and he will drop you off at your embassy. You are not a part of Grenada's Revo. Why are you here anyway?"

Felicity asked, "What did Claude mean about his father?"

"Oh, that. Never mind about that."

"I want to know. Tell me the truth."

Neville rolled onto his back. "Claude's father was killed during a strike when we were trying to get rid of Tibbs."

"I know that," said Felicity. "Why was he mad at you?"

"There were lots of meetings," Neville said. "Claude always went to them. But then you showed up on the island, Felicity. Claude began to disappear during the day. I knew he was seeing you. I couldn't go to all the meetings by myself; it was too much. So I trusted Lee to go to some of them, and I found out later that he didn't. When we started the march, the Nutmeg Squad was waiting for us. There were nurses, teachers, students. Claude's dad was trying to get the women and children to safety when he was shot." Neville's voice was a saw, chopping down the tall tree of his image. "We fucked up," he said. "I fucked up, and Claude blamed me, but really, I think he blamed himself."

No, Felicity thought as a vine strangled her heart. *He blamed me. Had I not been there distracting him, he would have gone to the meetings, done the work Neville and Lee failed to do, saved his father.* She knew now why Claude had never sent for her. Neville reached out a hand through the darkness to touch the tears on her cheeks. "That's why you're still here, isn't it?" he said. "You're still in love with him after all this time. I did wonder." Felicity made a choking sound, and Neville said, "Felicity, he loved you too, but after you left here, I told him, and he knew, it could never be. He couldn't be with a Canadian, and one who was half-white, with a mostly white child, and help lead the Revo."

"I'm a Black woman," Felicity said. It was an automatic response; she already knew what Neville would say.

"Not in Grenada. In England, yes. In the States, yes. In Canada, yes. But not here. I've been with white women in the States, but never here. White tourist women come to my parties, and I don't even look at them. I'm Mr. Black Power, right?"

Felicity remembered the Grenadian children taunting her, calling her red-skinned, mocking her absent white father. She hadn't told Claude what she had learned about her father; it was further proof of the distance between them. She had been closer to Claude than anyone in her life; and, yet, she had never belonged in his world. She had never belonged anywhere. Neville and Claude's Grenada was one that had sent them off carrying the hopes of a people and had welcomed them back as heroes. Felicity's Grenada was a place from which people fled, unwanted and never missed.

Through her tears, she made a decision. She would tell Neville about Adele and leave him to tell Claude. "Neville," she said. "There's something else." The downstairs toilet flushed.

"Shit!" Neville handed Felicity her T-shirt and reached for his pyjama bottoms. A moment later, the light flicked on, and Pat stood in the doorway.

"Hi, Pat," said Neville, not in the least abashed.

"We're just talking —" Felicity began, but the look on Pat's face quelled her.

"What are you doing down here?" Neville asked. "You have the bathroom in my room upstairs."

Pat put a hand to her stomach. "Dinner didn't agree with me," she said. "I have terrible heartburn, and my tummy is upset. I didn't want to stink up the bathroom we're sleeping next to."

"Do you want an antacid?" Neville jumped up. "There's some in the kitchen."

Felicity wondered if Pat would tell Claude that she had seen her with Neville. If she would tell Alison.

The next morning, as Alison handed around the porridge for breakfast, Felicity studied her closely. Her eyes seemed slightly red and her manner towards Felicity slightly cooler, but perhaps this was Felicity's imagination. Neville was nonchalant, talking about the newspaper he was going to try to create and smuggle out to the journalists beyond the fence. Claude was quiet. Pat was absorbed with complaints about her stomach, still upset from the night before. She sipped at the bush tea Claude had made her as he rubbed her feet.

Felicity's stomach churned with guilt. To sleep with Neville was to betray Claude. Neville had always taken everything Claude had and Claude never complained. Claude's class notes, his homework, his trial strategies, his speeches, his own ambition — all were subsumed by Neville's needs. And, when it was time for Neville to plan his own demonstration to bring himself to power, he didn't do the work. Claude only did what Neville had always done — took time off to chase a woman — but disaster ensued. And Felicity had just slept with the architect of that disaster.

There was a loud bang. A window shattered. Someone screamed. Someone else yelled. Felicity became aware that there was glass on her shoulders. Before she could move, a dreadlocked head poked itself through the window frame. "Carpenter!" said a cheerful voice. "We've come to free you!"

Felicity jumped up and looked through the broken window. The crowd had finally prevailed. What looked like thousands of protestors had flattened the fence and pushed past the helpless soldiers. People swarmed into the house, shouting "We want we leader! No Carp, no Revo!" Neville stood in the middle of the fray, his face lit by the rising sun, appearing almost holy in his delight.

A seething mass of people coalesced — soldiers, journalists, and regular Grenadians — and pushed into the yard. This was Felicity's chance to go, to get lost. She hurried to the bathroom, put on the sundress and high-heeled sandals she had arrived in, added her sunglasses, grabbed her purse. She began to walk through the courtyard, when a hand grabbed her arm. "Felicity?" Her cousin Arnold held two long guns and wore a military-style beret with his street clothes.

"Arnold? What are you doing here?" she asked, as if he were the one out of his element.

"I came to free the Carpenter," Arnold said. "What are you doing?"

"I was here for a showcase. Wrong place, wrong time."

"Is your mother here with you?"

"My mom and my daughters. But they're staying at your mom's."

"They're in Vincennes?"

"Yeah. I need to get back there."

"Shrimps, Felicity, you can't go up there," Arnold said. "The buses aren't running. And Henry's men have that place surrounded. No one in or out. There's a curfew. They'll shoot you. You need to go to the Canadian embassy, get out of the country quick quick. They're getting all the foreigners out." Arnold began moving off, looking back at her. "Get out of here, Felicity, now! Is not safe!"

Felicity tried to push her way through the crowd, but it was impossible to move against that tide of humanity. She turned and went back inside, to the living room. Shattered glass, smashed dishes, and splintered furniture were everywhere. The occupants of the house ran around, gathering items.

Neville said, "We need to get to Fort Albert before they do." Felicity followed the group through the front door where a convoy of cars stood waiting. The chants swelled. "We want we leader! We want Buck and Carp! No Carpenter, no Revo!"

"Thank God, the Cubans are here," said Neville.

As Felicity stood still, trying to make a decision, Claude came to her. "Felicity. We cannot guarantee your safety. You need to seek the protection of your government. You need to go to your embassy."

"Can you take me?"

Claude didn't hesitate. "No," he said. "We need to get to Fort Albert before the army does. It's not far. You walk that way, turn left —"

Felicity said nothing, did not move.

"Think of your child," Claude said, and she realized he still thought she had only one child. She had already decided not to tell him, but that decision could still be undone.

The staccato rattle of a machine gun intervened. "Oh my God," said Claude. Bodies collapsed in Neville's yard, amid shrieks and shouts. Felicity saw the blue striped shirt Arnold had been wearing falling to the ground. She started towards the place where he lay, and her ribs tightened at the sight of a thick dark pool radiating out from under him.

"That's my cousin," she said. Claude pulled her back.

"Get in the cars!" he shouted. "Everybody!" As more gunfire sputtered behind them, he pushed Felicity into the back seat of one of the vehicles where Alison and Pat were already waiting. Neville sat in the front seat. Claude dived after Felicity, spoke to the driver in rapid Spanish, and the car headed up the hill. Crammed between Pat and Claude, their child pressing against her through Pat's dress, Felicity breathed in and out, feeling her ribs unclench, life still thudding through her veins as Arnold's life seeped away. These events might have begun as a game, boys playing at pretend battles, but they had summoned a real war to this island, where, even now, the lush green hills and the slender palm trees rushing past the car window invited peace and relaxation.

CHAPTER 47.

St. George's, Grenada, October 19, 1983

"I'M NOT STAYING here," Alison said. They had arrived at a small house where chickens pecked in the front yard and the noise from the streets below was muffled.

"Come on, Alison," Neville said.

"Why?" Alison said. "It's men's work, is it? I took the training. I know how to use a gun. You said I was one of the best shots you've seen, Neville. And I'm a nurse. You always said we might need nurses."

"I don't want to stay here either," Pat said.

"It's going to be dangerous," Claude said, his face pinched. "I don't want my child, our child, in danger." He paced alongside the car, his hands on his head.

A woman came out of the house, holding the hand of a little boy. "Pat!" she shouted. "Thank God, thank God. I knew you were at Carp's; you're back, you're back."

"Ma," said the little boy, but he stood at a distance with his thumb in his mouth.

Claude bent down. "Hi there, little fella," he said. "Come and give Pa a hug." The boy turned away and buried his face in his grandmother's skirt.

"He ain't seen you long time, Buck." The grandmother looked tired, shrunken beyond her years under her headscarf.

"These ladies are going to stay here for a while," said Claude, straightening.

"Alison, hello," said Pat's mother. She pointed to Felicity. "Who this American?"

"My name's Lydia," Felicity said. "I'm just a friend in the wrong place at the wrong time." She was speaking through what felt like layers of heavy, wet cotton. Arnold had been shot in front of her. He had walked to school with her and defended her from bullies and showed her how to play marbles. Now he was dead.

"I'm not staying," repeated Alison. She turned and walked back to the car.

"Pat, you'll stay, won't you?" Claude pleaded.

Pat's eyes swivelled between Claude and the cars and her mother and her son. Then, she said, "I am the Minister for Women's Affairs. I must show that women are an equal part of this Revo. We cannot be written out." She sprang forward and hugged her mother, both women crying now. She bent down and tried to kiss her son, who continued to bury his face in his grandmother's leg.

"Be careful," her mother said in a resigned tone.

Felicity looked up, into the branches of a lemon tree, wondering if the child's grandmother made him fresh lemonade the way Felicity's mother once did. The sky was blue, so blue. The colour of Mara's eyes. It was funny that it was Mara's eyes she thought of and not Adele's, whose father was right here beside her, handing her a lifeline to safety. She could stay with Pat's mother and make her way to the embassy in the town below when the crowds dispersed. But she didn't know Pat's mother at all, and she didn't like the hostile gazes she was giving her.

Claude said, "We need to go. Move, move!" He turned to Felicity. "Well, Felicity," he said, and she imagined that his expression shone with remembrance and regret. "I wish you the best."

"I'm not staying either," Felicity said. Arnold had died for Grenada. She was not going to leave it now. She was not going to be the foreigner Neville and Claude thought she was.

Claude looked at his watch. "Please, Felicity."

The Cuban stuck his head out of the window and shouted something in Spanish. Felicity ran to the car and wrenched open the door. Claude followed, shaking his head.

Neville said, "Well, that was a waste of time. One big commess."

Pat said, "Abegunde wouldn't come to me."

Claude put an arm around her. "He was surprised to see us, that's all."

The car careened back down the hill and into the capital. The streets were thronged with people, chanting and waving signs that read "NO CARP, NO REVO." The car had to honk to move people out of the way for the convoy to pass. Neville and Claude hung out of the windows, shaking hands and greeting people as the car rolled past. The crowds gradually thinned as they approached the large stone fort at the top of the hill, overlooking the capital. The car stopped in a large grey courtyard surrounded by steep stone walls with cliffs on one side, the ocean on the other.

"We made it first," said Neville. The Cuban opened the trunk, and a large screw drilled into Felicity's chest as Claude pulled out armfuls of weapons and began carrying them inside, as casually as he had once brought home groceries. They headed up a set of stone steps to a large suite of rooms. "We need to call Cuba," Neville said, heading to a table that held a switchboard.

"Why?" asked Melvin, who had arrived in the second car.

"They'll send troops to subdue Henry," Neville said. "They promised."

"Neville!" Claude said, aghast. "You want to use violence against our own people? Against our own Revo? Against Grenadians?"

"You're going to bring the Americans here," said Lee.

"The Cubans will hold them off." Neville shrugged.

"Not forever!" Lee shouted. "America will crush them! You know it and I know it! Fuck, Neville!"

Speaking with an exaggerated calm, as if he were medicated, Neville said, "Americans don't want any more bodies coming home in body bags. Not so soon after Vietnam. We just have to keep them back for a while, cause them enough losses for them to stand down."

"Since when is this Cuba's fight?" said Claude. "We don't need them here anymore than we need America here. This is our Revo. A Black Revo."

Neville said, "It's too late for that, Claude." He put a pair of headphones on, flicked some buttons on the switchboard, and directed Claude to address the Cubans in Spanish.

Having realized where Neville was, a stream of people began flowing into the room. A crowd had followed the convoy of cars up the hill. Looking out the window, Felicity saw an ancient basketball hoop, its iron ring glazed with a flaky green sheen, listing to one side. Schoolboys in uniform hefted a soccer ball towards it and cheered whenever someone managed to hit their target. Music blared from radios in the courtyard and people blew on conch shells, the watery echoes travelling over the din of the music and laughter. This was a celebration. The people had their leader back.

"I'm almost finished your speech, Neville," said Claude. "What do you think of this? 'The people are the Black pearls of freedom, and we are all precious. Each one of us has our place on the string'?"

"Whatever you think is best," said Neville.

"You should go down to the Square and do the speech there," Claude said. "Not up here."

"No," Neville said, his eyes glowing with Revolutionary fervour. "I'm not running away. I'm staying to fight."

A rumbling began outside. Lee ran to the window. "Shrimps," he said. "Neville, come see." Five large army Jeeps filled with soldiers were entering the courtyard.

"They're here," Neville said. "Henry's people are here." He began giving orders. "Fortify the doors. No one in or out."

Guns rattled below. Felicity watched with a growing sick feeling as bodies fell and lay in red patches on the concrete. Other terrified people ran and began to jump over the stone walls of the fort. Their bodies hung in the air like black crows, a final voyage past the sun's weary eye before they plummeted out of view. She retched and grasped at the windowsill.

"Maybe we should send the women and children out," Claude suggested.

Neville said, "Not yet. They're safer here."

The people remaining in the room began to arm themselves. Alison and Pat lifted heavy guns over their heads as easily as did the men, Pat's stomach protruding below the ammunition belt. Felicity heard bangs, pops, screams, and then booted feet running up the stairs. There was a hammering on the door. "Neville Carpenter and all supporters, come out and surrender!"

"Ssh," Neville cautioned. The pounding on the door grew harder.

"Never!" shouted someone in the room. "Never surrender! Forward together!" The chant was taken up by others. A few seconds later, the tick of gunfire began. Felicity dropped to the floor as small round holes appeared in the metal door. The bullets clicked against the stone walls and fell to the floor. Others hit their marks, and people cried out as bursts of blood spattered the room. Neville shouted, "All right, we'll surrender, but we're sending out civilians first. Women and children. Some wounded. Let them pass, and then you can deal with us."

The machine gun fire stopped, and a voice said, "That will be acceptable."

"Go now!" Neville said. "All of you, go, go, go!"

"I am not going," Alison said, serene in her certainty. She stood next to Neville. "There are people in here who need medical assistance. Whatever happens to you, happens to me, and so be it."

Felicity looked at Claude. He was whispering to Pat, his hand on her belly. Pat broke away and went and stood by the mangled door, tears rolling down her cheeks. Then Claude beckoned to Felicity. She made her way through the smoke, past the groaning bodies of those who had already been shot, to where he stood by the shattered window.

"Felicity," Claude said. "You have to go now." Felicity nodded. Claude took her hand between his, and said, "You were never here, you understand? You go home and do what you were always meant to do. You're one of the world's greatest singers now, and the world needs you." He tried to smile but his face contorted into a grimace. "We'll bring you back for another showcase when this is all over."

Even now, as all their lives hung in the balance, she thought of pushing him against the wall, kissing him, begging him to take her again, right in front of everyone. Even now, she thought of spilling the news about Adele. But then Claude said, "Pat's agreed to leave too. Go with her to her mother's. Take care of her for me, please. Take care of my child." There was no more time, Felicity thought. There was time only to leave. She had a mission. To get her daughter's half-sibling to safety.

Felicity and Pat waited in the crush of people trying to get onto the stairs. Soldiers pushed them with the butts of their guns. Eventually, there was space for them. Near the bottom, Felicity stopped. A rubber tire was burning, fire blocked their way. It wasn't large, she reassured herself. She could jump over it. Soldiers stood at the top of the stairs and at the bottom. She told herself she would not miss. She bent, took off her high-heeled sandals and held them in her hands, took a deep breath, jumped, and soared over the fire. The heat of the flames washed against the bottom of her feet. Thudding down safely on the other side, she winced as she jarred her ankles. She put her sandals back on and saw Pat, stricken, on the other side of the growing fire. A soldier stood behind Felicity, making no attempt to help. The stench of burning rubber made Felicity cough as it tore through her lungs.

"Pat!" Felicity shouted. "Pat, jump, quick!"

Pat was cradling her stomach. "I can't! I'm too big!" she yelled over the crackle of the flames.

"You can do it. Come on. Do it for the baby," Felicity shouted. "Back up and run!"

Pat hesitated. Felicity thought she would go back up to Claude, and he would think that Felicity had taken off and left Pat to fend for herself.

"Patricia!" she shouted again, and Pat did it. She jumped, landing in Felicity's opened arms.

The soldier behind Felicity turned and called to the one standing outside the door to the courtyard. "Pat? Patricia Jack? Don't let her pass!" He approached Pat and pressed her against the wall, motioning to Felicity to go through the door. Felicity took a step towards Pat, reaching for her hand to drag her to safety, but the soldier turned his gun on her. "Leave her and come!"

"It's all right, Felicity," Pat said, her voice bending around the words. "Go now. Go." The smoke thickened. Bangs continued from upstairs. The soldier pushed Felicity to the door. She stumbled through. The sunlight smacked her in the face, blinding her. As her pupils adjusted, she saw that the courtyard was thick with people screaming, bleeding, running. Plumes of smoke billowed from the windows ringing the yard. People were fighting to get through the only gate out of the fort. She headed in that direction, stepping over abandoned signs — "No Carp, no Revo." Pushing through the crowd, she heard someone shout "Brother Carp!" She turned and saw soldiers marching a group out into the courtyard. Neville, Claude, Alison, Lee, Melvin, Lawrence, Frank, and Kingdon, their hands in the air, no sign of the weapons they had had earlier. The soldier who had forced Felicity out of the stairwell led Pat to join the group. They were marched at gunpoint to stand against the wall beside the rusted basketball hoop.

Felicity sensed time shimmering above her head, sliding through her fingers. She saw Pat, her hand on her stomach, looking down at a pool glinting on the ground between her legs. She saw her head turn to the soldier behind her and knew that she was pleading for her baby's life. The soldier prodded her back with the tip of his gun. She faced the wall.

There was a scuffle behind Felicity, and yet another soldier shoved her out of the way, pushing someone else towards the group lined up against the wall. It was Elrick, the young soldier from Neville's house. "You told them we would be coming to the fort!" the soldier accused.

"No, I never did!" Elrick said.

"You were at the house. You talked to them. You told them —" The rest of the conversation faded into the roars of the crowd as Elrick, too, took his place against the wall. Felicity's ribs seemed to collapse inward, crowding the breath from her lungs.

A crackling sound came from high up on the wall above the basketball hoop. A voice projected from the loudspeaker affixed there. "Attention, people of Grenada!" it said. "I speak on behalf of your prime minister, Mark Henry —" There was a hail of boos.

"We want we leader! We want Carp! We want Carp and Buck! No Carpenter, no Revo!" Undaunted in the face of the unfolding brutality, the people in the courtyard raised their voices to the sun above them, sent their chants out to the rim of the Caribbean Sea, gleaming outside the walls of the fort.

"These are enemies of the state!" shouted the voice. "They are obstacles to a true socialist Revolution. They must be eliminated!"

If Felicity hadn't been watching the exact spot where the murder took place, she might have missed it. It happened faster than her eye could blink, faster than her head could turn, faster than two decades of memories could tumble through neurons and synapses. Faster than those whom death was rushing to claim could roar and flinch against it, or stretch out their arms to receive it, it came.

The line of soldiers lifted their guns, and in an instant, Felicity was looking at the place where Claude had been, at the parts of Claude now littering the ground, the parts of Pat, the parts of their child, the parts of Alison intermingled with the parts of Neville, forever linked with him at last, the parts of Elrick, his young dreams dashed. *Kopf und Schultern, Knie und Zeh,* she thought. She remembered cradling that head, being held to that chest, weeping in those arms. Those big brown eyes that would never turn their warmth on her again. *Augen, Ohren, Nase und Mund.*

The guns cried out again, this time firing on the crowd. More bodies scrambled over the stone ramparts of the fort, backlit by the sun, falling. On one side, rocks, on the other, the sea.

Felicity allowed herself to be borne by the swirl of bodies through the gate. Part of her longed to die with Claude, to end this agony, not to have to live the rest of her life seeing him explode into pieces before her. She stumbled as she was vomited out onto the road by the crowd. The heel of her sandal snapped. She could hear herself wailing, but the sound was trapped in her body, absorbed by the noise around her, the screams and chants, the Jeeps roaring up the hill to the fort, the guns still barking out metallic death.

Claude was dead. The final lines from "Laurie's Song" echoed in Felicity's mind as she stumbled down the hill of this beautiful, deadly island. *The time has grown so short, the world so wide.*

CHAPTER 48.

St. George's, Grenada, October 19, 1983

FELICITY TRIED TO remember Claude's directions to the Canadian embassy, but she couldn't pull them from the howling chaos in her brain. Current sensations tumbled about and tangled with memories. She had an overpowering urge to see the ocean. The first time she had floated in Grenadian waters, as warm and soothing as a bath, Claude had been at her side. The crowds thinned as she got to the Carenage, and she walked along it until she saw a quiet place to sit. The undulating waves broke the sun's light into luminous shards, just as they had at the fort. Seagulls circled overheard or dove in dark blurs to the water. Bodies teetered on the edge of the fort and dropped from view. Felicity blinked; the fort turned into into the seawall again. She wanted to swim now, but it was too much effort. The ocean was dangerous; it was a graveyard. Her eyes closed as the sun edged towards the horizon.

Claude loped up to Felicity and took one of her curls in his hand. "There you are, Cinnamon." He bent to kiss her and she threw her arms around his neck. "Bon jay, I'm a lucky man."

"Where are we going?" Felicity pressed her face to his chest, placing her ear over his heartbeat. He smelled like musk and marijuana.

"Wherever you want, my love." The setting sun streaked the sky with red, reminding Felicity of the night skies when the workers of Grenada stood tall together. This redness was darker, more viscous. It began to drip onto Felicity. It was blood. Claude's face disappeared into its thick haze, accompanied by a loud roar.

A Jeep approached. Felicity lay curled on the sea wall. Claude was gone. A warm moistness between her legs told her she had wet herself. She needed to get to the embassy, she remembered. She swung her stiff legs over the wall. The Jeep screeched to a halt in front of her. A man jumped out of the driver's seat and walked towards her. Felicity, now fully awake, braced herself. Maybe this was the end for her. After surviving Fort Albert, she would be shot here, against this wall. She would be united with Claude in death, a character in an opera. But then, she realized that this man was white, not Grenada white, but the white of someone newly arrived on the island, without having had time to get sunburned.

"Well, hello, little lady," said the man. "You're out awfully late."

Felicity opened her mouth to say that she was a Canadian, that she needed to go to the Canadian embassy, but nothing came out. She struggled to communicate, but her tongue was heavy in her mouth, trapping sound in her throat.

"Nothing to say? You know you can be shot for being out this late? They've imposed a curfew. You're lucky we're US Marines and not your people. Come, get in the truck."

They were American troops. Claude and Neville had feared the arrival of the US army; but she was Canadian. America was Canada's friend. They would not act as brutally as the Grenadian forces whose work she had witnessed. She followed the man to the truck. There was another man in the passenger seat and two crouched in the flatbed. One Black, the others white.

"What's your name?" her rescuer asked. She debated whether to say "Felicity" or "Lydia." Deciding on Lydia, she opened her mouth, but, again, the words were a baby bird, frantically beating its wings, unable to fly. She, the owner of one of the world's best known and loved voices, was silent.

"Aw, maybe she doesn't speak English. Do you speak English?" he asked. When she did not respond, he said, "I'm Hank. That's

Buster. That's Buddy. And that's Junior." Nicknames, Felicity thought, and wondered why that felt ominous. "Get in," Hank said, motioning to the cabin, and Felicity did. She hoped her stench of urine and sweat wasn't too obvious, and wondered where they would take her if she couldn't tell them where to go.

As the Jeep began to move, Buster said, "You sure this is a good idea, Hank? You know we're not supposed to be here yet."

Hank shushed him, with a look at Felicity.

"Aw, she doesn't understand," Buster said. "They told us they speak English here. Didn't they tell us? They said get in, make the preparations, get out. We're not supposed to fraternize with the locals." Hank shushed him again. The Jeep rumbled through the dark, deserted streets, until Buster said suddenly, "How about over there?"

Hank pulled the Jeep over. He leaned over the back of the driver's seat to where Felicity crouched at the bottom of the cabin. "You ready, little lady?" he asked. Felicity's deadened senses came alive and she scrabbled backwards but met a steel wall. "You ain't saying no," Hank observed. Felicity was saying no, as hard as she could. She just couldn't speak her no. "Well, here we go." Hank came over the seat, already starting to unbuckle his belt. Felicity squatted, trapped against the cabin wall, as he pulled his underwear aside, grabbed her hips, peeled off her sodden panties, wrinkling his nose at the stench. "No," she cried, inside her head. She grabbed his arm and sunk her teeth into his wrist.

Her father had done this to her mother. Brian had done it to her. She would rather die than allow a United States Marine to violate her. These were the people who were coming to kill the Revo. They would rape Grenada, but they would never rape her. She bit deeper.

"Ow!" Hank snatched his hand back, his flesh dragging across her teeth. "Bitch!" he snarled. He slapped her across her face. Her lip stung. She tasted salt. He swung a fist at her face, once, twice, three times. She felt her eye swing crazily in its socket as she tried to scratch his cheek. She swung a punch. She kicked at him, aiming for his crotch. He grabbed her leg and a handful of her skirt. "Help me out here," he called. The fabric of her dress came apart in his hands as Buster swung over the back of the seat. Felicity yanked her leg free of Hank and aimed it at Buster. She connected with his knee.

"Fucking bitch!" Buster grabbed Felicity's shoulder. She tried and failed to wriggle free.

Hank cocked his arm once more. The blow caught her on the temple, knocking her backward. She struggled to right herself. Another punch connected with her nose. Hank grabbed her hair, yanked her head backwards. A long arc of pain sizzled through her neck. Felicity's screams rang out so loudly inside her head, she could not believe that the whole island could not hear them. Hank's face and Brian's were one. Was this agony what she deserved for sending so many people to their deaths? Alison had shown her loyalty, dying with Neville, adoring him to death, despite Neville's casual indifference to her feelings. She had loved Neville more than Felicity loved Claude. Felicity had left Claude to die, and she had not protected his lover and child. She had got Elrick killed too. She grew limp, accepting her fate, waiting for the beating to be over.

"What are you doing?" said Buster. "She ain't worth the trouble."

Hank let go of her hair and she flopped back against the wall of the Jeep. He bent over, breathing hard. She hoped he would shoot her quickly. Her scalp felt tender, screaming in pain. But he had not entered her. She had won.

Buster said, "Now what?"

"We could just leave her here," Hank said.

"No," Buster said. "All she has to do is say 'American'."

"Well, she comes with us, then."

"Hey, what's the hold up?" came a shout from outside the truck. The Black Marine poked his head into the cab. "Aw, man," he said. "Hank."

Hank said, "We go to the base and she stays with us till we get the all-clear." He zipped up his pants and vaulted back into the driver's seat. Felicity touched her cheek. It was wet, and she assumed she had been crying, but when she looked at her fingers, they were red.

The Jeep stopped in front of a small house labelled "Sun 'n' Sand Guesthouse." It was a home repurposed into a bed-and-breakfast for tourists, similar to the one where Claude had taken her in Sauteurs. There was a small American flag in the window. Hank opened the door of the truck. Felicity refused to move, fearing the horrors that might await her inside. She didn't want Hank to touch her again.

"For fuck's sake." He reached in and pulled her out of the Jeep, carrying her in his arms as she kicked and flailed.

"We don't go out again unless it's for the mission," Buster said. "That was stupid, Hank."

"It was dark," Hank said. "They're all under curfew. One Jeep looks like another."

"Our job is to keep a low profile," Buster said. "Report back when the conditions are right for the operation."

The Americans are coming, thought Felicity. *This group is the vanguard. They will wait until the Grenadians have weakened themselves fighting each other, and then they will pounce. They will land from the sea and from the air and then it will no longer matter who was a Henry supporter and who was a Carpenter supporter.* The guns at the fort today had brought death not just to the people they had mowed down, but to the Revo, the collective work and agony and hope and blessing of the people of Grenada, so beloved by Neville and Claude. Without them, the Revo would suffocate, it would shrink, it would blow out to sea. Its black fist would be broken by the landing of the eagle on its white sands.

Hank deposited Felicity on a bed. He said to Buddy, "You're going to have to guard her. And get her cleaned up. She reeks."

Buddy said, "You, um, you want to have a shower?" Felicity curled up on the bed and turned away from him. He persisted, "Maybe in the morning?" He retreated to a chair near the door and placed his gun beside him.

OUTSIDE THE WINDOW, the rising sun filtered through the serrated leaves of a stand of cabbage palm trees, blending with the patterns on the window shutters to create a latticed design on the walls. The light washed against Felicity's face with the same rhythm as the ocean. Claude would be back soon with breakfast, she thought. He would have walked out to the wharf to get some fish, and they would cook it together. Her stomach griped, wanting the food now. Her hair was loose and tangled on the pillow. She had forgotten to wrap it before bed. She would have to fix it before Claude came back. She rolled over, preparing to sit up. One eye wouldn't open; it throbbed with a smarting syncopation. Now that she thought of it, her whole face felt sore and swollen. She touched her left cheekbone with one finger, causing a stabbing response.

Claude was sitting in a chair by the door. She would ask him what had happened to her face. No, she knew what had happened. She was with Hans. They were arguing. She was trying to get away from him and she tripped. Now all her cast mates would think he had beaten her up. But if she was with Hans, how could Claude be here? Why was Claude holding a gun? Had the Revo happened? She was at Neville's house. The army were outside. Claude didn't love her anymore. He had Pat. She was pregnant. She looked at Claude again, but the man she thought was Claude didn't have Claude's face. How could he? She remembered now. Claude's face had exploded into pieces at Fort Albert.

Acid from her stomach surged to her mouth. She leaned over the side of the bed and spat onto the floor. She was pregnant and it was Claude's baby, but everyone thought it was Anthony's. No, this was Brian's baby and Claude was mad at her. She didn't want a baby. No, her babies weren't babies anymore. They were adolescent girls. She had left them in Vincennes. She struggled to right her mind, to keep it from lurching between present and past. She would need it to be steady if she was going to escape.

"Hold up, hold up." The man sitting in the chair stood up, put his gun down, picked up the garbage can, and hurried over to Felicity with it. "Oh, damn," he said. He held the garbage can close to her mouth. Felicity remembered his name. Junior. She didn't want him near her. She tried to push his arm away, but she couldn't make her fingers work.

"Okay," Junior said. "Okay." He took the garbage can out of the room. Felicity tried to sit up. She could run away while he was gone. But her eye wouldn't open and the stinging behind it drilled into her skull. Her brain was bursting through her eye socket. Lines of dizziness forced her to put her head back on the pillow. Junior came back with a glass of water and a wet face cloth. "Here, girl," he said. He handed them to her and retreated to his chair. Felicity tried to drink from the glass, but she couldn't lift her head. Prickling spears pinned her to the bed. The glass fell from her hand and shattered onto the tiled floor.

"Damn," Junior said again.

Glass was breaking. The crowd outside Government House had come to free Neville, to free everyone. People swarmed into the house, shouting "We want we leader! No Carp, no Revo!" Neville stood in the middle of the fray, his face lit by the rising sun, appearing almost holy in his delight. A seething mass of people coalesced — soldiers, journalists, and regular Grenadians — and pushed into the yard. This was Felicity's chance to go, to get lost.

"Here, girl." Someone was holding a straw to her lips. A straw that went down into a fresh glass of water. Not someone. Junior. Felicity forced herself to stay. If she went back there, she would have to answer the questions that hammered her swollen brain. Why hadn't she left and gone to the Embassy? Why hadn't she told

Claude about Adele? There had been reasons, she remembered that, but she couldn't recall what they were.

"Drink up," said Junior.

FELICITY WANTED HER mother. She wanted her mother to smooth her hair back from her forehead, to wrap her arms around Felicity and pull her close. Her mother had gleaming, dark skin and she smelled like carbolic soap and peppermint. She wanted her mother to rock her, to croon to her that it would be all right. Why couldn't her body conjure the sensation of her flesh and her mother's, almost connected? She was an actress. It was her job to feel these things. She shifted in the bed. Through her one working eye, she saw the figure by the door. Junior. He was a US Marine and she was his prisoner. She couldn't remember her mother hugging her because she never had. Her mother didn't love her. Felicity had two daughters, and she couldn't remember if she had ever hugged them. She must have. But when she tried to bring the feel of those hugs into her arms, she couldn't.

Junior came over to her. "Do you need to use the bathroom?" he asked.

She did. She hadn't realized it until he said it. She nodded, and the motion made the pain in her head spike. Junior helped her up from the bed. As soon as she was on her feet, with his arm around her waist, she dug her elbow into his ribs, wanting to stand unaided. He let go and her knees gave.

"Whoa, whoa." Junior grasped her again and pulled her to the bathroom. He allowed her privacy, and when she was done, he led her back to the bed. He brought her more water and helped her drink. "I'll check on you in a bit," he said.

Felicity closed her eyes. She thought she could hear the ocean splashing against the Carenage. She could make things happen. If she visualized them clearly enough, her dreams came true. She could bring Claude back, if she tried harder. She had been wasting her thoughts on too many other things. She needed to focus on Claude. Claude, outside the South African embassy armed only with a placard and an unerring sense of justice. Pigeons scattered as she ran towards him and his lips raised into a smile. That was yesterday. Now, she could feel Claude in the bed beside her, the length and weight of him, the way he dragged his fingers slowly across her stomach. She turned over on her side to kiss him.

The door opened, and three people came in. *Neville*, thought Felicity. *And Lester, and Gerald Mason.* Gerald who had a crush on her. But no, they were white men. She pulled the covers over her head. She blinked. Claude was gone. She wanted Claude back, but she had to stay. She struggled to remember the men's names. Hank, Buddy, and Buster. They had busted her face. The smell of cloves and thyme swirled under the covers along with the aroma of coffee. Her empty stomach wailed.

"What did you get?" asked Junior.

"Dunno," said one of the man. "Goddammit, no McDonald's anywhere in this fucking place, and only one restaurant was open."

Felicity struggled to hear the rest of their conversation, but her brain buzzed too loudly. She reached for Claude and pulled him close.

"This is for you." Someone yanked the covers from her face. Sunlight concentrated on her one good eye. She squinted, tried to breathe evenly as the throbbing intensified. Hank, she remembered. It was Hank, and he was a threat. She rolled away. "You gotta eat," said Hank. "Look, it's meat and some kinda potato, and spinach."

Felicity looked over at the paper plate he had shoved at her. It held stewed beef, dasheen, and callaloo. In London, she had learned to say "Grenadian dasheen" and "Grenadian callaloo," because those names meant different things in other islands. In Trinidad, dasheen was the leaves of the plant and callaloo was the soup made with it. Claude had said, "They tried to unite us all into one West Indian Federation, Cinnamon, but it didn't work, because each of us has our own culture, our own aspirations. The smaller islands like Grenada didn't want to be subsumed by the bigger islands like Jamaica and Trinidad, and now those big islands have their independence, but we still don't. So little Grenada will have to find her own way." The food smelled like her mother's kitchen, but she didn't want to take it from Hank.

"She puked before," said Junior.

"Fuck," said Hank. "Maybe just a little, then." He put the plate down on the bedside table, loaded a fork, and approached Felicity with it. She pursed her lips and turned her head away. He jabbed it at her. She pushed his hand and a chunk of meat plopped onto the sheet. "Fuck!" he said.

"Let me." Junior approached. He sat down on the bed. "Come on, girl."

"She's not right in the head," Hank complained. Felicity agreed. She wasn't right in the head, and never would be again.

Junior reloaded the fork and lifted it to Felicity's lips. Claude had done that. He had fed her like a baby at Alison's house, on Christmas. If she closed her other eye, she could almost believe that Junior was Claude. The scent of the food was overwhelming. She opened her mouth.

"Look at that. She'll only take food from another nig- Negro," said Hank.

"Jesus, Hank," said Junior. "Look what you did to her face."

After they had eaten, the three Marines dragged backpacks into the room and set up equipment — radios, phones, tangles of wires. They talked as they worked. "We gotta get those kids out soon," said Hank. "Who knows what could happen to them here."

"Some of them don't wanna go," said Buster. "They say they're fine."

"They're not fine!" said Hank. "They're living in a fucking jungle full of savages and the shit is about to hit the fan."

It already hit the fan, thought Felicity. She made herself stay, made herself listen.

"What do we tell them if they refuse to evacuate?"

"Tell them American lives are the highest priority to the president. He doesn't want one American life lost. We're bringing them to safety, and they can come back when things are stabilized, after a change of government."

They began testing the equipment, reporting to someone named Flynn. "Hey, Flynn, you gotta hear this," they said. "Hey, Flynn, get a load of this." The radios crackled and sizzled. The air around Felicity hardened and then it shattered. Pieces of light and sound floated past her ears and her one good eye.

FELICITY WAS SUFFOCATING. Every breath felt like her last. Each time she drew air, she sucked it through a pipe stoppered with ice. This dressing room was smaller than normal; it had a bed, and the mirror was small too. Curtain was in fifteen minutes. She needed Jack. She needed Claude, but Claude was gone. She would call Jack. There was no time. The orchestra had already started playing the *Traviata* overture. She was late. She didn't have her wig on. The general manager would fire her. She tried to sit up. Her vision blurred and her brain banged against her skull. She'd never had a headache this bad before. How could she sing like this?

"Felicity Alexander is a regular performer at the Metropolitan Opera, and next week, she should be taking the stage with the lead role in Verdi's *La Traviata*," said a voice. Felicity opened her working eye. A man was adjusting the volume on a television. A soldier. Junior, she remembered. "But Felicity Alexander is missing in Grenada, where she was to appear in an arts showcase organized by the Neville Carpenter government. The death of Neville Carpenter has now been confirmed, along with that of his deputy, Claude Buckingham —" She was lost. Claude was dead. Was she dead? She wanted to be dead, if Claude was dead.

After the news, Junior switched to late night TV. He chose Bob Fernandes. He was Zebediah's friend. Zebediah had called her once from his condo. Thinking about Zebediah made him appear on the screen, sitting opposite Bob in a leather chair. "As news of the possible killing of Neville Carpenter reaches the world," said Bob, "We're talking to people who knew him. Tonight, we have Zebediah Miller in the studio, host of *Late Night With Z.* Now Mr. Miller, Neville Carpenter was a famed playboy and party animal, wasn't he, but he was also a radical —"

Zebediah interrupted the host. "No more radical than any Black American. I heard Neville Carpenter speak less than a month ago at Emerson College here in California, and that cat spoke the truth. And man, could he talk."

Claude wrote those speeches, thought Felicity. Claude, who had the ideas, Claude who saw the danger and warned against it even as Neville walked right into it.

"Your ex-girlfriend, opera singer Felicity Alexander, is missing in Grenada, isn't she?" A picture of Felicity popped up on the screen. She cringed, waiting for Junior to recognize her, but the made up, styled, smiling woman on TV bore no relation to who Felicity was now, a beaten Grenadian in a torn dress.

"She is," Zebediah said, and he looked genuinely sad when he said, "Wherever she is, I hope she's okay."

She was not okay. She would never be okay again. Claude was dead, and she was lost. She reached for the tears that had evaded her so far, but they did not come. The pressure on her chest refused to be relieved.

IT WAS SNOWING. There was a tear in the sky, and big white flakes spiralled down to the ground, coating leaves and grass as they fell. The wind spun them, whirled them, shook them down onto the roof.

It didn't snow in Grenada, so Felicity must be back in Winnipeg. She was at Salvation Baptist, standing at the fence where the church property met the edge of a field. Out beyond it lay the beginning of the prairie, flat land glazed white, a gleaming sheet stretching out past the highway. The sky was white too. The sun wasn't visible, but it shone so brightly that if Felicity looked up, her eyes squeezed shut in the painful light. The clouds were invisible above the telephone wires. Felicity's bare hand was striking in its brownness against all the white. The snowflakes swirled past the window, and with them came a thumping, whirring noise overhead. They were pieces of paper, not snow. And the noise came from machines. The noise of war. The sun was rising, and Felicity had no idea how many days had passed. Hank came into the room and said, "All right. Time to move. Get her out of here." Where were they taking her? She curled her body into itself, tried to anchor herself to the bed.

Buster said, "Let's go." He reached towards Felicity to pick her up. She attempted to kick him. Her leg flopped weakly to the bed. She forced her mind to sharpen, to clear, to plan.

"I got it." Junior stepped into the room and sat down on the bed next to Felicity. "Where do you need to go, girl?" He unfolded a map before her. Felicity looked at it, amazed that the US Marines were using tourist maps to plan their invasion. She was a Grenadian to them, so she could not ask for the Canadian Embassy. She seized the map, looked for St. David Parish, lowered her finger to the spot.

"St. David," Junior said, following where she was pointing, and she nodded. "Windsor Castle, that's where you want to go?" She shook her head violently, the effort almost too much for her. "Providence?" he guessed again. She stabbed the paper emphatically, and he said, "Oh! Vin — Vins —" he gave up trying to pronounce *Vincennes*. "I'll take you there," he said. "We're not landing up there, so it should be safe for you. Come on, now." He helped her off the bed. She struggled to stand, unsteady on her legs. She had to walk. She remembered first Mara and then Adele toddling so proudly across the room. Her two fatherless girls, one born in hate and one in love. She wobbled through the door towards them.

As Felicity settled herself in the Jeep, Junior said, "Listen, I'm sorry. Hank — he — I should have — oh, fuck." Felicity felt a sudden urge to lay her head on his shoulder, but she huddled stubbornly against the door as Junior consulted the map. "This place is beautiful," Junior said. "Do you take it for granted, living in a place this beautiful?" As he drove, he said, "Know where I'm from? Detroit, Michigan. Ever heard of it? It's not as gorgeous as it is here, but it's home." As they twisted and turned through the hills, sheets of paper floated in the breeze, fluttered up to stick to the windshield. Junior reached out of his window to grab one and handed it to Felicity. "Here," he said. "Our choppers dropped these this morning."

Felicity read, *The United States Army is replying to cries of distress from Grenada. Cries of distress*, she thought. Who had heard Claude's cry of distress? Who had heard Neville's, Alison's, or Pat's, or the cries she had made when a member of the United States Army battered her flesh and drew blood?

Junior said, "You don't agree with us coming in, do you?" He dropped his voice, even though no one else was around. "I don't, either. Truth is, I only joined the Army to go to college and when I'm done my service, I'll be getting out." He stopped the Jeep and consulted the map. "This is it, that Vins place. Somewhere around here, right?"

Felicity opened her mouth to thank him, but, again, her words clung to the inside of her chest. "Well, then," Junior said, "I'll be on my way. Take care of yourself." He reversed down the hill, rushing back to his war, leaving Felicity alone with the sound of the breeze through the trees, the quiet fluttering of the birds, the insects, all the life in these hills that had no sense of the calamity about to befall them, or of the one that had already occurred.

CHAPTER 49.

Vincennes, Grenada, October 25, 1983

FELICITY RECOGNIZED THE place where Junior left her. She was near the old sugar mill, the one Claude had brought her to twelve years ago, where he had told her that her ancestors were enslaved. Then they had made love, bringing their youth and life and beauty to a scene of sorrow. She trod softly through the undergrowth, remembering Claude's warnings to look out for snakes. Or maybe that would be a fitting way to die, expiring quietly and alone from a snake bite, sinking into the ground to join those who had gone before her, those who had poured their sweat and blood into this earth.

According to her coach at the Met, Cleopatra had died like this. She had encouraged an Egyptian cobra to bite her. It sounded insane, and yet Felicity understood it. To kill her, it would take an infusion of poison even stronger than the one already running through her veins; the poison in which she had been conceived and had conceived.

The old walls were still there, becoming one with the jungle. She ran her hand along their mossy contours. She had sat here, with Claude. He had asked her to be his mistress, and she had refused. They had ended here.

"Cinnamon," said Claude. She turned and scanned the rainforest for him. "I'm here," Claude said. "With you."

"Claude." She said his name, inside her head.

"Cinnamon, you have to go to your family," said Claude. "Your mother, your daughters."

It was what she had been planning to do; but, here at the old plantation, she breathed in the suffering of her ancestors. She stood on their graves; she wanted nothing more than to join them.

"My mother doesn't love me," she told Claude.

"Bon jay, Cinnamon. She's from a country that survived slavery, which broke the original family structures of Africans, and still lives under harsh colonial rule. You don't show love if everything you love has been taken from you."

If her mother couldn't love her, she couldn't love Felicity's daughters either. And Felicity had failed at that also. Her girls were carrying the same hurts she was, because pain was all the world had to offer.

"And music," said Claude.

"I don't know which way to go," Felicity told him.

"You do," said Claude. "I showed you, before. You go out to the road. Turn right at the rum shop. Walk past the big sandbox tree."

"I'm not strong enough."

"You are."

She walked with Claude, legs unsteady but holding her up. They passed the fruit stand, the church, the school. The graveyard where Grandma was buried. A goat, tied to one of the gravestones, looked at Felicity and bleated. It was a longer walk than she had thought it would be. Her mind flickered like a faulty television, but her body did the work. She walked, uphill, her calves burning, her back sweating. Past standpipes, past trenches, past abandoned cricket stumps.

She could see the house. It was the last one before the jungle had taken over. Its creepers spilled onto the gravel. Her one goal was to reach that house. As she staggered uphill, she looked down at herself through her one good eye. The other was still swollen shut. Her blue flowery sundress was torn, the skirt stained and hanging down in frayed ribbons. Her arms and legs were bruised and scratched. The air was unusually still, without a finger of a breeze. The sheets hanging on the clothesline did not move. No birds chirped.

Claude was dead. Neville was dead. Arnold was dead. The Americans had invaded. Claude was dead dead dead, he was dead.

When she reached the yard, she collapsed to her knees. "You're home, Cinnamon," said Claude, and before she could thank him, he was gone. She began to retch, vomiting a small puddle of bile and mucus onto the stepping stones. She lay down, gasping, her cheek pressed to the ground. The sky must be cracking; but, no, its blue sheet still hung pristine above her. Shouts of unknown voices collided in her brain.

"Oh Lord Jesus." Mom ran from the house. "We thought you were dead. We haven't seen you in over two weeks, Felicity."

I am dead, Felicity thought. *Claude is dead, and I am too.*

"Who did this to you?" Felicity turned her head away. "Come on, let's get you cleaned up." Felicity curled up into a ball and moaned.

"Felicity." Mom yanked on her arm repeatedly. Felicity allowed herself to be pulled up and into the house. Mom suggested that Felicity take a shower, but she headed straight for the mattress that lay on the living room floor and collapsed onto it.

"Mom!" Adele shrieked and hurtled down the ladder to where Felicity lay. She threw herself on top of her mother. "You're back! I can't believe you're back!" Felicity swatted at her daughter as if she were a fly, turned over to face away. How could she tell her daughter that she had just seen her father murdered, that the dead man she thought was her father had not been her father, while all the time, the real father lived?

"Mom!" Adele cried again.

"Adele, leave her alone. She isn't well."

Aunt Beulah shuffled into the room. "I see Her Highness come back," she said, her voice raspy. Then she took another look at

Felicity. "Who do that?" she whispered.

"I don't know," said Mom.

"Must be Mark Henry's men," said Aunt Beulah. "They execute Carp and Buck, they kill my son, and they do that to her too."

"DRINK THIS." MOM knelt beside Felicity, pushing a glass of water against her lips. Felicity drank. "Eat." She banged a spoon against a bowl.

"If she don't want it, leave she," Aunt Beulah said. "We ent got enough food as it is. This beh-beh curfew."

Whatever was in the bowl could not compete with Felicity's smell. Her stench filled the room, but she didn't care. She deserved to stink. She was dirty. Mom jabbed her lips with the spoon. They parted, and the metal scraped along her teeth. She opened her mouth the rest of the way and let Mom feed her.

Mom took the bowl away and came back with a bucket. She lifted Felicity onto it. She emptied her bladder and lay back down. She was reduced to a machine that took in fuel and eliminated waste. She tried to summon Claude, but he was gone.

Mom opened her Bible. "The Lord himself goes before you," she read, "and will be with you; he will never leave you nor forsake you. Do not be afraid; do not be discouraged."

The suggestion that God could help her, that God had anything to do with this, was obscene, but Felicity could not form the words to tell her to stop.

Mom turned the pages. The sound of paper fluttering against Mom's fingers took Felicity back to her childhood. Whenever she was sick or sad, Mom would sit by her bed and leaf through the Bible. "Out of the depths I cry to thee, O Lord," Mom read. It was a psalm, Felicity thought. Psalms were meant to be sung, but Felicity couldn't sing. She couldn't speak. "I wait for the Lord, my soul waits," said Mom. Felicity wondered who had written that psalm, what abyss they had dwelt in, who had hurt them.

Mom sighed. "I don't think she's hearing anything." She closed the Bible and stood up.

Felicity's cousin Adam, Arnold's brother, came into the room and turned on the radio. It was jammed, Felicity remembered. There was only the offshore station. Adam found it, and the stories flooded into the room. Cuban forces were helping the Grenadians. The Americans planned to use a nuclear bomb. They were throwing bodies into the sea. "Oh shrimps! Oh God!" said Aunt Beulah. Six Caribbean nations had joined the American forces, had invited them in. "Traitors!" said Aunt Beulah.

"How they could invite the Yankees to we country?" asked Adam.

"They paid them," said Aunt Mary.

The announcer moved on to the evacuation of the American medical students from Grenada. They had been lifted by helicopter from their campus at True Blue Bay, and they had kissed the ground on the airstrip in Miami, their hands raised to the sky in thanksgiving, as if they had ever been in danger. The description of their entitlement reminded Felicity of Brian. They were oblivious to the devastation coming to Grenada because of them.

The terrible visions were back. She saw Claude's head exploding. She fantasized about how she could stop them. A knife? She could plunge her head into a sink full of water. Hang herself from the rafters? Eat the rat poison in the cupboard? It didn't seem to be effective, as she heard scratching and scampering all night. She remembered standing on the cliffs at Sauteurs with Claude. On one side, rocks. On the other, the sea. But that made her think of the people who had jumped from the walls of the fort. They leaped as the original inhabitants of the island had leapt from the colonizers centuries ago, but now it was their own people they fled. Felicity should have jumped with them. She would have chosen the sea. She would have let the waves take her out and under, allowed them to drag her down.

THE AFTERNOON WAS hot. The leaves of an almond tree bent slightly in the breeze. That tree had shaded the house for decades. Felicity remembered looking up into its branches at ten years old, newly arrived on the island. Her heart contracted with the memory of herself walking up the hill towards the tree on her first day of school in Grenada, wearing the unfamiliar school uniform. Her mother had said that school in Grenada would be good for her with its proper British teaching and discipline. Loose frizzy hairs had escaped from her braids; they appeared golden in the sunlight.

Felicity was still crying as she approached her grandmother's house. At the end of the day, the Grenadian teacher had asked the class to sing. Then she walked around the room and stopped behind Felicity. She called Felicity to the front of the class and asked her to sing by herself. When she did, the class had erupted with shrieks of laughter. All the way home, her cousins imitated her with warbling, hooting sounds. They said that she sounded like a fat white lady, and she looked like one too. Her father was a white man, they said. She was different, she was not like everyone else. But in Winnipeg, kids teased her because her mother was Black, and she was Black, and she didn't look like them either.

Arnold told her not to mind the teasing, but she couldn't block it out, and she couldn't stop the tears from coming. Her distress only made her cousins taunt her more. Mom would be mad that Felicity was crying. She said Felicity cried more than any child she knew. But Felicity couldn't help it. When sadness filled her and it just kept pouring in, she had to let it out.

When they got home, Felicity tried to go up to her room, unnoticed, but her aunts saw her tears and sensed that something had happened. Her cousins broke out in fresh laughter as they described the spectacle of Felicity regaling the class with strange and hilarious sounds. Mom listened to their yodelling for a minute, and then she asked Felicity what she had been singing. "'Over the Rainbow,'" Felicity answered. Aunt Ida said she liked that tune and started to sing it. She didn't make the octave leap, and her voice petered out shortly after.

Forgetting the teasing and the tears, Felicity stepped into the middle of the room, opened her arms, and began the song again. The sadness and isolation lifted from her. She could almost believe that there really was a place where nothing and no one could hurt her. About halfway through, Grandma called for Mom. Grandma was sick and lay all day on a camp bed wedged into the adjacent laundry room. Mom went to see what she wanted, and then she asked Felicity to come.

Felicity didn't want to see Grandma's gnarled skin or smell her staleness. But she went. Her aunts followed. Grandma had heard Felicity singing in the living room, and thought it was someone on the radio. Mom wanted Felicity to sing for Grandma, to prove that it had been her all along. Felicity took a deep breath and began the song again. Grandma nodded along. Her lips peeled away from her puffy, toothless gums into a smile, the first Felicity had seen from her. Mom's face flickered with an unfamiliar expression. Most of the time, Mom looked at Felicity with disappointment and exasperation. But she thought that maybe, just maybe, here was some pride. Perhaps love.

Felicity closed her eyes as she spread her song through the little room, filling up every crack in the wall and sending it out through the shutters into the street. When she was finished, her aunts and her grandmother talked about how she was better than that Shirley Temple.

Lying on a mattress in the same living room twenty-five years later, Felicity realized that her father hadn't mattered then, and he didn't matter now. She may have inherited her talent from him, but it was her mother who had nurtured it, who had worked extra shifts to pay for her lessons. She had never intended for Felicity to become an opera star, but she had sought to restore her dignity, to keep bullies from crushing her spirit. Her mother had seen the harshness of the world by then. She knew what people were capable of, and she knew that she could not shield her sensitive, precocious daughter from cruelty or pain. She didn't give Felicity the affection she needed, but she had taught her who she was, where she was from. Felicity's gift of song and her Grenadian heritage were her birthright. She was meant to share them both with the world.

Through the window, Felicity could see the green edge of the hills that ringed the house, capped by a tangle of vines. A layer of mist sloped above. Wafting down from the jungle, she smelled nutmeg, cinnamon, and mace, and the rain, steaming onto the flat leaves of the palm trees. From somewhere in the distance came the salt scent of the sea. Birds called to one another up in the branches of the almond tree. Soon, they would spread their wings and fly.

CHAPTER 50.

Vincennes, Grenada, October 29, 1983

THE VOICE ON the radio was American. "Coalition forces are capturing towns along the coast," it proclaimed. "The airport is under United States control." Adam sucked his teeth and twirled the dial, searching for the resistance radio. The Grenadian voice sounded faint, but the message was clear. "Keep fighting. Block the roads. Do not offer assistance to foreign troops." Planes and helicopters had been passing over the house since sunrise, letting loose a blizzard of paper. One flyer blew through the window shutters and landed next to Felicity. She picked it up. SURRENDER, it read. *Never.* Felicity skimmed the paper. Coalition forces. We do not wish to hurt you. The helicopter sounds receded and, in their place, came the sound of a vehicle driving up the hill. A door slamming. Next, she heard her mother's voice and an unfamiliar male voice rolling in from the street. A moment later, Mom came running into the house. "Girls!" she shouted. "We are being evacuated by the Americans. Pack your things!"

Aunt Beulah came out of her bedroom. "So, you decide now you not from Grenada? You a foreign, and you go back to foreign."

Mom said, "I'll ask if we can bring you too. Maybe we can sponsor you."

Aunt Beulah put her hands on her hips. "No, thank you. This me country, even if it mean shit to you. My son's body here, so I ain't going. And if you think you taking the girls and leaving that one, you wrong," she declared, pointing to Felicity.

"I'm not leaving her!" Mom said. She strode over the mattress. "Felicity Alexander, you listen to me right now," she said. "You get up this minute, do you hear me?" She yanked on Felicity's arm. Felicity tried to push her away, but Mom pulled harder. Felicity, weakened and undernourished, rolled off the mattress to the floor. Mom yanked again until Felicity was on her feet, swaying. She marched Felicity to the laundry room and began stripping off her ripped, stained dress.

Mom pushed Felicity under the shower and turned it on. When Felicity just stood there, Mom sucked her teeth, grabbed the bar of soap, and washed her daughter as she hadn't done in decades — under the arms, under the breasts, reaching between her legs into her thicket of hair. Felicity couldn't remember the last time her mother had touched her in her intimate places; not roughly, but not exactly gently. She swayed as Mom pushed her head under the water, letting it dampen the knots and tangles. She looked down and saw it running dark red. Mom dried her off and dressed her in clean clothes pulled from Felicity's suitcase; Felicity had no interest in what she was wearing or whether it matched.

"Girls!" called Dolores. "Take your cases out to that Jeep and tell them we'll be right there. Use the bathroom first." As they complied, Mom grabbed her large metal comb and tub of grease. She gripped Felicity between her knees, as she had when Felicity was little. She didn't tackle all the knots, but smoothed Felicity's hair enough to gather its wet curtains together and weave them into a semblance of a French braid. Then she pulled Felicity up on her feet and shuffled her through the door.

"So, you off." Aunt Beulah's voice cut through the thick, hot air.

Mom turned back. "Beulah. There's the children, and I have to get Felicity home."

"All of you think you special? There's children in Grenada. Sick, hurt people in Grenada. They ain't leaving."

I don't want to leave, Felicity howled, but no words came out. Mom turned and guided her to the Jeep, looking back only once.

They were being evacuated by American soldiers. One Black, one white. Felicity thought she might vomit. Her feet planted themselves on the gravel. The Black soldier smiled and said, "Hello, Ma'am." Felicity's chest heaved. She stood there.

"What's wrong with her?" the Black soldier asked.

Mom shrugged. The Black soldier approached but Felicity flinched. She could not let him touch her. Mom sucked her teeth. Felicity tried to lean against Mom, but she pushed her away. The white soldier came back from throwing the suitcases into the back and asked to see their Canadian passports. After perusing them, he said, "The plan is that we'll get you to safe ground and onto a chopper to Barbados, and from there, your embassy will take over and fly you to Toronto and from there to wherever your home is."

"Winnipeg," Mom said, the word sounding like *hallelujah* on her tongue.

"What on earth are you still doing in this country?" the solider continued. "Everyone else evacuated days ago."

"We don't have a phone," Mom explained. "How did you find us?"

"Our men captured some enemy forces, and one of them said one of his colleagues who was killed had family from Canada up in — how do you say it — Vincennes."

Arnold, thought Felicity. Even in death, Arnold had sent help. He had said the magic word, *Canada.* Canada had accepted her mother, however unintentionally, however reluctantly, and now it had to give her family shelter. Canada was where Felicity had learned to sing. It was where Claude had told her to return. Canada was where she would be when her voice came back to her.

Felicity forced her shaking legs to climb into the Jeep unaided. She was going where she needed to go. All her life, she had been confused about whether Canada or Grenada was her home, but they both were. She was not Claude, with roots firmly planted in one patch of soil like the almond tree outside her family home. She was a child of the world, travelling from city to city, but always with her heart anchored to Grenada as a ship returning to port.

As the Jeep rattled down the hill, the white soldier said he was from Minnesota, which began a brief conversation with Dolores about her best friend Rose whose parents were from Minneapolis. The Black soldier said he was from Alabama. After these pleasantries, the occupants in the Jeep fell silent. Felicity watched the houses, stores, churches, nursing stations bump by. She tried to memorize everything she saw: the trees, earth, and sky of Grenada flashing past the window.

When they reached the highway that led to St. George's, American soldiers in uniform stood atop ladders, stretching up to the billboards, removing the words "Black is Beautiful" and "Education is the future" and "Forward Together" and replacing them with ads for soft drinks and baby formula. The grief came in waves of pain washing against her chest, but she forced herself to keep looking at the last of Claude's words emblazoned against the sky. She imagined each letter resisting the soldiers' efforts to remove it. Even when they were gone, Felicity would remember those words. The Americans could strip the Revo from the roadside, but they would never strip it from her.

Jeeps and tanks lined the side of the road. They passed through a checkpoint where a group of young soldiers holding guns almost as big as themselves had a conversation with their driver before waving them through. The rough dwellings beside the highway appeared to be deserted, with no sign of the vendors who sold peanuts, fruit, and corn to the commuters who normally passed by.

As they approached the capital, the hills that ringed it flashed intermittently with blossoms of brightness. Felicity realized that she was witnessing the fighting between Mark Henry's people and the United States. The Jeep proceeded to a bank, where a helicopter sat on the rooftop, its blades churning. Felicity stepped out of the Jeep into thick, hot air. A soldier jumped out of the chopper, yelling

"Hurry, hurry." He guided the girls up the ladder and reached back for Felicity, who breathed in Grenada one more time. She waved away the soldier's arm. She clambered up, slowly, feeling her leg muscles clench. Her head spun with the heat and the noise of the turning rotor. She fought the urge to faint. She lifted a foot, then a hand, then a foot. Behind her, Mom grunted as she climbed, and the soldier encouraged her. "That's it, keep going."

"Welcome," shouted a voice at the doorway of the helicopter. "I'm Corporal Hanson. We're going to try to avoid the heaviest fighting, so it may be a bit more complicated of a flight path." Felicity's legs gave out. She crawled over to the closest seat. Her fingers scrabbled to fasten her seat belt. She glanced at her daughters, noting the terror etched across their faces, comforted to see them already belted in. Mom came over to her with some blankets taken from a corner of the helicopter and wrapped them around her shoulders. Then she strapped herself into her own seat.

Corporal Hanson gave a signal to the pilot and the helicopter lifted into the long arms of the sun. It rose over green forested hills. From above, Felicity saw dark figures scrambling, more brilliant flashes, and other, bigger choppers, like malevolent birds, hovering above the figures. The Grenadians were resisting the Americans, even after losing their leader. Pride thrummed through her body with the rhythm of the propellers.

The helicopter zigzagged sharply to the left and the pilot yelled something that was lost in the whirl of the blades. Felicity's stomach roiled with sudden nausea, both at the movements of the helicopter and the realization that they could die. They could be shot down by either Grenadian or American forces. It would be the ultimate injustice: after she had decided to live, a tumble to oblivion at the bottom of the Caribbean Sea. The girls remained silent, but Mom begged Jesus for protection. Felicity pulled the blankets tightly around her and shuddered with the weight of the words she could not speak. She looked down at Grenada, the place her mother had left, decades before. Like Laurie in *The Tender Land,*

Mom had gone out into a great shining unknown, armed only with her dreams and determination. Felicity was raised away from her mother's homeland, but it had not failed to grow within her. She, too, had ventured into the world so wide only to find her way back to the tiny island.

She breathed in the feeling of sadness, the feeling of the loss of Claude, and she let herself go down with it. She pressed her chest. *Good morning, heartbreak*, she thought. *Hi there, Claude.* She didn't expect him to respond, but it felt right to talk to him.

"Hi, Cinnamon," said the heartbreak. She jerked back in her seat and her head bounced against it. "You're going to be one of the greatest singers in the world. And I'll be there cheering you on."

She had missed her performance of *Traviata* at the Met, but there would be others. As she had learned from Will, operas were meant to be seen again and again, the stories familiar, the music a balm. Everyone knew the ending when they went to the opera. They wanted to discover how each singer told the story. As she prepared the role, she had thought of her life with Claude as following the three acts of the operatic tragedy. Act I was their time together in London, the breathlessness of their young love and shared dreams. Act II was their parting at the announcement of Felicity's pregnancy; Violetta throwing herself at Alfredo's feet, telling him that someday he would know how much he loved her. In Act III, Violetta died, but from now on, when Felicity was singing it, it was Claude who would die. She would sing the story of Grenada and its Revo in every opera she performed.

She visualized her return to the Met for her rescheduled *Traviata* debut. The desire winged across the Caribbean Sea with the path of the helicopter. She imagined how she would enter through the stage door, and as she always did inside that building, she would surrender to a sense of smallness. There were so few artists in the world who got to sing leading roles at the Metropolitan Opera, let alone return again and again. And even fewer Black singers who did so. And out of those, Felicity knew of no others with Grenadian heritage, and certainly none who had been present for the death of the Revo, and who were awaiting its rebirth.

She would sit in a chair in the wig department, and she would not apologize for the fullness and texture of her hair. It was miraculous, this hair. It could do anything. It claimed space for itself; it announced itself; it was hers. Costumed in an elaborate gown, she would wait backstage as the chorus milled about, the skirts of the women's less-spectacular gowns rustling. Her ears would absorb the familiar cacophony of the orchestra warming up in the pit: string players practicing their runs, flautists perfecting their trills, and the soft thud of the timpanist tuning. The audience would chatter and flip through their programs.

Then the oboe would blow an A440, the one note that instantly banished the trills and scales, bringing order from chaos. The sections of the orchestra would play the A in turn, the lowest of the brass first, working up to the strings, stacking fifths upon fifths, the flutes pealing above them, until, satisfied, their sound tapered off. Near-silence, broken only by the occasional cough from the audience, until applause signalled that the conductor had taken his place for the overture. Real silence, followed by a cascade of melody. Felicity would breathe it in, her ribs expanding, her throat relaxing.

The stage manager would give the cue, and Felicity would sweep out onto the stage, her skirts bustling behind her. She would feel the familiar hush fall over the audience. She would sing, and maybe she would cry. Tears for Claude, for Neville, for Pat, and Elrick, and Alison, for Arnold, for Philip, and, yes, even a few for Anthony. She would weep too at the beauty of the music, especially her favourite moment at the end of Act II. Humiliated by Alfredo, Violetta swoons, collapses, and then revives. Felicity would sing as she knelt on the floor, her gown spread around her, shimmering under the stage lights.

She would start with the most plaintive sound she could produce, almost child-like in its purity. Then she would allow her voice to build to a glorious shimmer as she sang, *I shall be dead, but I shall love you still.* As it should be for any great love. The swell of the violins, the full-throated abandon of the chorus behind her, would lift her up, providing the scaffolding for her voice to soar. No one in the audience would cough or shift in their seats as she spun out her sound for them on this stage, her altar. She wondered that this music held the entirety of human existence; its deepest misery and its greatest glory.

Such beauty demanded her all, including her tears. It was a beauty matched only by that of the scene spinning below the helicopter: an island with lushly treed hills that rolled downward to shores of white sand, melting into a clear blue sea. Across it, its people were fighting for that land. She pressed on her chest again.

"To the Revo," said Claude.

As the helicopter neared the ocean, a wash of sunlight spread through the window. It lit the skin of Felicity's arm, turning it a gleaming bronze. Cinnamon, Claude had called it. A spice of Grenada from the bark of a tree; sweetness, sharpness, medicine. In her peripheral vision, a few stray curls that had escaped her mother's braiding glowed in the bright yellow beam. "To the Revo." Felicity lifted her arm and squeezed her sore, bruised fingers into a fist.

FINALE
Acknowledgements

PRAISE TO THE ancestors and the Most High, who gave me life and who give me the stories.

This book was written on Treaty 1 territory: Original lands of the Anishinaabeg, Cree, Oji-Cree, Dakota, and Dene peoples, and the Homeland of the Métis Nation. I am thankful for the water, the land, the air, all the life in this place and most of all, its people, for providing me with shelter and community.

Thank you to my fabulous agent Léonicka Valcius for always having my back and for your unwavering solidarity, support, and belief in me; and to my former agent, Chelene Knight, and everyone at Transatlantic Literary Agency. Thank you to my amazing editor, Marc Côté, for your extraordinary vision, and for the love and care you gave to my novel and to me. And to Gillian Rodgerson for the astute copy editing and beyond. Thank you to the entire team at Cormorant Books, especially Marijke Friesen for the gorgeous cover in Black liberation colours that embodies the spirit of the book so perfectly.

This novel first took shape when I was selected for the Sheldon Oberman Mentorship of the Manitoba Writers Guild. Eternal gratitude to mentor extraordinaire, Angeline Schellenberg, for your insights that gave Felicity her voice.

I am also grateful to the Manitoba Arts Council for its support of *The World So Wide*. Thank you to Aeman Ansari for your early editorial assistance and encouragement.

In researching this novel, I read many accounts of the Grenadian revolution. These include: *Skyred: A Tale of Two Revolutions*, *The Grenada Revolution*, and *Forward Ever: Journey to a New Grenada* by Bernard Coard, *Maurice Bishop Speaks: The Grenada Revolution and its Overthrow, 1979–83*, *Unchained* by Phyllis Coard, *My Mother and I* by Kamau McBarnette, *We Move Tonight* by Joseph Ewart Layne, *Grenada Morning* by Chris Searle, *The Grenada Revolution* by Wendy C. Grenade, *The Grenada Revolution in the Caribbean Present* by Shalini Puri, and two works of fiction: *Angel* by Merle Collins and *In Another Place, Not Here* by Dionne Brand. I am also indebted to two websites: grenadarevolutiononline.com and grenadarevo.com, and the *Washington Post* podcast "The Empty Grave of Comrade Bishop."

Thanks to my music teachers and coaches, who opened the world of opera to me and insisted that I do my own translations.

Everlasting gratitude for my writing community and especially "The Write Clicks": Danie Botha, Phyllis Cherrett, Brian Hughes, Gloria Moodrey, Mitchell Toews, Erika Uustalu-Nicholson, and Leslie Wakeman; "The M&Ms": Donna Besel, Lauren Carter, Carrie Hatland, Rowan McCandless, and Jennifer Robinson, and "The TTs": my writing sister Rowan again, and Vincent Anioke, Christina Brobby, Jedidiah Mugarura, Dianah Smith, Chanel Sutherland, and Iryn Tushabe. Black writers matter! Also, Mike Blouin and Chris Fash, and the gang at Canada Writes. Thank you also to the many Canadian literary journals and contests who have chosen my work, and to the CBC, for your ongoing support of my short fiction and your faith in my long fiction.

To my many friends, too numerous to list, except for a special shout-out to Rifah Khan Blackburn and Tejinder Chohan Beschel, who were there since the beginning.

I would not be a writer without readers, and I am so appreciative of all of you who picked up this book and took this journey with me.

And finally, thank you to my family: Mummy and Daddy for their love and support and to Mummy for putting that pencil in my hand when I was three and watching in wonder as stories poured out. To Aunty Marion, for writing first and for making sure we were brought up in the struggle. My brilliant siblings and my extended family across the Caribbean, the Americas, and Europe. My fabulous in-laws, the Strachans and Hazzards, who lived through Grenadian history and shared their experiences with me. And finally, thank you to Larry, for giving me the space to create and taking pride in what emerges, and most of all to my bright suns, Jericho and Kamil, the revolution that I am raising. Everything I do is for you, and who you are becoming is everything to me.

Wire bend,
Story end

We acknowledge the sacred land on which Cormorant Books operates. It has been a site of human activity for 15,000 years. This land is the territory of the Huron-Wendat and Petun First Nations, the Seneca, and most recently, the Mississaugas of the Credit River. The territory was the subject of the Dish With One Spoon Wampum Belt Covenant, an agreement between the Iroquois Confederacy and Confederacy of the Ojibway and allied nations to peaceably share and steward the resources around the Great Lakes. Today, the meeting place of Toronto is still home to many Indigenous people from across Turtle Island. We are grateful to have the opportunity to work in the community, on this territory.

We are also mindful of broken covenants and the need to strive to make right with all our relations.